ORPHAN
LAMB

ANN PURSER

ORION

Copyright © 1995 Ann Purser

The right of Ann Purser to be
identified as the author of this work has been
asserted by her in accordance with the
Copyright, Designs and Patents Act 1988

First published in Great Britain in 1995 by
Orion
An imprint of Orion Books Ltd
Orion House, 5 Upper St Martin's Lane, London WC2H 9EA

A CIP catalogue record for this book
is available from the British Library

ISBN 1 85797 761 0

Typeset at The Spartan Press Ltd,
Lymington, Hants
Printed in Great Britain by
Clays Ltd, St Ives plc

ORPHAN LAMB

Because of Harriet

ORPHAN LAMB

CHAPTER ONE

'It could kill his father,' said Olive Bates, staring blankly out of the window of Round Ringford Post Office and General Stores.

A small, worn-looking woman with short grey hair and stubby-fingered hands, roughened by years of work on the family farm, Olive Bates had come into the shop ostensibly for a jar of instant coffee, but actually because she needed someone to talk to, and Peggy Palmer, postmistress and storekeeper, was likely to be a sympathetic ear.

'But does your Robert really mean to move?' said Peggy. 'After all, he and Mandy have lived in Bridge Cottage for such a short time. And you'd worked so hard to get it nice for them when they came back from their honeymoon.'

Not that you'd get me living there, however nice Olive had got it, thought Peggy. Robert was Olive Bates's only son, and lived with his very new wife Mandy, a young hairdresser from town, at the old house built on low-lying land near the narrow stone bridge over the River Ringle. Its nearest neighbours were the quiet folk in the graveyard and a cantankerous old woman living in the Hall Lodge.

Peggy Palmer, small, plump and quick-moving, ran the village shop on her own, fighting a constant battle against her bank balance. As she totalled up takings at the end of each month, she still had doubts about her decision to carry on alone after the death of her husband Frank in a road accident, only one year after they had left a lifetime's town dwelling and taken on the village stores. Her experience as a newcomer to Round Ringford gave her some insight into what awaited young Mandy.

Olive Bates looked desperately at Peggy's pleasant face, blue eyes full of concern, and blurted out the real cause of her anxiety.

'It's not just that they want to move, Peggy,' she said. 'We're only guessing about that, ever since Ted saw Robert poking around behind that empty bungalow. No, Robert himself says he's going to give up on the farm and set up a garage. Well, not a petrol sort of garage, but mending cars and trucks and that, and there'd be no room at Bridge Cottage.'

Peggy stared at her. 'Robert? Give up the farm? But who else will take it on, Olive? Your Ted is still a fit man, but nobody goes on for ever, and he'll need Robert. Oh no, I'm sure he doesn't mean it. It must just be a silly idea he's got from one of his friends.'

'I blame Mandy,' said Olive. 'She never liked the idea of living in a village and being a farmer's wife, her being a townie and never getting her hands dirty. Can't see her being much help at lambing time, motherin' the orphans, can you?'

'I don't know about that, Olive,' said Peggy with a small smile. 'A hairdresser has to handle all kinds of heads of hair . . .'

Olive looked at her closely, suspicious of being teased, but decided Peggy wasn't like that, and turned away again to look across the sunlit Green, with its shady chestnuts. Over towards the willow-fringed river, she could see the roof of Bridge Cottage in the trees.

'Robert *is* serious, Peggy,' she said. 'He's been to see the Council already.'

The springing bell over the shop door jangled, and Peggy

welcomed the next customer with relief. Poor Olive is a bit of a misery, she thought, but if it's true, it must be a real blow to her and Ted.

'Mornin' Peggy,' said the bent old woman as she came laboriously into the shop, clutching the counter to steady herself. 'Lovely mornin',' she continued, 'though to look at your faces, you'd never know it.'

Olive handed Peggy the correct money, picked up her jar of coffee, and left the shop with barely a grunt to old Ellen Biggs, who shrugged. 'Please yerself, Olive Bates,' she said. 'Ain't nothin' to me whether you speak or not.'

'She was very worried, Ellen,' said Peggy, 'very worried indeed.'

'About her Robert?' said Ellen, in a matter-of-fact way.

Peggy sighed, put her hands flat on the counter and leaned over towards Ellen Biggs. 'So you know all about it, Ellen,' she said, pretending to accuse.

'O' course,' said Ellen. 'Everybody knows. Robert's goin' to set up on 'is own, mending cars and that. And why not, I say. He's a good boy, and deserves to do well. He's put up with his father for years, old Ted carpin' and criticisin' everythin' Robert wanted to do on the farm. Now Ted'll reap what he's sown, and see 'ow he likes it.'

'Olive blames Mandy,' said Peggy, resigning herself to the impossibility of anything being secret in Round Ringford.

'Rubbish,' said Ellen. 'She's a good girl, that Mandy, does what's best for Robert. They're very 'appy together. Can't 'elp noticin' it from the Lodge – does the 'eart good to see it. But then, Olive always 'ad it in for Mandy, right from the word go.'

Peggy straightened up and tidied the counter, putting away the blue marbled cash book where a number of villagers ran up accounts, some paying their bills more regularly than others. 'Well,' she said, 'we shall see. Now, Ellen, what can I get you this fine morning?'

★

5

Round Ringford was a small village in the middle of England, enclosed by a ring of wooded hills which gave visiting strangers the dramatic sensation of coming suddenly upon a lost community. Its golden stone houses were grouped around the Green, a spacious stretch of grassy common land on which villagers no longer pursued their right to graze cattle and sheep. Children now played in their specially dog-proofed corner, and a comfortable wooden seat had been placed under the chestnut trees in memory of the late squire of Ringford Hall, the father of the present owner, and inheritor of a family estate going back to the days when England was carved up by the Normans.

Ringford had its share of new houses, most of them in Walnut Close, a small but, in its time, controversial development up the Bagley Road. A plain and unambitious group of council houses, Macmillan Gardens, sat squarely off the main street. Now that some of these houses were owned by their occupiers, touching personal improvements had been made; new porches and bedroom extensions, wrought-iron gates and fancy front doors. Heritage nuts, who would preserve the village in what they imagined was its ancient perfection, were in the minority. Round Ringford was wholeheartedly in the twentieth century, however rural and remote it seemed to newcomers, and close-knit in many different and not always comfortable ways.

Bridge Cottage was on the Hall estate, and the Bateses were tenants of the Ringford Hall family. Several of the surrounding farms still belonged to the estate, and the standing of their tenant farmers was subtly different from those who owned their own land. It was hard to define, but it was there in the village subconscious, in the gatherings of the farming community, in the pecking order in the pub.

Mandy Bates couldn't have cared less about all this. She was a trained hairdresser, good at her job and popular with her ladies, and she had loved Robert since their first year at

Tresham Comprehensive. She had no particular fondness for the countryside, but wherever Robert was, she wanted to be there too. After a wonderfully romantic wedding, they had returned from Tenerife to Bridge Cottage, where Mandy had worked with a will to make a bright and cheerful home for her beloved Robert.

'It isn't because of me, is it?' she had said to Robert, when he first mentioned the garage idea. They had had their ups and downs on the subject of farmers' wives and carrying on in Olive's footsteps. But Mandy had determined to do her best, and it was quite a surprise when Robert came up with his new plan for their future.

He looked at Mandy, washing up their new crocks, absorbed in her task. Her sweet face, with its snub nose and big dark eyes, pleased him so much that he put down the drying-up cloth and took her in his arms, all soapy and wet, and kissed her with unclouded love.

'Come and sit down a minute.' Robert said. 'I want to tell you something.'

Mandy wiped down the draining board and the work-tops, looked at them with pride, and then took off her apron. 'Out with it, then, Rob,' she said. 'Is it good news or bad?'

'Not sure,' said Robert, 'but with luck it could be very good news indeed.'

The daylight was fading outside the cottage, and with its small windows the little front parlour was quite dark. Mandy switched on a couple of reading lamps and sat down, looking expectantly at Robert.

'You know the bungalow behind the playing fields, where old Miss Hewitt used to live?'

'No,' said Mandy. 'At least, I think I know the bungalow, but you know perfectly well I couldn't have known Miss Hewitt. It's been empty ever since I started coming to Ringford.'

Robert nodded. 'Yep, well, it belongs to the Hall estate.

7

Built for Miss Hewitt, I think. She was some kind of distant aunt, and retired there. Anyway, now it seems they're going to sell it.' He paused, waiting for Mandy's reaction, but she continued to look attentively at him, registering nothing more than polite interest.

'Well,' Robert went on, 'it does have a very big garden, and good access from the lane by the playing fields. If we could raise the money . . .'

'Ah,' said Mandy, 'now I'm with you. It would be the ideal spot for Bates Motor Engineering Plc.'

Robert looked hurt. 'Don't laugh, Mandy,' he said. 'It's a serious suggestion. We'd have the land to put up a building, and you'd have a nice modern bungalow instead of this old dump.'

It was Mandy's turn to look wounded. 'Old dump?' she said, looking round at her sitting room, newly decorated and fresh with flowered curtains and cushions. A crudely painted fiesta scene in bright, hot colours, souvenir of a magic honeymoon, hung over the fireplace, and Mandy reached up and adjusted it a fraction, defensive and hurt.

Robert hastily backtracked. 'No, you know what I mean, Mandy, you hated the idea of this cottage at first. And whatever we do to it, it'll still be a cramped, damp old house with small windows and low ceilings. Fine for weekenders who seem to like that kind of thing, but I know you're making the best of a bad job.'

'Mm,' said Mandy unhelpfully.

'And,' said Robert, playing his trump card, 'there's a really nice little bedroom overlooks the garden, big window . . . plenty of room for a cot . . .'

Mandy looked at him, her face softening. 'Robert Bates,' she said, 'don't count your chickens. Still,' she continued, drawing the curtains against the dark garden, 'no harm in having a look.'

CHAPTER TWO

Although Bates's Farm was only a short walk from the centre of the village, its high laurel hedge and narrow muddy track made it seem isolated and dismal, so dismal that paperboys new to the job were not keen on delivering the papers on dark winter mornings. But behind the farmhouse the land sloped away to the river, and when Olive went out into the vegetable garden to cut a cabbage or hang out her washing, she would straighten up, hand on her aching back, and be comforted by the gentle beauty of the view. Ted had never believed in grubbing up hedges and felling mature trees in the interests of super-mechanised farming, and their fields were still small, dotted with sheep and, in the spring, with leaping lambs. The hedges were alive with sparrows and rabbits, and on hot summer noons motionless cows found plenty of shade from spreading oak and ash trees.

The Bates family had lived there for several generations, and it was expected that a Bates son would take over from his father as a matter of course, as had happened in an unbroken line for at least as far back as Ted Bates's great-great-grandfather.

'It's your fault, Olive,' said Ted, sitting in a depressed huddle at the kitchen table, stirring and stirring his tea until Olive thought she would scream. 'Lettin' him spend all his spare time at Peter Barnack's garage in Tresham instead of comin' straight home from school and helpin' me on the farm. And all 'is Saturdays . . . Never thought about nothin' but cars.'

'You never said much at the time,' said Olive defensively. 'You used to be proud when Peter Barnack said he had a real way with engines. And what he learned there has been very useful on the farm.'

'You spoilt him, Olive,' insisted Ted, stubborn and full of bile. 'Always stood between him and me, makin' him think he was somethin' different, and now look where it's got us.'

'Maybe,' said Olive, but thanking God that Robert was different from his father. He had been such a clever boy at school and agricultural college, and yet Ted had never let him have his say on trying out new things. Like that time with the pigs. Robert had said they should diversify – 'Do what?' said Ted – and have a go at pigs. Prices were good, and he'd studied modern methods of pigkeeping at college. He had put his ideas to his father one day over tea, and Ted had growled his disapproval. 'Never bin any money in pigs,' he'd said. And that was that.

Now Ted was equally scathing. 'How does he think he's goin' to make a livin', fiddlin' about with other people's cars?' he demanded. 'And what about the work here? Have we got to hire a man? You know as well as I do that this farm's not big enough to pay a worker's wages.'

Olive thought to herself that Ted should have considered that before, instead of taking Robert for granted. He couldn't blame Robert, now he'd got a wife and home of his own, if he had ambitions for something more than playing second fiddle on the farm.

There were so many things she'd like to say to Ted, but old habits are hard to change. If only she could get through to him that if he wasn't careful they'd lose their only son altogether, make him see that a serious quarrel over all this could land them in a mess like the Waltonby Bateses, a family split down the middle by a feud that nobody could mend.

As it was, she quietly made a practical suggestion, hoping to defuse Ted's anger.

'We could ask young Dan, Fred's youngest, if he'd like to come and work here. There's too many sons there for one farm, and he might be glad of a change, things being what they are.'

'So I have to pay Fred's son to help me on my farm, when I've a great healthy lad of my own?' said Ted, frowning angrily at her.

'He's not a lad,' said Olive, under her breath. 'He's a grown, married man.'

'What did y'say?' snapped Ted. 'Speak up, woman, don't mutter like your old mother.'

But Olive's courage had ebbed, and she picked up a pile of newly-ironed clothes and left the kitchen, shutting the door carefully behind her.

In the shop, where the current chief topic for gossip was Robert's intended split with the farm, Peggy Palmer tried to limit speculation.

'But Ellen,' she said to the old woman across the counter, 'there's nothing to say he'll get permission from the Council. You can't just set up a garage business in a village without taking a lot of things into account.'

Ellen Biggs had walked down to the shop slowly, feeling the warmth of the early summer sun on her old bones. Her knees were painful this morning, and she'd drunk several cups of strong tea, feeling ancient and gloomy. But then, over her garden fence, she'd seen a new foal in the Hall park, its spindly legs splayed out at all angles, being coaxed and encouraged by the old bay mare, and Ellen had cheered up. A new life, she thought, new lives for old.

Pensioned off from her job as cook up at the Hall, Ellen

lived in the old lodge, surrounded by furniture which had seen better days with the Standing family. She grumbled at the damp coming up through threadbare carpets put down straight on to an uneven brick floor, but when advised to have a proper surface laid, she refused. 'It'll see me out,' she said. 'I couldn't stand all the mess and bother with workmen in the 'ouse.'

In the summer she was fine. She sat out at the front of the lodge on a rickety canvas chair, watching the occasional passer-by, warm and undisturbed amid scented roses and border pinks, listening to the birds and counting her blessings. But in the winter, when the cold draughts whistled through ill-fitting windows and doors, and damp logs wouldn't burn, Ellen put on extra layers of clothes and retired early with a hot water bottle, hoping her arthritis would be no worse by the morning. The dread of not being able to get out of bed was always there in the back of her mind.

'So long as I can get about,' she said to her old friend and sparring partner, Ivy Beasley, 'they 'on't have no reason to take me off to the workhouse.'

Now she stood in the shop, leaning against the counter, smoothing down her voluminous denim skirt and hitching up wrinkled cotton stockings.

Miss Ivy Beasley lived next door to the shop, and this morning had followed Ellen in, having seen her from her watching post at the front window, and feeling in the need of a few words with someone alive. Her long-dead mother lived on in Miss Beasley's head, and their conversations were lengthy and often acrimonious. But impossible as her mother's echoing voice was to ignore, Ivy was perfectly aware that she lived quite alone, and was often lonely.

'If,' said Ivy Beasley with emphasis, 'by "the work-house" you mean Tresham House, you might find them not all that keen on taking in an obstreperous old woman like you.'

A third customer, a neatly-dressed, compact little woman, wearing glasses and with a black leather handbag tucked under her arm, climbed the worn steps to the shop and nodded to Peggy Palmer, taking in the bristling pair as they squared up to each other like a couple of cockerels.

'Morning, Doris,' said Peggy to the newcomer. It was only latterly that she had felt able to call Mrs Ashbourne by her Christian name, although Doris Ashbourne had been owner and postmistress of Round Ringford Stores before Peggy, and so had been closest to her for the first few months of new ownership. Peggy had soon learned that instant friendship in the village was not encouraged. A probationary period was always advised. 'After all,' Ellen Biggs was fond of saying, 'it's no good gettin' too close too soon, and then wishin' you 'adn't.'

Doris Ashbourne returned Peggy's greeting, and then directed her attention to the other two women. 'If you two can stop spitting at each other for two minutes,' she said, 'perhaps I can remind you it's your turn to come to me this afternoon.' She folded her arms over her shopping basket, and looked warningly at Ivy Beasley.

'We've not forgotten, Doris,' Ivy said. 'We're looking forward to sampling what you baked for us today, aren't we, Ellen?' Ivy was a demon baker, supreme champ at the WI, and highly critical of others' efforts.

None of the three would have forgotten, of course. Their weekly tea-time meetings were a high point in their lives. Each living alone, confined to the village, except for an opportunity to go on the shopping bus twice a week, their days were bounded by village events. And the most important event this morning was Robert Bates's rumoured defection from the farm.

'What about your Robert, then?' said Ellen, returning avidly to the subject. She appealed for information to Ivy Beasley, because the one chink in Ivy's spinsterly armour was her love for Robert Bates, whom she had helped to nurse and cherish when he was born, a weak and sickly baby, in need of constant attention. Olive Bates had reluctantly accepted Ivy's help, and Robert had grown to love his Auntie Ivy.

'What Robert and Mandy decide to do is their business,' said Ivy Beasley primly, 'but I must say it's not a great surprise that he's aiming to get loose from that father of his.'

'Yes, well,' said Ellen Biggs, with a sly smile at Doris Ashbourne, 'you'd know all about heavy-handed parents, Ivy. That mother o'yours were twice as bad as a cartload o' Ted Bateses.'

'Come now, ladies,' said Peggy. 'I'm sure you've all got jobs to do, and so have I, so what can I get you, Miss Beasley?'

Next door neighbours, Peggy Palmer and Ivy Beasley did not get on. Full of resentment at newcomers and village prejudice against townies, Miss Beasley had been prepared to dislike Peggy from the start, and she had no intention of relenting.

'Pound of cooking apples,' she said, 'and I hope they're not full of brown spots like the last lot.'

'I am always willing to replace unsatisfactory goods, as you know,' said Peggy, tight-lipped.

With Ivy served, and Doris Ashbourne's pension counted out in the Post Office cubicle, Peggy watched the three women leave the shop slowly, and exchange a few last words on the wide pavement outside before making their way home.

Peggy watched them go with relief. She came out from behind the counter and stood at the door, looking out over the Green. Her view was for the moment interrupted by a huge trailer of fresh grass for silage trundling noisily past the shop. There goes Robert, she thought. Wonder if he knows how the village is talking? The trailer turned off down Bates's End. It was enormous, oddly out of scale in a street of houses built two or three hundred years ago, when even the biggest wagon and horses would have been dwarfed by Robert's tractor.

Now she could see Ellen stumping slowly across the closely mown grass, pausing at the Standing seat ·to exchange banter with a couple of old men taking the sun. The petals of fallen chestnut candles lingered on the grass around the seat, brownish, like old snow. But the tree was in full leaf, its swaying branches sheltering a hidden population of birds, creeping nuthatches, noisy sparrows, and always the flapping, conversational pigeons.

The pigeons were not popular. When the Parish Council had voted to put a seat under the tree, they'd thought of providing shade from strong summer sun and shelter from sudden storms, but forgotten about the pigeons. It was just as well, as Ellen Biggs said, that pigeon shit was lucky.

Ivy and Doris had disappeared through Ivy's gate, and Peggy's irritation began to evaporate. She heard heavy footsteps approaching, and stood back to open the door for a tall, fairish man with thick, wheaty hair and blue eyes, and a brown skin weathered by outdoor life. His arrival could not have been better timed. He was the one person she was always pleased to see, especially if there was nobody else around.

'Hello Peggy, my love,' said Bill, with a quick look behind him to make sure the shop was empty.

'Bill,' said Peggy. 'How are you today, my dear . . . and how's Joyce?'

Bill Turner's smile faded, and he shook his head. 'Just the same,' he said. 'She doesn't know me from the Reverend Nigel Brooks. He turned up, too, by the way. I suppose it's worth going to see her in that place, but honestly, she doesn't seem to care whether I go or stay.'

Peggy leaned across the counter and took Bill's hand. 'What a lousy situation,' she said. 'It's almost worse than when she was at home. At least you spoke to each other,

15

even if it was always a quarrel.'

'I can't think of anything to say to her.' Bill stroked the palm of Peggy's small, warm hand with his muddy forefinger. 'She just chatters on about that non–existent world she lives in. I can see the appeal. She just makes things happen how she wants them, nothing goes wrong and nobody disagrees with her or makes her do things she doesn't want to do. But there's no place for me, even if I wanted it. Which I don't.'

'Did Nigel Brooks find anything to say to her?'

'Oh yes, you know our Nigel, smoothly professional and at ease in all situations. No, to give him his due, he was good with her. Entered into her conversation as if he knew what she was talking about. You know, Peggy, you've seen him with batty old folks in the village.'

Peggy looked at Bill's downcast face and changed the subject. 'How're you getting on with Mrs Standing's bird–watching hide?' she said, smiling sweetly.

Bill looked at her and grinned. 'Coming on well, gel,' he said. 'It should be finished in a few weeks. Depends on other jobs around the estate, but Mr Richard's keen to get it finished before madame gets too heavy to go up a ladder.'

'When's the baby due?'

'Don't ask me,' said Bill. 'That's more in your line.'

'Well, it's around the end of September, I think,' said Peggy, 'though nobody knows exactly. Jean Jenkins hasn't dared to ask yet, but she'll find a way, you can be sure of that!'

Jean Jenkins lived in Macmillan Gardens, next door to Bill Turner, and she cleaned up at the Hall. She was regarded as the unofficial newsgatherer from Ringford Hall, but as yet not many details had emerged.

'Anyway,' said Bill, 'there'll be plenty of time for me to take you to do a bit of birdwatching, if that's your fancy. Mr Richard needn't know, though I don't suppose he'd mind, being a bit of a birdwatcher himself.'

All of this was quite clear to Peggy Palmer and she looked pink and pleased. She took a deep breath, closed the till drawer with a snap, and asked Bill if he would like a cup of tea.

He followed her into the kitchen, and watched her filling the kettle, her plump bottom neatly skirted in blue linen, and her legs bare and tanned from gardening in the sun. He put his arms around her, his hands leaving muddy marks on her blouse.

'Mm, Peggy . . . You couldn't shut up shop for an hour or so, I suppose?' he said into her ear, tickling her with his breath.

She turned around inside his arms and kissed him firmly and with finality.

'Home, Bill Turner,' she said. 'I've a shop to run and a living to earn. I'll see you this evening. It should be nice for a walk in Bagley Woods.'

It was only when he reached his garden gate that Bill remembered he hadn't got his cup of tea. And I forgot to ask Peggy for the latest on Robert and Mandy Bates, he thought. Still, I shall see her this evening. This pleasant thought spurred him on, and he unlocked the back door to let himself happily into his silent, empty house.

CHAPTER THREE

'You've got bits of Bagley Woods in your hair, Mrs Palmer,' said Mandy, carefully extricating an entangled piece of twig from Peggy's curls.

Peggy was sitting at the kitchen table, a mirror in front of her and a towel round her shoulders. Mandy stood behind her, wielding scissors and comb, and wondering whether she should have said that. But Peggy smiled at Mandy in the mirror and made no excuses.

'It was lovely up there this evening, Mandy,' she said, 'with the sun coming through the trees, and the woods full of colour. That ugly old piebald horse was in the top field, and even he looked better than usual surrounded by dandelion clocks. A bit like Eeyore and the thistles . . .'

Mandy looked gloomy. She'd never heard of Eeyore. 'I suppose you know all the names of wild flowers and that, Mrs Palmer,' she said. 'Robert and me go for walks at the weekends, and he explains about things, but they just go right out of my head, and next time he has to say it all over again. Give me a walk round the Grosvenor Centre in Tresham any time. Only flowers you see there are geraniums, and even I can recognise them.'

Peggy laughed. 'You should have seen Frank and me a couple of years ago,' she said. 'When we first came to Ringford we'd take a book of wild flowers on walks and look up every new plant. But that was a waste of time. The village kids have got their own names for things anyway, haven't they? You'd not catch Warren Jenkins calling cow mumble "umbellifera".' Mandy looked blank. She was rescued by a sudden streak of tabby scattering the cut ends of hair under Peggy's chair, and Gilbert slithered to a halt beside the Rayburn. The cat's golden eyes looked reproachful, and she miaowed in a cracked, starving voice.

'Oh Lord,' said Peggy, 'I forgot to feed her before I went out.'

'Do you want to have a break for a minute?' said Mandy. 'That's just about the right length now, so I'll be getting out the drier.'

Mandy still worked in the salon in Tresham full-time, but was slowly building up a clientele of ladies in Ringford and around, going along in the evenings and turning the necessary business of having a haircut into a social occasion. For Peggy, of course, it was wonderful not to have to waste her precious free time going into Tresham, inevitably waiting beyond her appointment time, and coming out into the chilly streets of town looking like a boiled lobster.

Peggy put down a saucer of catfood for Gilbert and returned to her seat. Mandy had plugged in the drier and began to brush and blow Peggy's hair into shape.

'I wish all my ladies had hair like yours, Mrs Palmer,' she said. 'It just goes whichever way you want it, no trouble.'

Peggy smiled at her again, unwilling to shout over the noise of the drier. She looked at Mandy's young face, absorbed by her task, sure of her skill. But there was a downward turn to her mouth, and Peggy wondered if all was not well down at Bridge Cottage. She had made up her mind not to ask Mandy about the garage rumours unless Mandy brought up the subject herself, but now she thought perhaps a small nudge might be helpful.

'Your mum-in-law was in the shop this morning,' she said. 'Not an easy woman to talk to, but she seemed a bit upset about something.'

Mandy looked at Peggy's reflection and grimaced. 'Well, Mrs Palmer,' she said, 'if *you* find it hard to talk to our Olive, how do you think it is for me? I'm the girl who stole away her only son, the girl who knows bugger-all about farming, and cares even less, and what's more won't even join the Women's Institute and learn how to turn the heel of a sock.'

Peggy laughed loudly, disturbing the smooth curve of her hair, and causing Mandy to turn off the drier.

'If only you knew how I suffered when we first moved here, Mandy,' Peggy said. 'I joined the W.I. because Frank said it would be good for business, and anyway, Doreen Price was so friendly and nice I couldn't really refuse. But half the time I had no idea what they were talking about – not so much the official side of it, but when they got together in groups after the meeting for the coffee.'

'There you are then, Mrs P.,' said Mandy. 'I sometimes think I'll never make a farmer's wife. I have nightmares about it, though I don't tell Robert.'

'Maybe you won't have to, from what I hear.' Enough pussy-footing around, thought Peggy.

'Ah,' said Mandy, 'so it's common knowledge, is it?'

'More or less,' said Peggy, 'but I wouldn't mind hearing a few facts instead of endless gossip.'

Mandy put away the drier, held up a hand mirror so that Peggy could see the back of her head, and began to put away her things, explaining to Peggy that it had been all Robert's idea, nothing to do with her, and that he wanted a career of his own, to build it up from scratch.

'Means we'd have to move, of course,' said Mandy, 'to get the land. But Robert has his eye on that bungalow behind you. Wasn't it a Miss Hewitt used to live there? Anyway, the estate is selling, and Robert hopes to buy. Plenty of room to put up a building, he says. What would you think about that, Mrs P.?'

Peggy had already thought about it, and decided that so long as it didn't impede her view across the fields she wouldn't mind. She said as much to Mandy, adding, 'but how will you feel, having a mucky old business right on your doorstep, customers coming and going, and the noise of car engines all day?' Peggy had certainly thought of that, too.

'No different to being on the farm, really,' said Mandy, 'except on the farm there's no customers, just smelly old cows and sheep, and my charming in-laws for company. I think we'd do better on that new estate outside Tresham.'

Peggy reached for her handbag, and fished out a note which she handed to Mandy. 'Thanks, Mandy, it looks lovely. What would I do without you?'

'It's nice to come and talk to you, Mrs Palmer,' said Mandy. 'I'd do your hair for nothing, just to speak to someone who understands.' She pocketed the note, nevertheless, and picked up a clothes brush.

'Just let me brush you down,' she said. 'There's a few bits of hair on the back of your jersey. And here,' she continued with a smile, 'hold still a minute, I'll get these bits of grass off your skirt as well.'

Fox Jenkins, husband of the large and amiable Jean, cycled along the empty lane from the Hall, whistling, looking forward to his breakfast. He had been up since five, and was hungry. The hedges on either side were high, and he looked at them critically. Old Ted Bates don't cut his hedges like he should, thought Foxy. Probably economising on the cutter. Still, he had to admit that the pale pink dog roses climbing high in untrimmed elder and hawthorn made a very pretty sight. Should be some good sloes, too, he thought, sizing up the blackthorn thicket by the Glebe Field gate.

He whistled, shrilly now, for his terrier, who had dived off into the hedge in pursuit of a baby rabbit. The dog reappeared, looking foolish, having lost its prey in the thick, grassy undergrowth.

'Come on, boy,' said Fox, and free-wheeled over the bridge hump, his legs up in the air like a young lad, sure of being unobserved at this hour of the morning. Unfortunately the post van was on its way to a farm up beyond the woods, and narrowly missed him.

'Watch where you're goin', you berk!' yelled Fox.

The driver, who had been at school with Fox, stuck up two fingers in reply and drove on, grinning. Fox cycled fast now, along the Green, round by the pub and into Macmillan Gardens, breakfast uppermost in his mind.

Swirls of wonderful frying bacon smells filled the room, and Jean, a big, generous girl with a head of fair, frizzy curls, stood at the gas stove, turning fried bread with a fork, shouting at the twins to get up at once, and talking to Fox about Robert's plan, all at the same time, with practised ease.

'It's Olive I feel sorry for,' she said, 'what with her precious Robert left home, and a daughter-in-law she don't like, and on top of that there's that miserable old sod Ted Bates takin' it all out on her. I reckon Robert has a right to do what he wants, and good luck to 'im.'

'Not everybody thinks like you, Jean,' said Fox, draining his big cup. 'Down in the Arms last night they were sayin' Robert shouldn't have done it. There's always bin Bateses on that farm, and some'd give their eye teeth to have a farm to step into.'

'Well, he hasn't done it yet,' said Jean, turning out the gas, and going to the door. 'Gemma! Amy! If you're not down here in one minute, I'm coming up there after you and you'll wish I 'adn't.'

'They get worse,' said Foxy fondly. He was a kind man, proud of his three boys and twin girls, and though they heard the rough end of his tongue at regular intervals, they were an affectionate family and lived happily at very close quarters in their small council house in Macmillan Gardens. Foxy's real name was Ernest, but from an early age his reddish hair and sharp features had earned him his nickname, and very few people in the village had ever called him anything else. He was a good six inches shorter than his wife, but she saw to it that he ruled the roost, or at least thought he did.

'Here's your coffee, Fox,' said Jean, handing over his flask. 'I'm goin' in to Tresham this morning on the bus, so it'll be cold dinner. Come on, my duck, let's get cleaned up.' She turned to a small, round, red-faced toddler sitting up to the table, raised to a convenient height by a couple of cushions. 'No, don't do that, Eddie!' she said. Eddie, whose grin stretched in an exact horizontal across his chubby face, had perfected an annoying habit of curling his small feet round the legs of the chair so that it was impossible to lift him down. This had raised a good family laugh the first time he did it, and now he repeated his trick at every mealtime in the hopes of another rousing success. This morning, however, Jean was in a hurry, and she jerked him out of his chair, leaving one scuffed shoe to fall on the floor, where the Jenkins terrier picked it up and made a furtive attempt to bury it in his basket in the corner.

Two ten-year-old girls, one the exact replica of the other, walked quietly into the kitchen and sat at the table. Jean put down plates of food in front of them and they began to eat, neatly, almost in unison.

'Did you put clean socks on?' said Jean, peering under the table.

''Course,' said Gemma. 'Don't we always do what we're told?'

Jean pursed her lips and looked across at Fox, struggling with his canvas haversack and making for the door. 'A couple of clever buggers we've got here, Fox,' she said. 'Bye, my dear, see you later.'

★

With a few minutes to spare, the house quiet and Eddie ready in his pushchair for the walk down to the bus stop, Jean went out into her back garden and leaned over the fence.

'Bill!' she called. 'Bill, I'm goin' into Tresham. Anything you want?'

Bill Turner appeared round the corner of his shed. 'I don't think so, thanks Jean,' he said.

'Want me to go and see Joyce this week?'

'Best not at the moment,' he said. 'They seem to want to keep her as quiet as possible. Mind you, I don't see any improvement whatever they do.' He smiled sadly at Jean, and she hurried back into her house, collected Eddie, locked the front door and made off for the bus, moving very fast, considering her bulk.

'It's a crying shame,' she said, and the little boy twisted round in his pushchair to look at her. 'Poor old Bill, he's still not free of that Joyce. And there's nothin' we can do to help. She's got him tied to her with different strings, that's all. Could go on for years.'

Eddie nodded wisely. 'Years and years and years and I want a sweetie,' he said.

Doris Ashbourne, sitting in the big window of her old person's bungalow, with a good view of the Gardens and the Green, watched Jean disappear round the corner. 'A good girl, that,' she said to Ivy Beasley, who sat sipping tea on an upright chair just to one side of the window, so that she could see but not be seen.

Ivy nodded. 'Jean's a good mother. Had those children as easy as shelling peas. And she's a faithful wife and a hard worker, which is more than you can say for some.'

Now, thought Doris, who does she mean by that?

But Ivy had no more to say, and finished her tea, getting up to take the cup and saucer into the kitchen. 'That was a nice cup of tea, thank you, Doris,' she said. 'Very nice, considering it was a tea bag.'

★

24

It was a blustery morning, and with the wind behind her Jean reached the bus stop in good time. She looked back down the street, and could see a brewer's lorry unloading beer for the pub, rolling barrels down a ramp into the cellar. Old Fred Mills had hobbled down from his bungalow in Macmillan Gardens and sat with a crony on the seat under the chestnut, clouds of pipe smoke enveloping them, happy in the sunshine and sheltered from the wind. Jean watched the children in the playground, out for the first playtime of the day, rushing about in the joy of release from the classroom. She couldn't see Mark, her middle boy, and wondered if he'd been kept in again. He didn't say much, Mark, but he managed in a subversive way to get into quite a lot of trouble. Nothing serious, mind, but Fox was always warning him. If only he'd be a bit more like Warren, Jean thought. We've never had no trouble at all with Warren.

'Here, Ellen,' she said to Ellen Biggs, who was voluminously dressed in violet cotton and sat on the bench inside the bus shelter. 'That's Olive Bates comin' down the road. She's running, too. Must be coming for the bus.'

'Since when did Olive Bates catch the bus?' said Ellen. 'Goes in regular as clockwork with Ted on a Saturday afternoon to the Supashop. Never misses.'

'Well, see for yourself,' said Jean. Ellen heaved herself to her feet and peered round the corner of the bus shelter just as Olive arrived.

'Oh, sorry, Ellen,' she said, coming to a halt inches away from the old woman. 'I thought I'd missed it, couldn't see anybody waitin'.'

'Nicest thing I've heard this mornin',' said Jean. 'My diet must be working if you couldn't see *me*!'

'We're shelterin' from this wind, Olive,' said Ellen. 'It may be summer, but old bones don't like the wind. And what's brought you to the bus this morning?'

Olive looked embarrassed. 'Had to get out of the house,' she said. 'I just thought I'd go into Tresham for a few things

I forgot on Saturday. I've a lot on my mind right now, Ellen.'

'Ah, well,' said Ellen, 'you'd better sit by me and we can 'ave a nice chat on the bus. Here it is now. Jean, look lively with that pushchair. Come on, Eddie Jenkins, up the steps and in we go!'

CHAPTER FOUR

An ancient footpath, used years ago by farm workers on their peregrinations from one farm to another, began at Ringford Hall and went through the fields and into the old spinney without touching the road. It was seldom used now, except by the occasional group of ramblers, but Susan Standing had taken to walking that way on a sunny summer's afternoon, particularly since she had become a little heavier with the baby. She strolled at her own pace along the grassy paths and rested on broken stiles and fallen trees when she felt weary.

Today she had company. Her husband Richard walked by her side, helping her over low fences and making sure stray, rusty pieces of wire did not scratch her legs. They passed through a flowering bean field, and the scent from the flowers was heavy and wonderfully sweet, but strong, and Susan began to feel queasy. She quickened up, and Richard opened the gate for her at the end of the field, helping her over the ruts and ridges of dried mud.

Richard was tall, dark-haired and rubicund, inheriting his looks from his mother, rather than from his late father. Charles Standing had been a thin, austere man, with a stoop and an air of faint bewilderment at having produced this energetic, often wayward son.

But Richard Standing had settled down now, apart from

a few passing fancies, and the estate and its farms were his whole life. The excitement of a new child, long after his son and daughter had left home more or less for good, had taken him by surprise. He spent as much time as possible with Susan, making sure she took a rest every day and helping her to resist the odd cigarette.

Now they walked slowly, hand in hand, chatting idly about the village and the current chief topic of gossip.

'I shall have to think about it seriously, of course, if Robert does decide to abandon the idea of taking on Bates's Farm when his father retires,' said Richard. 'We'd have to go into it with old Hawkins. See where we stand.'

Hawkins was the elderly solicitor in Tresham who, like his father before him, advised the Standing family on all matters legal affecting the estate.

'Never thought it would be the Bateses, though,' said Susan. 'I suppose we'd expected something of the sort at Hall Farm, where there's no son to carry on. But we'd always taken it for granted that Robert would take over. Still, maybe that's it. Robert doesn't want to be taken for granted. He's a nice lad, Richard, very polite.'

She bent down and picked a scarlet poppy from the edge of the field of ripening corn. 'How about calling the baby Poppy, if it's a girl?' she said, bored with the subject of Bates's Farm. She folded back the flower petals, leaving the smooth seed pod and hair-like, blue-black anthers exposed.

'Give me a piece of grass, Richard,' she said, and he dutifully handed her a slender green blade. She wound it round the petals, making a waist, and then snipped the hairy stalk into three parts with her fingernails. One piece went through the poppy lady's shoulders to be skinny arms, and the other two were carefully inserted under the petal skirt to become legs, adjusted to a jaunty angle.

'There,' she said. 'A poppy lady for our Poppy.'

'Not so sure about that name,' said Richard apprehensively. 'But where did you learn to do that?' He took the little figure from Susan and put it into his big pocket.

'Oh, I've always known how,' Susan said dreamily. 'We used to make whole families of them when we were children, when the long hot summer days went on for ever.'

'Oh, come on, Susan,' said Richard. 'You're not that ancient. But you do look a bit tired, darling. Let's take the short cut and get back for a cup of tea.'

Susan got to her feet and tucked her arm through Richard's, allowing him to lead her back through the spinney, across the little stream which finally broadened out to swell the Ringle, and down the sloping fields full of lark song into the grounds of the Hall.

In Bridge Cottage, Mandy Bates sat on the edge of a new armchair, watching television. That is, the television was on, and her eyes were focused on the screen, but she wasn't taking in a single word.

She had been to the Health Centre in Tresham after her sandwich lunch in the salon, and there they had confirmed what she both feared and hoped for. She was indeed pregnant, they told her. The test had been positive, and they said the baby would be born around the middle of February.

That means I am eight weeks pregnant, she thought, and stood up, feeling that this momentous news, if kept to herself, would cause her head to explode. She went out into the garden, leaned over the wooden gate, freshly painted white by Robert, and looked up the lane towards the farm.

No sign of Robert yet, but then he's bound to be late. It's a busy time on the farm, and he could be another hour or so. Mandy looked in the opposite direction, over the bridge and across the Green. It was a perfect evening, a little cool after the warm afternoon, but the wind had dropped, and the air was clear and fresh. A blackbird perched on top of one of the churchyard yews, and sang a duet with another sitting precariously on Mandy's television aerial. The perfection of the sound and the birds' total absorption in their song, oblivious to Mandy at her garden gate, made her feel even more in need of some human being to hear her earth-shattering news.

She looked again, almost conjuring Robert from a patch of shadow in the road, but there was not a soul in sight, not even a dog. Then she heard footsteps, slow and shuffling.

''Ow you doin', Mandy?' The harsh voice came from the lane, and Ellen Biggs walked painfully round the corner and into Mandy's vision.

'Not so bad, thank you, Mrs Biggs,' she said. She couldn't see herself announcing the momentous news to Ellen Biggs.

Ellen was tired, and leaned on Mandy's fence for support. 'Lovely day, it's bin,' she said, looking over at the young Bateses' garden. Their little patch of grass needed cutting, and the roses were disappearing in a thick growth of chickweed.

'Don't suppose you get much time, the pair o' you, for gardenin',' she said. That young William Roberts'll always do a bit o' weedin' for a consideration,' she added, 'but you 'ave to be sure 'e don't shirk when you're not watchin'.'

The Roberts family lived in the Gardens, opposite the Jenkinses, and were an untidy, hard-talking lot. William Roberts was Warren Jenkins's best friend, and envied him his cheerful, loving home life. William had several redeeming qualities, such as a kind heart and a friendly nature, so far intact, in spite of his father's best endeavours to knock them out of him.

'I think I've seen William,' said Mandy. 'Doesn't he do the papers on Sundays? I shall have to have a word.' She hesitated, then said, 'Do you fancy a cup of tea, Mrs Biggs?'

Ellen looked at her in surprise. She'd noticed that Mandy was not usually keen on a chat when she passed, and put it down to youth and shyness. She stood up as straight as she was able and smiled.

'Save my life, that would, young Mandy,' she said, 'or should I say Mrs Bates?'

Mandy looked embarrassed. 'Mandy will do fine,' she said, and held open the gate for Ellen to come through.

Settled in Mandy's comfortable new chair, Ellen sipped her tea and looked around. 'Got it very nice in here, you 'ave,' she said. 'Pity you'll be movin'.'

'I beg your pardon?' said Mandy.

'Well, it's all round the village, my dear,' said Ellen. 'Can't keep nothin' secret in Ringford.'

Mandy laughed shortly and, without realising it, held her hand, fingers widespread, over her stomach.

Ellen looked at her through half-closed eyes, and said slyly, 'You got some other secret you're not tellin', Mandy?'

Mandy stared at her.

'Not expectin', are we?' said Ellen.

'Mrs Biggs!' said Mandy.

'Ah, I see,' said Ellen. 'Well, you can trust me, I shan't tell a soul. Told Robert yet? I expect you've just found out, you bein' home early and that.'

Mandy was speechless, but old Ellen chatted on. After a number of revelations about past pregnancies she had known intimately, though not, as far as Mandy could discern, her own, Ellen finished her tea and struggled to her feet.

'Ta very much, dear,' she said. 'That was very welcome. You must come and 'ave a cup with me when you're passin' by. Bye bye, now, look after yerself.'

Mandy saw her out of the gate and returned to the house. She turned on the television again and thought about old Ellen, and then, when she realised that Robert would not be the first to know, she burst into tears.

CHAPTER FIVE

William Roberts was late. He always tried to get the Sunday papers delivered by ten o'clock, so that he could join Warren at the church in time for ringing. But this morning Dad had been yelling at Mum more than usual, and William had not wanted to leave, fearful that the row would escalate.

He shoved hard at a huge bundle of supplements and magazines, tearing newsprint as he pushed it through the narrow letterbox of School House. The headmistress no longer lived there, having moved over the hill to Fletching, and a strange, tall Welshman had just moved in. He had several times shouted at William because his papers weren't there by nine. God knows what he did with them. Ate the business section for breakfast, shouldn't wonder, thought William.

He pedalled home at speed, dumped the newspaper bag by his back door, and yelled into the kitchen, 'Goin' to church, Mum.' His father's voice came from upstairs, still angry, thick and heavy after last night's session in the Arms. 'Waste o'bloody time! Better be gone before I come down, else there'll be no bloody bell ringin' for you, boy.'

William had had plenty of practice at vanishing, and he vanished. At the bridge, he stopped. He'd had such a quick turn-round at home that now he had a few minutes to spare.

Just time for a quick drag, he thought. He propped his bike against the low stone wall, and scrambled down to the river bank, edging his way along until he was under the bridge. A large flat piece of stone formed a ledge overhanging the water, and William squatted down, fumbling in his jeans pocket for a flattened pack of fags and a plastic lighter he had nicked from his Dad.

The cigarette alight, he leaned back against the damp, green underside of the bridge and closed his eyes. He knew every sound in the village. Ringford had been William's world since the day of his birth, and its sounds and sights were in his head. That was Ted Bates's old Land Rover going over the bridge now. Don't say he was going to church! Not likely. Christmas and Harvest Festival, that was old Ted's lot. Prices' bantam cock's crowin' his head off down the spinney. Times Dad threatened to put it in the pot. It could start up as early as four o'clock some summer mornings. That screaming was Eddie Jenkins. Wonder what he'd been up to. Still, he wouldn't get a thumpin'. Fox Jenkins didn't believe in it. Pity Dad did. William listened to the water, always the sound of the water running on and on, out of Ringford and far away . . . Then a whirr and a clang brought him to his feet. That bloody clock!

William threw his dog-end into the river, and climbed back to the road. The clock was still striking when he rushed into the bell chamber, out of breath, and smelling strongly of cigarette smoke. Warren Jenkins frowned at him, and he took his place among the adult ringers, pulling the rope with a will and enjoying the heady sound of the bells.

'Got a gardening job,' he mouthed at Warren.

Warren frowned, unable to read William's lips.

'Tell you later,' said William silently.

When the bells finally came to rest, they crept into the back of the church. The Reverend Nigel Brooks had said that if they wanted to come into the service after ringing, and only if they wanted to, they could sit there and be quiet, really quiet and no misbehaving. They couldn't have explained why, but most Sundays they attended.

The church was quite full by Ringford standards. Ivy Beasley sat upright and stern in her usual pew, with Doris Ashbourne beside her. The third member of the trio, Ellen, was absent, not being a regular churchgoer.

'Old Poison Ivy's got a new hat,' whispered Warren.

'It's not,' said William. 'She had it for Mandy Bates's wedding. That's where I got the gardening job.'

Warren smiled. 'Nice looker, that Mandy,' he said coolly.

Ivy Beasley turned round and glared at them, and Warren nudged William. 'Sshh,' he said innocently.

They stood when the others stood, and kneeled when the congregation knelt, and had a reasonable stab at the hymns in voices on the verge of breaking. There was plenty to keep them amused. Sparrows were nesting in the church rafters, and the din made by baby birds, as their parents refuelled them with a continuous supply of insects, nearly drowned Tom Price's hesitant reading from St Paul's Epistle to the Ephesians. 'Not his mornin',' whispered William, as Tom peered at the old Bible and tried switching on the lectern light. 'It's not plugged in!' spluttered Warren, and this time Ivy darted them a look of such icy disapproval that they were quiet.

At last the joyful retiring voluntary struck up, and, weaving their way between the twos and threes coming out of church, William and Warren emerged on to the road and collected their bikes from where they'd left them, propped up against the church wall, under the black yews.

'Should be worth a couple of quid a week, down at Bridge Cottage,' said William, 'if I can spin it out. My Dad says there's not above two weeks' work in that little old garden, but I reckon I can do better than that.'

Warren looked miffed. 'If you need help,' he said, 'p'raps

with the heavy work, let me know.'

'Some hopes you got,' said William with no trace of Christian charity. 'It's rainin',' he said. 'I'm off.' He rode off at speed, narrowly missing old Fred Mills as he reached the pub door for his midday Sunday pint.

Robert Bates woke up in the front bedroom at Bridge Cottage, and for a moment wondered why he felt so good. It had been the same for the last three mornings . . . Then he remembered, sat up and looked for Mandy beside him and, seeing a vacant pillow, he leapt out of bed and rushed down the narrow stairs. They ended at a door which led straight into the living room, and there he found Mandy, kneeling like Cinderella at the hearth, cleaning out the remains of last night's fire.

'You mustn't do that, Mandy!' he said, pulling her gently upright.

'Don't be ridiculous, Rob,' she laughed. 'I'm pregnant, not ill.'

'Doesn't matter,' said Robert, taking the brush and ashcan from her. 'Let me do this, and you go and put the kettle on. I'm dying of thirst.'

'Not celebrating in the Arms last night, I hope?' said Mandy.

Robert shook his head. 'No, no. Better tell the old folks first, yours and mine, before we let the news loose on the good folk of Ringford. We can break it to Mum and Dad when we go up for tea this afternoon.'

Mandy didn't answer, and Robert looked worriedly after her as she disappeared into the kitchen. He knew she hadn't really settled in Ringford, that she missed her busy town life, and he was sad that she still felt uncomfortable and out of place at the farm. He also saw that his mother, although she never said anything, did not feel that she had gained a daughter, not for one minute. Lost a son, yes. And now with this plan of his, Robert knew that they blamed

Mandy. There is one good thing, though, he told himself brushing a few cinders off the rug. It would let Mandy off the hook. She hasn't said anything lately, but I know she doesn't fancy being a farmer's wife for the rest of her life.

By midday it was raining, a steady downpour, filling the gutters and making puddles on the Green. The sky was heavy, no breaks in the cloud and uniformly grey in all directions. A full-blown, yellow rose outside the cottage window shed its petals in a sudden shower, unable to withstand the force of the driving rain.

'Fancy a half at the pub, Mandy? I could drive you up, save getting wet.' Robert was concerned. Mandy had been looking miserable all morning, and she usually loved Sunday mornings, preparing dinner, putting the roast in the oven, playing house.

'Can't leave the beef,' she said, shaking her head. 'Needs basting – it says every half hour in the book.'

'Turn the oven right down,' said Robert knowledgeably. 'We wouldn't be much more'n half an hour.'

Mandy hesitated, then nodded. 'Okay Rob, it would be a bit more cheerful than watching the rain fall.'

The public bar was full. Sunday morning was a favourite time for the locals, as well as groups of ramblers and a few young people who drove out of Tresham in fast cars for a drink in the country.

The Standing Arms had been a small alehouse at the turn of the century, but over the years had been smartened up by successive landlords, until now it had a long, warm bar with an open fireplace at one end, and solid oak benches and tables for its regulars. Every blackened beam and crooked post was decorated with twinkling brass – horsebrasses, old bits of harness, warming pans, post horns – all cleaned regularly by Bronwen Cutt, the publican's sturdy wife.

Robert opened the door for Mandy and they pushed their way into the crowd. Robert was hailed by several young farmer friends, and Mandy went to sit at a table by the fire.

She felt uneasy, sure that everyone was staring at her. In the corner, Fred Mills was leading the regular dominoes school, and by the bar a group of girls tossed back their long hair and flirted with the lads. Mandy wished Robert would hurry up with the drinks, but could see that he had been nobbled by one of his friends.

'Hello, Mandy! Don't often see you in here . . . What can I get you?'

Colin Osman's voice was cheerful, welcoming, from the next table where he sat with his wife Pat. The Osmans were newcomers – had lived in Ringford for only a couple of years – but Colin had become a leading light in village activities. He had rejuvenated the cricket team, started a newsletter, and had an embryo group of junior footballers for whom he planned a great future. He was tall, bouncy, and very pleasant.

'Thanks,' said Mandy, 'but Robert's getting me one. He'll be here in a minute.'

'Come and sit with us,' said Pat Osman, smoothing her dark fringe and smiling at Mandy with lively brown eyes. 'We just came to cheer ourselves up on this dreadful morning.'

They agreed that the weather forecast had been wrong, that the day had started well enough, that it was possible it would clear up by teatime. The topic exhausted, Mandy looked anxiously for Robert, and was relieved to see him walking slowly towards her, bearing two brimming glasses of beer.

'Oh, Robert,' said Mandy, 'do you think I should have beer . . . you know?'

'Good gracious yes, girl,' said Robert with a smile, happy to see Mandy talking to the Osmans. 'It'll do you a power of good, all those hops and that.'

'Have you been poorly, Mandy?' said Pat politely.

Mandy looked uncomfortable. 'Not really,' she said, and then in a moment's inspiration, 'just trying to watch my weight, that's all.'

'No worries there, I should have thought,' said Colin gallantly, and then turned to Robert and began to talk about his plans.

Pat Osman twisted in her seat and looked surreptitiously under the table. 'Sit still, Tiggy,' she whispered, and pulled at a narrow, tartan lead. 'It's Tiggy,' she said apologetically. 'Don Cutt doesn't mind dogs, so long as you keep them under control. And Tiggy is so small . . .'

Mandy, too, looked under the table. A small whiskery brown face looked at her, melting blue-black eyes fixed on her, and she put out a hand to stroke the hairy head. The little Cairn licked her hand, and Mandy smiled at Pat.

'She's my new baby,' said Pat Osman, with a meaning look at Colin. 'Still just a puppy, really. I take her everywhere, if I can.'

By now, Robert and Colin were deep in the complications of planning permission, business rates and VAT thresholds. Colin had transferred from a London printing company to its branch in Tresham, and had ambitions to become a Parish Councillor first, and then, who knows, to reach the dizzy heights of the District Council. He was very happy to advise Robert on his idea for a motor engineering business.

'I'd need to put up a building, a workshop,' said Robert enthusiastically. 'And you've got to have good equipment to attract customers. People are very fussy about their cars.

Unnoticed by either Robert or Colin, a young man with pale hair and light coloured eyes hidden behind thick lenses frowned. He had been trying to listen to their conversation without appearing to eavesdrop, and turned to order another half pint from Don Cutt at the bar.

'Morton's, was it, Mr Dodwell?' said Don Cutt.

The young man nodded, and with his refilled glass in hand went over to sit at a table just behind where Robert sat with Colin, now talking to the girls and annoying them with heavy-handed teasing.

There was a loud roar of laughter at the bar, and a knot of middle-aged men, all farmers in their Sunday tweeds, rounded on one of their group. 'Don't believe you, Ted,' said one. 'Tell that to your missus, she might believe you, but we don't!'

Robert turned, hearing his father's name, and saw the bent shoulders and beaky nose of Ted Bates, just come in for his regular pint, or two, or more. 'Well, Mandy,' Robert said, 'we'd best be off to look at that meat. Drink up, my duck, we'll make a dash for it.' The rain was still beating against the small windowpanes of the pub, and Robert held his jacket like an umbrella over Mandy's head as they rushed for the Land Rover.

'Bye Dad, see you later,' called Robert as they left, but Mandy did not even glance in Ted's direction.

The pale young man returned to the bar and put his empty glass down on the counter. 'Another half, Mr Dodwell?' said Don Cutt, but the young man shook his head.

'No more, thanks,' he said. 'But tell me, what do you know about plans for a motor engineering workshop in the village?'

'Come again?' Don rattled empty glasses on a tin tray.

'Motor repairs,' said the young man. 'Where exactly does Robert Bates intend to set up his repair workshop?'

'Search me,' said Don Cutt, who knew perfectly well every detail of Robert's plans. 'Better ask him yourself, Mr Dodwell. Now, if you'll excuse me, I must see to these glasses.'

CHAPTER SIX

For the first time in many years, Olive Bates's Victoria sponge had failed to rise. This was such a bad omen for the family tea that she had thrown it into the dustbin, well wrapped in old newspaper to disguise the waste from Ted, and quickly started again. This time the cake had risen to its proper height, and Olive put the light, golden sponge to cool on a wire tray.

But she could not forget the heavy, lumpen mess in the bin, and, more importantly, the reason for its abysmal failure. I'm just not myself, she thought, and the house is an unhappy one. Cakes won't rise when the heart of the house is cracking open. It was all round the village now, Robert's proposed application to open a garage workshop at Miss Hewitt's old bungalow, and Ted had been so angry Olive had retreated to the garden in fear.

Why didn't Robert tell us first? thought Olive. His father may be a miserable old devil, but he was really hurt to have to hear about the bungalow from Fred Mills in the pub.

Well, Ted was snoring in the front room now, after a session at the Arms and his Sunday dinner. The day had not improved, and Olive had lit a fire, putting the guard in front so that no spitting red-hot sparks should land on the sleeping Ted.

It's that Mandy, I expect. Olive put the best china cups

and saucers on a tray, ready to take into the front room when the young ones arrived. Those Butlers have lived in Tresham all their lives. How could Robert expect Mandy to take on the farm without any knowledge of what it meant? She'd had a go at warning Mandy before the wedding, then tried to help her by telling her as much as she could about the farm, what had to be done, and what Robert would expect from her. But farming was a thing you had in your bones, and Olive had felt she was getting nowhere.

She had been dreading this afternoon all week. She knew exactly what would happen. Robert would start off all reasonable and nice, and then Ted would argue, and lose his temper and shout, and before Olive could smooth it all out, Robert and Mandy would leave and never come back.

A tear dripped into the milk jug, and Olive poured off a little and watched it disappear down the sink. The kettle was singing, and she moved it to one side of the Rayburn, putting the teapot to warm by its side. Sniffing sadly, she took off her apron and went upstairs to change.

'So who's going to tell them, you or me?' said Mandy.

'Whatever you think, Mandy,' said Robert, helping her on with her jacket. 'It might be better coming from you. I'm pretty much in the doghouse with Dad, anyway.'

'I wish we didn't have to go. Couldn't we just ring them up and say it's raining too hard, and by the way we're having a baby?'

Robert sighed. He'd never imagined it would be like this. His mother had always been so fond of babies, making a fuss of every new one in the village, and he'd looked forward to being able to give her grandchildren one day. Now everything had gone wrong. It was his fault, of course, wanting to leave the farm. But now he'd decided, he knew there was no going back. He just had to do it. It was something he'd always wanted to do. Nothing to do with Mandy, or anyone else.

41

'Come on Mandy, love,' he said. 'Let's go and get it over. I just hope Dad didn't have too many beers at lunchtime, that's all.'

They walked in silence up the wet lane, the big trees at the edge of the park hurling great sprays of rainwater at them. The old vicarage, tall and forbidding in the grey light, looked empty, deserted. Robert remembered how, as boys, he and his friends had trespassed regularly in the wild garden. The old vicar, Cyril Collins, had cared nothing for gardening, and then he'd got too old.

'We used to go scrumping round the back there,' Robert said, squeezing Mandy's hand. 'There was one apple tree specially, always loaded. Wonderful apples, they were. Wonderful. Sweet as a nut. Trouble was, it was just outside old Cyril's study.'

'Didn't you ever get caught?' said Mandy incuriously, picking her way round a mound of cow dung and straw turned to slush in the middle of the road.

'We thought we were too clever,' said Robert, 'but I reckon old Cyril knew quite well we were there. He didn't mind, you know. Funny old bloke, he was.'

As they passed the big vicarage gate, the black front door opened and the Reverend Nigel Brooks came out. He was a tall, handsome man, his wavy grey hair showing no signs of thinning, and his ready smile already well in place. He was quite new in Ringford, and apart from a shaky start over the Christmas Concert, had settled in well, popular with the old people and treading carefully before trying any more innovations.

'Not much like summer, Robert!' he called, hurrying down the path. Mandy and Robert slowed down and waited.

'Going to the farm?' he said. 'I'll walk along with you, if I may. Old Ricky has to have a walk, whatever the weather.' He whistled to a heavy black labrador, who walked crookedly out of the vicarage garden and into the road.

'He looks as if he'd rather be in a nice warm kitchen,' said Mandy.

'Quite so,' said Nigel Brooks. 'I just pretend he needs the walk, but it's really that I like a breather before going to Fletching to take the evening service.'

As he spoke he looked closely at Robert and Mandy, and noted their glum expressions. He had of course heard all about the garage plan, but said nothing. He saw it as his duty to know everything and say nothing until he was asked. Then he was wary, and tried to get others to unburden themselves to him before attempting anything in the way of advice.

'Quite settled in at Bridge Cottage?' he said, stepping out and not bothering to avoid the puddles in his big green Wellington boots.

Robert and Mandy exchanged glances. 'Not too bad,' said Robert. 'It is very small, of course. Not too much room for expansion.'

Nigel Brooks raised his eyebrows. 'Ah,' he said, 'I see. Well, I shall leave you to a happy tea party . . .' He waved cheerily and branched off on a footpath across the fields, whistling and calling to old Ricky, who unwillingly followed.

'That's all *he* knows,' said Mandy, and opened the gate in the laurel hedge.

Ted Bates woke with a start when he heard the farm dog barking and the back door open. He sat up hastily, and smoothed his thin hair with a hand that shook slightly. Picking up the newspaper from the floor, he hurriedly opened it and turned to the racing results. When Mandy and Robert came into the room he did not look up.

'Hello, Dad, rotten weather,' said Robert, with a brave attempt at normality. Mandy said nothing, but went to sit over by the window, looking out at the rain in the green, lush garden. The wet logs on the fire hissed, and a jet of

43

liberated gas from an old piece of oak burned brightly with orange and blue flames.

Robert tried again. 'We'll have to look at that bottom field tomorrow, Dad,' he said. 'There's standing water there. All this bloody rain, I expect.'

'No need to swear,' said his father, who was usually unable to reach the end of a sentence without blaspheming. 'Specially not in front of Mandy, here,' he added self-righteously.

Robert started to protest, but then shut his mouth tightly, and looked desperately at Mandy. She shrugged, and came to his rescue. 'Nothing to what I hear sometimes in the salon, Mr Bates, I can tell you,' she said, with her most winning smile.

Ted put down his newspaper and got up to kick one of the logs back into the heart of the fire. 'Well,' he said, 'I wouldn't know about that, would I? Not goin' much to ladies' hairdressing shops.'

The awkward silence that followed this was mercifully broken by Olive bringing in the tea. Robert jumped up to carry the tray, and Mandy returned with her to the kitchen to bring the cake and hot water to refill the pot. This was the one aspect of Bates's Farm that Mandy loved. The teatime ritual had never existed in her mother's home, and nobody else she knew had small sandwiches and biscuits and cake with their cup of tea in the afternoon. Her family had never used a hot water jug, and she couldn't remember seeing a cut-glass cake stand before she came to Bates's End.

'Will you have a sandwich, Mandy?' said Olive, when they had all settled nervously on the edge of the chairs. Only Ted sank deep into his armchair and glowered.

The conversation flickered and died, and was relit by each in turn as they desperately thought of something else to say. Finally the opening came.

'I saw Mrs Standing yesterday,' said Olive. 'She came

into the shop in a flimsy dress, and she's showing quite well now. September is it, the baby's due?'

'Think so,' said Mandy, taking a deep breath. 'And we'll have another Ringford baby in February, with any luck.'

Robert smiled encouragingly at her, and then turned to his mother. 'You've always wanted to be a granny, Mum,' he said.

Olive's mouth opened, and she tried to speak, but nothing came out. She swallowed hard, tried again, and managed, 'Oh, Robert . . .'

Ted's head had come up sharply after Mandy's announcement, and he too stared at Robert. 'Ain't you got enough on your bloody plate,' he said, 'what with leavin' your parents in the lurch, and takin' on new property an' all that, without fathering a baby s'soon?'

Mandy's face began to crumple, and Robert went quickly to her side. 'We thought you'd be pleased,' he said.

'And have you thought of the extra expense?' said Ted, warming up. 'Have you considered mortgage repayments and building costs and lawyers' fees, without havin' cots and prams and 'undreds of bloody nappies to buy on top?'

Mandy stood up, fumbling for her handkerchief. 'Take me home, Robert,' she said. 'This is no place for us. Take me home, please.'

After they had left, Olive washed up the tea things in silence. Ted followed her about, not saying anything, just snorting every now and then. She dried up the best china, and put away the untouched golden sponge cake. Leaving Ted sitting at the kitchen table with his head in his hands, she went upstairs and sat in the worn armchair in Robert's old room, and cried bitterly for a long time – but quietly, so as not to disturb Ted.

CHAPTER SEVEN

Half a week gone, and the sun had returned to Ringford. Doris Ashbourne locked her front door and set off down the little concrete path, pausing to pick a few dead heads off her roses, and then closed the gate behind her as she walked smartly down Macmillan Gardens. She had a word with Fred Mills, as he leaned on his gate, puffing his pipe in a reverie, like some old hookah smoker. Doris wasn't sure he'd heard her. He was a bit of a poor old thing since his sister died.

William Roberts came out of his garden on his bike and narrowly missed Doris. 'Sorry, Mrs Ashbourne!' he shouted, shooting straight across the grass and flowerbeds of the common area, and without losing speed disappeared up the Jenkinses' footpath.

'If I catch you, y'young bugger, I'll teach you not to ride across them flowerbeds!' Fred Mills had sprung to life at the sight of William's bike ploughing through the beds he lovingly tended on behalf of everyone in the Gardens.

Doris walked out of the Gardens and could see festive bunting fluttering in the school playground, stirred by gusts of light wind, ready for the evening barbecue organised by the Parents' Association. I hope Reverend Brooks is praying for the fine weather to last, thought Doris, looking at a distant bank of heavy clouds beyond

Bagley Woods. Tables and chairs had been set out by the children, and Foxy Jenkins had positioned the barbecue itself under the great sycamore tree, all prepared for lighting up after school. Several summers ago Doris had helped Jean Jenkins with the bunting, made out of triangular pieces of old summer dresses from the jumble sale, machined on to strong white tape. Done well, that has, thought Doris.

She stopped outside Victoria Villa, the red-brick, solid house where Ivy Beasley had been born and still lived. On the other side of the road, at the edge of the Green, the Jenkins terrier was tossing a dead shrew into the air and catching it again, shaking it viciously to make sure there was no life left. The breeze stirred the willows on the far side of the Green, and as Doris narrowed her eyes against the sun to make out a figure with a little dog strolling along the river path, William and Warren trudged past her, fishing rods over their shoulders, deep in conversation.

'I like the fizzy centres,' said Warren.

'Yeah,' said William, 'an' I like them middle bits.'

'Centres *are* the middle bits, you berk,' said Warren, guffawing.

'I know that,' said William, punching him on the shoulder. They clashed fishing rods for a few minutes, then set off again at a jog trot across the Green.

Doris turned, expecting to see Ivy appearing to join her. But the dark-green front door did not open, and Doris sighed. She knew Ivy spent most of her time keeping watch on village life from her front window, and must have seen her. Just making me go the extra steps. Done purposely, thought Doris.

Inside Victoria Villa, in her kitchen, Ivy Beasley was innocent for once. She had just slid a rice pudding into the range oven, just the right coolish temperature, and was hanging a cloth over the oven rail. She looked at the old wall clock and hurried to get her cardigan and handbag.

Time you got a new cardigan, said her mother's voice. Are you too mean, Ivy, to throw that one away? You'd never have seen your mother in such a shabby old garment.

Yes, mother, said Ivy wearily. She picked up a magazine to pass on to Ellen Biggs, and made for the front room to watch for Doris. Yes, she said, I'll look at Addenham's next time I go to Tresham.

Navy-blue would be best, said the voice. Can't be wearing bright colours at your age.

I was thinking of a nice pink, for the summer, said Ivy.

Pink! With your high colour? Anyway, it would always be in the wash.

Maybe, mother, said Ivy stubbornly. I'll see what they've got. She could see Doris coming up the path, and walked through to the front door. 'No need to ring, Doris,' she said, opening it just as Doris put her finger on the white china button.

They walked slowly in the sunshine, and as they passed the shop, Bill Turner's van drew up. He strode up the steps and disappeared.

'No shame, that man,' said Ivy Beasley.

'What do you mean, Ivy?' said Doris. 'He's got to go shopping, like anybody else, for goodness sake.'

'Not twice a day, every day,' said Ivy. 'A man on his own doesn't need that much to live on. One good shop a week would do him.'

'Perhaps he's lonely, now his Joyce is in the mental home,' said Doris, as they crossed the road and set off down Bates's End towards Ellen's. She hoped Ivy wouldn't go on about it. The romance between Peggy Palmer and Bill was common knowledge now, and most people accepted it, some with wholehearted approval and others with regret that poor Joyce Turner had been made worse by the affair. But the Turner marriage had been a travesty for many years before Peggy Palmer came to the village, and the general

48

view was that Joyce would have tipped over the edge sonner or later, anyway.

Ivy's abiding dislike of Peggy Palmer had not abated, however, and counting herself Joyce's only friend, she held on like the Jenkins terrier with a rabbit. 'He needn't have been lonely,' she said. 'Had a good wife, and didn't know how to handle her. And as for Mrs Peggy Palmer, no sooner put her poor husband under the sod that she's after Bill Turner full steam ahead.'

'Look at that river,' said Doris, determined to change the subject. 'It's come up inches in all that heavy rain.' They lingered on the old bridge, gazing down to where small shoals of minnows wove in and out of the waterweed, and Prices' ducks uptailed, far from home and over-confident that the fox was not about.

Bridge Cottage was quiet, doors and windows closed, and no sign of life. Robert was hard at work on silage, cutting the rich grass in the far fields, keeping thoughts of his father at bay with cheerful local radio in his tractor cab. And Mandy, fourteen miles away in Tresham, gossiped with her ladies, safe in the scented, humid air of the salon, catching up on clients' holiday plans and snatching a dry cracker between appointments when she felt queasy.

'You've heard, I suppose, about Mandy and Robert?' said Doris.

'Naturally,' said Ivy Beasley. 'I was the next to know, after Olive and Ted, of course. Robert came in for his cup of tea on Monday as usual, and he couldn't wait to tell, bursting out of him, it was.' She didn't reveal that Robert had been far from ecstatic, had told her about his father's reaction, and asked her to keep up Mandy's spirits if she had the chance.

As they passed the church and approached Ellen's Lodge, Doris stopped. 'Ivy,' she said, 'what's that in Ellen's garden?'

'Can't see anything,' said Ivy, walking on.

Doris caught her up and took her arm, slowing her down. 'No, Ivy, wait, there is something there. Look under that holly bush by the fence.'

The Lodge garden had once been a model of neatness and order, but that was when the Standings' old gardener had lived there. Ellen did her best, and Fred Mills would occasionally give her a hand with the digging. But it was a poor best, and roses and shrubs went unpruned, borders unweeded. 'Well,' Ellen had said cheerfully, 'I'm in the fashion. We all got to leave room for wild flowers, ain't we, Ivy.' Ivy had replied tartly that that didn't mean the whole garden had to be devoted to weeds.

In spite of neglect and confusion, The Lodge still had a rustic, battered charm. Twisted brick chimneys and ecclesiastical windows, shrouded in ivy and climbing roses out of control, an arched porch and clumps of lime-green moss on the stone slates, all added to an air of mystery and romance. At least, that's what Doris thought, but wisely never said so to Ivy.

As far as Ellen was concerned, it was a damp, dark old cottage, but it was home.

'Here, Doris,' said Ivy, peering over the garden gate, 'hold my handbag. You were right. I reckon it's a sheep, got in from the field. Mind you, it can't do much damage, might even eat down the grass a bit.'

Doris took Ivy's handbag. 'What are you going to do, Ivy?' she said apprehensively.

'Get rid of it, of course,' said Ivy, opening the gate. 'Can't see Ellen Biggs chasing a sheep, can you?'

Ivy grabbed an old broom that Ellen kept for sweeping up leaves, and approached the sheep. It stared at her stupidly, in the way of sheep. 'Go on,' she said, 'get out!' She approached it and waved the broom. With a resigned expression, the sheep turned and, without hurrying, eased itself under the fence and back into the park, where it continued to nibble the short grass.

'There!' said Ivy, scarlet-faced and triumphant.

'Very brave, Ivy,' said Doris. 'Here, take your handbag. I can see Ellen at the window.'

Ivy looked meaningly at Doris, and said, 'I wonder what delights she's cooked up for us today?' Ellen, in spite of having been cook at the Hall, now lived on very simple fare. She could not be bothered, seeing no point in spending hours on making meals for herself which took all her pension money and gave her indigestion.

'Mr Kipling as usual, I expect,' continued Ivy, but Doris frowned her into silence, and called out, 'Yoo hoo! Ellen, are you there!'

'I ain't deaf, our Doris,' said old Ellen, materialising from her dark little bedroom. 'Leastways, not very. Just bin changin' me shoes. Yer feet don't 'alf sweat in this weather.' She didn't mention the sheep.

Ivy wrinkled her nose, and sat down gingerly on the edge of a cane chair by the window.

'I'll just see to the kettle. It 'as boiled already,' said Ellen, and hobbled into the tiny kitchen. Doris followed her, offering help, but Ellen shook her head. 'Only room for one in 'ere, Doris,' she said. 'You go and cheer up our Ivy. Looks as if she's swallowed a lemon, poor thing.'

Doris went back into the sitting room and surreptitiously tried to open one of the leaded, ecclesiastically arched windows. It was welded shut, however, with old paint and years of grime, and she sat down on the sagging sofa without looking at Ivy. One glance would be enough to provoke a scathing remark, so she kept up a conversation with Ellen, shouting through the open kitchen door.

'Did you know about the Bates baby on the way, Ellen?'

'What you say, Doris?'

'I said, did you know about the Bates baby?' Doris raised her voice, articulating each word.

''Course I did,' said Ellen. 'I knew before anybody else, even 'er Robert.'

Ivy sat up straighter, bristling. 'Don't be ridiculous, Ellen Biggs,' she said. 'Mandy told Robert first, then Olive and Ted, and then Robert told me. They know the proper way to go on, Robert and Mandy.'

'Ah well,' said Ellen, appearing with a loaded tray, teacups rattling dangerously, 'they didn't exactly tell me, Ivy, I just used my head and guessed. Mandy 'ad it written all over 'er that afternoon. I only 'ad to read the signs.'

Ivy sniffed, and leaned forward. 'I saw that cake in the shop last week, didn't I? Peggy Palmer taken to selling things out of date now, has she?'

Ellen opened her mouth to retort, but Doris stepped in. 'You'll not be wanting any, then, Ivy?' she said. Ellen grinned. Good old Doris, she could be a match for Ivy any day if she put her mind to it.

Ivy glared at her. 'A fruit cake will last for weeks, Doris,' she said. 'At least, a home-made one will. Don't know about shop cakes. Never buy them myself. But I'm prepared to take the risk, if you are.'

Doris, who knew that any luxury such as a cake, however despicable in Ivy's eyes, made a big hole in Ellen's resources, smiled, and said, 'Well, I'm starving, Ellen, only had a quick sandwich for dinner, so me first, please.'

Ellen poured out strong, hot tea and cut the cake, giving Ivy a noticeably smaller piece and settled back in her armchair.

'Well, I reckon,' she said, 'them Bateses are in trouble. There's Ted so mad that 'e can't speak to anybody. He used to manage a grunt when 'e saw me, but he passed this morning and I could'a not bin there. And Robert with a face like a wet week, and Mandy slammin' her car door so's I can 'ear it from 'ere . . .'

'I did see Olive in the shop,' said Doris, 'and she looked pale. Peggy was saying that Olive's lost weight lately, too. She was trying to persuade her to buy some of those extra creamy yoghurts.'

'She don't want none o' that rubbish!' said Ellen. 'A few good puddins is what she needs.'

'If you ask me,' said Ivy, and Ellen and Doris exchanged glances, 'Olive Bates could do with a different husband, but as she's not likely to get one, a spot of arsenic in his tea might be the next best thing.'

'I've got some,' said Ellen helpfully.

Doris and Ivy both put down their cups with a crash. 'Ellen Biggs!' said Ivy.

'Well,' said Ellen, smiling a small smile, 'it's in that rat poison stuff, ain't it? That's all I meant. More tea, Ivy?'

It had been a long afternoon in the shop, people coming in dribs and drabs, so that although the takings hadn't swelled much, Peggy had been unable to get on with any pricing or stacking between customers. She pulled down the white blind with relief, and after looking up and down the street to make sure nobody was making a last-minute dash before she shut, she locked the door and went through into her kitchen.

She had just settled down with the newspaper and a cup of tea, Gilbert curled up warmly on her lap, when she heard the side gate click open. Now who is that? she thought. Bill, probably. He's telepathic where teatime is concerned.

But it wasn't Bill. Mandy Bates stood on the step, and when Peggy opened her back door she came straight in without being asked.

'It's not my appointment, is it?' said Peggy, looking anxiously at the calendar.

'No, no, Mrs Palmer,' said Mandy. 'I just wondered if I could have a word. I don't know who to talk to, and Mum would worry, so I can't tell her, and . . .'

Her voice tailed away, and she looked at Peggy pleadingly. 'Sit down, Mandy dear,' said Peggy. 'The tea's fresh in the pot. Here, put some sugar in it and sit quiet for a minute. I must tell you about the Standings, it's too good a story to keep to myself.'

She regretfully put aside all thoughts of an early start in the garden. All afternoon in the shop she had looked longingly out at the summer sunshine, vowing to be out among her flowers as soon as possible after closing time. She had planted a new herbaceous border, knowing little about perennials and annuals, but taking advice from Bill. It was all beginning to bush out now, and looked something like the covers of the seed packets. And those buttercups by the fence, she thought, I'd meant to dig all those runners out where they come in from the field. Damn it.

Instead, she launched into the latest on Susan Standing, thinking she could cheer up Mandy a little, and give her strength to come out with whatever was bothering her.

'And,' she said, 'you won't believe it, Mandy, but she's booked her nanny, already! A properly trained girl from Ireland, daughter of someone her sister knows. I don't know why people like her have babies, when they pass them on as soon as they're born . . . Still, Mr Richard's like a dog with two tails, and they say Mrs Standing's mother is so pleased it's given her a new lease of life . . .'

Oh, well done, Peggy, she thought, seeing a tear rolling down Mandy's cheek. 'Come on, Mandy,' she said. 'What is it? Better spit it out.'

Mandy shook her head and pulled out a small handker-chief.

If I'd had a daughter, Peggy thought, she would have been about Mandy's age, and I'd be a granny-to-be. Olive Bates should count her blessings. And that Ted, miserable sod.

She waited, turning the pages of the newspaper and pointing out a ridiculous fashion feature to Mandy. 'That would go down well in Ringford,' she said. 'I can just see Doris Ashbourne in that.'

With a glimmer of a smile, Mandy nodded. 'Or my precious mother-in-law,' she said. 'Baggy tweed skirts and hand-knitted jumpers is the height of fashion for them.'

'Still,' said Peggy, 'they have their good points, Doris and company. Olive too, in her way.'

And then it all tumbled out, Mandy speaking fast, almost without drawing breath, telling Peggy about the disastrous tea party at the farm, and how Robert had hardly spoken to her since, or to anyone, come to that.

'What am I going to do, Mrs P.?' she said. 'If we're going to live here for the rest of our lives, we can't have this between us. Just when we should all be happy and joyful, the whole Bates family is going around like a major tragedy has struck.'

Peggy wondered if she should tell Mandy that just the fact of being pregnant would have been a miracle for her all those years ago, overriding all else, but decided against it. She'd learnt that lesson early on in the shop. Unhappy people did not want to hear of others' troubles.

'Patience, Mandy,' she said. 'Just keep your head down and let Robert sort it out. After all, its all because of Robert leaving the farm, and Ted not being able to forgive him. Don't let it get you down, my dear. Babies are great ambassadors, you'll see.'

CHAPTER EIGHT

The door of the Standing Arms stood open, and Bill Turner, elbow on the polished oak bar, watched his friend Tom Price walk towards the pub with a slight limp that dated from the day he had tipped his tractor into a ditch at Hall Farm. He saw William Roberts and Warren Jenkins emerge from Macmillan Gardens, dawdling behind Tom. Then he saw that Warren Jenkins was limping in exaggerated imitation of Tom. Tom did not look round, but slowed up by the stone cottages next to the pub. He bent down to pick up a bright purple chocolate wrapper, and then turned suddenly to face William and Warren, caught in the process of limping laboriously across the road.

Now they're for it, thought Bill. After a minute or two, during which Tom talked and the boys listened, Tom handed the wrapper to Warren Jenkins, and the two boys – their shoulders hunched in chagrin but walking absolutely normally – crossed the road again to the litter bin placed strategically under a poster for the annual Tidy Village Competition.

'Young buggers,' was all Tom said when he reached the bar.

Tom was chairman of the Parish Council, and his family had been farmers in the village for as long as the Bateses, if not longer. He was a tall, heavily built man, with short, greyish-white hair and a good-humoured expression. His wife, Doreen, was President of Ringford WI and a good third of the workforce on the farm. They had had only one child, a daughter who – to their disappointment – had married a young solicitor and gone to live in Manchester.

'Wondered if you'd be down tonight,' said Bill, 'it being such a grand evening. Finished the silage?'

'Nearly,' said Tom, 'but the forecast is good, and I was beginning to see bloody great glasses of ale coming over the fields towards me.'

'Time to stop, boy. You did the right thing. Is it a pint, then?'

Bill beckoned to Don Cutt and gave him the order. They settled down to an easy, inconsequential conversation, comparing the state of crops and gardens. Bill was involved in most things on the Hall estate, and worked closely with Tom when there were jobs needing the two most experienced pairs of hands in the village.

'How's your Joyce?' said Tom. The question was becoming a ritual, gone through by both of them, best got out of the way.

'About the same,' said Bill. 'Don't see much change yet, but thanks for asking.' He changed the subject. 'Seen Ted Bates lately?' He had been kept up to date on the unhappy story by Peggy, and felt some sympathy with the miserable old bugger. 'Mind you,' he continued, 'I suppose you know a bit how he's feeling.'

Tom shook his head. 'Worse for Ted,' he said. 'He's always taken it for granted that Robert would step into his shoes. At least I've always known there'd be nobody.'

'Robert's a good lad,' said Bill. 'It's very difficult to take sides.'

'Ah, now, you just remind me,' said Tom. 'I was going to ask you what you thought about co-opting Robert on to the Show Committee? We're one short, and I reckon Robert would be a real asset.'

Round Ringford Agricultural Show was one of the oldest in the country, and still accurately reflected the life of the farming community. It was sheep and cattle, goats and ponies, hunters and driving turn-outs that people came to see. Every August, the big Top Field at Hall Farm was given over to the Show, and Tom Price and the Committee, chaired by Richard Standing and his father before him, worked for most of the year organising an event regarded by the whole county as the jewel in its crown.

Ringford Show drew competitors from all over the country, and standards were high. To be on the Show Committee was a privilege, and Bill did not take Tom's suggestion lightly.

'He's got a lot to think about just now,' he said. 'I don't know if he'd have time for anything else. Still, it would cheer him up a bit, with all this unpleasantness with Ted. It'd be all right with me, Tom. See what the others think at the meeting on Thursday, but I'm behind it.'

The meeting, held officially in the Village Hall but mostly in the pub afterwards, agreed that it would be a good thing to ask Robert to join them. He had proved his worth on the Parish Council, was not too pushy with his opinions, and always willing to take on any jobs the more senior members did not want to do.

'Right, Tom,' said Richard Standing, as agreement was reached, 'would you like to approach Robert on the Committee's behalf?'

Robert Bates walked home through the fields, thinking about Mandy and his parents, and wishing things could be otherwise. He looked across the pale ripening wheat and knew that soon harvest would be upon them, and all hours would be taken up with the usual race against the weather. He climbed a stile and walked through the long pasture, keeping an eye open for the red bull, in with the cows to do his stuff, and saw him, short-legged and deep-chested, his curly red poll lowered as he grazed peacefully. Should be some good calves there in due course, thought Robert. A good bull, that.

He passed the giant muck heap, and a flock of feeding crows flew up, cawing in annoyance at having been disturbed. We shall have to spread that, find a new site, thought Robert. It's been there too long already.

He followed the hedge downhill to the back of the cottage and, with his eye on the ground to watch out for rabbit holes, he saw purple vetch, ox-eye daisies, iron-red spears of sorrel and giant sow thistles in the ditch. Shan't see much of this when I'm working on cars all day, he thought, but he shrugged. Plenty of time when I'm an old man to look at wild flowers. Now's the time to be making my way, specially with a family coming along.

'God, I'm hungry,' he said aloud, and quickened his pace, finally opening his gate with a new determination.

'Ah, Robert,' said Mandy, looking up from a motherhood book as he came in. 'Tom Price rang up and said he'd like a word. He's dropping in on his way to Bagley tonight, said it won't take long.'

Robert frowned. Surely not objections to his plan already. He had submitted preliminary details to the Planning Department, and awaited developments. Tom had warned him that when it came up before the Parish Council, Robert would have to absent himself as an interested party.

'What time's he coming?'

'Around seven, he said.' Mandy got up and stretched her arms high above her head.

'Tired?' said Robert, giving her a kiss. Things had quietened down on the farm, and he kept out of his father's way. His mother was pale and withdrawn, but occasionally touched his shoulder when he sat at the kitchen table with his coffee. He worried about her, but could think of nothing to ease her lot.

Mandy fortunately had a sunshine-and-showers nature, and had recovered from the traumatic tea at the farm. She kept well away from Ted, but when she knew he was out in the fields she dropped in to see Olive, taking magazines from the salon and trying to cheer her up. But she felt that Olive always had one eye out for Ted approaching, and so Mandy stayed only a few minutes.

'I had a very full day in the salon, today,' she said. 'Guess who came in.'

'Joan Collins,' said Robert, rolling up his sleeves and washing his hands in the sink.

'Close,' said Mandy. 'No, dope, it was madame herself, Mrs Susan Standing. She'd booked with Gerald, naturally, only the top stylist being good enough. Apparently she's too big with child to go trotting off to her London hairdresser, and has decided to have her hair done locally, at least until after the baby's born.'

'Did she speak to you?'

'Yes, as a matter of fact, she was very nice. She came over and said she believed we had something in common, and gave a really nice grin. Said we'd be able to compare notes, but she was glad she had a head start. Apparently she was very sick at the beginning, much worse than me.'

'Well, well,' said Robert, 'seems this baby thing has its good side.' He took the cup of tea Mandy handed to him and disappeared up the narrow stairs to have a proper wash and change before Tom came.

'Well, what do you think, darling?' said Susan, turning this way and that in front of her looking-glass. 'Will it do, until after Poppy is born?'

'It's very nice, Susan,' said Richard, without really looking, 'but I do hope you're not getting stuck on Poppy as a name. Sounds like some old flapper from the Twenties. And what if it's a boy?'

'Cyril?' said Susan.

60

Richard looked at her sharply, and then gave up. 'Shall we change the subject?' he said. 'I saw some papers today in the Council Offices, all to do with young Robert's plans. I think we may be in for a spot of bother there. It seems there's a pretty deeply-entrenched animosity to anything to do with the motor trade. And Ringford being a conservation village is going to make it very difficult for him to put up a commercial building on late lamented Aunt Hewitt's garden.'

Susan yawned. 'I should think so too,' she said. 'It's a nasty noisy business, repairing cars. Much better kept in towns, darling, don't you think? Now do come to bed, Richard, I need you to rub my back.'

'Certainly,' said Richard with alacrity, and pulled back the covers.

'Go away,' said Peggy, but not very firmly.

'Just want to say goodnight,' said Bill. 'Can't I come in?'

'No,' said Peggy. 'Don't forget old Ivy Beasley the Beautiful Spy will be watching. She has her binoculars trained on me night and day, especially night.'

'Who cares about old Ivy,' said Bill, a little indistinctly. He put his hand out, and Peggy took it. 'If I can't come in, you'll have to come out,' he said, and pulled her to him, holding her close on the back doorstep, kissing her with beery breath.

'What difference does it make? Everybody thinks we're at it at every opportunity, so why aren't we?'

Peggy drew away from him, and walked him slowly down the path at the side of the shop, out of sight of Victoria Villa. She stopped and turned, putting both hands on Bill's shoulders, peering up at him in the dark.

'Bill,' she said, 'you're clear-headed enough, I hope, to take this in. While your Joyce is in hospital, not able to think straight, I can't do it. Don't ask me what the difference is, why it would be so much worse than what we have already.

61

I don't know. It just would be.'

She led him to the gate, opened it and gently pushed him out. 'Go home, Bill, there's a love. See you tomorrow. Goodnight.'

Bill walked home reasonably steadily, pushing his bike, unaware of the shadowy face at the bedroom window of Victoria Villa. 'Bugger it,' he said, as he caught his shin on his bicycle pedal. 'Bugger everything.'

CHAPTER NINE

Show day dawned with a cool breeze across the Top Field, welcomed by the team of men putting the finishing touches to the three main rings. They hammered in stakes and tightened ropes so that onlookers would be kept safely out of the way of cantering horses and wayward cattle.

Bill Turner, out of breath and thirsty, straightened his back. He looked up at big white clouds, high and benevolent, and predicted a fine day. They'd been lucky the last few years, but he could remember one or two total washouts. Well, not total, because the exhibitors and competitors came whatever the weather. But it was the spectators, the crowds of families with excited children, that were the vital part of the Show. Without them, half the atmosphere was lost.

'We shall be all right today, Fox,' he called across to where Foxy Jenkins was testing out a gate on the goat pens. 'Should be record crowds today. All your lot coming?'

Foxy came across, rubbing his big hands together, grinning happily. 'Good God yes, boy,' he said. 'You try and stop 'em! Jean's in the WI tent, with the little 'un, and the rest'll be out and about round the Show. Warren is helpin' Tom Price, runnin' messages and that, and the twins will be hanging round the ice-cream van, most likely.'

Horse boxes and trailers arrived early, and William Roberts had been entrusted with the job of seeing that they parked in an orderly fashion. He was especially helpful to a family with two daughters of sixteen or so. William looked at their neat little bottoms in immaculate white riding trousers and was stirred to offer his services.

'Just ask me,' he said, 'if you want to know where to go. You know, register, and that.' On the whole, there was little argument from the exhibitors. Most of them had been coming to Ringford Show for years, and knew exactly where to go, what to do.

Colin Osman, whose help had been enlisted by Tom Price, turned up good and early for his stint of car park duty, and was not so lucky.

'You should have seen them,' he said to Pat, as she joined him for his coffee break. 'I don't know where they came from, the most incredible old wreck of a car, crammed to the brim with rat-faced men and scruffy children. Swearing and cursing at me, they were, because I wouldn't let them squeeze into the ringside. Tom had warned me, but I wasn't quite prepared for that lot.'

Pat Osman soothed his ruffled feathers, and praised him for the regular parallel lines of parked cars, all with a sensible distance between them.

'You done well, boy,' said Foxy, joining them for a couple of minutes before he went off to help in the collecting ring. 'Just be glad the ground is firm. I've known times when we've had to tow 'em off with tractors. An' that's a pantomime, I can tell you.'

By ten o'clock everything was in full swing. Miraculously, all the animals were in the right pens, the owners standing close by, or sitting on collapsible stools brought specially, guarding their valuable stock.

Mandy Bates had fallen in with Peggy as she walked to the Top Field from the village, up the lane with its queues of cars and dry summer verges. A film of dust had settled on the grass and the strong, rusty red sorrel.

'Convolvulus,' said Peggy, picking a white trumpet-shaped flower from the hedge and handing it to Mandy, 'or bindweed to you and me. See, all those walks with Frank were not in vain.'

'You must miss him, Mrs P.,' said Mandy, glancing across at Peggy. But Peggy's face was serene.

'Yes, I do,' she said, 'but while I can still remember what he said and did, he's not completely gone.'

They stopped at the entrance gate and looked across the showground. It was a scurrying, throbbing field full of organised activity.

'How on earth shall I find Robert?' Mandy said.

Peggy laughed. 'You meet everybody in the end,' she said. 'Keep walking and you're bound to bump into him sooner or later. It's the annual promenade, round and round the ring. The one place where you'll find everybody you know, Doreen Price says.'

'Is there a Secretary's tent, or something?' said Mandy, remembering Robert's last words to her when he had left her still in bed at an ungodly hour.

'Yep,' said Peggy. 'I'll walk with you.'

They passed pens of wonderfully clean woolly sheep, and rams with curly horns, no sign of the usual hanging globes of sheepshit adhering under their tails. A mad-eyed goat, bony and velvet-coated, reared on to its hind legs, scrabbling with its dainty cloven feet for a foothold on the tubular gate, and was patted soothingly by a white-coated owner. The Jenkins twins stood watching, each holding one of their small brother Eddie's hands, obeying their mother's warning not to let him go at any price.

'Goat done a poo,' said Eddie admiringly. Gemma and Amy collapsed into helpless giggles and dragged Eddie away to find less embarrassing attractions in the children's play area.

Families of feathery white geese, angry at being rounded

up, herded into transport and unloaded into strange confinement, hissed and swore at Mandy as she stretched out her hand. She hastily withdrew it. 'I could do with a Coke, or something,' she said, licking her dry lips.

'You all right, Mandy?' said Peggy. It was hot, approaching midday, and there was very little shelter from the sun. They continued past an enclosure with apparently nothing in it but a series of wooden logs, set on end. Peggy pushed closer through the crowd. 'Must be something there,' she said, 'or people wouldn't be staring like that.'

There, unblinking, sat several small hawks, the colour of the logs of wood, captive and sadly out of place. 'Yer gos is the experience of a lifetime,' said a thin, dried–up little man, setting the obedient bird on his wrist. It looked about, its orange-yellow eyes fixed on other worlds, ignoring the wary mothers and noisy children.

'They're like time-bombs, waiting to explode,' said Mandy with a shiver.

Must be pregnancy making her fanciful, thought Peggy. 'Oh, look there!' she said, guiding Mandy to a line of mellow cows and calves, the picture of successful motherhood. That would surely be the right thing.

It was. Mandy adored the small, curly brown and white calves, everything about them new, clean and soft. They looked at her trustingly with their huge eyes and ridiculously long lashes, and she beamed.

'Enough to turn you vegetarian, Mrs Palmer,' said Richard Standing, pausing to tip his hat to Peggy and Mandy. He was a happy man, in his element in the world he knew best. Full of pride, he helped a slow-moving Susan out of the Range Rover and across to have tea and strawberries with the biggest agricultural machinery dealer in the area. Here he was treated with courtesy and the respect due to a good customer.

The erratic public address system crackled, and Tom Price's voice announced the favourite event of the day.

'Once again,' he said, his voice careful and slow, 'we welcome the Master and hounds of our very own Bailee Hunt. Always the high point of our Show,' he continued, refusing to acknowledge on such a day, this special Show day, any objections, antis, disapprovers, 'the age-old, traditional sight of the English hunt stirs the blood.'

'Steady on, Tom,' said Bill Turner, sorting out rosettes on a rickety trestle table.

It was undeniably a beautiful sight, as the Master and huntsman trotted into the ring, the two magnificent bay hunters groomed and polished to perfection. The milling hounds, pale liver and white, soft ears flapping, obligingly followed commands, and all came to a standstill in the centre of the ring.

'As always,' said Tom, from his commentary box high up on a special stack of straw bales, 'all children are invited to go into the ring and say hello to the hounds. Contrary to reports in the local press, they will not be eaten alive! Come on, kids, in you go!'

In ones and twos, some accompanied by anxious parents, the children began to invade the ring. With growing confidence, the trickle became more of a stampede. The Master, well aware of the need for good public relations, leaned down to have a word with Gemma and Amy Jenkins, who were still hanging on tight to little Eddie. Surrounded by waving tails, Eddie wriggled one hand free and made a passing grab. A warning snarl sent him rushing for cover behind Gemma's skirt, yelling loudly. 'Eddie!' said Gemma, covering his mouth with her hand and feeling his sharp little teeth. 'Come on Amy,' she said, 'let's get him out of here.'

Tom judged that the hounds and children had had enough, and called for a round of applause. Ripples of clapping accompanied a final lap of honour, and then men, horses and hounds disappeared from the ring. It was a heart-warming fifteen minutes, and had absolutely nothing to do with the real business of the Hunt.

Peggy and Mandy strolled on, Mandy wiping her forehead and slowing up. Goodness, thought Peggy, she's gone pale. Better get her to the Secretary's tent where she can sit down. Must be the heat.

'I need the loo,' said Mandy, coming suddenly to a halt.

'Ah,' said Peggy. 'The facilities, as they say, are a bit rough, but over there, by the ice-cream van, you can see the Portaloos. You might have to queue for a bit. Are you all right, Mandy? Shall I come with you?'

'No, don't wait for me, Mrs P.,' said Mandy. 'I'll go to the tent and find Robert. See you later.'

In the tiny space allocated for each primitive lavatory, Mandy inspected her pants and her heart lurched in fear. The fine white cotton, edged with narrow lace, was stained with streaks of red blood, where no blood should be.

CHAPTER TEN

Mandy Bates dreamed that she had put her baby in a shoebox. It was very, very small and was wrapped in layers of cotton wool. She had placed it in the airing cupboard and gone away and forgotten it. Hours later, she remembered it would need to be fed, and she rushed to the airing cupboard to take it out. She was not sure that it was still alive.

She awoke, screaming for Robert, who rushed up the narrow stairs of the cottage and into the bedroom, where Mandy lay flat on her back looking desperate.

He held her hands tightly between his and soothed her until she stopped shivering. 'Mandy, Mandy, it's me, I'm here, don't fret, my little love, don't fret.'

When she had woken up properly and seen that it was still light, and heard the voices of pigeons in the trees outside the window, Mandy remembered.

Robert sat quietly by her, waiting for her to speak, and he also remembered. He saw her running towards him, pushing through the crowded Secretary's tent, her face white and terrified. And then he'd found his car blocked in by a trailer, and had to find Bill Turner to drive them home. He had telephoned Dr Evans and finally been reassured by his quiet and sensible advice.

Dr Evans had come and gone, telling Mandy to rest, saying that it was quite common to have slight bleeding during pregnancy, but that he would call in tomorrow on his rounds to see how she was. He advised Mandy to relax, not worry, just keep quiet and perhaps stay at home for a day or so until the bleeding stopped.

'I had this horrible dream, Robert,' Mandy said, but when he asked her to describe it, found she could not put it into words.

'Would you like something to eat,' Robert said. 'I could make you a sandwich . . .'

Mandy shook her head. 'I couldn't eat anything just now,' she said, 'but I am thirsty.'

Robert went downstairs and made Mandy her favourite orange juice and lemonade, put a couple of tinkling cubes of ice in the glass, and took it up to her.

'Mmm,' she said, sipping the cool drink, 'that's delicious. Stay with me, Robert, just for a while.'

'I'm here for as long as you want,' said Robert, and he did stay, until it was dark and Mandy had fallen asleep again. Even then, he sat watching her until he was sure she was peaceful, and then quietly retired to the tiny spare room, where he stretched out on the hard, narrow divan and, in spite of being absolutely exhausted, could not sleep.

Monday morning in the Post Office Stores was not usually busy, and Peggy stood on the top step looking over the Green. I've been here only a couple of years, she thought, and yet here I am, standing outside my shop wearing a pink overall, as if the village is all mine and I've been here for ever.

She could smell bread, although it was unlikely that anyone was baking at this time of day. Could be Ivy Beasley, she thought. A gust of warm air shook the leaves of the chestnut on the Green, and lifted a chocolate wrapper out of the bin, chasing it along the street, too fast for Peggy to catch. Peggy sniffed. The smell had come and gone with the wind. The temperature was rising, and Peggy pulled the white canvas blind down over the shop window, shading her display of detergents, dusters, mops and scrubbing brushes. Better change that, she thought, it's not really the weather for housework.

'Could you smell bread?' she said to Jean Jenkins, who rushed in for a packet of mints to keep her going while she cleaned up at the Hall.

'It comes off the fields,' said Jean. 'It's the ripe wheat. If you walk down the concrete road at the side of Barnett's wheatfield, you'll get it good and strong then. It's a lovely smell, always reminds me of my Gran. She was a great baker.'

Old Fred and Mr Ross from the neo-Tudor house in the Bagley Road stood on the shop step and had a long conversation about runner beans, but didn't buy anything. Then nobody came in for at least half an hour.

'I might just as well shut up shop and do some gardening,' Peggy said to Gilbert, who was stretched out on a clump of purple catmint bordering the back yard, soaking up the sun and watching Peggy through half-closed eyes.

But, as always when she decided to get on with a job while the shop was empty, the door bell jangled, and Peggy returned to find Ivy Beasley tapping her fingers on the counter in an impatient tattoo.

'Could have helped myself, Mrs Palmer,' she said sharply.

Peggy ignored this, and asked politely what she could get for her.

'One of them cartons of orange juice,' said Ivy. 'It's what she wants, apparently.'

'Ah yes,' said Peggy, knowing exactly what Ivy meant. 'Robert was in earlier and said Mandy was feeling a lot better.'

Peggy had wanted to rush off down to Bridge Cottage as soon as the news about Robert's hasty departure with

Mandy had gone like wildfire around the showground. But Doreen Price, solid and wise behind the homemade cakes in the WI tent, had said it would be better to wait until the doctor had been. And then Robert said on the telephone that Mandy had to take things easy for a few days, and he was not encouraging visitors.

'Shan't stay, of course,' said Ivy shortly. 'She'll not want a lot of gossipping and chatter.'

Point taken, thank you, Ivy. Peggy put the carton in a bag, and took Ivy's change out of the till. 'There we are, then,' she said. 'Give Mandy my love.'

Ivy Beasley sniffed, barely nodded, and left the shop. As always, she left a small chill behind her, and Peggy went into the kitchen to make a quick snack.

Ellen Biggs was the first afternoon customer, and she perched on the edge of the chair by the Post Office cubicle, gasping and fanning herself with a letter she had come to post.

'Shouldn't grumble, I know,' she said, 'but this heat ain't too good for me, not for gettin' about.'

'Just sit there and cool down, Ellen,' said Peggy. 'I'll get on with sorting these out, if you don't mind.' The rack of birthday cards had been jumbled up by Richard Standing, rushing in first thing before he shot off to catch the London train from Tresham.

'Couldn't see any sign o'life at Bridge Cottage when I come by,' said Ellen, homing in on the topic top of the list in Ringford that morning.

'I spoke to Robert earlier,' said Peggy. 'I think he's staying at home for a day or two, just to be sure.'

'It's 'er job what done it,' said Ellen. 'She's standin' on 'er feet all those hours every day. Stands to reason it won't do 'er no good in 'er condition.'

'Lots of women seem to manage without any trouble,' said Peggy. Never having been pregnant, she had no store of knowledge on babies, none of those tales of the labour ward passed down generations of mothers waiting in ante-natal clinics, relaxing in group exercises, wallowing like clumsy dolphins in the swimming pool. Still, come to that, Ellen hadn't had children either. At least, there had been a rumour years ago, when she'd been a young maid up at the Hall, and been sent off to her relations in Yorkshire for a 'rest' for a couple of months. But it had all died down, and Ellen had returned, perky as ever, thin as a rake.

'Well, she'll 'ave to give up now,' said Ellen. 'She's 'ad the warnin', an' let's 'ope she heeds it.'

Jean Jenkins climbed the steps wearily, leaned on the counter and looked across at Ellen. 'Back again! My head'll never save my steps,' she said. 'It's all right for you, young Ellen, but for us poor workers it's a very tirin' day.'

Ellen grinned, showing a flashing full upper set, and smoothed down her bright Indian cotton skirt. She was not impervious to flattery, and returned the compliment.

'You got more energy than most I know, Jean,' she said, 'slavin' away up at that barn of a place, doin' the work of half a dozen maids. I remember a time when them servants' attics were full. In old Mr Charles's early days, that was.'

'You ought to write down all them memories, Ellen,' said Jean. 'When you go it'll all be lost.'

'I ain't goin' yet,' said Ellen, rising to her feet. 'Second class stamp, please, Peggy.'

Peggy came over to the cubicle and gave Ellen her stamp, then returned to serve Jean Jenkins. It would soon be time for the school bus, and the daily influx of schoolchildren, hot and thirsty after their journey from Tresham. She had to be on her toes then, eyes everywhere for the one or two children with lightfingered reputations. The Robertses had a talent for sliding small items into their sports bags, but they were not the only ones, and Peggy sometimes thought it hard on young Andrew Roberts, who as far as she knew, had never taken anything he hadn't paid for. William had been an early transgressor, but he had settled down to a respectable early teenage and, if approached in the right way, could be very helpful.

'It's young Robert Bates's planning application comin' up at the Parish Council meeting tonight,' said Jean. 'Are you going, Peggy?'

Peggy knew about this, and couldn't make up her mind. She certainly did not want to give Robert any extra trouble just now, and had almost decided not to go. She didn't have any major objections, but would have liked to look at the plans and made sure motor repairs wouldn't invade the peace and quiet of her back garden too much.

'Are you going, Jean?' she said. Jean Jenkins nodded. 'I enjoy a good meeting in the Parish,' she said, 'especially if there's likely to be a few fireworks.'

'Who's goin' to cause trouble, then?' said Ellen, looking out of the doorway into the bright sunlight spreading across the Green.

'Oh, one or two moaners have said it'll spoil the village, havin' cars parked everywhere outside Miss Hewitt's bungalow, an' all the noise an' that,' said Jean.

'The noise will affect nobody but me,' said Peggy, 'and maybe one or two of the new houses in Walnut Close.'

'I think it'd be a good thing,' said Ellen firmly. 'Robert's a very nice lad, and I'm warmin' to that Mandy, an' if I 'ad a car I'd be glad to get it serviced or whatever in the village.'

Jean Jenkins laughed her big, generous laugh, and said, 'Thank God you haven't got a car, Ellen! We'd none of us be safe if you were at the wheel. What do you say, Peggy?'

But Ellen was on her way, shaking her head at Jean, and shouting, 'You wait, Jean Jenkins, 'til I get my Rolls Rice, then you'll see!'

Tom Price arrived early at the Village Hall, a wooden building put up by public effort sixty years ago, and beginning to look its age, with worn floorboards and a leaky roof. Time we had a bit of a go at this, Tom thought.

Still, the playgroup had brightened it up with big collages of Our Village. Tom looked at one labelled 'Macmillan Gardens'. There was old Fred, clearly recognisable from his pipe and cloud of grey woolly smoke. He held a cut-out garden fork at his side like a rifle, and his vegetable patch boasted regular rows of cabbages and carrots. The children had been kind to number eight, the Roberts' house. Only the Alsatian, tamed and smiling, peered through a hole in the hedge.

Tom moved on to 'Bates's End', and laughed at the vicar, cloak flying, marching down towards the church. The big silver car emerging from the Hall avenue must be the Standings. And there was old Ellen at her garden gate, talking to a stern figure in black, with thick, frowning eyebrows. Must be Ivy, little devils, thought Tom. He heard steps, and turned to greet Mr Ross, Parish Clerk. A trickle of councillors and several members of the public followed.

Peggy and Jean had walked down to the Village Hall together, and sat attentively at the end of the row. Colin Osman took the seat next to the pale young man who had listened so intently in the pub that day, and the last to come in was Greg Jones, who taught geography at Tresham Comprehensive. He was deaf, and leaned forward to catch the councillors' comments.

This was quite a crowd for Ringford. It was seldom that anyone except Colin Osman attended the Parish Council meetings, and tonight Tom Price held a tighter rein than usual on contributions from the public. He had one eye on the clock. It was only three minutes' walk to the pub, but Parish Council business was thirsty work.

Robert Bates' proposal was last on the agenda, and when they came to it he stood up to go. 'I'll be off then, Tom, having an interest, and that,' he said.

'Right, boy,' Tom smiled encouragingly at him. 'See you down at the pub in a while.'

After he had gone, Tom continued. 'The plans for Robert Bates' proposed workshop and hardstanding area are laid out on that table. Perhaps it would be helpful if we gathered round and took a good look.'

There were ten minutes or so of close examination of the plans, and then Tom said they should go back to their chairs and get down to a decision. 'We don't have the power to veto, as you know,' he said, 'but any recommendations we make are very seriously taken into account. I will now take any comments or complaints from the general public present.'

His formal language made Peggy smile, but the smile faded when the pale young man stood up and said, 'I would like to object most strongly. That workshop will be only a few yards from my back fence, and from what I know of the motor trade, there will be screeching and crashing at all hours. My wife and I would like to register our serious concern, and are willing to take it further, should it be necessary.'

Mr Ross was writing busily. He was the perfect Parish Clerk, and everything was recorded carefully. He sorted the correspondence, answered bureaucratic demands with speed and efficiency, and never failed to draw Tom Price's attention to anything particularly affecting Round Ringford. He was taken for granted, but didn't mind, because he loved the job.

'Er, what was your name again?' said Tom, squaring his shoulders and looking benevolently at the young man.

'Dodwell,' he said, colouring slightly. 'Peter Dodwell. I live at number seven, and we bought the house because of the views over Walnut Farm fields. We like a bit of peace and quiet, and thought we'd found it in Ringford. Didn't expect to have light industrial buildings setting up behind us, with machinery going night and day.' He looked along the line of village representatives, and added acidly, 'And from what I know of Robert Bates, I don't expect much in the way of co-operation. He was very unpleasant when I complained about a heap of straw and slurry right outside the entrance to Walnut Close.'

'Doesn't sound like our Robert,' said Tom, less benevolent now. 'Anyway, you've had your say, Mr Dodwell. Anybody else?' He had a sinking feeling that this would not be the end of it, and was not surprised when Jean Jenkins stirred and put up her hand. Tom nodded at her, and she stood up.

'Jean Jenkins, Macmillan Gardens – the council houses,' she said.

Tom smiled at her and said 'Right-oh Jean, we all know where you live. What've you got to say?'

Jean Jenkins did not like being patronised, and she cleared her throat firmly. 'Lovely country views are all very well,' she said, 'but people are more important. And as for peace and quiet, if Mr Dodwell is so worried he'd better go and live next to the cemetery – there's plenty of peace and quiet in there.'

Peter Dodwell put up his hand, but Jean Jenkins hadn't finished. 'It's all very well for the likes of Mr Dodwell,' she said, 'comin' up to the village and complainin' when one of our own wants to set up a business that'll be a good service to us all. Good luck to our Robert, I say, and a bit of workin' noise around the place will keep this village alive.'

Peter Dodwell once more put up his hand, but Greg Jones had begun to speak, and Tom Price waved him on.

'My sympathies are with Mr Dodwell,' said the bearded schoolteacher. 'If we'd wanted to live next to an industrial estate, we'd have bought houses in Tresham. I value the tranquillity of Round Ringford, and consider Mrs Jenkins is taking her usual parochial view.'

Jean Jenkins rose angrily to her feet. As she did so, a giant tractor and trundling harrow roared past the Village Hall, deafening the meeting and enforcing a short pause in the proceedings.

'There you are!' said Jean triumphantly. 'I suppose you'd like my Fox to be out there with a horse and cart! You're another of them, Mr Jones, with your barn conversions and your letters to the Editor . . .'

This reference to a recent effort on Greg Jones' part to discredit the new vicar of Ringford was not lost on the meeting, and Tom considered enough was enough. 'Stick to the point, else we'll never get through the business,' he said, and glared at Jean. She was not, however, in the least daunted.

'The pub'll still be open,' she said tartly. 'I've just got this to say. If this village ends up full of commuters and weekenders havin' their smelly barbecues and doin' all their shopping in Tresham and gettin' their cars serviced in Bagley, the place will die. It'll be quiet enough then, Mr Dodwell!' She sat down with a bump, and the old chair creaked under her weight.

There was a small silence, and then Peggy put up her hand.

'Yes, Mrs Palmer?' said Tom.

'Robert's plan for repairing cars would affect me in much the same way as Mr Dodwell,' she said, 'but I've thought a lot about it and come to the conclusion that if we want young people to stay in Ringford, we have to compromise. Robert will be giving a service to the village, his children will eventually go to the village school, and we shall have Mandy too, hairdressing in our own homes at half the price of Tresham.'

Tom smiled at Peggy, grateful for her moderate contribution, and hoped it would be the last. He moved quickly on to take a vote from Council members, but to his amazement the majority were against the plan. Peter Dodwell's vehement objections had worried them. They were, however, sympathetic to Robert, and took refuge in compromise. They asked Mr Ross to record in the Minutes that their main concern was an ugly new building which would be out of keeping with the rest of the village.

Robert, leaning against the bar and sipping his beer nervously, turned to see the pub door open and the drinking members of the Parish Council walk in. As soon as he saw Tom's face, he knew it had gone against him.

'Sorry, old lad,' Tom said, putting his hand on Robert's shoulder. 'It was that Dodwell chap put the kybosh on it. He was dead against it, and not too polite about you, I'm afraid. What you done to offend him, Rob?'

'Dodwell?' said Robert. 'That weedy bloke from the new houses?' Tom nodded, taking a deep swig of beer.

'Well, bugger him!' said Robert furiously. 'I had a ding-dong with him last week over a heap of muck in the road. Silly fool claimed it was unhygienic, and I nearly told him where to put it. Now I suppose he's getting his own back!'

'Beats me why the likes of Dodwell come to live in the country,' said Tom soothingly. 'Still, all is not lost. The decision went down in the Minutes as an objection to a new building. Now Robert, you know them barns of Barnett's, behind Miss Hewitt's bungalow, well . . .'

Peter Dodwell walked home through the village, and was passed by a car belting out pop music with a thud, thud, thud. There were loud voices around the telephone box as a bunch of youths, belligerent from a night at the Arms, fought to make a call. A motorbike screeched round the corner in front of him, but he noticed nothing. He opened the front door of his house in Walnut Close, and banged it shut behind him.

'Peter! You'll wake Hugo!' His wife Caroline came into the hall and looked anxiously up the stairs. But all remained quiet, and she followed Peter Dodwell into the sitting room, where he slumped heavily into an armchair. 'Bloody village!' he said loudly.

'What on earth's the matter?' said Caroline, bending

down to pick up her knitting from the floor, her long wavy red hair falling over her face. She pushed it back behind her ears, revealing a sharply pretty face with features like a small, sandy vole. 'Did he get his permission, then?' she asked.

'It's not up to them,' growled Peter Dodwell, 'they just make a recommendation. And no, they turned down his plans.'

'Well, that's good news, isn't it?' Relief flooded through Caroline at the thought that Peter's current obsession would now be over, and she smiled.

'No, it's bloody not good news,' said Peter. 'It was only the look of the building they didn't like, and you can be sure Tom Price and Peggy Palmer and that bloody Jean Jenkins will find a way round it for their precious Robert Bates. Oh yes, the old village guard will see him right – one of their own, our Robert. Well, he'll see he's got me to reckon with!'

He was shouting now, and Caroline moved to shut the sitting-room door.

'His wife's nice,' she said sadly. 'And for someone who wants peace and quiet, Peter, you're making an awful lot of noise.'

CHAPTER ELEVEN

'I shall be fine, Rob,' said Mandy, picking up her handbag and taking her car keys from the hooks Robert had fixed by the back door. 'Dr Evans said it would be best for me to go back to work, and not brood. You must admit there's not a lot to occupy me here in Ringford when you're up at the farm.'

Harvest took up all Robert's time, from very early in the morning until late at night. It was as if his whole world had shrunk to endless fields of ripe corn, nothing but waving golden heads, all to be gathered in before the weather broke. It was the same every year. The Bateses looked at the Barnetts' fields, and the Barnetts looked at the Prices', and they all compared notes in the pub when they snatched time for a quick pint.

Ted Bates worked on in silence. But he had a quiet smile every now and then, when he thought of Robert's reversal. He assumed that his son had given up.

'Stop all his bloody nonsense, that will,' Ted said to Olive.

Olive would not join in with Ted's crowing. She knew Robert well enough to know that he wouldn't admit defeat that easily. 'He's got enough to worry about, with Mandy and that,' she said, but Ted would not comment. He had set his face implacably against the young couple, would hear no talk of babies or grandchildren, and raised his newspaper if Olive approached the subject, effectively shutting her out.

She had been deeply hurt that Robert had not asked her to help when Mandy had taken to her bed. 'Fancy having to find out from Peggy Palmer at the shop!' she said to Ted in a rare burst of anger, but he had pulled on his boots and stumped out into the yard, banging the door behind him.

Robert reluctantly waved Mandy off to work. But he continued to return to the cottage for breakfast each day, to keep an eye on her and make sure she was feeling fine. He kept his nagging anxiety about her to himself. She seemed happily restored, all tests had been reassuring, and she had begun to talk about looking at prams and pushchairs. Robert smothered his superstitious fear that if they were over-confident, things would go wrong again.

High summer passed quickly, and the end of harvest was finally in sight. Robert sighed with relief as he finished combining the long field at the back of the farm, and he climbed down from his cab to sit for a while under a shady hedge, exactly as Bateses had done for hundreds of years.

It was a warm day, sunny, with a soft wind and high, fluffy clouds. He looked at the ditch, choked with a summer growth of rushes and weed, and put it on his mental list of jobs for the winter. The combine had missed a thin line of ripe heads on the edge of the field, and Robert peeled off a few grains and chewed them. He was very thirsty, and was just climbing to his feet when he saw his mother running up the field from the farm.

'Telephone, Robert!' she yelled, still fifty yards away. 'It's the hospital, they've had to take Mandy in!'

Robert's stomach turned over so fiercely that he thought he would be sick. He hared out of the field, through the old stackyard with its crumbling dovecote, and into the farm kitchen, where he picked up the receiver.

'Ah, there you are, Mr Bates,' said a cool voice. 'Please

don't worry. Mandy has had another spot of bleeding, and was brought in from the salon. Just to be on the safe side, you know. You can come and see her at any time.'

The old spaniel licked Robert's big, dusty hand, sensing trouble. Olive panted into the kitchen and stood by the Rayburn looking anxiously at Robert. He put down the telephone and for a moment covered his face with both hands. Then he straightened up and looked at his mother.

'Another crisis, Mum,' he said. 'I'll have to go to the hospital, she'll want me there.'

Olive nodded, but then said, 'How's your father going to manage for the rest of the day?'

Robert lost his patience. 'I don't know and I don't care!' he said. But seeing her shrink back, he added, 'Oh, Mum, I'm sorry, it isn't your fault. Better ring Waltonby and see if Dan can come over and give us an hour or two. I must be off now.'

Olive stretched out a hand to him, but he didn't see it. 'Hope she's all right, son,' she said in a small voice.

Bill Turner saw Robert speed off down the village street, and wondered what he was up to. Combine broken down again; gone to get a spare part, I shouldn't wonder, he thought. Old Ted Bates should spend a few bob and get his machinery working properly. Young Robert's had to make do and mend for long enough.

Bill got into his van and set off along the Fletching road, turning after about a mile down a rutted track that led through a spinney of silver birch, and into denser woods. The old van rattled and shook, and Bill bounced about in his seat, steadying the vehicle like a jockey with a wayward racehorse. When he reached a mossy clearing, he turned off the engine and got out.

He walked through the trees, carrying a bag of tools and some lengths of new wood. There was still a fair bit to do to Susan Standing's bird-watching hide, and Bill climbed the solid ladder he had made, up into the green light of the treetops. There was no hurry now. Mrs Standing certainly wouldn't be wanting to come here for a few months, probably not until next spring. Bill sat back and looked over the unfinished floor and out into the woods.

Could be miles from anywhere, he thought. A darting movement caught his eye, and he watched a flycatcher sally out and return to its oak tree with an insect caught in mid-air. Must be a young one, thought Bill. Not so spotted when they get older. 'Whee-tucc-tucc!' chattered the flycatcher, suddenly aware of Bill. It flew off through the clearing, its undulating flight deceiving the eye, and Bill lost sight of it.

The warm wind rustled the top leaves of beech, oak and wild cherry, and at the fringes of the wood crab apple trees swayed with their tiny fruit, survivors of Fox Jenkins' depredations with the hedge cutter. Bill was glad of the movement of air as he mopped his forehead. Down at ground level it was quite still. As he watched, a shadow moved by a narrow runnel of water in the soft, boggy ground. It became a small fallow deer, a doe, walking delicately along the edge of the stream. She lowered her head to drink the cool water, and Bill held his breath, wishing Peggy were with him to see the beauty of it.

Never mind, he thought. If I get this hide finished in good time, we'll have it to ourselves until spring. The thought spurred him on, and he started work again, whistling happily to himself, betraying his presence to every creature in the wood.

In Tresham General Hospital, Mandy dozed and listened to the quiet conversations of other women in her ward. This time she had not panicked, just told the salon manager that she must go to the rest room, and asked him to send for a doctor. There was more blood than before, but even so, Mandy was confident. It had stopped before, and would

84

stop this time. She was quite surprised, therefore, when the doctor sent for an ambulance and had her admitted to hospital.

'Just to make sure,' he said to her reassuringly, but she heard him telling the nurse that this was the second bleeding in the pregnancy, and must be taken more seriously. Now it was her second day in hospital, and sedatives had made her drowsy. She drifted in and out of sleep, wondering when Robert would arrive to see her. A strange voice in the ward woke her from a dream about cutting Mrs Standing's hair much too short, and she was surprised when the curtain round her bed was drawn back and Sister came in with Caroline Dodwell following behind. Caroline was biting her lip anxiously and clutching a bunch of carnations.

'Just a few minutes then, Mrs Dodwell,' said Sister. 'Mandy must be kept as quiet as possible for a while.'

Too late for me to say I don't want to see her, thought Mandy, smiling weakly. She was well aware of the coolness between Peter Dodwell and Robert, and felt too drugged and confused to conduct a tactful conversation with Caroline.

'I heard in the shop you'd been taken in,' said Caroline Dodwell, sitting nervously on the edge of a chair by Mandy's bed. She did not say anything else, and Mandy struggled to think of something to break the silence.

'What's the weather like out there?' she said. In hospital, nothing impinged on the routine of ward life, least of all the weather. It was like being in a spacecraft, occasionally visited by creatures from another planet.

To Mandy's dismay, Caroline did not answer, but fumbled for a handkerchief to mop up a tear which escaped and ran down her cheek.

Oh God, thought Mandy, this is all I need.

'So sorry, Mandy,' said Caroline. 'I meant to come in and cheer you up, but all this bad feeling with Peter and your Robert is getting me down. I'd better go . . .'

85

'No, no, stay for a few minutes.' Mandy managed another smile, and Caroline sat down again. 'It's all a storm in a teacup, anyway,' Mandy continued with an effort. 'These things blow over. I've not lived in Ringford myself for very long, but I have learned that much.'

'Peter gets so worked up,' said Caroline. 'In our last house, we lived next door to a family with three dogs, and he couldn't stand the barking. Got it stopped in the end, but the neighbours never spoke to us after that and I was really miserable. It was one of the reasons we came to Ringford, so you can see . . .' Her voice petered out, and another tear plopped on to the carnations.

'Don't worry, Caroline,' said Mandy, wishing that Sister would come in and put an end to all this. 'They'll come round. We shall just have to get them talking to each other. Over a pint, that's the usual remedy.' She was pleased to see a small smile on Caroline's face.

'You're right, Mandy,' said Caroline. 'As soon as you're out of here, you can come up for coffee and we'll make a plan.'

Great, thought Mandy, that'll be something to look forward to. But she nodded as best she could with her head flat on the hospital pillow, and said, 'Hope you don't mind me saying, but you've got lovely hair, Caroline. Who does it for you?'

'Nobody special,' said Caroline, 'but if you'll have me, it will be Mandy Bates's salon in Ringford from now on.'

Robert walked swiftly along the hospital corridor, head down, deep in worrying thoughts. He didn't see Caroline Dodwell walking in the opposite direction, and looked up in surprise when she said 'Hello, Robert,' and continued on her way. Robert stopped and watched her retreating back until she was out of sight. What was she doing here? Oh well, perhaps she had been seeing a friend or relation or something.

He walked into the ward and was met by Sister. 'Hello, my dear,' she said, 'you're the second visitor Mandy has had today.'

'Who else, then?' said Robert sharply.

'A nice young woman, long red hair, about Mandy's age, said she was a friend of the family.'

Robert contained himself with difficulty. Caroline bloody Dodwell! So that's where she'd been. 'I'm surprised you allowed Mandy to have visitors,' he said stiffly.

'Oh, she didn't stay long,' said Sister, 'and Mandy seemed a lot brighter after she'd gone.' She put her hand on Robert's arm and gently guided him to where Mandy lay, smiling at the sight of him.

'There she is, still in one piece, and pleased to see you, Robert dear.' Sister bustled off, reassuring and competent, queen of all she surveyed.

At the end of the week, Robert was waylaid on his way in to visit Mandy, and asked for a word.

'We think it would be safe for Mandy to go home tomorrow,' Sister said, 'but we do strongly advise that she should not go back to the salon. It would be worth slowing up for the last few months. Perhaps she could keep her hand in with some hairdressing in the village? Not too much, but enough to stop her being bored. It's not that she is ill, but we'd like to be just a tiny bit cautious, in view of her history so far.'

Robert tidied and cleaned the cottage, too proud to ask his mother to help, and clumsily arranged a bunch of purple and crimson asters in a vase on the windowsill to welcome Mandy home. He had stocked up the fridge with ham and eggs and salad, and the fruit bowl on the kitchen table overflowed with apples, bananas and grapes. The washing machine had been spinning all day, and the line in the back garden sagged with the weight of Robert's shirts and overalls. She won't want to be washing straight away, he thought.

He was early at the hospital. 'Come in about three,' Mandy had said, but he was there by two-thirty, and she was still packing her few things into a bag.

'Let me help,' said Sister, zipping up Mandy's holdall with capable hands. 'Look after her, Robert. We don't want you back in this ward again, but let me know when baby arrives. February, isn't it? Best of luck my dears.'

Robert put his arm around Mandy and led her slowly out of the ward.

He drove home carefully, as if any sudden movement would shake the baby loose. Mandy looked out of the window, noticing the bright autumn gardens in the suburbs of Tresham, neat and geometrical, like her Dad's. Heavy rain in the night had beaten down chrysanthemums and dahlias, big shaggy heads hanging sadly. Mum and Dad had been in to see her, but they seemed like strangers. I don't really belong anywhere now, Mandy thought. I'm not a country girl, but Tresham's not my home any more, not really.

'Put your foot down, Rob,' she said, with a small shiver. 'I'm dying to get back to the cottage.'

As they drew up outside Bridge Cottage, William Roberts straightened up from his labours in the garden. He came down after school two afternoons a week, and had made quite an impression on the untidy, dying flowers and shrubs. The more he worked in the quiet garden, the more he liked it. Turning up only for the money at first, now he came down regularly and did not always charge for the full amount of time he spent there.

He raised his hand to Robert and Mandy, and said shyly, 'Are you better, Mrs Bates?'

Mandy smiled at him and nodded.

'My mum says you should be taking it easy now,' he said seriously.

'Thanks, William, I certainly will. I am sure your Mum's right.'

'Yes, well,' said William, 'she's had plenty of practice, thanks to my Dad.'

Robert and Mandy exchanged a swift smile, and then William shouldered his spade and made for the shed at the bottom of the garden. 'I'm off now,' he said, 'see you next week.'

It was chilly in the evenings now, and after the sun had gone down Robert lit a fire in the small front room and settled Mandy in front of the television.

'I don't really want to watch anything, Rob,' she said. 'I had enough of that in the hospital. Let's just talk. Tell me what's been happening while I've been in there.'

'Nothing that I haven't told you at visiting,' said Robert. But maybe now was the time to tell her about Tom's idea. He'd not wanted to worry her with it before.

'Tom Price has suggested something else we could do, now they've turned down the workshop building,' he said. Mandy looked into the fire, and said, 'Oh yes.'

Robert could see she'd rather be talking about something else, but he pressed on. 'You know the paddock at the back of Macmillan Gardens,' he said, 'belongs to the Barnetts up at Walnut Farm?'

'What about it?' said Mandy.

'Well, the paddock also backs on to the garden of Miss Hewitt's bungalow, and there's a couple of old cow barns near the fence, a bit dilapidated, but still quite solid.'

Mandy turned to look at him, her eyebrows raised. 'And?' she said.

'Tom thought the Barnetts might let me use the barns for a workshop, take down the fence and get access that way. I'd need permission, and the council might be against it again, but Tom thought it would be worth a try.'

Mandy looked at Robert, sitting on the edge of his chair, his short fair hair sticking up in stubbly spikes where he had repeatedly combed his fingers through in his anxiety to get everything right for her return. He was chewing his bottom lip, and looked like a puppy begging forgiveness.

'I do love you, Robert Bates,' she said, 'and if you want a workshop in a smelly old cow barn, it's all right with me. Mind you, I'm not so sure it'll be all right with Peter Dodwell . . .'

CHAPTER TWELVE

'Do you want to buy something, Andrew, or are you just filling in time?' said Peggy.

There had been a thunderstorm in the night, lightning playing over Bagley Woods and claps of thunder reverberating round the village for hours. Peggy had got up with a bad headache, pain shooting up the back of her neck and head. Now it was settling into the left side and she had difficulty in focusing on her list of supplies for the wholesalers. Another migraine, I suppose, she thought. I should take a pill, but they're beside the bed and I can't leave Andrew Roberts in here by himself.

Andrew Roberts, brother of William and the last in the line of the Roberts tribe, was thin, dark and sharp. His eyes flashed in a fight, and his dark skin earned him unpleasant nicknames at school. His looks came straight from his Italian grandmother on his mother's side, and his fiery temperament along with them.

'Not doin' no harm, am I?' he said belligerently. Peggy sighed. They always win, these kids, no matter what. I've never seen him take anything, but things go missing, always small things, nothing worth making a fuss about. But small things mount up, and in the end they do matter, in a business like this.

Andrew brought a packet of crisps to the counter, and

handed Peggy the right money. 'You heard about Mrs Standing?' he said conversationally.

Peggy shook her head, and then wished she hadn't, as the pain ripped up through her left ear.

'Bin took to Tresham, early this mornin'. Mum says it's bound to be a girl, the way she was carryin'.'

In spite of herself, Peggy smiled. 'That's exciting, Andrew,' she said. 'I expect we shall hear some news later on.'

As he left the shop, Peggy debated whether or not to take a pill and decided against it. The pain was unbearable and her new pills would eventually blot it out, but the side effect was an irritating muzziness that made concentration in the shop very difficult.

There was usually a reason for her migraine attacks, but Peggy did not always want to face up to reasons. For one thing, she would have to admit that avoiding certain things would probably prevent the pain, things like chocolate and cheese, and seeing Bill.

She and Bill had gone for a walk along the old railway line the previous evening, and in the late sun had wandered along, hand in hand, sure of being unobserved. The cinder track, pitted with rabbit and badger holes, no longer had sleepers or rails, and tall, spindly birches had taken root soon after the line had been closed. Nettles were dying back, and Bill had picked hazel nuts, cracked them open with his teeth, and given the sweet kernels to Peggy to eat.

High above the fields, the embankment was built up to carry the rails over streams and marshy ground, and a walk along the track was like traversing a cross-section of the landscape.

'I love this dark wood,' Peggy had said, as they became surrounded on all sides by dense fir. 'Can't you just imagine a knight riding through on his white charger, fighting all obstacles to rescue his lady, imprisoned in the high castle?'

'No,' said Bill, 'not really. I can imagine trying to find the

Jenkins' terrier in there, disappeared down a hole after a rabbit, and stuck in the boggy clay.'

'You have no romance in your soul, Bill Turner,' said Peggy

'Oh yes I have,' said Bill, turning to face her. 'Come here and I'll show you.'

William Roberts and Warren Jenkins, plodding along with their heads down, looking for scrapes in the cindery ground where squirrels might have been, hadn't seen the couple until they were nearly upon them. They stopped dead, and Warren signalled to William not to make a sound.

Bill had just put his arms round Peggy when he heard a twig snap. 'Warren bloody Jenkins!' he said. 'What d'you think you two are doing?'

'Nuthin', said Warren automatically, but William was quicker.

'Could ask you the same thing, Mr Turner,' he said, and pushing Warren in the back, continued along the track. 'We ain't trespassin',' he shouted back over his shoulder. 'Got permission from old Bates. Doin' a school project.' He had paused, and smiled sweetly at Peggy. ''Lo, Mrs Palmer,' he said. 'Nice evenin'.'

And now, here in the empty shop, Peggy flushed, remembering the awful embarrassment. No wonder I've got a migraine, she thought.

It was pension day, and she could see old Ellen coming slowly down Bates's End, using her umbrella to lash out at a stray dog that appeared from under the stone bridge and menaced her threateningly. Poor old Ellen, thought Peggy, I wonder if she'll last through this winter. Not if it's a hard one, she won't. Not in that dreadful Lodge.

One of the symptoms of migraine, she had noticed, and not easily dealt with by a pill, was a dreadful pessimism which took hold of her, made her unable to see the bright side of anything. Even though she knew the attack would be gone by tomorrow, she couldn't shake off a terrible

93

gloom. Much better to go to bed and hope for the oblivion of sleep, Peggy thought, but that was impossible.

'Yer lookin' peaky, my dear,' said Ellen, stamping her wet shoes on the doormat inside the shop. 'Eaten somethin' what disagreed with yer?'

'Could be,' said Peggy. That was another thing about migraine. It was difficult to own up to being a victim, as if it was somehow your fault.

'Got some news to cheer you up,' said Ellen, smiling broadly. 'Madam has been took in to 'ave her baby. Started up about five this morning, so Jean Jenkins said. Probably the thunder and lightning. Jean said a good storm always got her goin'. The nanny's there already, and I saw Mr Richard go by about hundred miles an hour lookin' like somethin' possessed.'

At least six more people gave Peggy the news during the day, and then, just as she was about to lock the door and retire gratefully to bed, Mr Richard's big silver car drew up, and he made for the shop steps at a run.

'Ah, just caught you, Mrs Palmer,' he said. 'Just in time.'

Peggy smiled at him. He was grinning broadly, and she nodded encouragingly.

'It's a girl,' he said, 'a dear little girl. And how am I going to stop Susan calling her Poppy?'

They both laughed, and Richard paid for his bottle of mineral water, leaving the shop without his change, so that Peggy had to call him back. They laughed again, and Peggy congratulated him with all her heart.

Bless him, she thought, and as she locked up and filled the kettle for a cup of tea, she realised that the sky had cleared and her migraine had gone.

94

CHAPTER THIRTEEN

'Who's that then, comin' up the street?' Ellen leaned forward from her upright chair in Ivy Beasley's front room. Her royal-blue smock dress, with its drawstring neck and pentiful folds of material, had appealed to her at once when she'd pulled it from under a pile of jumble. 'Covers a multitude,' she had said to a critical Ivy. 'You should get one like it.'

She peered round Ivy's lace curtain to follow the progress of a tall, blonde girl approaching the shop.

Ivy, whose turn it was this afternoon to host the tea party, and Doris Ashbourne, sensibly dressed in navy-blue and white, positioned themselves discreetly behind Ellen Biggs.

'Never seen her before,' said Ivy.

'She doesn't seem to have parked a car anywhere,' said Doris, 'so she must be staying locally.'

'Not even a bike,' said Ivy.

The girl walked on, coming closer now, and the women drew back.

'Pity she's wearing glasses,' said Doris, 'else she'd be a stunner.'

Ivy sniffed. 'All for the best, if you ask me,' she said. 'It goes to a girl's head if she's too good-looking.'

Old Mrs Beasley had never praised Ivy's looks. Ivy had

not been much of a stunner, but she had had her good points: thick, dark hair, and good teeth. The dark hair was grey now, but her teeth were still her own, and flashed white and even, when she allowed herself to smile.

'I've remembered,' said Ellen, turning back into the room, pleased at having solved the mystery. 'It's the new nanny up at the Hall. Name's something foreign-soundin'. Hang on a minute, it'll come to me.'

'She's gone into the shop,' said Doris, returning to her seat and sipping her tea.

'Lovely figure,' said Ellen, hoping to annoy Ivy. 'Not many in Ringford could wear them tight-fittin' jeans and top and get away with it.'

'Let's hope Mr Richard is well occupied with his new daughter, and doesn't notice, then,' said Ivy, removing the crinoline lady tea cosy from the pot. She stalked out to the kitchen for a refill.

Doris and Ellen looked at each other, and then began to laugh. 'Leopard don't change its spots that easily,' said Ellen. 'Perhaps that young lady should be warned.'

The room was cool and smelt strongly of furniture polish. Ivy returned with the pot and poured fresh tea into the fine china cups. 'Another piece of sponge, Ellen?' she said.

'Wouldn't say no,' said Ellen, anxious to prolong a comfortable afternoon of gossip and excellent refreshment.

'How is Mandy Bates coming along?' said Doris, settling with another wedge of rich chocolate sponge.

Ivy got in quickly, there being some competition between her and Ellen as to who got first news from Bridge Cottage. Ellen had some advantage in living so close, and Ivy hadn't seen Robert for his Monday cup of tea since harvest began.

'Doing all right,' Ivy said. 'She was in the shop yesterday, showing quite nicely now, and says she's taking it easy.'

'Still doing people's hair in the village,' said Ellen. 'I saw 'er this mornin', puttin' 'er things in the car and goin' off up Walnut Farm to do Deirdre Barnett's stringy old stuff.'

'You got no call to be critical,' said Ivy. 'You couldn't describe yours as a luxurious head of hair, Ellen Biggs.'

'Well, what does it matter?' said Doris the peacemaker. 'Get to our age, and as long as it's neat and tidy, there are other things more important to think about .'

'Such as what?' said Ellen grumpily.

'Such as who is that girl talking to in that Land Rover? Isn't it Bates's? It certainly isn't Robert at the wheel.'

'It's young Dan Bates from Waltonby, givin' an extra hand with finishing off the 'arvest,' said Ellen. 'He's always 'ad an eye for the girls. Look, 'e's givin' 'er a lift. Blimey, that's quick work, ain't it?'

'There's not a lot you don't know, is there, Ellen Biggs?' said Ivy, outclassed.

Ellen smiled triumphantly. 'It's Bridget, that's 'er name,' she said.

'That's not foreign,' said Ivy.

'Sounds foreign to me,' said Ellen stubbornly.

'Irish, perhaps,' said Doris.

'There you are, then,' said Ellen. 'I told you it was foreign.'

'How's young Dan getting on?' asked Mandy, setting a large and fragrant steak in front of Robert.

Robert took a forkful and said indistinctly, 'Very well. He doesn't seem to mind Dad peering over his shoulder all the time, telling him what he knows perfectly well already.'

Mandy settled herself in a big armchair, crossing her hands over her nicely rounded stomach. 'I can't wait to be really huge,' she said, and then shifted in her seat. 'Here Rob,' she said, 'just feel this kicking!'

Robert put his large hand over Mandy's bump and smiled. 'Definitely a boy,' he said, 'and a great little full-

97

back already.' Robert was a keen Old Treshamian rugby football player, enjoyed getting together with his old school mates, and he and Mandy supported all the social events. He had always been proud of his attractive wife, and now the thought of introducing his baby son to the lads filled him with excitement.

'Dan gave the new nanny a lift this afternoon,' he said. 'He came back to the farm singing her praises. Name's Bridget, and very friendly, he said.'

'Wears glasses, doesn't she?' said Mandy, widening her own brown eyes.

'Doesn't put our Dan off,' said Robert. 'Says he's taking her to the pictures on Saturday night.'

'I haven't seen the baby yet,' said Mandy. 'What are they calling her?'

'Mrs Palmer said something like Polly or Poppy, but that doesn't sound grand enough for the Standings.'

'Mrs P.'s been really nice to me lately,' said Mandy. 'She made me sit down in her kitchen yesterday, just because I was a bit out of breath. It was that wretched Jenkins terrier, took my bag of rollers. I'd just put it down on the pavement for a minute and he grabbed it and made off. I caught up with him by the bus stop. Gemma and Amy Jenkins were there, but all they could do was laugh. They're weird, those twins, they do everything together. I'm glad I'm not having twins.'

'You shouldn't chase after a dog, not now,' said Robert, frowning.

'Don't be silly, Rob. I'm not an invalid. Mrs P. was very kind, made me a cup of tea and sat chatting while the shop was empty. I must say, I don't know how she makes a living there. Well, anyway, she'd got a magazine with some baby knitting patterns in, and asked me to choose one and she's going to knit it. Isn't that lovely, Rob? My mum's not much of a knitter, never was, so all contributions will be gratefully received.'

Robert broke off a piece of bread and mopped up meat juice and tomato sauce. He loved it when Mandy rattled on.

'That was very tasty, Mandy, thanks,' he said, and took his plate out to the kitchen. 'I'm washing up,' he called. 'You put your feet up.'

They watched the news and then Robert switched off the television. 'I've been up to see John Barnett,' he said, 'about the paddock.'

'I know,' said Mandy. 'Deirdre told me.'

'Might've known it,' said Robert. 'Well, what else did she tell you?'

'That's all,' said Mandy. 'I didn't encourage her to gossip.' Her expression was smug.

Robert hid his disbelief, and said, 'We had a good talk. Old John wasn't too keen on my plan to use the cowsheds, but young John was all for it. Says they're no good for anything any more, too small for the big stuff we use on farms nowadays. And he doesn't put stock in that field, only when he needs to isolate an animal for some reason.'

'So, what next?'

'Get some proper plans drawn up, and go to the Council again. Young John suggested going round the village talking to people and getting support. I might do that.'

'I could help,' said Mandy. 'I know quite a few people now, what with hairdressing and that.'

Robert pulled her gently to her feet and put his arms around her. 'You look after yourself, Mandy Bates,' he said. 'Both of you.'

CHAPTER FOURTEEN

I shall leave Dodwell until last,' Robert said. He had had a good day on the farm, with nothing breaking down and Ted keeping out of his way. He'd washed and changed, and now, well fed and full of good intentions, he intended to tackle the known opposition to his plan. Peter Dodwell was the primary objector, but Robert knew that Greg Jones had also supported the view that Ringford was the wrong place for a motor repair shop. And then there was Mr Ross.

Strictly speaking, Alec Ross was not supposed to express any opinions on Parish Council matters – at the meetings, that is. But in the Arms, perched on a bar stool with feet up on the long brass rail, with his regular Guinness in front of him, and immaculately dressed as ever in neat grey flannels and tweed jacket, he was forthright in his views, and his air of authority had been known to sway many an undecided villager.

'Right, Mandy,' said Robert. 'I shall start with Greg Jones, then go up the hill to the Rosses', and end up in Walnut Close with Peter Dodwell. It's probably a waste of time with Dodwell, but he's supposed to be an intelligent bloke, isn't he? Might at least listen to my side of the argument.'

Mandy wasn't so sure, remembering Caroline's reference to Peter's obsession, but she brushed a tiny piece of straw out of Robert's hair and kissed him.

'Best of luck, love,' she said. 'If you need help, send an SOS.'

It was a perfect evening, still and cool. As Robert walked over the bridge and past the pub, he looked across the Green to where Mark Jenkins and friends were throwing sticks up into the chestnut tree, determined to collect the last of the conkers. Their shouts echoed around the village, and Robert was at once carried back to his boyhood in Ringford. He could feel again the silky smoothness of the ripe conkers, smell old Fred's annual bonfire of leaves, see the gathering mist of late autumn. Ah well, he thought, that was a long time ago, and he walked on past the pub and turned in at the Joneses' gate.

Greg Jones lived at Barnstones, a former granary barn which Richard Standing had converted to a house to raise a bit of ready cash. It was reasonably well done, but village people had been used to the barn with its stone staircase up to a loft, and the horizontal stripes of dark and light ironstone which had now been broken up by picture windows and a modern front door. The Joneses were more or less accepted in the village, after a nasty period when rumour had been rife of an affair between Gabriella Jones, who played the church organ, and the new vicar. Their daughter, Octavia, had been trouble, too, with her passion for Robert Bates and its embarrassing consequences.

Robert had not forgotten the Octavia episode, and felt ill at ease as he pushed the bell button by Barnstones' front door.

'Robert?' said Greg, opening the door wide. Greg Jones, geography and football, was not a tall man, but trim and athletic. He had added importance to a rather weak face by growing a dark, piratical beard, and his smile was warm. 'Come in, please do,' he said.

Robert walked into the cool, comfortable sitting room.

He remembered the day the Joneses had tackled him about a supposed amorous lunge at their daughter. God, that Octavia! He looked round quickly, but there was no sign of her, and he began to explain his visit.

'The workshop will be inside a good solid stone barn,' he said. 'Now the Barnetts have agreed to rent to me, I shan't need to have a new building. The noise won't be nearly so bad. And anyway, it's only now and then. Most of the work is me down in the inspection pit workin' away with me hands.'

'But do we need a repair workshop in Ringford?' said Greg. 'Everybody seems to manage perfectly well at present.' His voice was loud, unnaturally loud because of his deafness, and he fixed his eyes on Robert's face to catch his reply.

'We don't *need* motor repairs in the village any more than we *need* a school, or a post office or a shop – or, come to that, a pub. Or a church. Lots of villages don't have any of 'em – well, most have a church. Which is daft, because not many folks go. But them villages are dead. Every time they want something they have to get the car out.'

'That should suit you, then,' said Greg Jones illogically.

Robert ignored this, and blundered on, feeling Greg was not really listening. The prepared speech had got all muddled up, and Robert had lost track of how to get to the end.

'Suppose,' he said, 'nobody could buy a stamp or a bag of sugar in Ringford. Suppose you couldn't walk down to the Arms for a pint. Suppose the schoolchildren, even the littlest, all had to get on a bus every day, and we didn't see them till they got back in the afternoon – how would you like that?'

'Ah, now then,' said Greg, 'now you have got a point there, Robert. But I still don't quite see the parallel between schoolchildren and motor repairs.'

'Well I do,' said Gabriella Jones, coming into the room

and smiling kindly at Robert. 'It's all to do with what kind of village you want. I'm on your side, Robert. And so is Greg, really, but he does like to take the opposing view, just for love of an argument.'

She smiled so sweetly at the bridling Greg that he deflated like a burst balloon. 'She's probably right,' he said, patting Robert on the arm. 'No, on second thoughts, she's always right. Count on us, lad. We'll support you if you need it. Now, how about a beer?'

Robert sighed with relief, but declined the drink, saying he had a couple more people to see. On his way, he met Octavia coming up the path, and he automatically gave her a wide berth. But Octavia had lost interest, and did not even answer his cautious hello.

'What does Robert Bates want coming here at this hour?' said Mr Ross, stationed at his front window, smoking a cigarette and surveying his manicured garden.

His wife sat in an armchair watching television, and, without taking her eyes off the screen, said, 'I expect it's to do with the repair business.'

'Very possibly,' said Mr Ross, and walked swiftly from the room to open his front door.

Robert accepted a seat, though he perched on the edge, saying he would not take up too much of their time. He wished they would switch off the television, but Mrs Ross continued to stare at it, although occasionally making a relevant remark. This unnerved Robert, and he found himself stumbling once more.

'Hold on a minute, Robert,' said Mr Ross. 'You're assuming we're against you. But we're not. Let me tell you why.' He stood by the empty fireplace and leaned one elbow on the mantelpiece. He was careful not to obstruct his wife's view of the screen.

'No doubt you remember when Walnut Close was first mooted,' he began. Robert wasn't quite sure what this had to do with his workshop, but he nodded politely.

'The wife and I were dead against it, as you probably know,' continued Mr Ross. 'Our view would be ruined, and from being up here on our own with perfect peace and quiet, we were going to be overrun by new families, kids, cars, footballs, lawnmowers, hedgeclippers – you name it. Naturally, we objected strongly.'

Again Robert nodded, though he still couldn't see quite where this was leading – or rather, how it could be leading in his direction.

'Now, there they are,' said Mr Ross, pointing out of his window and across the road to the new development. 'And just as we expected, our peace and quiet has gone for good.' Mrs Ross nodded strongly, but her attention to the screen did not waver.

'Um, so what are you saying, Mr Ross?' The elderly man seemed to have come to a halt.

'Just this, Robert, just this.' Mr Ross was not without a sense of drama. 'As well as the kids, the cars, the noise and the lost view, we have got new friends. The wife goes babysitting, the young husbands come to me for gardening advice. We've got neighbours, and we've discovered we were wrong.'

As Robert walked across to Walnut Close he felt decidedly more confident. Two down, one to go. But then he remembered that he'd left the worst to last, and he knocked nervously at the Dodwells' door, aware that his progress from Mr Ross and into the lion's den had been closely monitored by Peter Dodwell at his bedroom window.

'Yes?' The watcher had come quickly downstairs and reached the door before his wife.

'I wondered if you could spare a minute,' Robert said.

'Sorry?' said Peter Dodwell unhelpfully.

His wife Caroline appeared at his elbow, and eased him to one side. 'Robert!' she said. 'How nice to see you. How's

Mandy? Come on in, we're just about to have a restoring drink after getting Hugo off to sleep.'

Peter Dodwell looked furious, but he stood aside and allowed Caroline to draw Robert into the house.

They sat in a stiff group and Robert tried to explain his point of view, stressing the practical benefits to the village and assuring Peter Dodwell of the minimum of noise disturbance. Peter Dodwell said nothing, just sat and stared at Robert with a disconcertingly blank expression.

Caroline made up for her husband's silence by agreeing enthusiastically with everything Robert said, until even she was overcome by the complete absence of reaction from Peter Dodwell.

Acutely embarrassed, Robert began to get to his feet.

'Just a minute, Mr Bates,' said Peter Dodwell slowly. 'Do I not have the right to reply?'

'Oh, don't be so stuffy, Peter,' said Caroline, with an attempt at a smile.

She might have been invisible. Peter Dodwell glared at Robert and said rudely, 'Sit down. You've taken up my precious free time with your ramblings. Now it's your turn to listen.'

It was the same argument as he had put forward reasonably mildly at the Parish Council meeting, but this time his voice grew loud. He stood up and pointed accusingly at Robert, and then he marched up and down the room, and began to shout. His face was red, and his eyes bulged.

'Peter,' pleaded Caroline, 'you'll wake Hugo. You know he's only just gone off.'

Peter Dodwell rounded on her. 'So what if I do bloody well wake him,' he yelled. 'He'll be lucky if he ever gets to sleep when bloody Bates has got going! Night and day, screeching and whining and hammering! How dare you come up here with your explanations and excuses! Get out, go on, get out!'

Caroline was crying now, and Robert frowned. He felt quite calm, and put his hand on Caroline's shoulder. 'Don't upset yourself because of me,' he said. He turned to face Dodwell, who was shaking with rage.

'I don't need your support, Mr Dodwell. There are enough sensible people in Ringford, thank God, willing to back me.'

Robert walked without hurrying to the Dodwells' front door, and did not look back. As he turned out of the gate, Peter Dodwell screamed his parting shot.

'I shall do everything in my power to stop you! You and bloody Round Ringford! You'll see!' And as he slammed the door, the thin wail of a child woken from sleep drifted over the darkening Close.

CHAPTER FIFTEEN

Round Ringford Horticultural Show, after years in the wilderness of any old field that was available, now had its regular venue in the grounds of Ringford Hall. The Show Committee were in luck again this year, and the day was fine and warm, encouraging a good crowd to make their way up the chestnut avenue, chattering and scolding children, and greeting acquaintances they had not seen since last year.

Outside the elegant, pale-gold stone facade of the Hall, a large blue and white striped marquee had been erected on newly-cut lawns. Bagley Studio Band, red-faced and sweating with effort and hot sunshine, were seated in a grassy hollow which had once been a lily pond, until a visiting two-year-old had drowned there. Bill Turner had been instructed to fill it in, and a delicate-leaved acer, giving no shade to the unfortunate Band, had been planted in memory of a life cut horribly short.

Entrants for classes came from every village within the radius allowed, and the standard was high, the competition cut-throat. Certain names – Price, Turner, Ross, Beasley – dominated. Miss Layton, the village school headmistress, who had defected to live in Fletching for a bit of peace and quiet in her leisure time, had come over to judge the children's art and craft entries, and this year a magnificent exhibition of amateur photographers' work almost stole the show.

'That's my favourite,' said Doris Ashbourne to Ellen, as they meandered up and down. 'That one of the vicar on his bike. Must have been a windy day, his cloak flying up like that. Who took that, I wonder?'

Ellen peered at the label. 'Looks as if 'e's about to take off,' she said. 'I can't read this, the print's too small, and I 'aven't got me glasses.'

Doris had a look, and nodded. 'Of course, we might have known,' she said. 'It was that Colin Osman took it. Always about the village with his camera, he is.'

'Regular little Anthony Hamstrung Jones,' cackled Ellen.

A brisk wind had got up, slapping the marquee, and outside on the sunlit lawns the crowds held on to their show catalogues and were glad of the cooling air. Mr Richard, after opening the Show ith his usual speech, spent much of the afternoon with Susan, proudly pushing their new baby around from one display to another, showing her off to the village people, who obligingly cooed and admired.

'What you calling her, Mr Richard?' said Doreen Price, leaving her station at the WI refreshment tent to come and have a peek. Doreen was a large, comfortable woman, who inspired confidence and justified it, being capable and unfussed. She looked at the little pink-cheeked face, and the baby's blue eyes stared back at her without blinking.

'Elizabeth Alexandra Poppy,' said Susan, with a sideways glance at Richard.

'Very nice,' said Doreen, smiling, and the baby suddenly smiled back.

'Dear little soul,' said Peggy Palmer, coming to stand next to Doreen. 'What's her name?'

'Elizabeth Alexandra Poppy Standing,' Doreen told her, with a twinkle in her eye.

'Poppy for short?' said Peggy, remembering the day of

her birth.

'Yes, that's right,' said Susan firmly, and Richard at the same time said equally firmly, 'No, of course not, we shall probably call her Lizzie.'

'Afternoon, sir.' It was Robert Bates, smiling at Mr Richard and holding tight to Mandy's hand.

'Ah, hello Robert, Mandy,' said Richard Standing, and Susan proudly straightened Poppy's sun hat. Mandy shyly put out her finger for the baby to grasp. 'She's lovely, Mrs Standing,' she said.

The group of admirers had grown, and now blocked the way of passers-by, among whom was Peter Dodwell. He had lost Caroline and Hugo in the big tent and was impatient, bored and irritable. 'Excuse me!' he said loudly, pushing his way through.

Robert caught his eye, and because he had a sweet and forgiving nature, smiled apologetically. 'Sorry,' he said, and moved to one side.

'Trust you, Bates,' said Peter Dodwell, with no answering smile. 'Can't move without tripping over you.'

Peggy and Doreen, Mr Richard and Susan, and even Poppy Standing, stared at Dodwell's retreating back.

'What a very unpleasant young man,' said Mr Richard. 'Not a Ringford man, is he?'

'New here,' said Robert tersely, 'lives in Walnut Close.'

'Let's hope his manners improve,' said Susan Standing. 'Come on Richard, we must look for Nanny.' The group dispersed, Mandy looking shocked and upset, and Peggy Palmer and Doreen doing their best to restore order and calm.

The prizes were all presented, and the main tent had a bruised look. Displays of giant dahlias and chrysanthemums had been plundered, some taken off to present to the hospital, others snatched away in pique by disappointed owners and taken home to be appreciated in front rooms and on hall tables.

'The auction will begin in five minutes,' said Tom Price, using a microphone which whined and spluttered. Fruit cakes and Victoria sponges, shiny jars of blackcurrant and gooseberry jam, thick-cut and thin-cut marmalade, mammoth leeks and bunches of orange carrots, fine green cooking apples and perfect, tiny shallots – all would come under the hammer and raise large sums of money far above their worth. But this was for charity, and Ringford was proud of its record of giving.

The Standings had found Nanny Bridget and handed over the baby, now tired and grizzling, and Peggy walked back into the W.I. tent with Doreen.

'Poppy Standing,' said Peggy. 'I think that's really pretty.'

'Well, that's what it'll be, mark my words,' said Doreen. 'Mrs S. is used to getting her own way. What about Nanny Bridget, though? If I'd been Susan Standing I'd have advertised for a sixty-year old widow, plain and homely, with a life devoted to looking after babies.'

'Sounds like me,' said Peggy, 'except I've never had the babies.'

The sadness in her voice made Doreen change tack. 'Getting darker in the evenings now. Summer's almost gone when harvest is finished. Soon be time to think about the Jumble Sale and fireworks night.'

The auction successfully completed, the big marquee gradually emptied, until only Ivy Beasley and Tom Price were left, Ivy packing up the judges' papers, and Tom stacking the final trestle table.

'Went well, Ivy, don't you think?' he said.

Ivy nodded. 'Very well indeed,' she said. 'There were some excellent entries, and nicely presented. Only one small thing I think should be considered.'

Tom looked at her with raised eyebrows. There was always a sting in the tail with old Ivy.

'It is surely time for someone else to get the prize for best allotment. Bill Turner gets it year after year, and a great many other prizes as well.'

'He's a very good gardener, Ivy,' said Tom, puzzled.

Ivy's voice rose. 'He's not the only one,' she said, her face screwing up in irritation. 'I think we should encourage other exhibitors, some of the younger ones, maybe someone who would set a better example.'

'Nobody could set a better example than Bill Turner. I've never seen better onions or runners anywhere,' said Tom, with an innocent smile.

Ivy glared at him and, gathering up her bags, marched off out of the tent.

Tom and Doreen wandered along the Top Field together, taking the evening air after the long afternoon in the hot show tent.

'You should've seen our Ivy's face, Doreen,' said Tom. 'I thought she was going to hit me with her handbag for a minute. Of course, I knew exactly what she meant about poor old Bill and Peggy, but I wouldn't let on.'

It was almost dark, and chilly without the warmth of the sun. The pale stubble crackled under their feet, and Doreen shivered, slipping her hand through Tom's arm. A blackbird, settling in to roost in the hedge, flew up in noisy protest, alarming Doreen, who tripped on a dried clod of stubbly earth. A tiny, shadowy creature fled across their path and into the long, tussocky grass at the edge of the field. 'Not another ruddy plague of voles,' Tom said. Several years ago, there had been hundreds of field voles in the new spinney down by the river, but they'd moved out when the grass got sparse under the growing trees.

'They don't do any harm, Tom,' said Doreen.

'Belligerent little buggers, though,' said Tom.

Down in the village the church clock began to strike. The sound carried up to the Top Field, booming and echoing into the woods on the hill.

'Better be getting back, Tom,' said Doreen, turning him round with an affectionate hand. 'It was a busy day, boy, and early Communion tomorrow.'

They walked without speaking for a few minutes, then Doreen continued. 'That's a nice little girl, Tom,' she said, thinking of the baby's clear blue eyes and sudden smile.

'Very nice,' said Tom. 'Even those glasses seemed to suit her. I wouldn't say she was all that little, though. Quite tall, in fact. Bridget, wasn't it? I'm sure that was her name.'

Doreen could not think of a suitably cutting reply, and changed the subject. 'Nasty moment when young Dodwell was so rude. Did I tell you, Tom?'

Tom listened in silence to Doreen's account, and frowned. 'Seems he means to cause trouble. Still, he won't get much support from the village. They're all behind our Robert, solid as a rock. Bateses have been here too long to worry about the likes of Dodwell.'

'Hope you're right, Tom,' said Doreen. 'Now,' she said, 'about this Bridget . . .'

'You were talking to her a very long time, Rob,' said Mandy accusingly.

They too had discussed the Dodwell episode, but Robert had reassured Mandy that it was only a temporary hiccup, and they'd moved on to Nanny Bridget.

'Only being civil,' said Robert, taking off his shirt. Mandy was in bed already, half sitting, half lying, with a couple of pillows behind her head. Her face shone with moisturising cream, and she had brushed her hair until it flattened against her head like a cloche. She was aware that she was not looking her best, and now that they had been advised not to have intercourse because of the risk of bleeding, she felt unattractive and unloved.

'I know there's other ways,' she had said to Robert, 'but there's nothing like a good straightforward cuddle and that.'

'Specially "and that",' he replied.

Now he climbed into bed beside her and kissed her, messing up her hair and slithering about on the moisturising cream. 'It won't be that long, Mandy,' he said, 'then it'll be like the first time all over again.'

'Hope not,' said Mandy, and turned over on her side. 'He's kicking well,' she said. 'Always gets going three minutes after I've got into bed.'

'Got his timing right, too, then,' said Robert. 'That's my boy.'

Poppy Standing was getting into her stride. Every evening from around seven until half past nine she yelled lustily, the penetrating sound echoing round the old nursery and through the corridors of the Hall.

'Thank goodness for Bridget,' said Susan, finishing her pudding and putting the dishes on a tray to carry the half mile to the kitchen. 'She's asked for Saturday evening off this week, as well as the whole of Sunday, so I shall be a limp heap by Monday.'

'Who's the lucky boy?' said Richard, picking up a drying-up cloth. 'I hope to God it's not that ill-mannered oaf who turned up at the Show this afternoon.'

'No, no. It's the Bates boy, Dan Bates from Waltonby. He's taking her to the pictures. The lads don't waste much time round here, do they, Richard?'

'Never did myself,' he said. 'Got to strike before the others do. As in your case, my dear,' he continued hastily.

'Bridget seems very good with Poppy, a real talent for nannying,' said Susan.

'"Lizzie", my dear, don't you think?' said Richard.

Susan did not acknowledge this, and swished the water round the sink with a flourish. 'Dear little Poppy,' she said. 'When shall we have her christened?'

CHAPTER SIXTEEN

Bill Turner drove slowly along the lane leading out of Round Ringford, past Prices' farm, where the old sheep dog rushed out, barking frantically as always, chasing after Bill's old white van, until he outstripped her and she returned, looking foolish.

It was Wednesday afternoon, one of Bill's regular times for visiting his wife Joyce in the Merryfields nursing home for people unable to cope with the world outside. Loony bin, we would have called it in my young day, he thought, and then shivered at the idea of his wife, whom he had loved so much in the beginning, being shut up, put away.

The old van wasn't capable of much speed, but Bill knew he was driving more slowly than usual, putting off the moment of arrival. He passed Pat Osman, walking her little Cairn, Tiggy, and waved. Nice girl, that, he thought. Expect she'll be the next in the baby stakes. Pity some girls set so much store by it, like my Joyce.

Bill's marriage had sadly changed when Joyce had miscarried, and been too shattered and frightened to try again. She had passed long years in mourning and virtual reclusion, wrecking Bill's life as well as her own. Her final breakdown had freed him, but only conditionally, and he sometimes thought it had been better with her at home. He'd not felt quite so guilty, looking after her as best he could, allowing her to punish him with words and petty violence.

It was a misty day, the fine droplets of moisture gradually turning to rain. He switched on the windscreen wipers, and they scraped across the screen with a rhythmic, irritating squeak. Trees are turning, Bill thought, soon be winter. Could be a hard one, they say, but then they always say that, Fred Mills and his cronies in the pub. If the village gets cut off by snow, though, I'll not be able to go so often to see Joyce. This shameful thought cheered him, and he accelerated past a straggling flock of sheep, some already fat with early lambs.

The usual four or five cars belonging to family visitors were parked by the big Victorian mansion, restored and redecorated by the Health Authority to create a pleasant, peaceful place for those who would recover, and a haven for those who would not. As Bill walked through the tiled hallway, his footsteps echoing in the unnatural quiet, a young doctor came out of the office and approached him.

'Afternoon, Mr Turner,' he said. 'I wonder if you could spare a moment?'

Bill followed him, nervous and apprehensive, clutching a stiff bunch of gladioli from his greenhouse.

'Rather good news,' said the doctor. 'We are very pleased with Mrs Turner's progress, and if it continues for another week or so, we would encourage her to come home for a short period, just as a trial, to see how she copes.'

Bill started to speak, but choked and scrabbled for his handkerchief in his jacket pocket. He began again. 'But she doesn't even know me when I come to see her,' he said. 'I could be a complete stranger.'

'Ah,' said the doctor, with the air of a magician about to pull a rabbit from the hat, 'I think you'll find she does. She had a visit from her friend – Miss Beasley, is it? – this morning, and she greeted her by name, asked her about the village, and was more or less perfectly sensible. We knew you would be pleased.'

The doctor stood up, held open the door for Bill, and left him walking in a dazed fashion towards the big sitting room where he always found Joyce staring out of the window.

She was in her usual chair, but looked round and saw him coming. She stood up, smiling nervously, and tentatively put out her hand.

'Hello, Bill,' she said.

CHAPTER SEVENTEEN

The school bus lumbered along in front of Bill's van, occupying the entire width of the narrow road. Forced to crawl, Bill had plenty of time to look about him, and plenty of time to think.

Round every corner there seemed to be a memory of Joyce. The sharp turn coming out of Waltonby was still as dangerous as when he'd borrowed Tom Price's motorbike to take Joyce, his regular girlfriend by then, to the pictures in Tresham. They'd had a narrow squeak one night, but Joyce had kept her head, held on tight, and no harm was done.

And there was the oak tree with the secret hollow. He and Joyce, still at the village school, but well aware of each other, had sheltered there from a sudden storm. She'd offered to show him hers if he'd show her his. He'd shyly obliged, and then Joyce had run off into the rain, laughing, hanging on tight to her knickers.

The bus made dozens of stops, discharging children in twos and threes, but always at points where Bill could not pass. He sat resignedly in a depressed huddle, until finally they pulled up at the bus stop at Round Ringford Stores.

Coasting along, Bill peered through the shop window. Not a chance of seeing Peggy alone for a while. School-children, mothers and infants, all milling about inside, were deliberating over sweets, bags of crisps, cigarettes.

It's her busiest time, thought Bill. I shall have to come back later. He was still feeling confused and shocked. Joyce had not only recognised him, she had carried on a frighteningly normal conversation.

He turned up the Bagley Road, past Mr Ross's immaculate, newly-trimmed hedges, and stopped in a gateway at the side of the hill. There was an autumn chill in the air as he leaned on the cold metal gate and looked down across the village. The rain had cleared, leaving a damp haze over the woods. Bill watched a pair of wild duck flying like arrows along the line of the Ringle, and saw them disappear behind Prices' spinney.

That's grown tall, that spinney, thought Bill. Seems only yesterday we planted it. He could see straggling groups of children coming out of the shop, splitting up and regrouping, like tadpoles in their black uniforms. A car went past, and hooted a greeting. It was Robert Bates, with Mandy sitting beside him, waving cheerfully. Nice young couple, Bill thought. They deserve a break.

His own abortive attempt at becoming a parent came back to him, unwelcome and painful, and with it, the alarming news that Joyce might well be back home in two or three weeks' time.

He gazed miserably across the fields, and saw Tom Price ploughing in regular even swathes. White gulls, sharp against the grey sky, rose and fell behind the giant orange tractor, feeding from the freshly turned iron-brown earth. Bill wondered why he felt so moved. It was a very familiar sight, and yet this afternoon he was seeing everything as if through newly-opened eyes. Through Joyce's eyes, he realised.

Tom disappeared from sight behind the hill, and Bill's eye was caught by a brown and white spaniel appearing on the horizon and slowly bounding towards him. Tom's old Bessie, a bit stiff in her joints now, but still healthy and fond of a walk with her master, came up and licked his hand.

'Bill!' It was Tom's voice, and Bill climbed over the gate, following the spaniel across the newly ploughed field and through a gap in the hedge. Tom had descended from his tractor cab and was bending over a large piece of earth-ripping machinery which looked too lethal to be called anything as rustic as a plough.

'Here, Bill,' he said, looking up with a smile. 'Saw you at the gate, boy. You're just the man I need. Bloody thing's seized up. Can you hold this, while I get at it from underneath?'

They laboured until it was working again, and Tom straightened up. 'Thanks,' he said. 'I'll buy you a pint tonight.'

Bill nodded, unsmiling, and Tom climbed back on to his tractor. 'You all right, Bill?' he said. Bill did not answer, but seemed reluctant to go.

Tom got down again, and took out his pipe. He lit it, saying nothing, then stared Bill straight in the eye. 'All right, then, out with it. What's up?'

Bill sighed. 'It's our Joyce,' he said. 'She's better. Might come home soon.'

Puffs of smoke rose in the still, damp air, and neither man spoke.

Finally, Tom cleared his throat. 'What should I say, boy?' he said. 'It's good news, of course it is, in a way. But if it means you and Joyce taking up where you left off, then it certainly is not good news. That was no life for a man, as I said to you many times. And she was about as unhappy as it's possible for a woman to be. No, you can't have that again.'

'The doctor says they've been able to help her a lot. And with another two or three weeks, things could be a lot different. He wouldn't say she was completely better, but there'd be supervision and that, and coming home for a short while would be the next step, he said.'

'And another thing,' said Tom, looking away now, over his fields and back up to the farmhouse, where rooks were settling in the tree tops at the end of the home pasture.

'Yes,' said Bill, knowing what was coming.

'Well, there's Peggy. What about her?' This was the nearest Tom and Bill had ever come to discussing it, though Bill always felt he had Tom's tacit approval. Most people understood, he thought, but of course, you never knew in villages.

'I'm going in to see her, soon as the shop shuts,' said Bill. 'It's only fair. God knows how she'll feel. It's a bloody old mess, one way and another, Tom.'

He turned away and ducked through the gap in the hedge, heading back towards his van. 'Still,' he shouted to Tom, 'it's *my* bloody old mess, and I shall have to clear it up, somehow. Cheerio, boy, see you tonight.'

'I'm not sure I want your cousin's old cast-offs,' said Mandy, as Robert drove the car slowly up the long drive, and stopped in front of a low, stone farmhouse. Some unfeeling farmer had re-roofed it some years ago with red corrugated iron, extending the slope of the roof to include an unlikely-looking verandah.

'Funny looking house,' said Mandy.

'Uncle Alf is bit of a character,' said Robert. 'He breeds horses, and keeps the hunt terriers boxed up in the back yard. I'll bring you here in spring to see the foals.'

'Is Uncle Alf any more cheerful than his brother Ted?' said Mandy apprehensively, as they got out and walked over to the back door. It stood open, and Robert's cousin Stella turned from kneading bread on the kitchen table.

'Come in, Robert and Mandy,' she said. 'Nice to see you. I'll just put this to prove, then I'll make us a cup of tea.'

Stella had had three children, one after the other, very close together, and coped well. The children were plain and square, with rosy cheeks and sparse, wispy fair hair, but their smiles were broad and welcoming, and Mandy took to them at once.

'I've put all the stuff out in the sitting-room, Mandy,' Stella said. 'You can take a look, and say if you want anything. But for heaven's sake don't feel you've got to have any of it.'

'Sure you won't be needing it again?' said Mandy, warming to this pleasant woman.

'Not if I have anything to do with it,' said Stella. 'I love them dearly, but three's enough.'

The house was a big one, rambling and untidy. An extension had been added as the family grew, and now three generations lived there quite happily. Young Dan, who had helped with the harvest on Bates's Farm, teased his sister Stella, saying that if he was in charge he'd boot the lot of them out. But he loved his nephews and niece, and often took them off Stella's hands, showing them how to feed the horses and exercise the terriers.

Mandy sorted through the baby clothes and items of furniture. It was very clean, and smelt lingeringly of baby soap and lavender. It had all clearly been good quality when new. Stella tactfully left them alone to discuss what they wanted, and they agreed to have most of it, provided the price was right.

'Seein' as you're family,' said Stella, tying up her son's shoelaces in double knots, and pushing him firmly out of the back door, 'let's call it a round forty pounds, all right?'

This was so obviously a bargain that Robert agreed straight away, and they loaded what they could into the car. 'Cheerio then, and thanks, Stella,' he said. 'I'll pick the rest up next time I'm going by with the Land Rover.'

'Nice people,' said Mandy. 'I like to think of our baby in their cot.'

They drove down the farm road, the children running and shouting alongside the car until it pulled away out of sight. 'That's what I'd call a real home, Robert,' said

Mandy. 'It's kids make a home.'

'And that's what we'll have, Mandy, you'll see,' said Robert, swerving to avoid a rabbit which chose that moment to dive suicidally across the lane.

Peggy Palmer sat on one side of her kitchen table, and Bill sat on the other. They had been still and quiet for several minutes, and then Peggy stretched out and touched Bill's big brown hand resting on the table.

'What is it, Bill? You're beginning to frighten me, it must be something dreadful.'

It was dusk, and Peggy had not switched on the light. In the warmth and tranquillity of the kitchen, Bill did not know how to tell her the news. It was a complete stalemate, his love for Peggy and his feelings for a wife whom he no longer loved but could not abandon.

'Joyce is better,' he said finally. 'She's coming home, in a week or two.'

Peggy felt as if someone had punched her in the stomach. 'Oh,' she said in a small voice. 'Is she?'

'Yep,' said Bill.

'Well,' said Peggy. She got up, walked to the kitchen window and, with her back to Bill, said, 'Well, that's torn it.'

'She has every right to come home,' said Bill, his tone still without expression.

Peggy felt a chill in the small of her back and shivered. 'Of course she has,' she said. 'It is her home, after all.'

Then Bill had his arms around her, holding her close, and was kissing her in fierce desperation. 'Peggy!' he said. 'I love you! For God's sake, what are we going to do? I can't face it, I just can't.'

The old white van was still parked outside the shop as darkness fell, and it did not go unremarked by Ivy Beasley at her front window. All Peggy's rules and resolve in not allowing Bill to stay had had to be waived. There was much to talk about.

'It's no good, Bill,' she said finally. 'We've got to face it somehow. We've just drifted along, thinking Joyce would be in Merryfields for ever. Serves us right, really, for taking it for granted. Nothing's ever that easy,'

Neither of them felt hungry, but Peggy prepared a small supper and insisted that Bill ate it. When they had washed up and had a cup of coffee, Peggy looked at the clock.

'You'd better be off now. Go and meet Tom and have a couple of pints. It'll ease the pain, if nothing else.' She tried very hard not to sound resentful.

Bill kissed her again, and went towards the door. 'Can I come back here, after that?' he said.

'No,' said Peggy. For once, Bill did not try to persuade her.

CHAPTER EIGHTEEN

The Jumble Sale in Round Ringford was more than just Ellen Biggs' opportunity to provide herself with a new wardrobe for every season; it was a major social event in the village. Ivy Beasley masterminded a small committee of ladies, a sub-committee of the W.I., and each had her own established stall to look after, tasks to perform. Bill Turner and a tribe of children collected from every house, and most people were only too glad to get rid of unwanted items.

With a week or so to go, Ivy was standing at her kitchen window, holding her list of Jumble Sale Things to Do, but thinking about this morning's altercation with the hunt. They had jammed up the Green and the road, just when she needed to go out, and she'd given the Master a piece of her mind. Always been the same, she thought, and always will be. But although the arrogance of some of the hunting fraternity irritated her, she could not imagine Ringford without its annual meet.

She looked out at her garden, neat and tidied up, shrubs pruned and dead plants removed and chopped for the compost heap. It had been hard work this year, and Robert had not helped as much as usual. Busy with his Mandy, she supposed. She realised that for the first time she dreaded the onset of winter. Coal to heave in from the shed, logs to split, curtains to draw against the draughts, good hot meals to keep out the cold. Must be getting old, she thought. Still, my lot in life is a sight better than poor old Ellen's, struggling along in that dreadful Lodge.

She returned to the table, thinking now of Mandy and Robert. Not the best time for a baby, due in February, worst of all months. Still, if Robert's plan went ahead, and they could move into Miss Hewitt's bungalow before then, it would be a lot more suitable than that damp Bridge Cottage. Needs pulling down, that does.

Maybe, thought Ivy, taking up her list of Jumble Sale reminders, maybe Mandy'll need a bit of help with the baby when it comes, pushing it out in the pram, and baby-sitting . . .

She won't want you, Ivy, intruded her mother's voice. Got her own friends, surely. She'll not need you.

Ivy suppressed the stab of disappointment in her chest, and ignored the voice.

She had just ticked off 'See Doreen Price about refreshments', when a knock at her front door caused her to push Gilbert, Peggy's traitorous cat, off her lap.

Better get a move on, Ivy, else whoever it is will be gone.

I'm going as quick as I can, Mother, said Ivy. And anyway, if it's important, they'll wait.

She brushed cat hairs off her dark brown skirt, and opened the door into the passage. Her heels clacked on the lino, old lino, well polished, patterned to look like parquet flooring, but not deceiving for one minute in its shiny reflections of the hall stand and the hard wooden chair against the wall. Ivy reached the front door, and drew back the bolt. She opened up a couple of inches, not removing the chain.

'Oh,' she said 'it's you, Mr Osman, what do you want?'

Ivy had little time for Colin Osman, thinking him bumptious and interfering. He had no sense of decent village ways, of waiting until he was asked to join in, or respecting what had been done for years, perfectly adequately, suiting the village temperament, fitting in with the seasons and the farming year. In an unguarded moment, Ivy had expressed these opinions to her constant, ghostly companion. And then, when Ivy had been ironing and trying to listen to a gardening programme one afternoon, old Mrs Beasley's voice had sniped at her irritatingly.

He'll be on the Parish Council, next, mark my words.

Who will? said Ivy, keeping on ear on the radio. She tried to concentrate on the best way to deal with apples that fell before they were ripe.

That Colin Osman from Casa Pera, said her mother knowledgeably. Ivy, well aware that her mother could know nothing more than she herself had told her, had not answered. This always generated an impatient rebuke.

Deaf, are you, Ivy Dorothy Beasley? said the insistent voice in her head. I thought I'd brought you up to answer politely when spoken to?

I swear I shall stop talking to her altogether, Ivy had thought, and back came the voice without mercy: So who will you talk to, Ivy Dorothy? There's not that many callers at Victoria Villa these days.

At the front door, Colin Osman smiled sweetly at Ivy, his pleasant face determined to charm, his athletic body tense, ready for action. He had one foot on Ivy's scrubbed white step, and put out his hand. 'Could you spare a couple of minutes, Miss Beasley?' he said.

'What for?' said Ivy gracelessly.

'A suggestion, that's all, for the Jumble Sale,' Colin said, anxious not to alienate this stern, square figure blocking his way into her house. Once you're inside, his wife Pat had told him, experienced from calling with cosmetic wares, it's a doddle. They can't resist.

Ivy wavered. At least it would keep Mother quiet for a while. The voice was always silent if Ivy had a visitor.

The chain was withdrawn, and the door opened wider. 'Come in, then, for a few minutes,' said Ivy. 'I'm very busy on notes for the Jumble Sale myself, and I've a hundred and one things to do after that. Wipe your feet, please.'

Colin put his suggestion as tentatively and tactfully as his natural bounce would permit. 'I wondered if you would consider a special promotion on children's toys and games?' he said. 'Always popular, in my experience, and we could get the children to do the collecting, make them feel part of it all, teach them to be participating members of our community.'

'And what is your experience, Mr Osman?' said Ivy icily.

'Well, I don't want to boast, but in our town's Rotaract you wouldn't have found anybody better at running a Jumble Sale.' Colin looked encouragingly at Miss Beasley's ruddy face, dark eyes unrelenting, and mouth set in a thin line, and wondered what she would look like if she smiled. He was not about to find out.

'This is a village, not a town, and we've always managed very well without Rotaract, whatever that is. Collecting's always been done by Bill Turner and the children,' she replied, 'and Jean Jenkins always has a very successful toy stall. One of the first to sell out.'

'Ah,' said Colin. 'Then would you like an appeal for jumble in the next Newsletter? I could word it for you to make it absolutely irresistible!'

'Ringford folk are always very generous,' said Ivy, walking to the sitting-room door and opening it. 'And they don't need reminding,' she added. 'We've been having Jumble Sales to raise money for fireworks since before you came to Ringford. You'll see, Mr Osman, we don't need no irresistible appeals to make it a success.'

She walked down her narrow, dark passage and Colin Osman meekly followed. Dismissed, he thought, as he walked down the path, borders neatly dug and fallow for the winter. He latched Ivy's gate, and walked off down the windy street, a little downhearted, but planning other suggestions, determined to contribute in a way which would be noticed and applauded.

Old Mrs Beasley was right. His long-term aim was to be elected a Parish Councillor, and he had his strategy all planned out.

Not usually a lunchtime drinker, Colin Osman felt sufficiently squashed by Ivy Beasley to be tempted in for a quick half. The public bar was warm and welcoming, with a huge log fire sending out great waves of heat, and the small shaded wall lamps reflecting twinkling light from polished brasses and pewter tankards.

'Morning, Mr Osman,' said Don Cutt, large and proprietorial behind the bar. 'What can I get you?'

Robert Bates was leaning against the end of the bar, rough in his working clothes, and he greeted Colin with a smile. 'Let me get it, Colin. What'll you have?'

The quick half turned into a long pint, and Colin relaxed in the warmth of the Arms, a place of solace for villagers for hundreds of years. 'How're your plans coming along, Bob?' he said.

Nobody but Colin Osman ever called him 'Bob', but Robert did not mind. 'Still waiting for the planning decision,' he said. 'Old John Barnett is quite happy for me to use the barns. I'd have to spend a bit of money on them to make them suitable for the job, but not too much. Start small, I've decided. Then I can go on helping Dad on the farm for longer. God knows I'd be glad to get away altogether, what with the atmosphere there at the moment. But I feel sorry for the old bugger, and even sorrier for Mum, me bein' their only son.'

Colin nodded wisely and ordered another drink for them both. 'I hear Dodwell's sent a letter of protest to the Council Planning Office,' he said. 'He tried nobbling one or two people for support, but didn't get very far, so I heard.'

Robert sighed. 'He won't listen to reason,' he said. 'I did try, but he just flipped. Difficult man, I would say.'

'The more difficult the better, Robert,' said Colin. 'If the Council decide he's some kind of a nut, he'll get nowhere. Shouldn't give him another thought, if I were you.'

'Yep,' said Robert. 'Still, I don't like that kind of unpleasantness. We all have to rub along together somehow. And I know Mandy quite likes that Caroline.'

'It'll pass,' said Colin. 'Now,' he continued, 'how's our Mandy? Still keeping busy?'

'Fairly,' said Robert, 'but she's giving up altogether at the end of December, she's promised me.'

'Probably good for her to keep occupied while she can,' said Colin. 'There's nothing worse for women than being bored. That's when they get up to mischief.'

Don Cutt, polishing glasses and listening in, roared with laughter. 'Don't let your Pat hear you say that,' he said. 'She'll have your guts for garters!'

Robert pulled on his jacket. 'Must be getting back,' he said. 'It's a day off for you, Colin, is it?'

Colin nodded, and drained his glass. 'Thought I'd finalise the Newsletter this afternoon, get it off to the printers. Some good items this month, Bob, though I says it as shouldn't.'

He said an expansive goodbye to Don and Robert and made for the door. He felt much better, and, turning up his coat collar against the cold wind, set off along the edge of the Green, over the stone bridge and the clear, rippling water, down the deserted lane to his quiet house. I'll just sit down for a few minutes with the paper and then make a start, he thought. Three minutes later he was asleep, peacefully snoring off the effects of his liquid lunch.

'Where's he bin, at this time o'day?' said Ellen Biggs to Doris Ashbourne, as they stood at the dusty window of The Lodge, watching Colin Osman pass by jauntily on his way home.

'Down the pub, from the look of him,' said Doris. Her

late husband had more or less drunk himself into an early grave, and she could spot over-indulgence a mile away.

''E's not a bad bloke, yer know,' said Ellen. 'Ivy don't care for him, but I reckon 'is heart's in the right place. Tries very 'ard to be useful in the village. The likes of Ivy don't give 'im a chance, but there's precious few who'll put the time in, like 'e does.'

Doris turned away from the draughty window and looked around the room. 'This place could do with a lick of paint, Ellen, freshen it up a bit.'

'In the spring, maybe,' said Ellen, 'but it don't bother me. Mr Richard's promised me a new back door before the weather sets in. That'll make a lot of difference to keepin' the warm in.'

Doris shivered. 'Well, Ellen,' she said, 'you're always welcome to the bed in my spare room if it gets too cold down here.'

Ellen had a tempting vision of Doris's spare room, warm and cosy, with its pink walls, curtains bright with cabbage roses, and thick, fitted carpet. She could see herself curled up under fluffy blankets and crisp sheets, and Doris coming in with a steaming hot cup of tea, not too early in the morning.

'That's very nice of you, Doris,' she said, 'but what would our Ivy say?'

Doris walked out of the Lodge gate, and met Mandy Bates driving slowly down the lane. Time she gave up all that buzzing about, thought Doris. Time to settle down and wait for her baby. There was plenty to do here in Ringford, if you were prepared to join in. Not just the W.I., though that could take up a lot of time, one way and another. Doris wasn't a great one for the singing and drama, but she was in the Scrabble team, and always entered a piece of embroidery or patchwork in the craft classes.

Course, if you were used to being in town all the time, it

would be difficult, Doris could see that. I suppose a walk round the lanes doesn't mean much to Mandy Bates, she thought. Doris and Ivy could happily saunter up Bagley Hill and along the footpath through the woods for a couple of hours, finding endless topics of conversation and always something different to see, something new that hadn't been there last time they passed. Like that dead badger in the verge. Mind you, that had been there for weeks, and the smell was dreadful.

Doris chuckled. Maybe that wasn't such an attraction for a pregnant girl. And with the wind in the east, like it was today, the best place was indoors.

She smiled and waved as Mandy went by. You'd have thought her mother would have had a word, though, Doris thought. It's not really up to the rest of us.

Mandy took off her coat and hung it up in the tiny hall of Bridge Cottage. She felt tired, and put on the kettle for a cup of tea. Her day was punctuated with cups of tea and coffee, and she sometimes wondered if it was good for the baby. Her bump was quite unmistakable now, and her conversation with the ladies under her nimble fingers was all about babies.

'Start as you mean to go on,' said Deirdre Barnett at Walnut Farm, who had reared a wayward daughter and strapping sons, and was now an experienced grandmother. 'Don't be forever picking it up and dandlin' it. Leave it to cry for a while, and get yourself out of earshot. It'll soon learn.'

It? thought Mandy. No wonder John Barnett was so tough. Reared in a hard school, no doubt. And the girl, Josie, went off to America as soon as she could. No thanks, Mrs Barnett, that won't be my way.

'Love 'em and look after 'em,' said Jean Jenkins. 'Fox and me have never believed in being tough. If a baby cries, it's miserable. You're meant to do somethin' about it, and leavin' it to cry makes it worse. You do what nature tells you, Mandy, and you won't go far wrong.'

Mandy laughed. 'I'm not on such good terms with nature as you, Jean,' she said.

'Then come to me,' said Jean generously. 'I'll soon put you right.'

Now Mandy was on her own in the silent cottage, and she settled down with a cup of tea. She sat so that she could see out of the window into the lane. There was always a chance something exciting would happen, like a glimpse of Mr Richard's big silver car, or a passing sheepdog squatting outside the garden gate, just where they walked.

Gracious, that must be the nanny, thought Mandy, surprised that there was in fact a passer-by. The tall, blonde girl walked slowly, well wrapped up with scarves and gloves, pushing a pram.

Mandy got up quickly and knocked on the window. Any company's better than none, she thought. She opened the front door and called across the garden, 'Would you like a cup of tea, Bridget?' The chances were that Nanny Bridget was just as fed up as she was with the dreary half-light of the November day.

Bridget Reilly accepted with alacrity and sat gratefully in Mandy's comfortable armchair, sipping hot tea.

'My God, Mandy,' she said, 'this village is a dead-and-alive hole when the sun doesn't shine! Did you see the idiots on horseback this morning? And all their friends and relations, tramping about in their oilskin undertakers' coats, and hats like personal umbrellas, and the horses trampling all over the Green and churning it up into a mud bath! And Miss Beasley couldn't get to the library van because of the crush. If looks could've killed, there'd be a lot of dead bodies on the Green right now! Heaven save us, it's just like being back in Enniskerry . . .'

All this, spoken at cheerful speed, was as good as the sun coming out for Mandy.

'At least you won't have to be here for very long,' she said, laughing. 'I'm here for the rest of my life. Bateses have been in Ringford . . .'

'. . . for generations,' said Bridget. 'I know, I've heard it from Fred Mills and your mum-in-law in the shop, and god knows who else. They all live in the past in this village.'

Mandy thought about that, and tried to be fair. 'Well, there are some who don't,' she said. 'Mrs Palmer at the shop's not like that. In some ways I find her easier to talk to than my own mum. She's never had children, so she doesn't load me down with advice, and we have some good laughs. Course, she's not from Ringford, you know, not been here long.'

'Ah well,' said Bridget, 'that accounts for it.' They looked at each other, and then spluttered into giggles, like the pair of schoolgirls they so recently had been.

A cry from the porch brought Bridget to her feet. 'There goes Poppy,' she said, pushing her glasses straight on her elegant nose. 'Better be getting back now.'

'Oh, I must come and say hello, she's such a poppet,' said Mandy, following Bridget out to the porch.

Poppy's small face cleared when she saw Bridget, and she smiled, kicking her legs in gleeful recognition.

'Isn't she sweet,' said Mandy. 'If I have a little girl like Poppy, I shall be over the moon.'

'See you around, then, Mandy,' said Bridget. 'Perhaps you'll come up and have tea with me? And I promise you'll not get a lecture about babies. I want to ask you about Robert's cousin, Dan . . .'

When Robert came in for his tea, Mandy greeted him with a hug. He raised his eyebrows. 'Had a good day, Mandy love?' he said.

'A nice thing happened,' she said. 'I've found a friend.'

CHAPTER NINETEEN

The day of the Jumble Sale, the third of November, was decidedly wintry. Bill Turner got out of his lonely double bed and opened the curtains, peering out into Macmillan Gardens to see who was up and about.

Old Fred Mills had his front door open, and was stooping painfully to pick up a bottle of milk from his step. He had lost weight since his sister died, and his shapeless grey trousers hung loosely round his bandy legs. Rickets, thought Bill. Poverty and undernourishment, and then they all started work before they'd had time for childhood. He must be a good age, old Fred. This winter could carry him off, and one or two others in the village if we don't watch out.

His gaze moved round the Gardens and saw Mrs Roberts, slovenly in her dressing-gown, emptying rubbish into the dustbin they hadn't bothered to move back into their garden. Well, garden was not the word for it – more of a dump, with its broken pushchairs, bits of old cars, and always Michael Roberts' latest motorbike, propped up for essential repairs which never seemed to get done.

And there was Doris Ashbourne, washed and neatly dressed already, polishing the big front window of her old person's bungalow. She looked a lot younger and more spry than Renata Roberts, thought Bill, not in the least ready to be labelled an old person.

The sky was grey, and he could see from the way the trees were blowing in the paddock behind the Gardens that it was a cold morning. The barns that Robert hoped to use as a garage were in that field, and could be glimpsed through the line of bungalows. Bill had backed Robert in his venture, and he gathered from the nightly gossip in the pub that, except for Peter Dodwell, Robert had met with general approval in his efforts to sound out village opinion. Peggy had said that Mandy, too, had got a good response from her clients in the village, so with luck it should go ahead.

Bill got dressed and had a quick cup of tea. He had to load up his last batch of jumble and get down to the Village Hall to meet Ivy. She was a hard taskmaster, no mistake. Still, she got things done, old Ivy.

And tomorrow was Sunday. Not just any old Sunday, but the day that Joyce was coming home for a few hours in the afternoon. The doctor had said she was making excellent progress, and he wanted her to have a short spell away from Merryfields, back at home, to see how she coped. She would return to the hospital for a few days, then spend a whole day in Ringford, and so on, until she made the transition back to her home for good.

Bill could hear Foxy Jenkins in his back yard, emptying cinders into a bucket, whistling and talking to his dog. A happy man, Foxy Jenkins, with his big, comfortable wife and his brood of children. Life came easily to the Jenkinses, thought Bill, and then corrected himself. Fox and Jean had had their ups and downs, times when it was difficult to make ends meet, and worries over the children. There had been that time the twins went down with flu, and Gemma was near to pneumonia. Fox had looked a hunted man for weeks.

The old white van would not start, and Bill sprayed some damp-start over the plugs. Winter was on its way, and he shut his mind to the prospect of long evenings spent with Joyce in recrimination and argument. Don't know if I can stand it again, he thought, and trundled off down the Gardens with his load of jumble for the Village Hall.

'There's no need for you to do anything, Mandy,' said Peggy Palmer, sitting at her Treasurer's table in the Village Hall. 'Just sit here and keep me company.'

It had been a grand Jumble Sale, very well attended and with plenty of competition for the best bargains. The bric-a-brac stall had emptied first, just ahead of the home-made cakes, and the sub-committee was flushed and triumphant. Peggy had been asked to count the money. 'Should be child's play for you, my dear,' said Doris Ashbourne, while Ivy Beasley frowned her disapproval. 'You must count the takings in your sleep.'

'It doesn't take long,' said Peggy wrily, 'but yes, I'd be delighted, if you trust me.'

'Looks like a sizeable total,' said Mandy. 'We should get a really good firework display. I love it all, the fireworks and the bonfire and the baked potatoes and soup, and everything. Robert's got a good stack of wood in the Long Field already.'

She twisted in her chair, and winced. Peggy noticed, and said, 'Are you all right, Mandy?'

Mandy nodded. 'Just these practice contractions. It's perfectly normal, it says in the book. Still, I think I'll be getting back to the cottage now, if there's nothing I can do. I'll see you next Friday, anyway, for your trim. Bye, Peggy.'

Peggy watched her walk slowly across the wooden floor of the Village Hall, and felt uneasy. Then she shook her head, dismissing pessimistic thoughts, and returned to her piles of coins.

Mandy walked slowly away from the Village Hall and

crossed the road by the school. She heard footsteps behind her and looked round. It was Caroline Dodwell, half running to catch up with her. Oh no, thought Mandy, I can't be doing with her just now. She quickened her pace, but Caroline was determined, and caught Mandy by the arm, drawing her to a halt.

'Mandy! Are you all right?' she said. 'I thought you looked very pale as you left the Hall . . .' She was panting, out of breath.

'I'm fine,' said Mandy, walking on and disengaging herself from Caroline's hand. 'Nice of you to bother, though. Thanks.'

'Well, I'll just walk home with you to make sure,' said Caroline, and would not listen to Mandy's assurances that she could manage perfectly well on her own. 'I expect your Robert's still mad with Peter,' she said, and slowed down as they approached the bridge.

But Mandy was not in the mood to linger and look into the Ringle's weedy depths. 'More the other way round, isn't it,' she said shortly.

'I wish Peter wasn't so obstinate,' Caroline continued, too concerned with her own worries to see that her company was unwelcome. 'And he has such a quick temper.'

'Well, that's your problem, Caroline,' said Mandy. 'And anyway, Robert's much too busy to let it bother him.' She opened her gate, and made to shut it behind her. Caroline put out a hand. 'I must just say this, Mandy, before you go in.' Mandy sighed and waited. She could feel another contraction coming on, and was longing to go indoors and put her feet up.

'I think Peter would like to stop all the nonsense and put it right with Robert, but he doesn't know how.' Caroline looked helplessly at Mandy, who was losing patience.

'An apology might help,' said Mandy. 'However much he disagrees with Robert, I don't see he has to be so rude.

See what you can do, Caroline. Now, I must be getting in. Bye.'

Sunday afternoon was a welcome reprieve from threatening winter. The sun shone, and the cold wind had changed to a balmy, almost spring-like breeze. All the Jenkins children were out on the Green, Mark and Warren playing football, and the twins swinging backwards and forwards in exact unison in the play area. Even Eddie, well wrapped-up, was toddling about after the terrier, trying in vain to interest him in a piece of stick about three inches long.

Bill drove down the village street on his way to pick up Joyce, and wished he could be out on his allotment instead.

He slowed down at the cuttings, so called because the dangerous double bend had for some long-forgotten reason been cut deep into a bank, between high hedges and trees. It was a notorious spot for accidents, and although the locals always slowed down to a crawl, there was always some young lad, reckless after a night in the Arms, who whizzed through this tempting chicane at full revs and top speed. Bill sounded his horn, and remembered the icy morning when Maureen, the postwoman, had skidded into the milk float, both of them going at a snail's pace, but unable to stop. She'd hurt her knees badly, but when the Parish Council had suggested that the road might be widened, they had been dismissed with excuses of greater priorities elsewhere.

Bill approached Waltonby, and waved to Stella, who was shepherding children into the little shop. It had been there as long as Bill could remember, and he wondered if it would survive. So many village shops had shut down, and once they were gone the heart seemed to go out of a place. Bill thought of Peggy and her brave determination to carry on in Ringford Stores, in spite of overwhelming odds against her.

If I could go in as a partner, he thought, as he had many

times before, we could make a good go of it. But that possibility was receding ever further from him, and he accelerated out of the village, up the long hill with its overhanging sycamores, and on to the long straight Roman road which led into Tresham. With nothing much to look at but open ploughed fields and rising flocks of lapwings, he checked off in his mind the tasks he had set himself before fetching Joyce.

He had cleaned the house from top to bottom, declining Peggy's tentative offer of help, and then hosed down the white van until it looked as respectable as it ever would. He'd prepared an appetising salad of ham and tongue, lettuce, tomatoes and cucumber, and left the table set for tea. Freshly shaved and bathed, his rough hair brushed flat, Bill had set off, wishing he could feel something more than fearful apprehension on his journey to reclaim his wife from the breakdown which he felt had been largely his fault.

Oh Joyce, Joycey, he thought, as he saw her standing in the big tiled hallway of Merryfields, round-shouldered and vulnerable in her best coat, her hair newly washed and set, twisting a pair of unworn gloves in her thin hands.

He walked towards her, a frozen smile on his face.

'There you are, Bill,' she said in a quiet voice. 'I'm all ready to come home now.'

CHAPTER TWENTY

Peggy shivered as she opened the back door and emptied last night's ashes into an old galvanised pail. The wind whipped round the corner of the house, circled the concrete yard and whistled off down the garden and across the fields, taking fallen leaves from their neatly brushed heaps and scattering them over the scrubby lawn.

'I'd really like to crawl back into bed,' said Peggy to Gilbert, putting down a saucer of catfood and stroking the cat's thick tabby coat. She remembered for no reason the day – her birthday – when Frank and Bill had conspired to give her a tiny, orphan kitten, too young to have left its mother, barely able to lap its milk. Like a couple of schoolboys, they were, she thought, delighted with their secret. She picked up Gilbert impulsively and gave her a fierce hug. The cat miaowed, anxious to get back to her breakfast, and Peggy put her down.

'Sod it,' she said, wiping her eyes with a piece of screwed-up kitchen paper from her dressing-gown pocket. 'Why do I feel so low this morning?'

But of course she knew. Yesterday afternoon Bill Turner had brought his lawfully wedded wife, Joyce, back to her rightful home. Peggy had gone for a walk by herself, up into Bagley Woods and along familiar tracks. It was cold and quiet. Dark firs dominated the bare branches of oak and beech, twiggy hazel and spindly birch. Tall, vicious nettles had at last died back, exposing earth pitted with burrows and treacherous snaking brambles. It was a time for hibernating. Rabbits and badgers and small, scuttling mice were lying low. Peggy had felt like an intruder, and wished she hadn't come.

Hard as she tried, she had not been able to avoid a flood of memories of other, pleasanter walks through the woods . . . Sauntering along in her wellies, marvelling over drifts of snowdrops and primroses, finding Bill waiting for her in their own grassy clearing . . . Coming home with armfuls of bluebells, not sure whether she should have picked them, hoping that she wouldn't meet Ivy Beasley, certain that Bill would come and rescue her . . . Gathering wild strawberries and putting them carefully in Bill's big handkerchief, sharing them out equally in the warm sunshine, savouring their sharp, almondy taste . . . Oh hell, what was the point? She had returned home, praying that she would not catch sight of Bill with Joyce.

Peggy made herself a cup of tea and decided she wasn't hungry. Maybe later, when I have my coffee, I'll have a sandwich, she thought.

Dressed and ready for the day's work, she went into the shop and pulled up the blind. Not a soul about. The older children had all gone on the bus to Tresham, and the bell had called the little ones into the classroom of the village school. The playground was empty, the rope slapping the flagpole. A solitary red anorak had been forgotten, abandoned in the middle of the grey asphalt. As Peggy watched, a small girl, her blonde hair brushed into a bobbing ponytail, rushed out of school and scooped it up. She looked around, startled at the strangeness of being alone in the playground, and then ran back inside.

Peggy unlocked the shop door, and with her broom began to brush the pavement outside. No matter how many rubbish baskets I put out, she thought, there'd always be an Andrew Roberts to throw his sweet wrapper on the ground where he stands.

She did not hear Bill cruising towards her on his bike, and went back into the shop, leaning against the counter, weary already from the effort of brushing and lack of sleep the night before.

'Morning,' said Bill.

Peggy withdrew hastily to the other side of the counter. What am I doing? she thought. This is Bill, my dear Bill. But he wasn't any more, he was Joyce's Bill again. She managed a weak smile.

'How's everything, Bill?' she said.

'Fine,' said Bill.

Peggy nodded. 'Good,' she said.

'Could I have a quarter of ham, please,' said Bill.

Peggy began to weigh out the slices of ham, and the silence was unbearable. 'Um, how was Joyce?' she said.

'Fine,' said Bill.

'Good.'

Bill took the ham from Peggy and put it on the counter. He reached out to hold both her hands and looked straight at her, the counter solid between them. 'You haven't asked me how I am,' he said.

'Well, how are you?' said Peggy.

'Bloody awful,' said Bill.

'Oh, Bill.'

By the end of November, Joyce was back home for good. She and Bill lived side by side, rather than together. There were no more dreadful rows, no more violence. Joyce was taking pills every day, and she still would not leave the house, except for an occasional hurried venture into the garden. But the weather was dismal and uninviting, and Bill had been warned not to push her into anything she did not want to do.

He continued to shop for supplies, and did most of the cooking. But Joyce would now and then offer to make supper, and she began to dust and clean the house, quietly sitting down in front of the television when her jobs were done. After their rackety life together before her breakdown, Bill felt uneasy with the new Joyce, not quite believing that the calm would last.

His meetings and walks with Peggy had ceased, and he snatched only the occasional cup of coffee in her warm kitchen when the shop was empty. His feeling of guilt was worse than ever, now that he had nothing to complain of in his compliant wife.

December arrived with mild, unseasonal weather. With Christmas only three weeks away, the school windows were bright with cut-out silver stars and scarlet bells. Bill stood in the playground, mending the netball post which had been split as a result of a tussle amongst the Chargers, a Ringford school mafia which had held ruthless sway through a succession of generations. At nine years old, Bill had been leader of the Ringford Chargers, and Tom Price his deputy.

He straightened up and looked across to the shop. Nobody there, as far as he could see. A good time to nip across and see Peggy. He was just opening the school gate when he saw the ambulance. It was coming along the street at speed, its blue light flashing and siren wailing.

Good God! thought Bill, stepping back. Where's he going in such a hurry?

CHAPTER TWENTY-ONE

Robert Bates sat in the back of the ambulance as it sped towards Tresham. He held Mandy's hand and tried desperately not to show his anxiety.

Mandy had woken up early, and nudged Robert awake. 'I feel funny,' she had said. 'The contractions seem a bit strong for just practice ones. Robert, I'm a bit scared . . .'

And then, when she had got out of bed to go to the lavatory, she had suddenly yelled from the bathroom.

'Robert!' He had rushed in to find her staring at a small pool of water round her bare feet.

'Didn't get there quick enough?' he'd said, but she shook her head, dumb.

'Never mind, Mandy love, calm down, you've not woken up properly, that's all.'

They had got back into bed, and Robert could feel Mandy lying rigid and unrelaxed beside him. 'Try and get some sleep,' he had said, 'you'll be fine when you've had some breakfast.'

But she had not slept, and at eight o'clock she refused to get up. Robert began to feel alarmed. 'Shall I get Dr Evans?' he said finally, as Mandy clutched her back and groaned. She nodded and burst into tears.

'It isn't time, Robert, the baby's not ready yet. Please make it stop, please stay with me.'

Robert had stayed until the doctor came twenty minutes later, and then things happened very quickly indeed. And now here they were, speeding along the familiar road in an unfamiliar ambulance, on their way to the maternity hospital in Tresham.

An injection as soon as they arrived had stopped the contractions. 'Twelve weeks to go, hum,' said the doctor. 'We'd like baby to have a bit more time before we meet him!' His joviality, and the efficient way the nurses got Mandy into bed, smoothing her hair and making her comfortable, reassured both Mandy and Robert.

'Maybe it was just a false alarm,' whispered Mandy. She seemed drowsy, and after a few minutes she fell asleep, still holding Robert's hand.

The ward sister beckoned Robert into her office, and smiled kindly at him. 'We shall keep her quiet and resting for a while. It's probably all she needs, just for a few days. Has she been doing too much, Mr Bates?'

Robert shook his head. 'Not really,' he said. 'She's been doing a few appointments in the village and around, to stop her getting bored, really.' Perhaps she should have stopped all together, put her feet up more, he thought.

'Well, we shall keep a close eye on her, and you can come and visit whenever you like, of course. Don't worry, Mr Bates, she's in the best place now, and I am sure everything is going to be fine.'

Bridge Cottage was gloomy and cold when Robert got back. The light was going, though it was only teatime, and he wondered whether he should have a fire. Perhaps I should go down the Arms a bit later on, get a snack and have a pint to take my mind off it, he thought. Then he realised he must stay by the telephone, so he laid and lit a fire in the small front room, and switched on the television.

Should I tell Mum? he thought. He silently shook his head. It would only alarm her, and he couldn't take the reproach in his father's face, not just now. What about

Mandy's mum? He couldn't do that either. She was such an emotional woman, she'd probably steam straight into the hospital and upset Mandy with her worried-hen act. No, best not to say anything, he thought.

But the television programme did not hold his attention, and he wandered about, picking up things of Mandy's – a matinee jacket half-finished, a book on bringing up baby, the magazine she had been reading last night. He switched off the television, and went upstairs to the box room, where Mandy had set out the things from Waltonby. A carrycot, already made up with snowy sheet and small blanket folded back, the baby bath on its stand in the corner, the little chest of drawers, already quite full of sleepsuits and tiny vests.

'Oh God,' he said and went back downstairs, where he picked up the telephone.

'Mrs Palmer?' he said. 'This is Robert here, are you busy just now?'

Peggy checked the locks on the shop door and the post office cubicle, set the alarm, and went to find her coat.

As she crossed the road and set off across the Green, she saw a chink of light through the curtains of Victoria Villa. The chink grew wider, and Peggy wondered how Ivy knew when she was walking by. Witchcraft, probably, thought Peggy, and the hairs rose on the back of her neck.

There were no street lights in Ringford, just the one high up on the wall of the Standing Arms, but there was still a trace of light in the sky, and Peggy's eyes soon grew accustomed to the dark Green. She passed the chestnut tree and its wooden seat, deserted most days now, the weather being too cold for Fred Mills and his cronies to linger. Peggy pulled up her coat collar, The weather was changing, and she wondered if there would be snow for Christmas.

She could see a light in the vicarage, high up in the attics, where Sophie Brooks had a studio and painted strong, colourful scenes of circus and pantomime. She liked to

146

think of Sophie, up there in the warmth under the eaves, absorbed in her painting. Sophie was a good friend, quiet but loyal, and Peggy and she sometimes escaped up to that studio to swap comforting incomers' stories.

Wonder if there's any truth in the rumour that the vicarage is going to be sold, thought Peggy. Sophie won't like a modern box to live in.

She walked on over the bridge, and the invisible, murmuring water. There had been days of rain, and the river was high. Peggy heard the splash of a water rat, and shivered.

The lights were on all over Bridge Cottage, and Peggy walked round the back, knocking and opening the door. 'Robert?' she called.

She was not expecting a smiling Robert, but she was taken aback by the desperation in his face.

'I am sorry, Robert,' she said, 'but we mustn't be too gloomy, must we?'

Peggy's knowledge of the finer details of premature childbirth were sketchy, but Robert had said Mandy was resting and sleeping quietly, and there was no mention at the hospital of the baby coming too soon.

'She was so upset, Mrs P.,' he said, and then he put his hands over his face for a minute or so. Peggy waited, still and quiet, until he had pulled himself together, then she walked to the sink.

'I could do with a coffee, Robert,' she said. 'It's been quite a rush in the shop today. Well, quite a rush for Ringford . . .'

'It was very kind of you to come down,' said Robert. 'I couldn't stand the silence, and the television is mostly rubbish. It's very kind of you,' he repeated.

'Nonsense,' said Peggy briskly. 'I can do with the company myself. It can get very lonely on your own, and now that Joyce Turner is . . .' She petered out, unwilling to talk about it to a lad young enough to be her son.

147

'Bill's a good chap,' said Robert wisely, 'in a rotten situation.'

'Yes, well, let's talk about something else.' Peggy carried the coffee into the sitting room and they sat down. Inevitably, they talked about the time Robert had found Frank Palmer crashed in his car against a tree.

'It's the anniversary next week,' said Peggy quietly. 'Next Thursday, to be precise. I dread it, though it's two years now.'

It was Robert's turn to change the subject, and he asked Peggy what she thought of the new nanny, Bridget Reilly. 'Mandy likes her a lot,' he said. 'They have a lot in common. And, of course, she's started going out with our Dan from Waltonby. Hope she doesn't get too serious. Dan's had more girlfriends than I can count.'

Talk continued on this inconsequential level until Peggy looked at the clock and rose to her feet. 'Gilbert will be wanting her supper,' she said. 'Now, don't forget, Robert, I'm only a telephone call away if you need me.' Though what on earth I could do, I cannot imagine, thought Peggy. Still, Robert seemed calmer, and she walked back to the shop feeling neither hopeful nor pessimistic. As old Ellen would say, it was a case of wait and see.

The telephone was ringing as she opened the back door, and she rushed through to answer it.

'Peggy?' It was Doreen Price. 'Where have you been? Did you forget it was W.I. tonight?'

'Oh, Lord,' said Peggy, 'I'm sorry, Doreen. Robert rang up and asked me to go down, and it went right out of my mind.'

'Ah, well then,' said Doreen, 'perhaps you can enlighten the rest of the village. Just who was in that ambulance this morning? Was it Mandy Bates? Olive is beside herself with worry, and she's not liked to ring Robert. Old Ted watches her like a hawk. Well, Peggy, was it Mandy?'

Peggy hesitated. It was so silly, wondering whether she

should prevaricate.

'Yes,' she said finally. 'Yes, it was Mandy, but nothing drastic has happened. Not so far, anyway.'

CHAPTER TWENTY-TWO

'For God's sake, Olive, sit down!' Ted Bates was in his usual armchair, reading a farming magazine and sniffing heavily with irritating frequency. He had a cold, and the need to be out of doors in all weathers had made it worse. A barking cough kept him awake at night, but he had refused all offers of extra help from Dan, and snapped Olive's head off when she suggested he should go to see the doctor when he came to the village on Friday morning.

'I don't need no quack's remedies,' he said. He'd thought Robert had gone down with it this morning, when he hadn't turned up for work. Still, thought Ted, more likely off seeing the council about his garage plans, never considerin' his old dad trying to cope with a fluey cold. And not even a message to say why he didn't turn up. Serve him right if I went under, thought Ted, almost hoping he would.

Olive had also been worried, but Robert had been very taken up with the final decision on the barns, and she'd said nothing to Ted, glad that it was an easy day on the farm. Then, late this evening, she'd had the call from Doreen Price.

'I suppose they've told you, Olive?' said Doreen.

'Told me what?'

'Your Robert – has he told you Mandy's been taken in

again? I'm only ringing because Peggy said she wasn't sure you knew. Tell me to mind my own business if you like, Olive, but I thought you'd want to know.'

Olive muttered thanks to Doreen Price, and turned from the telephone in a daze. She made the Horlicks as usual, and then washed up, unable to think of a way of broaching the subject to Ted. She knew he'd either ignore her altogether, or fly off the handle again, shouting about Robert and Mandy and refusing to discuss anything to do with the baby.

Robert's my son, she thought, sitting down opposite Ted. And that baby will be my grandchild. She was near to tears and, unable to find a handkerchief in her pocket, got up again and made to leave the room.

'Where now, woman?' said Ted. 'Every time you open that door there's a howlin' gale round the back of my neck.'

Olive said she was just going to put the kettle on for hot-water bottles, and crept out of the room, opening the door only as wide as was necessary to squeeze through. She looked at the telephone on the windowsill and wondered if she dare make a call to Robert. Ted would be sure to hear. He claimed to be deaf when it suited him, but his hearing was as good as a rabbit's when he wanted. She tiptoed to stand outside the sitting-room door, and was sure she heard snores which deepened as she listened.

She went back to the telephone, and looked out of the window. It was very dark, no moon and a few drops of rain spattered on the small panes. Loud and insistent mooing came from the cow barn. That miserable old cow, thought Olive, she could go on for hours, shattering the night. Every so often other cows joined in, a bovine backing group.

Olive picked up the receiver and dialled Robert's number. 'Hello, hello? Who's that? Is that the hospital?' said Robert, his voice cracking with anxiety.

'No,' whispered Olive, 'it's Mum. How's Mandy,

Robert?'

'Oh, Mum,' said Robert. 'She's all right. I'll be up tomorrow, tell Dad. Sorry I didn't let you know. Thanks, Mum, see you tomorrow.'

Olive put down the receiver, and heard the kitchen door open.

'And just what do you think you're doing, Olive Bates?' said Ted.

CHAPTER TWENTY-THREE

Ellen Biggs walked out of her garden gate, well wrapped up in Mr Richard's old gabardine mackintosh and a pair of fur-lined rubber boots which needed only two extra pairs of socks to be a cosy fit. Her head was swathed in an acid green headscarf, and she added protection from the morning's driving rain by unfurling an aged umbrella with two or three spokes broken free of the stretched black covering.

Two small girls on ponies trotted past her, down the avenue of chestnuts which led from the Hall. Must be friends staying there, she thought. Mrs Standing had got very social since little Poppy's arrival. She seemed to have children there all the time. Could be something to do with Nanny Bridget.

Poor little souls, thought Ellen, watching the dismal, soaked ponies and their sagging riders. Wouldn't catch me sendin' my kids out on a morning like this. What do they see in it, these young girls? Covered in mud, wet and cold, when they could be indoors doin' whatever girls do these days. Watchin' telly, probably. Ah well, at least they're gettin' fresh air of sorts.

Ellen passed the church, and saw the Reverend Nigel Brooks emerging from the porch. He hurried down the shiny, wet flagstone path, and opened the lychgate. 'Morning Ellen!' he called. He rescued his bike from where it had fallen into a bank of thick, wet grass by the church wall, and wiped the saddle with the hem of his cassock.

'What brings you out on a morning like this?' he said, folding his trouser bottoms to accommodate bicycle clips.

'Got no choice, Vicar,' she said tartly. And if I was you, Reverend Brooks, she added under her breath, I wouldn't go biking round the village in the rain when I 'ad a perfectly good car in the drive at home. Just to show 'ow trendy we are, no doubt. Old Cyril Collins, God rest 'is soul, would have been tucked up in 'is study in the vicarage on a mornin' like this.

Nigel Brooks pedalled off at speed down the lane, not slowing up at the hump bridge, which lifted him comically in his saddle like a cartoon vicar in pursuit of an elusive congregation.

Bridge Cottage looked deserted, and Ellen – who had, of course, heard about Mandy's ambulance dash – shook her head as she passed. Poor child, she thought, bin in Tresham nearly a week now. She's not had it easy. 'Mind you,' she said to the Jenkins terrier, who had joined her along the side of the Green, 'sometimes them threats of a miss are meant. Best not to hold on if the baby's not right, my mum used to say.'

The terrier veered off across the rain-soaked Green, heading for the shop and the hope of a chocolate wrapper to lick.

By the time Ellen reached the shop, the rain was easing off, and she shook her umbrella before propping it against the wall. 'Don't want no puddles in your shop, Peggy dear!' she said, struggling up to the counter and leaning there to regain her composure.

'What a day, Ellen!' said Peggy. 'I could easily have brought down your shopping, you know. You could send a list by William with the papers.'

Ellen smiled. 'Very kind of you, my dear,' she said, 'but I'd go screwy shut up in that Lodge all day. A drop o 'rain

154

won't do me no harm. I'm well wrapped up, as you can see.' Ellen adjusted the knot in her scarf and hobbled round to take a packet of custard powder and a tin of mandarin segments from the shelves.

'Shan't need much supper tonight,' she said. 'It's Doris's turn to give us tea today, and she always does us well. Maybe not such a light hand with a sponge as our Ivy, but very acceptable.'

'Have you seen anything of Robert?' Peggy had not liked to bother Robert with telephone calls. It seemed that Mandy was being kept quiet in the hospital, and Robert spent as much time as he could at her side. Other visitors were not encouraged, and Peggy's heart went out to him as he rushed into the shop for chocolate biscuits or bottles of squash, thin-faced and worried as he drove yet again into Tresham.

'Only the tail end of 'is car every so often,' said Ellen. ''E don't stop to say hello even. Poor lad, 'e's on 'is own, what with that Ted 'avin set hisself against the pair of 'em.'

'I feel very sorry for Olive,' said Peggy, wrapping up a small piece of Cheddar cheese, and charging Ellen for a little less than it actually weighed. 'Robert's her only son, after all, and she's such a mouse where Ted's concerned.'

'There's a lifetime's habit there, Peggy my dear, Olive'll not find it easy to change. Mind you,' added Ellen, putting her small purchases in her old bag and walking towards the door, 'there's only one way to deal with a bully like old Ted. Face up to 'im, that's what, face 'im fair and square and 'e'll soon back down. Still, you couldn't tell that to Olive Bates, could you? Cheerio, my dear. Oh, and I ain't forgot what tomorrow is. We'll be thinkin' of you.'

Peggy hadn't forgotten, either, that tomorrow was the anniversary of Frank's death. The pleasure of approaching Christmas, which she had always enjoyed with childlike anticipation, was now marred by the memory of that awful day. If I could just stay in bed, she thought, let the day go by unmarked, it would be bearable. As it was, she had to serve in the shop as usual, be professionally cheerful and welcoming, and listen to other people's troubles instead of acknowledging her own.

Bill had been standing by, of course, but even his solid support was leavened by feelings of guilt, by memories of Frank's jealousy, even when there had been no real cause. And now Joyce was back home, everything had changed. Except, Peggy thought, checking the change in the till, opening up a bag of fifty-pence pieces and dropping them in with a clatter, except my love for Bill. That hasn't changed. And his love for me, she reminded herself, that hasn't changed either. Or so he says.

Robert slid his greasy dinner plate into the sink, where it rested on top of his greasy breakfast plate, and ran hot water into the bowl. A good squeeze of washing-up liquid produced enough foam, and he gave the plates a quick wipe and rinse, and stood them in the drainer. No doubt if things had been different, he would have stayed up at the farm for his meals, maybe moved back into his old room while Mandy was in hospital. But in a way he was glad to be here on his own, not having to answer Mum's questions and justify the answers to his grumbling father.

Although nothing was said, he knew his father resented all the time he was taking off to visit the hospital. His mum let him know how much she cared by slipping packets of homemade biscuits into his coat pockets, and whispering anxious questions when Ted was out in the yard. Robert had had the final green light on his plans for Barnett's barns, and in spite of feeling excited and proud of the village for backing him – at least, most of the village – he said nothing to his father, waiting for the right time, if there was one.

He washed his hands, and was just getting his coat from the hall, when the telephone rang.

'Mr Bates?' The voice was cool, professional.

'Yes, speaking,' said Robert, his heart beginning to thud.

'Ah yes, Mr Bates – Robert – this is Sister Westwater here. Are you coming in to see Mandy this afternoon?'

'Just on my way, Sister,' said Robert. He could hardly hear her, for the thumping in his ears.

'Oh good. We've just taken her down to the labour ward, my dear, her waters broke a short while ago. I believe she lost a little before coming in, is that right?'

Robert nodded, dumb.

'Are you there, Robert? Now there's nothing to worry about, we have every possible facility a small baby needs, and everything will be fine. Are you there, Robert?' she repeated.

'Yes, thank you, Sister. I'll be there in twenty minutes.'

'Just make sure you drive carefully,' said Sister. 'No point in hurrying if you don't arrive! See you later, then.'

Robert slammed the receiver back, and grabbed his coat. He looked wildly round the cottage, forgot to lock the back door, and rushed down the garden path, almost bumping into Ivy Beasley, who was turning into his gate.

'Robert!' she said. 'What on earth's the matter?'

He stood looking at her, saying nothing. Then he shook his head, and his mouth quivered. 'It's the baby, Auntie Ivy,' he said. 'The baby's on the way, and it's much too soon.'

Ivy Beasley, renowned for her hard heart and sour tongue, put out her hand and gently touched Robert's cheek. 'Best be off, then, our Robert,' she said. 'Your Mandy'll need you now.'

CHAPTER TWENTY-FOUR

'You might as well tell us what's up, Ivy,' said Doris Ashbourne, taking the cosy off the teapot and pouring out steaming tea into her best china cups. 'You've been sitting there like a wet week of Sundays ever since you arrived, and haven't spoken more than two words. What's wrong?'

'I knew there was somethin' different,' said Ellen. 'We've been able to get more than a word in edgeways for once, Doris.'

Doris frowned at Ellen, suspecting that something was really wrong with Ivy, and sure that this was not the time for the usual Biggs-and-Beasley sniping match.

Ivy Beasley shook her head, and lifted the full cup to her lips. But then her hand began to shake and she spilt a few scalding drops on her lap. Doris, alarmed at Ivy's expression, got up and took the cup from her, giving her a paper napkin to mop up the tea.

'Now, now, Ivy,' she said. 'This is not like you.'

Ellen was quiet, waiting to see what happened next.

Ivy clasped her hands together to stop them shaking, and cleared her throat. 'It was a bit of a shock,' she said.

'What was?' said Ellen.

'I bumped into Robert,' said Ivy, 'and he was in a terrible state. Seems Mandy's gone into labour. Can't hold on to the baby any longer.'

'Oh dear,' said Doris.

''As he gone in, then?' said Ellen.

'On his way,' said Ivy, 'when I met him.'

All three were silent for a minute or so. Then Ivy pulled her shoulders back and picked up her cup, taking a couple of sips, her hands quite steady now. 'Well,' she said, 'I remember our Robert when he was no bigger than a bag of sugar. Olive and me looked after him like he was one of her orphan lambs, and look at him now. What's been done once can be done again.'

'But not by Olive Bates,' said Ellen darkly.

'We shall see,' said Ivy. 'Now, how about cutting that fruit cake, Doris. It looks as if you've got it right at last.'

Wide awake for the first time in seven days, free of tranquillising drugs, Mandy Bates lay in Tresham hospital, Robert's hand clutching hers, and felt the unwanted, unplanned, unfair pains of premature labour.

For six days she had rested, and now, for some unknown reason, her body laboured to produce a baby eleven weeks earlier than nature intended. The nursing staff were kind but brisk. Robert looked pale and strained; and for Mandy time, in the form of morning, afternoon and night, had ceased to exist. The hours crawled by, and there was nothing for her but pain and a fruitless hope that it would all stop, and the baby stay in place, so that they could all go home and wait for the due date in pleasurable anticipation.

All that she had learned about the constructive joys of labour had been stood on its head, and in periods between contractions she and Robert talked fitfully of what they would do if their baby didn't make it.

'We could take a good long holiday. Maybe go to America,' said Robert. 'You've always said you'd like to go to Disneyworld, though I must say I can think of better ways of spending a fortune.'

'If the worst happens, Robert,' said Mandy, screwing up

her face as the pain began again, 'I think I'd like to emigrate. You know, if the baby doesn't come through it.'

Exhausted and desperate, she finally wanted nothing more than to get rid of the pain. She stopped thinking, stopped fighting against her body's extraordinary desire to do the wrong thing, and pushed as hard as she could.

She was vaguely aware that forceps were being used to help the fragile little head make its untimely way into the world, and then it was all over, the pain had gone, and she heard a faint, immature sound like a kitten mewling. It was her baby, and it was a boy.

Mandy clung to Robert's arm, and looked into the incubator separating her from her son. He weighed two and a half pounds, had brownish skin covered with a fine layer of hair, and looked like a skinned rabbit. His eyes were tightly closed, and he was unclothed, his movements jerky and spasmodic. He looked nothing like the pictures in Mandy's baby book, and his cry was so thin that she could hardly hear it.

This did not, however, mean that the crying did not have its effect. She didn't know how to bear the pain of not being able to hold him close, comfort him with the warmth of her body and her breasts. She was encouraged to stroke him gently and talk to him, but this increased her longing, and she hardly knew how to contain her anguish.

Her horror at the sight of all the machinery surrounding him, like some space-age experiment, was lessened by the careful explanations given to her by the staff. He was to be fed by a tube, because he was too weak to suck. The ventilator was there to help him breathe, if necessary, and the controlled and balanced environment of the incubator was designed to keep him as safe, warm and free from infection as Mandy's womb.

She felt horribly guilty. She remembered wanting to get it over with, pushing this little scrap on its way because she could no longer bear the pain.

Robert leaned over the incubator and smiled. 'Mandy, he's opened his eyes . . . Doesn't he look just like my dad!'

The hospital days dragged, and although Robert brought in Mandy's knitting and a pile of magazines, she couldn't settle to anything for very long. She knew what she should be doing, all her maternal instincts had emerged according to plan. In the mindless progress of her body's reactions to childbirth, no allowance was made for the fact that she could do nothing about it. Her baby was in someone else's hands. The balance of his life depended not on Mandy, but on an assembly of machines.

At one point, when the natural drop in birth weight had taken the baby down to less than two pounds, Mandy was asked if she would like to have him christened. Taken by surprise, she said she would ask Robert. They agreed that it might be a good idea, though neither of them wanted to acknowledge that this little scrap might be taken from them before they could reach a church.

When Mandy was confronted by a vase of freesias on a plastic lace mat, placed by the incubator by Sister with the best of intentions, she was consumed by a sudden feeling of undirected anger. As the sombre figure in black cassock and white surplice smiled and shook her hand, she wanted desperately to escape, to rush out into the hospital corridor and scream at a remote, incompetent deity, shift the unbearable guilt to where it must belong. But instead, she stood rigidly hand in hand with Robert as the hospital chaplain went quietly through an abbreviated version of the christening service. Joseph Edward Bates did not once open his eyes, and Mandy was glad.

He slept through visits from his grandparents, too. Mandy's mother and father had come, looking terrified, not knowing what to say. Piles of cards had arrived, including an effusive one signed Caroline and Peter, and

Olive Bates had appeared unannounced one afternoon, carrying Christmas roses from her garden. In her inarticulate, stilted way, she had given Mandy comfort. Ted Bates had not visited, nor sent any messages.

When it was suggested to Mandy that she should go home, that it was doing her more harm than good hanging about the hospital, staring at the baby for hours, monitoring all the alarms and setbacks, and getting thinner and more hollow-eyed by the day, she refused hotly.

She was expressing milk to be given by tube, and used this as a reason for staying. 'Supposing it gets infected at home. Wouldn't it be safer for me to stay here?'

All her objections were patiently countered, but she was never made to feel in the way or a nuisance. In the end, she allowed Robert to persuade her.

'I need you, Mandy,' he said. 'I'm just so lonely at home.'

She glared at him, wondering how Robert, a great healthy, hulking farmer, could possibly need her as much as tiny Joe. And then she saw the tears in his eyes, and knew that he meant what he said.

When little Joe was three weeks old, his mother left hospital without him, climbed into his father's car, and cried all the way back to Round Ringford, where she was met by Peggy Palmer and Olive Bates, the only people who knew she was coming home, with flowers and home-made cakes and the smallest, most exquisitely knitted layette that Olive Bates's stubby fingers could produce. When Mandy saw the small Christmas tree in the corner by the fire, she sat down and wept again.

CHAPTER TWENTY-FIVE

In preparation for Midnight Mass, Mr Ross had put out all the spare folding chairs from the vestry, knowing that on this one night of the year the church would be full.

For several days, Doreen Price, Peggy Palmer and Sophie Brooks had worked alongside Olive Bates, Ivy Beasley and Jean Jenkins, winding trailing ivy and boughs of berried holly round the ancient stone pillars of the church. They had arranged scarlet candles and vases of shaggy white chrysanthemums, bought from a man Doreen knew in Bagley market for half the price of blooms in the shops. The children from the Sunday School, encouraged by their teacher, Mrs Ross, had taken out the chipped plaster figures from their old wooden box once more and arranged them in clean straw from Hall Farm, making a crib scene by the Christmas tree.

Every year, Tom Price set up the huge tree in an old half barrel, and he and Bill Turner decked it with fairy lights, replacing dud bulbs and heaving a sigh of relief when they all twinkled into life.

It was a perfect night. A slight breeze hardly stirred the black yews lining the path up to the church porch, and as Nigel Brooks made his way along Ladies Path to the side door into the vestry, he stopped and looked up in wonder at the starry sky. It was cold, and he could see frost already glittering on the slate roof of Ellen Biggs' Lodge. Looking at the church, ancient stone walls black in the shadow of the trees, he felt a surge of affection for the squat little building, with its pinnacled tower and brightly lit windows.

How comforting, he thought, expansive from the warming punch Sophie had made him drink before setting off. How comforting to consider all the Christmas congregations who had sat in the oak pews and sung the old carols of welcome to the newborn babe.

And then he thought of Mandy and Robert, and sobered up.

What comfort could he offer them? Little Joe was still in special care, sometimes fighting for breath, still needing the ventilator, and Mandy drove in to the hospital every day, living on a knife edge of worry and dread, the milk that she expressed and carried in to him the only contribution she could make to her son's welfare.

There was a festive atmosphere in the church, helped by a faint smell of cigar smoke and alcohol accompanying many of the men who had spent the evening in the Arms, practising carols, swapping Christmas anecdotes, and reminding each other that they must not be late for church.

Nigel Brooks glanced around and judged it time to start the service. He noted with pleasure that Richard and Susan Standing were in the front pew, and next to them old Ellen, who had been given a lift in the big silver car and sat preening herself and occasionally darting smug looks at Ivy Beasley, sitting a few rows behind.

Peggy Palmer sat with Tom and Doreen Price, and directly behind her Bill Turner, who resisted the temptation to stroke the back of her neck, just where the hair curled into hollows behind her ears. He had suggested that Joyce should make the effort and come to the service with him. But she had politely declined, and gone quietly up to bed at half past ten, after rinsing their tea mugs and tidying the kitchen. She could be a guest in the house, thought Bill, a well-mannered guest.

As Nigel welcomed his congregation and announced the first carol, the big oak door creaked open, and Robert Bates came in, holding Mandy by the hand. They took a carol sheet from Mr Ross and tiptoed their way to a pew at the back of the church. In the Bates pew, Olive looked round anxiously, but Ted stared straight ahead.

The service progressed with lusty singing punctuated by winter coughs and sneezes. Mandy found herself sitting next to Jean Jenkins, who sniffed constantly and blew her nose with unashamed vigour. Mandy moved as far away from her as possible, terrified of catching a cold and passing it on to little Joe.

'And they found Mary and Joseph and the babe, lying in a manger,' read Mr Ross, and Mandy choked. 'I want to go home,' she whispered to Robert.

He held her hand and squeezed it comfortingly. 'Can't do that,' he whispered back. 'Everybody would stare.' So Mandy swallowed hard and looked round the church, willing herself not to cry.

In her pew with the Prices, Peggy was thinking about Joe, and how it should have been so different. There'd not been much rejoicing there, she thought, and she glanced round, looking for Mandy and Robert, wondering how they were feeling, with all this talk of babes in mangers and swaddling clothes.

She caught Mandy's eye, and saw the bleak expression on her face. Poor thing, she thought. There's no preparation for the shock they've had to cope with. And it's not over yet. She smiled, and was moved to see the flicker of a smile in return.

'Unto us a boy is born, unto us a son is given!' sang the choir, the children looking like angels, strictly watched over by half a dozen adults standing behind them. They had lasted out well, considering it was long past bedtime, and now the service was nearly over.

In the silence that followed the end of the carol, Nigel Brooks bowed his head. He knew that the usual prayer would not do. Andrew Roberts and Mark Jenkins, over-tired and over-excited, anxious now for Christmas Day to arrive, rustled in their choir stalls, making faces.

Still Nigel Brooks said nothing. Ivy Beasley looked up crossly from her folded hands, wondering why he didn't get on with it. It was late, and if he didn't get moving, the clock in the tower would strike midnight before the end of the service.

Tom Price looked at Doreen enquiringly, but she shrugged and raised her eyebrows, puzzled.

And then Nigel Brooks cleared his throat and began to speak, to pray in a quiet and even voice.

'Dear Lord,' he said, 'tonight we have a special prayer. We ask your blessing and protection for Ringford's own newborn babe, Joseph Edward Bates.'

The silence was profound.

'Guard this child with your blessing, and give strength to his young parents, Mandy and Robert. Amen.'

The congregation fervently echoed the amen, and then sang with more than usual enthusiasm the final carol, 'Hark the Herald Angels sing, Glory to the New born King!'

Robert and Mandy left the church, carried along by the warmth of feeling from well-wishers who approached them and said encouraging words. Behind them walked Olive and Ted, a space between them, not talking. And then Ted turned to Olive in the darkness and said, 'He'd no right.'

'What do you mean, Ted?' said Olive.

'He'd no right, no right whatsoever, to go namin' people in the church. Never been so embarrassed in my life. Old Cyril Collins would never have done that. He knew 'ow to go on, Cyril did.'

Olive said nothing. She watched Robert and Mandy walking away down the lane towards Bridge Cottage, and then followed Ted back to the farm.

'It's Christmas Day, Ted,' she said, as she climbed into the high marriage bed and addressed her husband's bony back, 'and I thought Reverend Brooks was quite right to say what he did. It was very nice, I thought.'

But Ted had fallen asleep the moment his head touched the pillow, and did not hear her. He began to snore, and Olive sighed. 'And a merry Christmas to you too, Ted Bates,' she said, pulling up the bedcovers round her ears.

CHAPTER TWENTY-SIX

Every morning without fail, Bridget Reilly pushed little
Poppy Standing in her pram, more suited to Kensington
Gardens than Bateses End, down the lane from the Hall to
call on Mandy Bates. When it rained, she covered the baby
with waterproofs and herself with a huge oilskin jacket
borrowed from Mr Richard, and tramped in her wellies
through the mud. In her young, straightforward way, she
helped Mandy through the dreadful weeks of watching
little Joe lying in his glass box, taking one step forward and
then two steps back.

Well aware of her inexperience, Peggy Palmer did all she
could to help, calling in at Bridge Cottage when the shop
shut, knowing that Mandy would be at home alone.

'It's nice talking to Mrs P.,' Mandy told Robert. 'She's
the one person who knows even less about babies than I do.
Everybody else knows it all, and I've had so much advice
from my mum that I could scream.'

The playgroup in the village, celebrating its first anniversary at the end of January, invited all mothers of young
children and babies to a party. Jean Jenkins was in charge. It
was a welcome change from cleaning, and a job which
made best use of her considerable talents. She knocked at
the cottage door one afternoon, and handed a personal
invitation to Mandy.

'We shall quite understand, dear,' she said, 'if you don't want to come, but we wanted to ask you. It's only as if little Joe was lent out for a bit, and you're just as much a mother as the rest of us.'

'You can come with me,' said Bridget, bouncing Poppy on Mandy's sofa. 'Mrs S. will be in London, and anyway, I can't see her hobnobbing with Ringford young mums, can you?'

Robert encouraged Mandy to go, saying she might pick up a few hints. This was meant as a joke, but unfortunately Mandy did not see the funny side of it, and went upstairs to the bedroom, slamming the door behind her.

'She's bound to be on edge, Robert,' said Peggy Palmer, dispensing wisdom from behind the shop counter. 'Baby Joe must be on her mind all the time, and that journey into the hospital every day would get anyone down. Is there any news about when he might come home?'

'We've got to wait until he's a decent weight, but they're going to take him out of the incubator soon, get some clothes on him. Mandy's terrified they're taking him out too soon.'

He looked worried and uncertain, and Peggy thought how he had changed. It seemed no time at all since she had first met Robert, and then he had been the life and soul of the Young Farmers and the Rugby Club, and his only worry had been how to avoid the unwelcome teenage crush of the Jones girl.

Fortunately for Robert, he had a lot to do. In deference to Peter Dodwell's protest, the Planning Office had laid down restrictions on hours when he could use noisy machinery, but otherwise, with the final go ahead on using the barns, he and the estate office had exchanged contracts on the bungalow. It was structurally sound, but dirty and dingy, and he spent every spare moment decorating and cleaning. Mandy helped, scrubbing and making curtains, and finally allowing herself to stick transfers of teddy bears and balloons on the walls of the small bedroom. They worked together, not talking much, and taking comfort from the routine they established. The high point of each day was Mandy's visit to Joe, and her report on his progress to Robert when she returned.

With the help of his beefy mates from the Rugby Club, Robert moved house one Saturday morning. Every vehicle was mustered, and the sight of Mandy's furniture trundling through the village on newly-swept farm trailers gave her moments of alarm. But nothing was damaged, and by evening everything had been sorted out and settled in the right place. Mandy cooked a huge mound of spaghetti for the lads in her new kitchen, bottles were opened, and a noisy toast to the Bateses' new home was drunk.

One beautiful early February morning, when the cold east wind had veered, and children in the school playground were tempted out without their coats, Mandy set out on the now boringly familiar road to Tresham.

I reckon this car could find its own way, she thought, stopping at road works just outside the village, where they were repairing the drains. Temporary traffic lights had been set up, and she waited impatiently for green. She was later than usual, having been held up for ten minutes by old Ellen Biggs.

The lights changed, and she went through the narrow stretch of road, thick with mud from working vehicles. It was a waste of time Robert cleaning this car, she thought, and pulled out to pass a woman walking alone on the verge. She looked in her driving mirror and saw a strange, thin face, pale and serious. I suppose I'd better offer her a lift, she thought, and reluctantly stopped the car again. After all, suppose it was me, trying to get to Tresham to see Joe, and nobody would stop for me.

She wound down her window and called out. 'Would you like a lift anywhere?'

To her surprise, the woman turned round immediately,

and began to walk back towards the village. 'How strange,' Mandy muttered, and set off again, thoughts of Joe driving the woman's odd behaviour out of her mind.

She parked the car as usual, and climbed the steps up to the main entrance. It was a tortuous route to the special care unit, but Mandy could have done it in her sleep, round innumerable corners and along wide, shiny corridors. She made her way over to Joe's incubator, and her heart stopped. It was empty, quite empty.

She turned round, wild-eyed, and saw a nurse coming towards her. She opened her mouth, but no sound came. The nurse was smiling, and, taking her by the arm, led her over to one of the hospital cradles.

'There he is, look. There's Joey, fast asleep.'

The nurse prodded Mandy gently until she bent over the cradle and looked. Sweetly sleeping, dressed in Olive Bates's fine wool jacket and bonnet, Joseph Bates, ten weeks old, had finally entered the same world as his mother, and her tears fell on his warm little cheek, until she smoothed them away with a shaky hand.

Four weeks later, Robert and Mandy were told that they could take Joe home in a day or two, and they returned to Ringford in a state of panic. 'I'm just terrified,' said Mandy honestly. 'After all this time in the hospital, how can I look after him as well as they do?'

Robert tried to bolster her self-confidence, but felt nervous himself. Bridget Reilly came to the rescue, forthright and amused.

'Buck up, Mandy!' she said. 'You'll take to it like a duck to water. Here,' she said, thrusting a grizzling Poppy Standing into Mandy's arms, 'have a practice with this one!'

Mandy took the warm, powdery-smelling baby in her arms, and thought how much there was of her. When she held Joe, there was so little to get hold of. He had taken to the occasional feed from the breast with little trouble, but feeding slowly, dropping off to sleep after the first minute or so. The nurse explained that the bottle was much easier, and his reserves of strength were still quickly used up.

'You'll be fine when you get him home,' she said. 'Take your time in peace and quiet, and he'll come along well, you'll see.'

Mandy nodded, but had agonies of doubt about whether he would take enough milk to keep him alive.

The day of Joe's homecoming arrived. Mandy had cleaned every room, corner and cupboard in the bungalow in a frenzy of anxiety lest there should be lurking germs. She was ready to go much too soon, and Robert made her sit down and have a cup of tea and a sandwich.

'You've eaten nothing all day,' he said. 'That won't do Joey any good.'

Mandy forced down the food, and took one last look at the little bedroom to make sure it was perfect for Joe. 'Have you got everything, Robert?'

'Of course,' said Robert confidently, but Mandy noticed that his hands shook as he picked up the box of chocolates for the sister and nurses.

They were almost exactly half way to Tresham when the car coughed and juddered to a halt.

'Robert! What's wrong?'

'Just a speck of dirt in the petrol, I expect,' he said. 'Don't worry, it'll be fine.'

He turned the key a couple of times, but there was no response.

Mandy grabbed his arm. 'Robert! It's not going to start, is it! And they'll be waiting for us at the hospital, and it will mess up Joey's feeding times, and . . . oh, Robert!' And she burst into tears.

Robert turned to look at her. 'You're not going to like this, Mandy,' he said. 'I don't suppose you'll ever forgive me.'

She stared at him wildly.

'We've run out of petrol,' he said. 'We must have

forgotten . . . what with . . . you know . . .'

'*We*!' yelled Mandy. 'It was *your* job to make sure the car was ready. It was just about the only thing you had to do. And you forgot to fill up with petrol! You . . .' Speechless with rage, she opened the car door and got out, looking up and down the road.

Robert joined her on the roadside, and said quietly that he would walk back to the nearest farm and get some petrol. It wouldn't take long, he said, and they'd be off again in no time. Mandy wouldn't even look at him.

'You'd better wait in the car,' said Robert. 'It's cold in the wind . . .'

But Mandy was not listening. She had seen a car approaching from Ringford direction, and as it drew nearer she walked to the middle of the road and stood with her hand up, like a small but determined traffic cop.

The car slowed down and stopped. Then the driver's door opened and out stepped Peter Dodwell.

The big clock over the hospital entrance reassured Mandy that they were only a few minutes late. As they climbed the steps, she allowed herself to address Robert for the first time since Peter Dodwell had rescued them. She had watched silently as Robert, scarlet with embarrassment, explained their problem.

'Well,' Peter Dodwell had said, looking rather pleased, 'I should have thought you'd have checked, you of all people.'

There'd been a small silence, and then, to her amazement, Mandy had seen a small smile flicker across Peter Dodwell's face. He'd choked it back, but then Robert's shoulders began to shake, and then there they were, the two of them, standing in the middle of the Tresham road, roaring with laughter.

Mandy had got quickly into the car and slammed the door, and this had brought the men to their senses. Peter

Dodwell had opened his boot and found a can with a gallon of petrol, and in no time they had rocked Robert's car and got it moving again.

Before they set off, however, Mandy had seen in the rear-view mirror Robert's hand outstretched and Peter Dodwell shaking it heartily. Robert was whistling softly as he got in the car, and he had turned to Mandy and said, 'Well, some good came out of it, anyway.' She could not bring herself to reply.

Now she put her hand in Robert's and squeezed. 'Sorry, Rob,' she said, as they pushed through the swing doors. 'It's easily done, specially when your mind's on something else.'

With reassurances from the nursing staff, and a return appointment for Joe, they finally left the security of the ward. As they said a last goodbye to Sister on the hospital steps, another young mother was leaving with her baby and husband. They laughed and joked with their nurse, and called across to Mandy and Robert.

'Another mouth to feed! We must be mad!'

Mandy smiled weakly at them, cuddled the shawl-wrapped Joe closer to her breast, and began to descend the steps slowly and carefully.

Peggy and Bill were standing side by side in the shop, not touching, looking out of the window and over the Green. They saw Robert's car go by, and Peggy grabbed Bill's hand. 'Oh Bill,' she said, 'there goes little Joe.' Bill nodded. 'Bless him,' he said. Then he released Peggy's hand and walked over to the other side of the shop.

'Joyce went out the other day,' said Bill.

'Out? Really out?' said Peggy, looking at him in disbelief.

'Yep,' he said. 'She just said she was going for a walk, and went. I was going to follow her, in case she needed help, but she just said, "I'll be all right," and walked off down the garden path as if she'd been doing it every day for years.'

Peggy was silent. She knew that every step of Joyce Turner's recovery was a step further away from Bill for her. They hadn't been out for a walk together for weeks, and apart from the few snatched moments between customers, she had no chance to talk to him, let alone show him how much she loved him. She ached for him to touch her, dreamed they were in the birdwatching hide, making love on long, hot summer afternoons, and then woke up to her cold, lonely bedroom with the photograph of Frank, eternally smiling at her from his silver frame.

A small, nasty suspicion came into her mind. 'Is she better in all ways, Bill?' she said.

He nodded, his face doleful. Jean and Foxy Jenkins were coming across the Green, hand in hand, and Bill sighed. 'After all them kids,' he said, 'just look at them.'

Peggy could not let it go. 'Does she, um, you know, still sleep in the spare room?'

Bill turned suddenly and looked at her. 'What do you mean, Peggy! For God's sake say what you mean, gel. If you mean do we sleep together like married couples should, then say so!'

'You might answer that it's none of my business,' said Peggy, flinching as if she had been struck.

'Of course it's your bloody business,' said Bill. 'What do you take me for? Some bloody Lothario who goes round the village knocking off the village girls while his wife's safely tucked up in hospital?'

Peggy turned away and began tidying up packets of sweets on the counter. 'Sorry,' she said.

Bill walked towards her, but stopped when the door opened with a jangle and Ivy Beasley stalked in. She looked at first one and then the other, and came to roughly the right conclusion.

'*If* I'm not interrupting,' she said, 'perhaps you could cut me a half a pound of strong Cheddar, Mrs Palmer.'

She turned to Bill, and looked at him speculatively. 'Good day, Bill,' she said. 'And how's your Joyce today? Tell her I'll be up with the magazines tomorrow as usual . . . or maybe she'd like to come down to me, now she's venturing out? That would be something to celebrate, wouldn't it, Mrs Palmer?'

Ivy turned back to the counter, and smiled in triumph as she saw the blood suffuse Peggy's cheeks.

'After all these years, Bill,' said Ivy Beasley, 'it looks like your patience with Joyce will be rewarded.'

CHAPTER TWENTY-SEVEN

The journey back from Tresham seemed to Mandy to take for ever. She kept her eyes firmly on Joe's face, checking that he was still breathing. At last Robert drew up outside the bungalow, and Mandy grabbed his arm.

'Rob! Look! Look what they've done!'

Across the front of the bungalow, attached to trellis and downpipes, flapped a long banner, with big, bright blue lettering. WELCOME HOME, JOSEPH EDWARD BATES! The banner belled out in the wind, and a bunch of festive balloons tugged at each end, blue and orange, announcing a party.

Robert leaned over and kissed Mandy's cheek. 'Come on, love, let's get him settled in.'

The baby stirred in his sleep, yawning and stretching his arms, red fists clenched.

As Robert opened the gate, three people appeared round the corner of the bungalow. Jean Jenkins, Bridget Reilly and Caroline Dodwell, smiling broadly, came down the garden path, each carrying a bunch of flowers.

'Present from Bill Turner and the Standings. Well, from the Standings' greenhouse!' said Jean, and leaned forward to kiss Mandy. The others followed suit, and then one by one peeped at Joey, well wrapped up against the cold wind.

Joseph Bates, disturbed by the change of temperature and

the absence of car movement, stirred again, and this time opened one cornflower-blue eye.

'Hello, little boy,' said Jean Jenkins. 'You took your time, givin' us all such a fright. But you're home now. Come on in, all of you, the kettle's on.'

Not only was the kettle on, but in the middle of the kitchen table, on an embroidered cloth, with tea things surrounding it, sat a large iced cake with 'Welcome Joe' piped in blue icing.

'Old Ivy made that,' said Jean. 'You have to hand it to 'er, she knows how to bake a cake.'

'Jean,' said Mandy, after three cups of tea and much smiling and laughing. 'Jean, and Bridget and Caroline, I don't know what to say. It was so kind of you to make Joey's homecoming a real celebration. Me and Robert want to thank you all, and I expect I shall be on all your doorsteps for help in the next few weeks!'

'Well,' said Jean, 'for someone who didn't know what to say, I reckon that was a pretty good speech. And you know you can always call on us if you get in a muddle. Couldn't have better advisers than us!'

They began to clear away the dishes, but Robert refused to let them do any more. 'Me and Mandy can do those in no time,' he said. 'You've done more than enough.'

With further farewells to Joey, who was now thrashing about and working up to a good bellow, they left, and Mandy and Robert were alone with their baby in the bungalow for the first time.

'You go and feed him,' said Robert, 'and I'll do these dishes. Amazing, isn't it, how many plates you can get through with a family?'

Ted Bates stood staring out of the kitchen window into his garden. A few daffodils were braving out the blustery wind, and Olive's border of bright polyanthus had attracted a pair of destructive bullfinches. He banged on the window to frighten them, and then turned round to Olive, who was sitting at the table, knitting.

'I suppose,' said Ted, 'you're just goin' to sit there, sayin' nothin', 'till supper time?'

Olive did not reply. She didn't even look up. Her needles clicked, and the pale blue baby jacket grew visibly as Ted watched.

'You can go round,' he said. 'I ain't stoppin' you. Just don't ask me to go with yer.'

Olive looked up at him. With great deliberation she stuck her needles into the ball of pale blue wool, and put it down on the table. 'If you think,' she said, 'that I am going round to the bungalow on my own, on our grandson's first day back from hospital, without his grandfather, and making some feeble excuse, you can think again. No, I shall just stay here until you decide to stop all your stupid nonsense and come with me.'

This was quite a speech for Olive, and her hands, which she clasped out of sight under the table, were shaking.

Ted stared at her. 'What . . . ?' He choked, and cleared his throat. 'What did you say?' he said.

'You heard,' said Olive.

'Oh well,' said Ted, 'two can play at that game, m'lady,' and he marched across to the door into the hall, slammed it behind him and clumped upstairs. Silence followed, and Olive bit her lip, sniffed, and took up her knitting once more.

''Ere,' said Ellen Biggs, 'who's that goin' past?'

Doris Ashbourne and Ivy Beasley had walked down to Ellen's together, keeping an eye open for Robert Bates' car, but they had missed it, and now sat uncomfortably in Ellen's dingy parlour, drinking lukewarm tea and eating jam tarts. Ivy Beasley was deeply suspicious of the fluorescent red and green filling. 'You can't call it jam!' she whispered to Doris. But this afternoon she had agreed that she would try not to hurt Ellen's feelings. 'She's an old woman,' Doris had said, as they walked over the bridge. 'You have to make allowances.' 'We're all old women,' Ivy had said, but so far she had been unusually polite.

'Where?' said Doris.

'There, just past the church now. Looked like Ted and Olive, but 'e don't never walk when 'e can ride.'

Ivy got up from her rickety chair and went to the window. 'It is,' she said. 'It's Ted and Olive, all dressed up. He's walking a bit behind our Olive, but then he always does. They're not saying much, that's for sure.'

'Like them Indians,' said Ellen.

'What Indians?' said Doris.

'You know,' said Ellen. 'Them Indians in Tresham. They all live over the far side o' town. Yer see 'em shoppin', and the bloke always walks a couple o' paces in front of 'is missus. Shows 'er 'er place, they say.'

'Ellen Biggs,' said Ivy, hands on hips, ignoring Doris's warning glances, 'I have never heard such rubbish in my life. And anyway, in case it has escaped your notice, Olive was walking in front of Ted, so it's nothing like "them Indians".'

Ellen shrugged and raised her eyebrows. 'No need to get aeriated, Ivy,' she said. 'I'm sure you know what I mean, Doris.'

'Don't bring me into it!' said Doris.

Ivy turned back to the window. 'Never mind about Indians,' she said. 'What we want to know is where are they going?'

There was silent speculation, and then Ellen voiced the unthinkable. 'D'yer reckon they're goin' round Robert and Mandy's?'

'Ted Bates?' said Ivy. 'Going to see the baby? Him! Pigs might fly!'

Robert was standing at the window by the sink, rinsing out

the last teacup, when he heard the garden gate, and then footsteps coming up the concrete path. He frowned. They'd had enough excitement, he thought, best to have a bit of peace and quiet now. He backed away from the window, not wanting to be taken by surprise.

'Robert!' called Mandy, 'come here quick, love, I need some help.'

He rushed into the sitting room, and saw Mandy sitting on the sofa, Joey at her breast, his little hand tucked into hers. 'I've forgotten the tissues,' she said. 'I need them for mopping up. Thanks, love.'

'I think someone else is coming, I heard steps,' Robert said, and was just turning to go back to the kitchen, when they heard the door. Mandy looked up in surprise, and as they both stared, Olive Bates came quietly into the room.

'Mum!' said Robert. 'You never said . . .'

'Hello Robert. Hello Mandy,' she said, and turned round. 'Come on, Ted, babies don't bite.'

Joe choked, the milk flowing too fast for him to swallow, and drew away from Mandy. She hastily pulled her cardigan across her breast and sat the small bundle up, stroking his back.

Ted Bates, face unsmiling, walked past Olive and over to the sofa. He bent over, hand on his hip, and looked closely at the baby's face. Joe stopped choking, opened both eyes and was completely still, looking up at Ted. His milky mouth made a crooked movement, and then, without any question of doubt, he smiled, straight at his grandfather.

'Bless me,' said Ted, putting out a roughened finger and allowing Joe's small fingers to curl round it. 'If 'e don't look just like 'is granddad! 'E's a Bates, no mistake. Bateses was always fighters, Joseph, always were.'

He turned round and glared at Olive. 'Well, don't just stand there, woman, get the kettle on, do,' he said.

CHAPTER TWENTY-EIGHT

The old barns in Barnett's paddock looked much the same from the outside. This had been a condition of Robert's being allowed to use them for his workshop. But he had put a decent concrete floor in, and made a hard-standing area outside. The drive into the bungalow had been extended, so that it was now properly surfaced and led round to the barns, and over the new sliding doors Robert had proudly fixed his modest sign: R B ENGINEERING.

This sign had been a subject of discussion in the pub, some siding with Robert, who said how the hell would people know he was there if he didn't put it up? And, of course, there were others who complained that it was out of keeping with the residential character of the village.

Mr Richard, in the pub for a quick half-pint and, as he put it, testing the water, before going on to meet his brother, chairman of the District Planning Committee, had unexpectedly defended Robert's position.

'If you'll forgive my saying so,' he said, 'I think some of you are forgetting the historical precedent.'

'Never 'eard of 'im,' said Fred Mills from his dominoes corner.

'I mean,' said Richard Standing patiently, 'that in the old days villages had a dozen different trades. Your grandfather, Fred, was baker, undertaker and wheelwright all rolled into one.'

''Ad to be,' said Fred. 'Didn't 'ave no choice. What you couldn't get in the village in them days, you didn't 'ave.'

'They didn't 'ave bloody great signs up, though,' said Michael Roberts, who had been standing for some time at the bar, fortifying himself against his return home to Macmillan Gardens and a slovenly, unresponsive wife.

'I wouldn't say *your* front garden was a real asset to the village, Michael,' said Tom Price. The Roberts' house and garden was like a betrayal in the neat, clipped rectangle of the Gardens. Even the old persons' bungalows were kept tidy and colourful, if not by their owners, then by charitable neighbours. But number eight, where the Roberts had lived for nearly twenty years, was a dump. The hedge had grown straggly from lack of attention, and inside the ever-open gate were piles of junk, old toys and dolls' prams, pushchairs and ironing boards. Some of it had been there so long – 'Waiting for the skip' said Michael Roberts – that the grass had grown round it, leaving the bones of rotting umbrellas and high chairs sticking out like a neglected household graveyard.

The planning officer had jibbed at a sign outside Robert's bungalow. Even the suggestion of a properly signwritten sandwich board, taken in at night, had caused solemn head-shaking. 'See how you go, boy,' Tom had said. 'Bide your time, and they'll think again. If you give the village good service, you'll find they'll be behind you.'

Robert had equipped his workshop with the minimum necessary to carry on his trade. 'Start small,' he had repeated to Mandy, 'and work our way up.' He spent reserves of savings on essentials, and then heeded his Grannie's wise words: 'Neither a borrower nor a lender be'. The more expensive items would have to wait.

The late Grannie Bates had been Ivy Beasley's mother's lifelong friend, and they had an unshakeable faith in the old sayings. Now buried next to each other in the cemetery by the church, their wisdom still surfaced now and then, when a handy summing-up was needed.

Robert's first customer was Bill Turner, whose old van limped past the bungalow and round the back to the barns on the first morning R B Engineering opened up. 'I can usually fix it myself,' said Bill, 'but not this time. Can you take a look?'

The truth was that Bill could quite easily have fixed it himself, but being a nice man and a sensitive man, he had made sure that Robert would have at least one customer on his first morning.

'Can you leave it with me, Bill?' said Robert. 'Looks like the plugs to me, come back at dinner time and we'll have it all tickety-boo.'

Dividing his time between the farm and workshop, Robert managed to keep on reasonably good terms with his father. He had never been wholly at ease with him, and knew that there was no likelihood of any better relationship now. But the old man's animosity had been dispersed by Joe's continuing delight at the sight of him, showing marked preference for his grandfather over other visitors, and the two generations rubbed along well enough.

The real bonus was Olive. Her stand against Ted had given her a quiet confidence that had not been there before. She had the sense not to let him see it, but now she often made decisions where before she would have bowed to Ted's better judgement. Sensible and naturally shy, she was not always popping in and out of the bungalow, but let Mandy know that she was there if needed, and continued to knit so many small garments that Mandy ran out of storage space.

'Reckon we're over the worst,' Robert said to John Barnett, as they drove in together to the game in Tresham. 'Got quite a few customers now, and I've just found a secondhand welding kit at a good price. Dad's been quite fair, really, keeping up my wage from the farm.'

'Good God, man,' said John, tough and blunt, 'you worked for next to nothing for the old bugger for years. I reckon he owes you some.'

As the weather grew warmer, Mandy pushed Joe round the village in his pram. He loved these walks, reaching out his little hand in a fruitless attempt to grab the Jenkins terrier, or trailing his fingers through the new growth of grasses in the verges. The Prices had installed a pregnant goat in the home close next to the farmhouse, and Doreen had encouraged Mandy to bring Joe round to stroke the velvety creature. 'She's talking to her sides,' Doreen had said mysteriously, 'the kids won't be long.'

One clear, sunny afternoon, Mandy stood on the bridge, Joey in her arms, looking at the water and pointing out the ducks. She felt rather than heard the presence of another person, and looked round. It was the woman who had been on the road that day by the traffic lights. She knew now that it was Joyce Turner, Bill's wife, occasionally seen out for a walk in the village.

'Morning, Mrs Turner,' Mandy said, with an encouraging smile. She knew the history of the poor woman's breakdown, and though she felt sorry for Bill and Peggy, Joyce's round-shouldered, thin figure also roused her sympathy.

'You're Mandy, aren't you?' said Joyce. 'Married Robert Bates.'

'That's right,' said Mandy, 'and this is Joseph, Joe for short.'

Joyce approached and took the baby's small hand. 'Hallo, Joe,' she said. 'You had a bit of shaky start, from what I hear.'

'But he's fine now,' said Mandy. 'Course, it'll take him a while to catch up, so we mustn't expect too much from him, but he's really strong now.'

'Can I hold him for minute?' said Joyce.

Mandy hesitated. She still had a dread of Joe catching an

185

infection he wouldn't be able to handle, but she saw the look on Joyce's face, and impulsively handed him over. Joyce cradled him in her arms, and then held him upright, supporting him with her hand at his back.

'Look, Joe,' she said, 'look at the quack-quacks!' She took her hand away from his back to point at the ducks, and he began to sway backwards. Mandy was immediately there, lifting him gently from Joyce's arms, and tucking him back in his pushchair.

'He likes you, Mrs Turner,' she said consolingly. Joyce was looking alarmed, as if she had done something wrong. 'Look how he's smiling! Say bye-bye to Mrs Turner, Joey. Bye-bye!' Mandy walked on, turning and waving to Joyce on Joe's behalf. Joyce watched them go, and then started back up the lane, walking slowly and frowning.

CHAPTER TWENTY-NINE

Richard Standing stood at the long windows of his drawing room and looked over the lovely aspect of the Hall park. One of his ancestors had taken advice from Capability Brown, and as a result groups of trees had been planted apparently at random, in imitation of nature, but at particular viewpoints from the Hall. Richard looked across to an artfully placed giant beech tree, and across sloping grass to the stone-built folly which he and his brother in their childhood had used as a secret retreat. There they had rolled string in brown paper and tried to smoke the disgusting result, making themselves sick, and nearly setting fire to a pile of old, rotting garden chairs stacked for a future use that had never come.

'What are you looking at, Richard?' Susan carrying baby Poppy in her arms, had come into the room. She put Poppy down on the floor, and Susan's small Yorkshire terrier, who had been in the family much longer than the baby, slunk away and growled in his throat. He was firmly ejected by Susan into the big hall, where he jumped on to a priceless tapestry seat and brooded on his displacement from being first in her affections.

Richard did not answer Susan, but turned and said appreciatively, 'You're looking very lovely today, my darling.'

He was right. This second flowering into motherhood had brought Susan to life. She even moved more quickly, with purpose. Her formerly limp blonde hair had thickened and shone, and her pale hazel eyes were lively, interested.

'Thanks,' she said. 'I wish I could say the same about you. When are you going to throw out those dreadful trousers? They're old and mucky, and totally shapeless. You look like Fred Mills from the waist down.'

Richard smiled. He knew he could look pretty good when required, and at other times he wore his most comfortable clothes. After all, hadn't he caught Bridget looking at him speculatively over the breakfast table? Still, perhaps he should please Susan by smartening up a bit. Couldn't take her for granted, not the way she had bloomed since Poppy was born.

'I was checking on that oak, the one over by the end of the kitchen-garden wall. Turner's got some men coming today to help him trim it up. It grew lop-sided because of the old elm next to it. That's gone now, but the oak is still unbalanced. No, Poppy! Leave the books alone!'

Poppy had begun to hitch along on her bottom, preferring that to crawling, and could get up considerable speed on the polished wood floor. Sometimes she trailed a rug in her wake, then got bogged down in its folds when she tried to reverse. Now she had arrived at the low bookshelves and was systematically pulling out valuable old books and throwing them carelessly to one side.

Susan grabbed her and held her high in the air. 'Naughty Poppy!' she said, shaking her gently and making her chortle. 'Let's go and find Nanny Bridget and maybe she'll give you your lunch. Bye bye, Daddy!' Poppy obligingly waved her small hand, and was carried out, wriggling and trying to escape.

Richard turned back to the window and saw a group of men had arrived by the oak tree, Bill Turner among them. One of them, young and lean, tanned from working outside, wearing a bright red vest, roped himself into a harness and began to climb the tree, a trailing chain-saw dangling from his waist.

That looks dangerous, thought Richard, but there was something smooth and accustomed about the way the young man climbed. The others stood on the grass beneath him, fooling about, kicking around an old tennis ball abandoned by Yorkie George, and shouting to each other confidently as if in a public park.

Perhaps I should go out and speak to them, thought Richard. But as he watched, he saw Bill Turner collect them together, and as the lopped branches began to fall, they organised themselves into what was obviously a familiar routine. Large branches were stacked neatly into a pile by the wall, and smaller, twiggy pieces fed into a noisy, violent shredder, which mashed them up and spat them out into a trailer as rough sawdust, to be taken away and put to good use.

Richard watched them sweep up the remaining debris, and then they were gone, shouting and mocking. Bill Turner disappeared through the arched doorway in the kitchen garden wall.

Must be nice, thought Richard, to have an immediately useful job like that, results apparent at once, orders obeyed and working hours rigidly observed. He suspected that the estate would carry on perfectly well without him. Bill Turner knew infinitely more about it than he did, and whilst he kept up the fiction of managing what went on, he was well aware that the seasons' routines of planting, harvesting, ploughing, lambing, and calving, would all happen just the same if he spent his time disporting himself in the Bahamas.

He turned away from the window, remembering his father, who had been even less involved in the estate. Charles Standing had cared only for the beauty of the landscape, the creamy scent of the lilies, and the quirky characters of those who worked for him. He had kept out of the way of mud and manure. His tenants were thankful, and respected him for it.

And anyway, thought Richard, he had Poppy to think about now, and all her lovely childhood to look forward to. His first daughter, now training to be a nurse and almost never in Ringford, had been a private, cool child, never wanting a cuddle and at quite an early age looking at him with a kind of pitying contempt.

Poppy is quite different, he reflected, crossing the high, black and white tiled hall and tipping Yorkie George off the tapestry seat. She loves to be cuddled and tickled. She's all girl, is darling Poppy, and will no doubt lead us all a dance.

'Just taking the car down to Bates,' he called, as he went out. 'He's got the new wing mirror and says he can fix it while I wait. Back for lunch!'

In the kitchen, Nanny Bridget spooned mush into Poppy's bird-like open mouth, and chatted to Susan. 'Would it be all right, Mrs Standing,' she said, 'if I asked Mandy and little Joe to come to tea this afternoon?'

'Of course,' said Susan. 'You can have a picnic in the garden. It's such a lovely day, and Poppy and Joey can make as much mess as they like. Not that he's getting around much yet, is he?'

'Not yet,' said Bridget, 'but he's got a lot of time to make up. Premature babies often have a slow start. He's such a little duck, isn't he, and Poppy loves him, bosses him about already.'

'Yes, well,' said Susan, 'we shall have to see that this young person doesn't get too spoilt. Though goodness knows how!' she added, popping a piece of banana into the rosebud mouth.

''E's never 'ere, these days,' said Ted to Olive, over the kitchen table. 'More and more work on the cars, and 'e just 'asn't got the time to give to the farm.'

'We should be pleased, I suppose,' said Olive, 'that he's making such a good go of it. Still, why don't you ask young Dan to come over a bit more often? I reckon he'd be glad of the chance. There's too many of them over at Waltonby.'

Ted nodded. 'I could do that, but then I can't afford to go on paying Robert if I 'ave to find a wage for Dan as well.'

'I'm sure Robert wouldn't expect it,' said Olive. 'After all, he must be raking in money for the work he's doing. Even Mr Richard takes his car to Robert now.' Olive was deeply proud of Robert's achievement, though she played it down in front of Ted. He had been trying hard to be reasonable lately, and Olive had noticed.

'Mandy's coming round this afternoon,' she said. 'We're going to push Joe up to the spinney to find some moss for the hanging baskets. They're putting them all along the front of the bungalow. It'll look really nice.'

'What will you do with the pushchair in the wood?' said Ted.

'Oh, we'll leave it on the edge and carry Joe,' said Olive. 'We shall manage with the two of us.'

'Be easier when he's on his feet,' said Ted, 'though 'e don't show much signs of it yet.'

'Give him time!' said Olive. 'He's such a dear little soul, and I swear he said "Gran" the other day.'

'Huh,' said Ted. 'You wait 'till he's chargin' about the yard, pullin' the dog's tail and yellin' like Robert used to, then you'll not be so b'sotted.'

'Oh yes, I shall,' said Olive, 'and so will you.'

Peggy and Bill sat in the yard at the back of the shop, tucked into a corner out of sight of Ivy Beasley's woodpile, drinking coffee and enjoying the sun.

'Isn't it wonderful, Bill?' Peggy said. 'I can see why the Incas worshipped the sun. If you close your eyes and let it soak into your bones you can get quite carried away.'

'If you close your eyes and relax,' said Bill Turner, 'I

reckon I could give you roughly the same effect.'

Peggy's eyes shot open, and she looked warningly at Bill. 'Don't forget old poison Ivy next door,' she whispered. 'She's probably just the other side of the fence right now, making notes.'

'Oh, who cares,' said Bill. 'I'm fed up with creeping around and pretending we're just occasional friends. Look, Peggy, I've finished the hide in the spinney now, why don't we meet up there after closing time this afternoon, and be by ourselves, without old Ivy's prying eyes for once.'

Peggy got to her feet and lifted Gilbert from her sunny bed in the catmint. She held her close and put her cheek to the purring cat's fur. 'I don't know, Bill,' she said. 'It's risky. And now Joyce is making such good progress, I'd feel guilty as hell if something I did set her back again.'

'She's going over to her sister's for tea,' said Bill. 'They're picking her up, and she won't be back until about eight. So it would be perfectly safe. Please, Peggy, do come. Maybe we could have a bit of a bunk up . . .'

Peggy put Gilbert back in the catmint, and lightly touched Bill's hand. 'How can I refuse,' she said, 'when you ask me so elegantly?'

The shop door jangled, and they got up, taking their mugs back into Peggy's kitchen.

'By the way,' said Bill, 'Joyce met Mandy and Joe on the bridge. She came home all shaky because Mandy had let her hold the baby. Mind you, she said she almost dropped him, the way he nearly toppled out of her arms. Said she must get in some practice, maybe offer to help at the playgroup. Doesn't seem possible, does it? Our Joyce, after all those years.'

'No,' said Peggy, wishing she could feel pleased. 'No, she's doing really well.'

She walked through to the shop and found Jean Jenkins collecting up groceries in her wire basket. 'Morning Jean, how's the world with you?'

'Great,' said Jean. 'Foxy's got hay fever, Mark's been kept in after school for insolence, Gemma and Amy left their new cardigans up in the woods somewhere and don't care tuppence, and Warren needs a hundred pounds to go on a school adventure holiday in Wales. Yep, everythin's fine, thanks, Peggy.'

'Oh my goodness, poor Jean!' Peggy said. 'And I was feeling sorry for myself . . .'

'Yes, well,' said Jean, dumping her full basket on to the counter, 'they say troubles never come singly, don't they?'

CHAPTER THIRTY

Bill cruised to a halt in the dry, sandy entrance to a field of dark gold corn, ripe and heavy. Poppies and marguerites soaked up the sunlight and turned the verges into strips of garden, scarlet and white against the yellowing dry grass. A soft, warm breeze stirred the corn in rhythmic, undulating waves.

Freshly washed and shaved, and wearing a thin, pale-blue cotton shirt, Bill got out of his van and took a deep breath. He walked slowly across the field to the spinney where he had arranged to meet Peggy. The penny-whistle song of an invisible lark hung over him in the hot blue sky, in an atmosphere full of the wild scents of high summer.

My God, he thought, if this isn't the perfect time and place, then I don't know what is. He had a pain in his side, as if he had run all the way from the village. He reflected that he hadn't been so nervous since he'd waited in Ringford church for Joyce to join him at the altar. Oh bugger it, he thought, why did I have to think of Joyce?

He climbed over the fence and approached the newly completed hide, securely built in the angle of branches, like a tree house and well disguised. He meant to sit up there and wait for Peggy to come along the footpath from the other direction. He'd passed no-one on the road, and if his van was seen by the field gate it would just be assumed that he was looking at the crop, assessing its ripeness for harvest.

He climbed the heavy ladder and stood looking around his hide. It was small, but not too small, and the last time he came he had brought a thick tartan rug and left it folded up in the corner. The boards of the floor were rough, and he was wary of splinters. He unfolded the rug and spread it out, then sat down, hands round his shins and head on his knees.

Come on gel, he thought, hurry up. Maybe Peggy had had second thoughts. She hadn't seemed too sure, and if she'd had a busy afternoon she might not feel like walking to the spinney. It was hot, and the road dusty and dry. No, she probably wouldn't come. Bill stretched out on the rug and closed his eyes. A fly buzzed round the hide, alighting here and there, not finding a way out. Bill felt himself drifting, the sound of the fly hypnotising him into sleep.

'Bill?' Peggy's voice calling from the bottom of the ladder jerked him to his feet. He leaned out and looked down at her warm, pink face.

'But, soft!' he said, 'what light through yonder window breaks? It is in the east, and Peggy is the sun! Or something like that . . .'

Peggy stared at him, then laughed. 'You fool!' she said. 'And anyway, Romeo's supposed to be down here, and Juliet up there, not the other way round. Shall I come up?'

Bill's inspired quoting had loosened the tension for them both, and he descended the ladder rapidly. 'Yes, my gel, up you go,' he said. 'You first and I'll come up behind you. Don't want you breaking a leg, now I've got you this far.'

Oh no, thought Peggy with renewed anxiety, what am I doing? But she felt Bill's strong arms supporting her as she climbed, caught a whiff of his aftershave, and knew she was lost. They stepped into the hide, and Peggy saw the rug on the floor. Bill took her in his arms, and they kissed, long and slow, the warmth of the hide enclosing them, the angrily buzzing fly still blundering round them.

'Oh, Bill,' said Peggy, all reservations submerged under waves of excitement.

'My love,' said Bill, carefully manoeuvring her on to the rug. The breeze stirred the tops of the trees with leafy sighs, and the fly finally escaped. It was very quiet.

And then the high, urgent sound of a crying baby burst in upon them.

'What on earth!' Peggy pulled away from Bill and stood up quickly.

'Bloody hell!' said Bill.

He looked sideways out of the hide, making sure that he could not be seen. Below, coming along the footpath, he could see two figures, one of them carrying a baby. It was Olive Bates, and Mandy holding Joe, and they were carrying bags of moss.

Olive's voice floated up into the hide. 'He's tired, I expect. We've been here a long time, what with our picnic and that.'

Peggy covered her face with her hands. Bill stepped back and put his arm round her shoulders, but she shrugged it off. They stood without moving for several minutes, until the picnickers had disappeared from sight and they could no longer hear Joey's grizzling.

'Phew!' said Bill, smiling at Peggy. 'That was a close one.'

He moved to kiss her again, but she turned away, shaking her head, all excitement and pleasure evaporated.

'It's no good, Bill, it's all spoilt now. I just feel cheap and dirty, hiding up here with someone else's husband. Suppose Mandy had seen me? She respects me, comes to me when she's in trouble. Oh, God, I'm going home. You'd better wait a while, in case there's other people about.'

She wouldn't look at him, not even when he helped her down the ladder, and he watched her retreating back, her brown, firm legs and her hair lifting in the wind, and then he sat down heavily on the rug.

Sod it, he thought, and then he began to laugh, and finally threw himself back on the rug, still laughing. 'So near,' he said aloud, 'and yet so bloody far!'

CHAPTER THIRTY-ONE

The summer months were set fair, with weeks of uninterrupted sunshine, and the village opened out like a flower, relishing the warmth of the sun, making the most of it. The Green was never without a group of children playing ball, or the old men gossiping under the tree. Bill Turner set the cutters high on the sit-on mower, and was the envy of Warren and William, who pestered to be allowed to have a go.

'In three or four years' time, boy,' said Bill, 'you can take over from me, but till then keep well clear.'

In an alarming new departure from routine, Ellen Biggs had carried an old, rickety cane table out into her front garden, and had there set it for tea on the small patch of grass which passed for a lawn. She had covered it with an embroidered cloth, now so thin that at the folds the fine linen was almost transparent. The teacups and saucers, cracks and chips very visible in the unaccustomed bright light of afternoon sun, rattled dangerously as she adjusted the table legs.

'Is this a good idea, Ellen?' said Doris Ashbourne, arriving first. Ivy had called in at the cemetery to change the flowers on her mother's grave.

Doris knew a great deal about Ivy's mother, mostly from Ellen Biggs. She knew how the old woman had blighted

Ivy's prospects on more than one occasion, and, although dead for some years, maintained a ghostly presence in poor Ivy's head, a cruel, ever-present alter ego, still dominating her ageing daughter.

'She nags on about it, Mother does, if I don't keep the grave fresh and nice,' Ivy said unguardedly to Doris, one damp afternoon when they had clipped the grass and pulled weeds from the granite chippings.

Doris Ashbourne had looked sideways at Ivy, thought of challenging her on the stupidity of her obsession, but in the end contented herself with saying mildly, 'She'll have nothing to complain of there, Ivy, it looks very nice, very nice indeed.'

Now she looked over Ellen's untidy hedge and up the lane, watching out for Ivy and wondering what she would have to say about Ellen's eccentric plan to have tea on the lawn.

''Ere,' said Ellen, 'give us a hand with this chair, Doris. If we get it all set up before Ivy arrives she won't 'ave no call to complain.'

This proved to be a vain hope, and when Ivy Beasley opened the garden gate and saw Ellen and Doris sitting uneasily on upright chairs which sank ominously into the dry, sandy ground, she was firm.

'Not on your life, Ellen Biggs,' she said. 'You'll not catch me sitting there for all the world and his wife to see and laugh at. Come on, Doris, help me cart all this stuff back indoors.'

But Ellen had spent a long time planning her tea on the lawn, and was not to be thwarted. 'Sit where you are, Doris,' she said. 'If our Ivy wants her tea indoors, then she's welcome to take it and have it there by herself. You and me are quite comfortable, and I'm just about to pour.'

She leaned forward perilously, and took off the tea cosy. Doris came to her aid, and held the cups while she poured. They both ignored Ivy Beasley, who remained standing, frowning and furious at this challenge to her authority.

'Well,' said Ellen, 'make up your mind, Ivy, are you comin' or goin'?'

Ivy snorted and gave up. 'I have never heard of anything so ridiculous,' she said. 'The likes of us don't have tea in the garden. If you ask me,' she added, 'you're enterin' your second childhood, Ellen Biggs. And you needn't look at me like that, Doris. I am not taking off my hat, and I am certainly not stopping more than five minutes.'

Silence filled the garden, broken only by the droning bees in Ellen's hollyhocks and the pigeons cooing high up in the thick-leaved chestnut trees.

Colin Osman, walking down from the Hall with his camera, stopped, taken unawares by the extraordinary scene before him. Framed by two great boles of chestnut, Ellen's tangled garden lay in a pool of sunlight. Roses rambled unchecked round the windows of the Lodge, and ventured in some places as high as the twisted chimneys. Clumps of self-sown cloudy blue larkspur and purple aquilegia bordered the grass where the three elderly women sat.

It's like a painting, thought Colin, raising his camera. There sits Ivy Beasley in her hat, dominating Doris, meek and self-effacing; and there's Ellen, square and belligerent, presiding over her teapot. He'd got it wrong, of course, as usual.

He took a couple of shots, and then walked quietly on, amused to hear as he passed Ellen's raucous voice. 'O'course I made it myself, Ivy, slaved away in an 'ot kitchen to make them shortbreads for your tea.' She turned, and caught sight of Colin. 'Afternoon, Mr Osman,' she yelled. 'Can I offer yer a cup o' tea?'

'Ellen!' said Ivy.

'Ellen!' murmured Doris.

'Very kind, but no thanks, Mrs Biggs. Got to get back. Good afternoon, ladies!' Colin Osman walked smartly on, wondering if he could incorporate a few photographs in his village newsletter. Shouldn't be too difficult with the new technology. He walked faster, stimulated by his new idea.

'Well!' said Ivy, getting up with difficulty from the sinking chair. 'This the last time we have our tea outside, if I have my way. Don't you agree, Doris?'

Doris smoothed her skirt, put her head on one side, and considered. 'As a matter of fact, Ivy,' she said, 'I've quite enjoyed sitting out in the fresh air. It's a warm afternoon, and Ellen has set it up nicely for us, so I think we should thank her for her efforts.'

Ellen beamed, but Ivy adjusted her plain straw hat and turned to leave.

'Oh look, Ivy!' said Ellen, also struggling to her feet. 'There's Mandy and Joe comin' with 'is pushchair. Now just go to the gate and ask them to come and have a quick cup with us. And take that sour look off yer face. You'll frighten the poor little mite.'

The last sentence was said for Doris's benefit, out of Ivy's earshot, and Doris laughed. 'You'll never change, Ellen Biggs,' she said. 'I suppose you want me to get another cup?'

'And you'll find a packet of rusks on the windowsill. Bring that too,' said Ellen.

Softened by little Joe's smile, Ivy returned with Mandy to the garden, and even brought out another chair for her.

'Sit 'im on the grass,' said Ellen. 'It's dry as a bone after all this sunshine. He'll not come to any harm.'

Mandy pulled out a small rug from her baby bag and spread it on the grass. She lifted Joe out of his pushchair and put him down on his stomach, where he kicked his legs and looked around with more smiles.

'Don't 'e sit up yet, Mandy?' said Ellen.

Mandy shook her head. 'He still topples over, just like those dolls,' she said, laughing. 'We shall have to let him take his own time. He's got a lot to make up, what with

201

being so little and premature.'

She leaned over and picked him up again, holding him protectively against her. 'Would you like one of Auntie Ellen's rusks, Joe?' she said, and helped him guide it to his mouth. He munched happily, and the women chatted about the likelihood of a good harvest, the need for a nice drop of rain, and the news that there was to be a Bonny Baby competition at the Church Fête in a couple of weeks' time.

'That was my Robert's idea,' said Mandy. 'He persuaded Mrs Brooks to organise it. He said it would be something new and bring more people in to the fête, but I know it's just because he's certain Joe will win!'

'We 'aven't 'ad a Bonny Baby contest for years,' said Ellen, 'not since Jean Jenkins and that woman from Fletching came to blows over it. D'yer remember, Doris?'

'I do,' said Ivy. 'You got to be very careful with a baby contest.

'Oh, well,' said Mandy, 'this time it will be fine. They're going to give them all prizes, and every one gets a photograph to take away. Mr Osman's doing that, I think.'

'Just as well,' said Ellen. 'We don't want no fightin' in the vicarage garden.' She rocked with laughter at the thought, and clutched Doris Ashbourne's shoulder to steady herself. 'And that reminds me,' she said, ''ave you 'heard the story that's goin' about? Fred Mills told me outside the shop this mornin'. They say they're goin' to sell the vicarage and build a new one for Reverend Brooks and 'is missus. It's the trend, Fred said, though what 'e knows about trends would go on the back of a postage stamp, I'd say.'

Mandy put Joe in his pushchair, thanked Ellen for the cup of tea, and set off for home. Ivy and Doris helped Ellen wash up, and then carried the table and chairs back into The Lodge. Ellen walked with them to the gate, and they sniffed the late afternoon air, cool and scented with Ellen's bed of stocks by the gate.

'A very nice afternoon, thank you, Ellen,' said Doris. 'And it was a treat to see Mandy and little Joe, wasn't it, Ivy?'

Ivy Beasley nodded, hesitated, and then frowned. She looked straight at Doris, and spoke with an uncharacteristic stumble in her voice.

'Yes, it was,' she said, hesitating. '. . . Doris, I know Joey was premature and that . . . but don't you think that child should be sitting up by now?'

CHAPTER THIRTY-TWO

During the week of the Church Fête, the Reverend Nigel Brooks rolled up his sleeves and set to work on the garden. He had Michael Roberts to help him in the evenings, and sometimes Warren came too, when he could spare the time from the Bates's bungalow. 'It's a challenge, Reverend Brooks,' he said, 'startin' from scratch. But Mrs Mandy keeps me goin' with drinks of Coke and pieces of cake.' He looked meaningly at the vicar, who dutifully made a mental note to ask Sophie to provide refreshment.

'Sometimes,' Warren rattled on, 'she pushes Joey out in his pushchair and he watches me. He's too little to help yet. Sides which, he don't move about much. Anyway, 'e's no trouble.'

The broad lawns of the vicarage had never looked so smooth, and the great cedar tree spread patches of welcome shade. Nigel dead-headed the late roses, and tied back flopping stems of golden rod. Gravel paths were weeded, and Michael Roberts scythed down the long grass in the orchard.

'You goin' to let the kids help themselves to apples, Reverend?' he said.

'They're not ripe yet,' said Nigel.

'That won't make no difference,' said Michael Roberts. 'You must've had gyppy belly from eatin' green apples when you were a lad?' He looked at Nigel's trim figure, his grey, clerical shirtsleeves neatly rolled, his thick wavy grey hair well brushed.

'Well,' he continued, 'perhaps not. Anyways, that Jenkins lot'll be after them, not to mention all them young Bates cousins from Waltonby. They always comes, the lot o' them.'

There was feverish activity on Fête Saturday morning, and this culminated in Ivy Beasley and Ellen Biggs having a stand-up row over who should have the stall in the shade of the cedar tree.

'I always have my home-mades under the tree, stops them melting and spoiling, you know that perfectly well, Ellen Biggs,' said Ivy, her face hot and red.

Ellen dumped on to the grass a cardboard box full of good-as-new clothes left over from last year's jumble sale, and folded her arms. 'You can't expect an old woman like me to stand in the full sun all afternoon, Ivy. Can she, Reverend Brooks?' she added, catching him by the arm as he walked by. He sighed. He had been warned about village life when he first arrived in Ringford from his parish in a grey Welsh town.

'Plenty of room for you both, I would say,' he said smoothly, and helped the warring parties to set up their stalls side by side.

'Don't know that that's such a good idea,' said Doreen Price to Peggy Palmer, as they sorted grubby books into piles of hardback titles nobody had ever heard of, and well-thumbed paperback novels by popular authors. 'Those two'll be at each others throats all afternoon.'

'Where are the Bonny Babies going to be?' said Peggy.

'Over there, by the summerhouse,' said Doreen. 'There's some shade from those cherry trees, and it's away from the general crush. Sophie's organising it, and she's welcome!'

'Who's judging?'

'Mrs Standing, naturally,' said Doreen. 'I don't know whether little Poppy is entered, but it wouldn't really be fair. You couldn't expect our Susan to be impartial.'

'Bridget will want to enter her. She's as proud as if the baby were her own. How many hopefuls are there?' said Peggy.

'Eight, at the last count, but anybody can enter, right up to the last minute.'

'We must see the line-up,' said Peggy. 'We'll have to take turns to leave the stall.'

Over by the stable wall, already radiating heat from the mellow rusty-pink and mossy green bricks, Sophie Brooks had set up a small trestle table for her entry forms and prizes. She had never run a Bonny Baby competition before, and was apprehensive. It was a good thing her daughter was staying, with Sophie's darling new grandson George, born at about the same time as Joey Bates, and a constant source of joy and pleasure. It was a shame they lived in Paris, but at least when they came over for visits they stayed two or three weeks, and the old vicarage came to life with laughter and tears and the clutter which seemed to surround baby George wherever he went. She could count on Millie to give her moral support, though she mustn't be seen to favour George above any of the others.

Susan Standing had been delighted to be asked to judge, and Sophie knew she would do it graciously and give the whole thing a sense of occasion. They had agreed that all babies would be given prizes, but one only would have a framed, portrait-size photograph, taken by Colin Osman. He had won one of the annual Kodak prizes for portraiture, and Sophie knew he would do a good job. All the other babies would have small prints, with the option of ordering enlargements.

She set out the prizes, little baskets of baby toiletries, donated by the local factory in Tresham, and put the notice acknowledging their generosity in a prominent position.

Proceeds from the fête were always given to charity, and this year Robert Bates had suggested Birthright, promoting research and better facilities for premature babies.

'Need any help, Mrs Brooks?' Pat Osman, carefully made-up and smoothly groomed as always, leaned on the table and looked at the prizes. 'These are nice. Wish I had a baby to enter. Still, maybe next year.'

'Plenty of time, my dear,' said Sophie. 'And you can always put Tiggy in the dog show. Yes, I could do with some help tying these balloons on the peach tree. We want to make it look festive and a bit like a children's party. Here you are, here's the balloon pump. You blow, and I'll tie them up.'

'I'm on the tombola later,' said Pat Osman. 'It's all organised. Colin helped me stick on numbers last evening, and there's nothing else to do. The old tombola drum sticks a bit, but Colin's going to oil it before this afternoon.'

'Who's on the bottle stall?'

'Greg Jones and Gabriella. They've been all round the village wheedling bottles out of people, and got loads. Should do well, there. And the lovely Octavia is selling raffle tickets. She should melt the heart of even the most stingy old farmer.'

Octavia Jones was in the sixth form at Tresham Comprehensive, and her teenage years so far had been far from uneventful. Tall and slender, with long blonde hair and a gift for showing off her considerable charms to their best advantage, Octavia was trouble. But at the moment, she had decided to devote her life to the service of others, and was willing and eager to sell raffle tickets at Ringford Church Fête. Next week, her mother had said gloomily, no doubt she'll be deep into caring for the homeless. And the next, added her father, with greater insight, she'll probably be pregnant.

At half past twelve, trays of squash and cups of tea were brought round the garden by Sophie Brooks and daughter

Millie, and all the helpers sat on the grass and ate sandwiches and contemplated the fruits of their labours. The vicarage garden had looked like this on summer fête afternoons for more than a hundred years. There were photographs, brown and faded, in the village hall, to prove it: ladies in big, floppy hats and dresses with dropped waists, and men in high white collars and their best caps.

The school's coloured bunting surrounded the garden, and the stalls had been set out in a rough circle. Ivy Beasley's clean, starched cloths were spread under tempting plates of sponge cakes, fruit cakes, ginger cakes, nut bread, tea bread, wholemeal bread, shortbread and more. Jars of preserves and trays of brown eggs from Doreen Price vied for space with neat bunches of radishes and half-dozens of perfectly ripe tomatoes from Bill Turner. Ivy had Doris Ashbourne to help, and the two of them could have done it in their sleep.

The old painted roulette game, kept from year to year in a cupboard in the village hall, had been set up by the roses, and publican Don Cutt, who had volunteered to give it a go, had insisted on plenty of space around it. 'You'll see,' he said. 'I shall get crowds. Folks can't resist a gamble, and I know how to make sure we win.'

The Reverend Nigel Brooks suppressed thoughts of the unsuitability of gambling in the vicarage garden, and took Don Cutt his float of coins in a polythene bag. 'Should be enough to get you started, Don,' he said. 'Good luck!'

The Women's Institute team had set up the refreshment tables and chairs, and had gone into a huddle in the vicarage kitchen, where hot-water urns were filled and crates of milk stacked neatly by the big table.

'Them pieces are too big,' Deirdre said to novice Caroline Dodwell. 'We'll never make a profit that way!' And she neatly halved the golden flapjack and almond slices.

Mr and Mrs Ross, composed and a little apart from the

gossiping tea-drinkers under the tree, had arranged their bric-a-brac stall with care. It was a work of art in itself, every piece of old china, glass bead necklace and poker-work toast rack carefully displayed on crocheted tray-cloths or lace dressing-table mats, and priced in Mr Ross's neat, parish clerk handwriting.

'All set then, Mr Ross?' called Tom Price, walking through with Bill Turner to the Glebe field next to the garden. The Dog Show was always held in the Glebe field, although some of the older villagers complained at the noisy barking and yelling of rougher supporters of the canine contestants. The Fête committee had reluctantly decided against terrier racing this year, though it brought in good money, in view of the fight that had resulted from two Jack Russells finishing in a dead heat last year. The dogs had fought, and so had their owners, until they all retired sulking, one with a bitten ear and another with a bloody nose.

Tom and Bill went through the field gate, and checked the ropes and posts marking out the ring. Some of the classes were serious categories of breed, but many were for fun, for the village children – The Dog with the Waggiest Tail, and Best Family Pet. Mrs Ross would not allow her black and white butterfly dog to be entered, certain that he would pick up something nasty.

'That's it, then, Ellen,' said Jean Jenkins, getting up from the grass and brushing down her skirt. 'We've done our sortin', and I must get back and give the kids their dinner. We'll be back in good time, don't fret.'

Ellen nodded. Nigel Brooks had brought out a comfortable chair for her to rest in, and she was quite happy to watch other people work and wait for the Fête to open. She saw Olive Bates giving final touches to the refreshment tables, fresh and inviting with red and white check cloths, and called out to her.

''Ere Olive, is Mandy puttin' little Joe in the baby show?'

Olive Bates walked over to Ellen and smiled. 'You've got the best place there, Ellen Biggs,' she said. 'It's going to be hot this afternoon. Yes, Joey's entered. Mandy's bought a new outfit for him, and he had his hair washed last night. Hates it, of course, like most babies! Still, he'll be looking his best.' She looked at Ellen, and seemed about to say something else, but didn't, and walked on, over to the book stall to have a word with Peggy Palmer.

'Did you have confirmation about the ice-cream, Peggy?' she said. 'Deirdre wants to know.'

Peggy said the ice-cream man had promised to be set up by two o'clock. 'He'll be here, Olive,' she said. 'Should make a mint in this weather.'

I wonder if Olive did see me that afternoon in the spinney, she wondered for the hundredth time, she hasn't said anything, not a hint, but she has been a bit off lately, as if she had something on her mind.

'Look, Joe!' said Mandy, holding him so that he could see. 'Isn't that pretty?'

The schoolchildren were dancing round a swaying Maypole, set up in the grassy space surrounded by the stalls. A good crowd had turned up, and proud relations watched as the children, sure-footed and serious, neat and tidy in their red and grey summer uniforms, wove in and out with the multicoloured ribbons, miraculously plaiting them into a basket-weave, and then, as the music changed, unplaiting them until the ribbons were free and swinging again.

'You'll do that,' said Mandy, 'when you're a bigger boy.'

Joe grinned and waved his arms about. His hair had a gingerish tinge now it was growing thicker, and his eyes had remained a clear, cornflower blue. In his new blue and white cotton suit, he was a picture of cleanliness and amiability.

Bridget stood next to Mandy, holding baby Poppy, and

trying to stop her wriggling down on to the grass. 'You'll miss the dancing, Poppy!' she said, and turned to Mandy. 'How am I going to keep her clean until three o'clock?'

'One thing about Joe,' said Mandy, 'he doesn't seem to get so dirty as other babies, thank goodness. There's enough washing as it is, what with Robert's oily clothes from the garage and that.'

By three o'clock, most of the people at the Fête had converged on the baby corner. The dog classes had finished, more or less, and all Ivy's cakes had sold in the first half hour. A good crowd had been sitting at the refreshment tables, chatting and greeting old friends, but were now gradually standing up and moving over to watch the Bonny Babies.

'You sit here, Mandy,' said Sophie Brooks, 'next to Caroline. Joey and little Hugo must know each other well, being neighbours.'

Mandy sat down and held Joe carefully, not creasing his suit, and supporting his back with her hand. Hugo Dodwell, thin and wiry, with pale curls and huge innocent eyes, reached out a probing forefinger and poked at Joe's arm.

'Sorry, Mandy!' said Caroline. 'He's like lightning, I have to have eyes in the back of my head.'

'I've got all that to come,' said Mandy, kissing the top of Joe's head. She was sitting at the end of the row of mothers and babies, and Susan Standing had begun to go along the line from the other end, having a word with each in turn. 'Like the Queen Mum,' said Caroline with a giggle.

The crowds laughed and talked, and Mandy could hear snatches of conversation about the babies, praising this one for his smile, and that one for a fine head of hair.

And then, in a sudden lull in conversation, she heard it. She heard the hoarse whisper of an elderly woman standing a few yards away from her. Mandy was never to forget it.

'What about that one then, 'im at the end?' said the voice. ''E don't look quite right to me, do 'e to you? Not quite right, if you know what I mean.'

CHAPTER THIRTY-THREE

Peggy Palmer stood on the stone base of an urn full of geraniums, and watched Susan Standing's royal progress along the line of mothers and babies.

'You have to hand it to her, Doreen,' said Peggy, looking across at her friend, who was perched insecurely on a rickety chair. 'She does it very well. And she did give Poppy a smacking kiss as she passed by.'

'Oh yes,' said Doreen. 'Madame certainly knows how to queen it when necessary. It's in the – hey, Peggy! What's Mandy doing?'

Peggy stood on tiptoe and peered above the crowd. 'She's leaving! What on earth's the matter with her, she looks as if she's crying, Doreen! I'd better go . . .'

Peggy jumped down from the stone plinth and pushed her way through the crowd to intercept Mandy on her way out. Heads were turning as Mandy half ran between the refreshment tables and headed for the vicarage drive. Peggy caught up with her as she emerged into the empty end of the garden and stopped to check the straps of Joe's pushchair.

'Mandy! What are you doing?' she said breathlessly, and when Mandy turned to face her, she knew it was something very bad.

'Can I come home with you, Mrs P., just for a few minutes?' said Mandy.

Peggy nodded, and put her arm round Mandy's shoulders, helping her to push Joey out of the vicarage garden and up the lane towards the bridge.

'Shouldn't we have told Robert?' she said, as they walked along the footpath across the Green. The grass was dry, and the path cracked and bumpy, jolting Joe from side to side. He was sleepy, and his head lolled on to his shoulder.

Mandy shook her head. 'I just had to get away,' she said. She didn't speak again until they were inside Peggy's quiet kitchen. Joey had fallen asleep, his hands sweetly folded on his new blue suit, and his legs dangling, completely relaxed, over the footrest of the pushchair. Mandy parked him across the far side of the kitchen and returned to sit at the table. Peggy said nothing, but made a cup of sweet tea and put it in front of Mandy.

'I know you don't take sugar,' she said, 'but drink it down, there's a good girl.'

Several minutes passed in the quiet kitchen, the clock ticking and Gilbert purring by the Rayburn, delighted that Peggy was home.

'Now then, Mandy Bates,' said Peggy, when the tea had been drunk, and Mandy leaned back apprehensively in her chair, 'are you going to tell me what happened?'

Tears ran unchecked down Mandy's face, and between gulps and sobs she told Peggy what the old woman had said.

'But Mandy,' said Peggy, 'you could have misheard her, or she might have been talking about one of the other babies, or anything! You can't be sure she meant Joe, and even if she did, why should she know anything at all about him? It was nothing, Mandy, I am sure it was nothing at all!'

Mandy looked at her so piteously that Peggy reached out and took her hand.

'It isn't nothing, Mrs P., Mandy said. 'There is something wrong with Joey, I know there is. I've known it for a while now, and tried not to think about it. I think Rob's mum knows too, though she's not said anything. But I can tell. That old woman . . .' She hesitated, and pushed her hair back, rubbing her eyes with her hand, smudging her make-up. 'That old woman,' she repeated, 'only told me what I know already. He's not quite right, Peggy, and that's the truth.'

Peggy stared at her uncomprehendingly. Mandy got up and gently took the sleeping Joe out of his pushchair. She held him close, and sat down again, cuddling him with her cheek against his soft little head. Peggy thought she had never seen such anguish, and had never felt so helpless.

'Dear God,' she said. 'I can't believe it, Mandy, I'm sure you're worrying about nothing, you'll see.' But Mandy shook her head, and hugged Joey so close that he began to wake up.

CHAPTER THIRTY-FOUR

Ted Bates looked at himself in the bathroom mirror and frowned. He saw an old man. His eyes were sunk deep into their sockets, and his thin, sandy hair barely covered the top of his head. His skin was rough and red, and his beaky nose shone from the good scrub he had just given himself after a hard day moving stock.

I shall have to get young Dan over here permanently, he thought. I can't keep up with the work without Robert, and his business keeps him full time now. Pity little Joe ain't of an age to help his old Grandad.

Ted walked into the bedroom he and Olive had shared since the day of their marriage thirty years ago. He took his grey flannel trousers off the hanger, and pulled them on over his thin, bandy legs. Buttoning his clean shirt, he looked again at his reflection in Olive's dressing-table mirror. Ugly old bugger, he said. And then the ghost of a smile crossed his face. Still, little Joe seems to like it. Wonder how he got on at the baby show. Mandy was so excited, and Robert was sure he'd win. Mind you, thought Ted, he's not a bad lookin' little chap, considerin' his shaky start.

He pulled on his comfortable tweed jacket, and brushed back the stray strands of displaced hair. 'Course, it were the lovin' care he got from Mandy and Olive. Like them orphan lambs of Olive's. She's never lost one, prides herself on it. Not that some of 'em wouldn't have bin better left.

Ted stumped down the shallow stairs and put his head round the kitchen door to say he was off to the pub. Olive sat at the table, her head in her hands. Ted, taken aback, stopped mid-sentence. 'What's up, Olive?'

She didn't answer, but raised her head and looked blankly at him.

'Did our Joey win, then?' he said. 'Good God, woman, whatever is the matter?' he continued, as Olive shook her head and still said nothing.

'Well, I'm late already,' he said. 'Whatever it is'll 'ave to wait 'til I come back.' He was half out of the kitchen door when Olive spoke.

'You'd better hear it from me, better than the crowd in the pub.'

'Hear what, for God's sake? Get on with it, do!'

'Mandy ran away. She never waited for the judging. She just got up and ran away with Joe. Everybody was staring. Peggy Palmer went after her, and I went and got Robert. He was still helping clear the dog-show ground. He went straight home, and I don't know what happened after that.'

Ted Bates stared at Olive, and then sat down heavily at the table. 'Go on, then,' he said.

'Go on with what? That's all I know.'

'No, it isn't,' said Ted.

'Yes, it is!' said Olive, banging her hand on the table.

'You might just as well say it,' said Ted. 'I know bloody well what you've been thinkin'. We ain't bin married for thirty years for nothin'.'

'If you know what I'm thinking, then I don't have to bother saying it.'

'Somebody's got to say it,' said Ted.

'Then we'll leave it to Mandy and Robert,' said Olive, getting up and turning her back on Ted. 'You'd better get goin', or you'll be pints behind.'

Ted slammed the back door behind him, and drove off in the battered Land Rover down the lane towards the pub. He caught sight of his angry face in the driving mirror and blinked. 'Poor little sod,' he said, 'and 'e looks just like me.'

Don Cutt had put up new fairy lights round the pub garden, and although Ted had been against it at the time, he had to admit it looked very festive, with families and young people sitting on benches, Bronwen Cutt's snacks vanishing rapidly, and foaming ale, even if it was canned lager, being downed with great goodwill.

Surrounding twilight made the pub an oasis of cheerful activity, and the evening air was pleasantly cool after the heat of the day. The Jenkins terrier roamed around the garden, mopping up dropped chips and crisps and anything else that descended to his level. Every so often he reported back to Foxy and Jean Jenkins, who sat at a long table in the corner of the garden, with Gemma and Amy side by side, drinking Pepsi through striped straws, and Mark wrestling with a Jumbo sausage.

'There goes Ted,' said Jean. 'He's late tonight. I expect they've been havin' a set-to about Mandy.'

'What about Mandy?' said Fox. He leaned forward and cut Mark's sausage into three manageable pieces, dipped one of them into a squirt of mustard, and popped it into his mouth. Mark squealed and retreated to the far end of the table, out of reach.

'She vanished, went off in the middle of the baby judging. It was really embarrassin', what with Mrs Standing doin' her bit and that. Goodness knows what it was about, but Peggy Palmer went after 'er, so I expect we shall hear about it in the shop on Monday.'

'That accounts for Robert not bein' here this evenin', then,' said Foxy. 'We were goin' to have a game of darts at seven o'clock, but 'e 'asn't turned up. P'raps I'll go an' buy Ted a pint, see what he's got to say.'

Ted stood by the bar, talking to Tom Price and Bill Turner. Tom had heard of the afternoon's drama from Doreen, and Bill had called in quickly on Peggy on his way home, but she had just said Mandy hadn't felt very well and needed to be on her own for a bit. Neither Tom nor Bill said a word on the subject to Ted, and the conversation centred on the harvest and set-aside, and the iniquities of the Common Agricultural Policy.

The bar was crammed full, and throbbed with loud voices, all shouting and laughing at such a pitch that Ted found it difficult to hear. He wouldn't admit to deafness, but found that in a crowded, noisy room it was at its worst.

He screwed up his face and leaned closer to Fox Jenkins. 'What you say, Fox? I can't hear a bloody word in 'ere tonight. God knows where they all come from.'

'I said, where's Robert?' Fox articulated as clearly as he could, directing his words into Ted's hairy ear.

Ted shook his head. 'Don't know,' he said. It was impossible to read anything from his expression.

'Should've been meetin' me for a game of darts,' said Fox.

'I'll give you a game,' said Ted, feeling an odd reluctance to get into close conversation with Tom and Bill. They were already discussing the Fête, disagreeing over the Best Terrier results, and he was glad to follow Foxy through the crowd to the dart board, where a game had just ended.

Ivy Beasley sat in Doris Ashbourne's front garden, a square of grass surrounded by straggling roses and clumps of pinks, all a bit gone over and brown at the edges. Doris had taken out two folding canvas chairs, and had persuaded a reluctant Ivy to sit with her in the twilight, listening to the children still playing in the Gardens and the distant hum of cars arriving at the pub.

'Nothing nicer than a summer's evening after a hot day,' Doris said, putting down an empty cup on the grass beside her. 'The fête was a grand success again, wouldn't you say, Ivy?'

Ivy nodded. 'My stall was, certainly,' she said. 'If they all did as well as I did, then we shall have a good total for the baby thing.'

'Birthright,' said Doris. 'It was a good idea of Robert's, a sort of thank you for having Joe safe and sound.'

'Safe,' said Ivy. 'Yes, safe he certainly is. Our Mandy has turned out a really good little mother.'

The two women said nothing for a few seconds, then Doris aired both their thoughts. 'What was it all about, then, this afternoon? I didn't see what happened, but Ellen Biggs was full of it.'

'She would be,' said Ivy. 'Loves a bit of drama, does Ellen.'

'Well?' said Doris.

'I know no more than you, Doris,' said Ivy sanctimoniously, 'and I don't mean to speculate. I saw Mandy leaving the baby show, looking like death warmed up, and my nosy neighbour goin' after her. Not feeling well, or something like that, I should say, nothing to get all het up about.'

'Mm,' said Doris, and leaned back in her chair. She stared up at the sky, now quite dark and with a speckling of early stars. Two of them were winking and moving along. She could hear the drone of an aeroplane high above the village, and wondered where it was going and who was aboard.

'When I said "safe and sound", Ivy,' she said slowly, 'you said "safe", and you didn't say "sound". Now, I know you very well, Ivy, and you choose your words with care. What exactly did you mean?'

Ivy stood up, picking up her handbag from the grass, and straightened her skirt. She put out her hand and rested it gently on Doris's arm. Doris could not remember her ever having done such a thing before.

'I only wish I knew, Doris,' she said, 'but I am very much afraid that our little Joe is not as "sound" as he should be. May God prove me wrong, Doris dear, let us all pray for that.'

CHAPTER THIRTY-FIVE

The garden at the bungalow was showing unmistakable signs of approaching winter. William Roberts had cycled down after school to do his usual hour or so, and realised that by the time he had cut down rusting Michaelmas daisies, done a bit of weeding and swept up piles of fallen leaves from under the cherry tree, the daylight was already fading. He could see the light on in Mandy's sitting room, and in front of the flickering television screen he saw little Joe in his high chair, Mandy beside him, feeding him with a spoon.

'Looks cosy,' William muttered to himself, thinking of his own cheerless home. He heard footsteps, and saw Robert's bulk above the border as he walked round to the back door. William stayed quite still. He didn't want to go home just yet. If he made himself invisible he could linger on in the garden for a while, then sneak out once Robert was safely settled indoors.

The back door was open, and he heard Robert call in as he took off his boots. 'Finished for the day, Mandy! Dad's back, Joey!'

William felt a kind of reflected warmth from thinking about them, sitting in their pleasant room, chatting about the day, eating their tea and playing with Joey. He took the leaves to the pile at the bottom of the garden and sat on the fence, looking across at Robert's workshop. It was very tidy, with the new sliding doors tightly shut and locked, and the concrete yard brushed clean. Mandy had put tubs of white cosmos daisies either side of the entrance, and they had flowered all summer, still sending out new buds. 'Dad says if you keep pickin' off the dead heads, they'll flower for months,' William had said, and his dad had been right.

If I could choose, thought William, that's what I'd do when I leave school. Wish I was Robert, he's got everything. Not much chance of Dad settin' me up in anythin'. Expect I'll end up workin' on the roads, like Darren. Darren was his elder brother, who lived in Tresham and came home as little as possible.

It was dusk now, and William looked hard at a dark shadow in the workshop yard. He made out what he thought was a wheel jack, a new, expensive one, only a few weeks old. It was resting by the wall of the workshop, and William supposed Robert had forgotten to put it away.

Better go and tell him, he thought, and jumped off the fence, making his way to the bungalow. As he came to the open door, he was about to knock when he heard what sounded like a woman crying, very different from Joey's yell. He was very used to this, as his mother cried a lot, and he stood still, making up his mind what to do.

Robert's voice, strong and firm, came through from the front room. 'This isn't going to help Joe, Mandy. I'm just as upset as you about it, but it doesn't necessarily mean bad news. Dr Evans is just being extra careful, that's all.'

William couldn't hear Mandy's muffled reply, but he suddenly knew that he was listening to something very private, and he quietly made his way down the path and out of the front gate without a sound.

CHAPTER THIRTY-SIX

Robert and Mandy, with Joe in his car seat in the back, followed the familiar road from Round Ringford to Tresham General Hospital. They had done the journey in many moods: fear, disappointment, anxiety, depression, hope, anticipation and elation. And on that joyful journey when Joe at last came home, they had hoped, had been confident, that all would now be plain sailing, that they could be like other young parents, with ordinary worries about nappy rash, teething and chesty colds.

They drove in silence. The car had, as usual, sent Joe off into a peaceful sleep, and his head had fallen to one side, his newly-washed hair curling in wisps over his ears, his long, gold lashes resting on warm, flushed cheeks.

Mandy had dressed him carefully, making sure he looked his best. As if it will make any difference, she thought, slumped in the front seat. She had eventually persuaded Robert that they should at least take Joe to Dr Evans, who knew them well, and wouldn't fob them off with the usual 'Give him time . . .'

'You take him, Mandy,' Robert had said. 'We don't want to spread undue alarm when, as far as I can see, there's no cause.'

Mandy had taken Joe in to the Health Centre in Bagley, crucified by contradictory thoughts. She still had a strong instinctive feeling that something was wrong, but at the same time was hoping against hope that she was mistaken. Dr Evans had not reassured her. He had taken everything she said very seriously, and examined Joe gently but carefully. 'Well, young man,' he had said, handing a grinning Joey back to his mother, 'I think we should get someone else to have a look at you.'

Mandy had left Bagley in a daze, driving home automatically along the sunlit lanes, scarcely acknowledging William Roberts in the garden as she carried Joe into the bungalow.

The appointment with a visiting paediatrician at Tresham General had come through quickly, and Robert put up a notice on the workshop door, explaining that R B Engineering would be closed for just this one morning. ' . . . owing to family business,' he had written.

Now they had arrived at the hospital, and were waiting outside the clinic door, hardly speaking. Mandy gently woke up Joe, and he emerged from sleep fractious and complaining.

The paediatrician, Dr MacArthur, was an elderly man, with thick grey hair and bushy eyebrows. He sat at a big desk in his consulting room and sunlight streamed in through the high, modern windows, opening up the room and inspiring optimism and confidence. He stood up as they came in, tall and distinguished, and welcomed them with a kind smile.

He took hold of Joey's hand. 'Now then,' he said, 'let's have a look at you.'

Joe had cheered up, and smiled at first, but soon protested at tests of his reflexes and at being held at awkward angles while his parents looked on, unsmiling and not coming to the rescue.

'There we are then,' Dr MacArthur said. 'All finished, young Joe, back to Mother.'

Robert moved his chair nearer to Mandy, and put out his

hand to Joe, who grasped his finger and tried to put it in his mouth. The three of them were joined together, physically connected, braced for whatever was coming next. It was not enough, however, to soften the blow.

'I am afraid, Mandy and Robert,' said Dr MacArthur gently, 'that little Joe is going to need a bit more help from us. We shall do further tests, of course, but his early difficulties with breathing have unfortunately resulted in some damage.' Mandy and Robert stared at him stonily. 'The best way I can describe it to you,' he continued, 'is that the messages are not yet getting through to encourage him to develop in the usual way.'

'Messages?' said Robert, holding on tight to little Joe's hand.

'From his brain,' said Dr MacArthur. 'Connections are made all the time with a growing baby, triggering off the usual steps of development. In Joe's case, some of the connections are not being made. You have noticed, haven't you,' he added, as gently as he could, 'otherwise you wouldn't be here, Mr Bates.'

It was Mandy who nodded, and said in a small voice, 'Yes, I knew there was something wrong. I was right, Robert.'

'Better get back to work, then,' Robert said. They had scarcely touched the cold ham and salad Mandy had prepared before they left for the hospital. Joe had eaten heartily, and was now on his stomach on the floor, reaching for a toy car and chortling to himself.

Mandy nodded, and Robert put his arms round her and held her tight. 'Don't worry, Mandy,' he said. 'We got through the last lot all right, we'll cope, you'll see.' But Mandy did not respond, and Robert walked across to his workshop with a heavy heart.

Mandy got up slowly from the table and looked down at her son. He could not yet roll over on to his back, and twisted his head awkwardly to look at her. His smile broke her heart, and she picked him up and hugged him fiercely. 'Come on, Joey,' she said. 'Time for your rest.'

She carried him to his cheerful little room, and lifted him over the rail into his cot. She bounced him up and down on his feet, and he laughed.

'That's it, Joey,' she said. 'Bouncey, bouncey! We'll have you right in no time, my lad!'

But as she drew his blue curtains with sailors dancing across them, and touched the mobile over his cot to send the bunnies leaping wildly, making Joe laugh, she knew in her heart that it was not going to be that simple.

CHAPTER THIRTY-SEVEN

In a few short weeks, autumn turned to winter. The chestnut on the Green deposited its remaining yellowing leaves on the Standing seat, but nobody wanted to sit on it now. The wind was too cold for Fred Mills and his mates. Fred was still to be seen, but busy in his garden, clearing the ground ready for planting in the spring, harvesting new young leeks and sniffing with pleasure the earthy, oniony smell as he trimmed the tops and bundled up a half-dozen for Ellen Biggs.

The pastures were empty, lying fallow whilst cows and bullocks had been taken into warm, noisy metal barns. In the school playground, the children's games were vigorous: follow-my-leader, and lines of nine-year-old toughs, arms linked, charging groups of huddled girls. The girls, well wrapped up in Marks and Spencer padded anoraks and scarlet scarves knitted by their grannies, dispersed in mock terror with piercing screams.

Joyce Turner, wearing her best coat, sat nervously on the edge of a chair in Ivy Beasley's kitchen, sipping a cup of tea.

Since her first impulsive walk into the village on her own, and the quick scuttle back when she suddenly felt lost and terrified, Joyce had continued to venture out, a little further each day, often stopping to talk to Mandy and little Joe, and then calling for a cup of tea with Ivy Beasley.

It had been Ivy who had stirred up so much trouble between Joyce and Bill before her breakdown, but now Joyce had the strength to discourage Ivy's gossip, and deliberately blocked any mention of Peggy Palmer in their conversations. In her perambulations round the village, Joyce had not once been into the shop.

This afternoon was to be a big milestone. Joyce was going with Ivy on the bus into Tresham, to do a bit of shopping and have a cup of tea at the new Iris Café by the market. 'It's full of stuff like my mother used to have,' said Ivy. 'All glass lampshades and fringed tablecloths. You'll like it, Joyce,' she added encouragingly.

Joyce set down her cup carefully in the saucer, and looked at Ivy's clock. 'Isn't it time we were getting out there?' she said.

The bus shelter was unusually crowded. The cold wind, having driven the early morning mist away from the Green, now blew paper wrappers from the wire basket outside the shop into the street, where they fell into puddles and finally came to rest, mud-soaked and soggy. Joyce watched the Jenkins terrier chasing a plastic ball, lifted by the wind from the school playground. She saw Mark Jenkins amongst a group of small boys bawling after the terrier, doubling up with laughter at the little dog's antics.

'It's very cold, Ivy,' she said, as they crossed the road to the shelter. 'Don't you think it would be better to go in to town on a warmer afternoon?'

'No,' said Ivy flatly. 'Come on, Joyce, nothing's going to eat you.' She marched into the bus shelter, where a space cleared for her on the bench, and sat down, motioning Joyce to sit beside her.

'Morning, Ivy . . . morning, Joyce.' It was Ellen Biggs, bizarrely dressed in a moulting rabbit-skin coat and a bright blue scarf wrapped several times around her head and neck. She carried her usual rexine bags, now empty, but to return full of bargains from the Supashop. Ellen felt sorry that many of her purchases were not made at the village shop, but economy was vital for her survival, and she could often pick up food which was past its sell-by date, going really cheap.

Jean Jenkins stood in one corner, with Eddie in his pushchair. 'Morning, Joyce,' she said, with a very kind smile. 'Nice to see you on the bus.'

Old Fred Mills, surrounded as always by a cloud of tobacco smoke, nodded towards Ivy and Joyce. 'Mornin',' he said. 'Nasty cold wind.'

The yellow and green shopping bus came slowly along by the Green, and drew to a halt.

'In you get, ladies,' said the young driver. 'It's nice and warm in here.'

'Cheeky little bugger,' muttered Fred Mills, struggling up the step. But Joyce Turner smiled shyly at the driver, and proffered her fare with a shaking hand.

'Here will do,' said Ivy, taking hold of Joyce's arm proprietorially, and guiding her into a seat at the front.

'Couldn't we sit nearer the back?' whispered Joyce.

'No point,' said Ivy. 'We'd only have further to walk when we get out.'

Joyce was overwhelmed by the noise and traffic smells of market day in Tresham. She had been a recluse for so long that she had forgotten what a busy town was like. Clinging on to Ivy's arm, she followed obediently from one shop to another, unable to make any decision about purchases, content to keep up with Ivy, and very relieved when they finally sat down at a small table in the Iris Café.

Ivy ordered tea and toasted teacakes from a waitress dressed in an old-fashioned uniform of black dress with tiny white apron, and the two women sat looking out of the window at the bustling market outside. Joyce slowly relaxed, and began to enjoy the teacake, full of currants and oozing butter. Ivy smiled at her.

'Not as bad as you feared, then, Joyce,' she said,

adjusting her grey felt hat to subdue a stray wisp of hair.

Joyce was about to reply when a stooping, middle-aged man stopped by their table. He was sombrely dressed in a dark blue coat and neat trilby hat, and his eyes were concealed behind tinted lenses in small, metal-framed spectacles. He lifted his hat a fraction, and spoke, directing himself to Joyce, who looked astounded.

'It's Mrs Turner, isn't it?' he said, and his pale face was transformed by his sudden smile.

'Donald!' said Joyce, sitting up straight, the blood rushing to her cheeks. 'Fancy seeing you!'

'I could say the same,' he said in a quiet, pleased voice.

'Well,' said Ivy tartly, 'aren't you goin' to introduce me, Joyce?'

Joyce hastily made a confused introduction, and Ivy nodded at the man. 'And where did you two meet?' she said, taking charge.

'May I join you for a few moments?' said the man, and sat down next to Joyce, taking off his hat to reveal thin, colourless hair brushed back close to his head.

'It was in Merryfields,' he said, with no trace of embarrassment. 'I was in hospital for a few weeks, needing a rest after failing to recover from the death of my wife. And Joyce here, dear Joyce, was a great source of comfort and contributed greatly to my recovery.'

Ivy, astonished, for once could think of nothing to say. And when Joyce and Donald Davie, who was, it emerged, a retired schoolteacher from Bagley, fell into close conversation and reminiscence about their time in Merryfields, Ivy relapsed into irritated silence. Finally she looked at her watch and announced that if they were to catch the bus back to Ringford they had better be getting a move on.

Joyce Turner and Donald Davie took amiable leave of each other, and to Ivy's increasing amazement, Joyce said, 'May see you again, then, Donald,' as they set off for the bus station.

★

When they got off the bus at Ringford's deserted, chilly bus shelter, it was already almost dark, and the light from the shop spread half way across the road.

'Right then, Joyce,' said Ivy. 'Now you've broken the ice, you can go into Tresham any time you like, with me, or on your own.' She hesitated, seemed about to say something else, but shut her mouth firmly and began to cross the road.

'I certainly shall,' said Joyce, in a voice that Ivy had not heard for many years. 'And thank you very much, Ivy, for all you've done.'

Sounds a bit final, thought Ivy, but she was already unlocking her front door, and her thoughts were directed to poking the fire into life and getting a juicy lamb chop straight into the oven for her supper.

CHAPTER THIRTY-EIGHT

Peggy Palmer woke up early, feeling cold. The bedcovers had drifted off during the night, and her legs and feet were frozen.

She pulled on Frank's old dressing gown, warmer than her own, and, pushing her icy feet gratefully into sheepskin slippers, went over to the window to draw the curtains. Outside, in the brilliant winter sun, fairyland awaited her.

Hoar frost had come in the night, and the great, bare chestnut on the Green dazzled and shimmered in the sun. Above the school roof, itself a sheet of glitter and rime, the sycamore that sheltered the children from the heat in the summer now spread its diamond-winking branches over the playground in an ecstasy of rainbow sparkles.

Peggy gasped, and opened the window needing to be part of it. The clean, bright air filled her lungs and she could have laughed with delight.

She pulled on yesterday's clothes, ran a comb quickly through her hair, and without washing or brushing her teeth, rushed downstairs, nearly tripping over Gilbert who, as usual, dogged her footsteps demanding food.

'You'll have to wait,' she said. 'I'll be back soon.'

Glancing at the clock on the mantelpiece, she saw it was early, but shook her head. 'Who cares?' she said to Gilbert. 'I might never see another morning like this!'

She opened the back door and walked quickly down the side of the shop, letting herself out of the side gate, and setting off at a cracking pace across the Green. She looked back once, and saw her footmarks in the frosty grass. How wonderful, she thought, and, in case Ivy was looking out of Victoria Villa, she waved gaily in that direction.

The lane up to Bagley Woods was shaded from the sun, and Peggy shivered, quickening her pace to keep warm. She turned off into the wood, through the broken fence and along the worn footpath, much used by village boys and courting couples. Everything snapped and crackled as she walked, and the sun through frosty trees picked out the brilliant colours of a rapidly disappearing cock pheasant.

I mustn't be too long, thought Peggy, but she couldn't turn back. The air was so clear and exhilarating that she could have walked on for ever.

As she approached the familiar clearing in the trees, where a giant oak had been felled, leaving a wide, mossy stump, she stopped suddenly. Someone else was there before her, and she knew who it was. They had met there many times before. She turned slowly, meaning to retreat, but trod on a thin, dead twig, and it broke with a snap.

'Peggy?' Bill Turner stared in amazement, not at all sure that he hadn't conjured her up from his deepest thoughts. He didn't move, and she walked slowly towards him.

'Morning Bill,' she said, as if they had met in the street. 'Beautiful morning, isn't it?'

He nodded, and laughed at her formality. Peggy felt uncomfortable, but took his outstretched hand. She looked up at him, his unruly hair spiked with bits of twig and leaf, and thought sadly that she had never loved anyone so much.

'How did you know?' Bill said.

'Know what? That you would be here?'

'No. How did you know that I had something very important to tell you.'

Peggy looked at him, puzzled. 'I didn't know,' she said. 'I woke up and saw this fantastic morning and had to be out in it. What important news?'

In spite of the sun, and the sparkling hoar frost, and Bill's warm, exciting presence, she felt a shiver of fear. Whatever it was, the news was not likely to be good.

'Sit down here,' said Bill, taking off his jacket and spreading it over the tree stump.

'I came back from the pub last night,' he said, 'and Joyce was still up. She's usually in bed early, so I was worried, afraid that she might be slipping back. But she didn't look angry, or mad, like she used to.'

Peggy tucked her hand into Bill's and squeezed.

'She said she was making a cup of tea, and did I want one. So we sat drinking tea by the fire, and then she came out with it.'

He was silent, looking away over the valley, where the village shone in the early morning sun. He could just make out the small figure of William Roberts on his bike, delivering the newspapers before school. The door of Victoria Villa opened, and he saw a tiny Ivy Beasley pick up a single milk bottle from her step and quickly vanish.

'Came out with what, Bill?'

He took his hand away from hers and stood up, turning away and looking through to the far side of the wood.

'Come on, Bill. What did Joyce say?'

Bill turned back and looked straight at Peggy, sitting like a plump, middle-aged wood nymph on the tree stump, and shrugged.

'It was a bit of a bloody shock, gel,' he said. 'She says she wants a divorce. That's what she said. "I want a divorce, Bill, and as soon as possible." Then she went to bed.'

CHAPTER THIRTY-NINE

It was pension morning, and the shop bell jangled non-stop. Peggy had worked all weekend setting out the Christmas corner, and now several children hung over the small, colourful bags of balloons, cheap books and packs of talc and soap, suitable for mums and sisters. They picked them up, changed their minds, and put them down again, eventually bringing their final choice over to the counter to give Peggy handfuls of hot coins.

She was busy, occupied and concentrating on her customers, and although her legs ached and her throat was gravelly, the unmistakable preliminary to a cold, she could not subdue a bubble of excitement in the pit of her stomach. Bill's news had been a bombshell, and she had hugged it to herself ever since. At last, there was hope. Maybe no more than that, but it was enough to keep her awake at night with possible, wonderful scenarios, and to send her whistling tunelessly out in the garden to hang out her few pieces of washing on bright, frosty mornings. On one such, Ivy Beasley had been standing by her woodpile, and Peggy called out 'Lovely morning, Miss Beasley!' Ivy Beasley had looked at her as if she was mad.

And now, this damp, chill morning, it was Mandy Bates's own very far from hopeful news that brought her crashing down to earth. The last customer had gone, and

Peggy waved Mary York goodbye as the faithful, hard-working girl set off back home on her bicycle.

Thankfully filling the kettle and taking bread from the bin to make herself a sandwich, Peggy heard the shop bell once more. 'Damn,' she said. 'Damn and blast. Just when I was about to – '

'Mrs P.!' It was Mandy's voice, and as Peggy reluctantly put the ham back in the fridge, Mandy appeared at the kitchen door, holding a smiling Joe in her arms. 'Can you spare a minute?'

Peggy nodded, and pointed at a chair. 'Sit down, Mandy, and let me have a cuddle of our boy.'

She lifted Joe on to her lap and undid his woolly scarf, took off his hat and smoothed down his soft hair. 'There,' she said, 'it's so warm in this kitchen, you'll not feel the benefit when you go out again.'

'Sorry to come at your lunchtime, Mrs P.,' Mandy said, 'but I need some advice.' Her voice was flat, quiet, as if she was reciting something well-rehearsed.

Peggy nodded encouragingly, and gave Joey a wooden spoon to bang on the table.

'You might have heard,' said Mandy, still in the same even tone, 'that we've been to see a specialist and he says Joey has brain damage.'

Peggy opened her mouth to speak, to say that she had heard rumours over the past few weeks and discounted them, but Mandy carried on relentlessly.

'That means he won't develop properly without lots of help, and even then he may not ever be quite normal, not like other children. Robert and me have got over the first shock.' She paused and swallowed hard, and Peggy thought, Oh, no you haven't, Mandy dear.

'I've told my mum and dad,' Mandy continued, picking up the spoon from the floor and handing it back to Joe, 'but we don't know how to tell Olive and Ted, and I thought – me and Robert thought – you might be able to help.'

My goodness, thought Peggy, trying to absorb the awful news about Joe and answer Mandy's appeal at the same time. She hugged Joe tight, and prayed for guidance.

And there it was, as if in answer, the jangling of the doorbell and Olive Bates's voice calling, 'Shop! Anybody about?'

'Sit there, Mandy, don't move,' said Peggy, handing Joe back to his mother. She went through to the shop and greeted Olive, who handed her a card of wooden pegs, saying, 'I'll have these, please. Where they go to is a mystery. I reckon the old dog chews them up.' She paid Peggy, who put the money in the till, and said, 'Now, Olive, you've come at just the right moment. Follow me.'

The three women sat round the table, and Joey was handed to his grandmother. He reached up to touch her face, and she laughed, giving him a smacking kiss on his red cheeks. 'Teething, is he, Mandy?' she said. 'He feels a bit hot.'

'It's this kitchen,' said Peggy. 'When the wind is in the east the Rayburn always goes mad. I can't control it. Take his coat off, Olive.'

After a few minutes' desultory conversation, silence fell, and Peggy looked at Olive. 'Mandy has something to tell you,' she said.

'I know,' said Olive.

'What do you know?' said Mandy, looking surprised.

'It's about Joey, isn't it?' said Olive.

'Yes, but it's difficult to find the words,' said Mandy in a muffled voice.

'No need,' said Olive. 'He's a bit backward, isn't he? I've known for some time, but it doesn't make any difference to Ted and me. He's our Joey, and we love him, and that's all there is and all about it.'

'And Ted?' said Mandy.

Olive nodded. 'He's not such a fool as he seems. Though God knows he often seems one. He won't say much, but he feels the same as me. Anything you need, Mandy, any help and that, you just ask. We're always there.'

Mandy put her hands up to her face, her shoulders shaking. The two other women said nothing, but Olive got up and put her arm round Mandy, while Peggy took down some mugs from the dresser.

The whistling kettle had a head of steam already, and when Peggy put it on the hotplate the whistle cap blew off and landed with a shriek on the floor, sending Gilbert scuttling off out through the cat flap. Joey, who had a taste for good old-fashioned slapstick, collapsed into helpless giggles.

Peggy smiled, and then, because the child's laughter was infectious, began to chuckle. Olive looked at her, surprised, but Mandy reached out and took Joey's hand. 'It's not bloody fair,' she said angrily. She turned to the other women, and Peggy's laughter died.

'You'd think he'd had enough, wouldn't you,' she said, 'what with his bad beginning, and struggling for life. And now this. Just don't let that Reverend Brooks anywhere near me, that's all. It's not bloody fair.'

In the silence that followed, Olive collected up Joe's outdoor clothes and began to put them on. Peggy stood with her back to the Rayburn, grasping the rail and feeling the comforting warmth. She cursed herself for being so tactless. Neither she nor Olive, in the face of such searing distress, could think of anything to say.

CHAPTER FORTY

The Standing Arms was looking its festive best. In the corner, by the huge log fire, Don Cutt had set up a tall Christmas tree, and his hard-working wife had found time to decorate it with golden bells and bows of scarlet ribbon. At the top, a tinsel fairy danced and played a tinkling version of 'Jingle Bells', to the delight of Eddie Jenkins. Eddie should not have been there, but he had followed his father, who was buying cans of Guinness to take home. Don Cutt, in a gentle mood for once, had shown Eddie the musical fairy.

'Come on, Eddie,' said Foxy Jenkins. 'Home to bed. Say goodnight to Mr Cutt.'

Robert Bates, leaning up against the bar with a pint of bitter in front of him, wondered whether his Joey would ever follow him into the pub, and jump up and down in delight at the sight of a dancing fairy.

Joe's first birthday party had passed quietly, with Bridget and little Poppy coming to tea, and Peggy walking up with Olive and Ted as soon as the shop shut to join in the celebration. This first milestone birthday was hard for Mandy, and she was well aware that Bridget and the others were doing their best to keep up her spirits.

Bridget had, of course, mentioned the party to Susan Standing, and had been shocked by her reaction. 'Is he really one year old, Bridget?' she had said. 'He does begin to look very odd. It's nothing catching, is it, Bridget? No, of course not. And I'm sure you're right – it will be a kindness to take Poppy along.' Bridget had said very firmly that Poppy loved Joey dearly, that he was her best friend and she would be buying something really nice for Poppy to give him.

Robert had taken photographs of the party, of Joey and his birthday cake and his presents. When he collected the prints and showed them to Mandy he was suddenly shocked by how different Joey looked, floppy and slack. And, he thought, punishing himself, his lovely smile just looks vacant in that one with Poppy. He said nothing to Mandy, and was quite unaware that her thoughts were painfully the same.

Now Christmas was almost upon the village, and the regulars at the pub embraced the festive spirit good and early. Robert had taken to nipping down for a pint straight after work, reluctant to go back to the bungalow and join in the exercises which made Joey scream and Mandy bite her lip in frustration and misery.

'Hello, Robert,' said Tom Price, coming in for a packet of cigarettes. 'You're down here early, boy.'

'Can I buy you one?' said Robert, hoping Tom would stay and keep him company.

'Well, Doreen will have the tea on the table any minute,' said Tom, 'but, yes, Robert, I could manage a quick half. Thanks.'

They talked about farming for a bit, and then Tom asked how the business was going. He took his own car to Robert for servicing, and was pleased with the result, and he knew many of his friends had followed suit.

'Going really well,' said Robert. 'I've got more than enough work already.'

'Raking it in, then, young Rob?' said Tom, teasing.

Robert shook his head and answered seriously. 'No, no,'

he said. 'I decided to plough as much back into the business as possible for at least two years, and I'm sticking to it. Mandy does a bit of hairdressing here and there now, while Mum has Joe, and she brings in quite a decent sum each week. So we're doing all right.'

'And is Joey doing all right, with them exercises and things?' said Tom. He was a big, bluff farmer, from generations of big, bluff farmers, but he was not wholly insensitive, and could tell from Robert's face that all was far from well.

'He hates 'em,' said Robert. 'Mandy steels herself to it, and I often wonder whether it's worth it. He doesn't seem to make much progress. Mind you, they've been talking for the last couple of weeks at the clinic about Joey attending a special class in Tresham. Seems a bit young to me, but they say the stimulation and that would help him.'

'What does Mandy say?'

Robert took a deep gulp of beer, and wiped his mouth with the back of his hand. 'She doesn't say much, but we don't really agree about what to do next,' he said.

Ah, thought Tom, here it comes.

Robert stared into his glass. 'If Joe's got to go to a special school in Tresham,' he said, 'maybe full-time later on, Mandy thinks it would make more sense if we moved to town, set up the business there. No long journeys for Joey, and her mother could help her out a lot with babysitting.'

'But Olive does that, doesn't she?' said Tom.

'Yep,' said Robert gloomily, 'and if we move to Tresham, it'll break her heart.'

Tom looked at his watch. 'Listen, Robert,' he said, 'I can't stop now, but why don't you and Mandy bring Joe up to tea with us on Sunday? We could put our heads together and maybe come up with something.'

Poor young buggers, he thought, as he walked back up the dark, wet street. It was mild, not at all seasonal, and across the misty Green he could see the lights of the Hall.

Makes you wonder, he said to himself, if there's any justice. Some folks have got it all, and others get nothing but trouble.

A bicycle came fast out of Macmillan Gardens, and swerved to avoid Tom, who was walking in the middle of the road.

'That you, William Roberts?' Tom said sharply. 'Why don't you look where you're going, you young fool!'

Inside the quiet, empty church, Peggy lingered over her flower arrangement, adjusting sprays of white chrysanthemums and dark green holly from her garden, unable to make anything like a satisfactory result. The other women had gone home hours ago, leaving perfect pedestals and pyramids of forced white lilies and yellow iris, scarlet-berried holly and trails of shining ivy. Peggy had turned off the strip heaters, conscious of economy, It was very still and cold.

It's warmer outside, thought Peggy. I suppose it's the stone floor holding the damp and cold. She had been allotted the big vase at the top of the chancel steps and, losing patience, rammed a prickly stem of holly into the middle of the flowers. The vase tipped, rolled precariously close to the edge of the steps, and water spilled out over the stone floor and strip of red carpet which led to the altar.

'Damn!' she said.

'Peggy Palmer!' said a voice behind her, and she turned round guiltily to see Bill, grinning broadly, standing just inside the studded oak door.

'Bill! That door usually creaks when it opens,' Peggy said, relieved that it was not the vicar.

'I oiled it last week, ready for Christmas,' said Bill. 'Saw the lights on, and thought I'd better check.' He walked up the aisle to where Peggy stood. 'That's a right mess you've made there, gel,' he said. 'We'd better clear it up.'

They fetched cloths and a mop from the musty vestry,

and got up most of the water, but there was still a spreading wet stain on the red carpet.

'What can I do about that?' said Peggy.

'Nothing,' said Bill unhelpfully. Then he saw that Peggy was really worried, and added, 'It'll be dry by tomorrow, just looks worse than it is.'

What would I do without you?' Peggy said.

'You don't have to,' said Bill. 'Come here.'

'No! It'd be blasphemous, or something.'

'Nobody's looking,' said Bill.

'That's not what the Reverend Nigel Brooks would say,' said Peggy, but she let Bill put his arms around her, and it was several minutes before she broke away.

'See,' said Bill, 'no thunderbolts.'

'Don't tempt fate,' said Peggy. 'Now, come on, make yourself useful and help me finish this wretched arrangement, then we can lock up and go home.'

They brushed up the broken stalks and leaves, and tidied away the broom and dustpan. Bill locked the church door and gave the key to Peggy. In the dark porch, its low beams almost brushing the top of Bill's head, they stood close to one another, arms hanging by their sides, with only their cheeks touching.

'I love you, Peggy,' said Bill.

'And I love you,' Peggy replied. She longed to ask him more about Joyce and her decision to get a divorce. But apart from telling her that Joyce now felt she had the confidence to move out, that she at last recognised that their marriage was finished, and that although there was no one else yet, there might well be, one day, Bill had not wanted to talk about the future. Still shocked, I suppose, she thought. Better bide my time, as we say here in Ringford.

'Goodnight, Bill,' she said, 'see you tomorrow.' She set off down the little path, feeling her way carefully for fear of slipping on wet leaves.

CHAPTER FORTY-ONE

One week before Christmas, the weather changed. The north-east wind blew down the valley of the Ringle like a scourge, and old Fred Mills, so wrapped up in scarves that only his eyes were visible, pronounced to the assembled company in the shop – all three of them – that there'd be snow by morning or he was a Dutchman.

The yellowish-grey sky hung over the village like a blanket in need of a wash. Daylight hardly seemed to arrive before it was waning again, and the school lights shone out, through the paperchains and bunches of holly, from the high windows and across the gloomy, slippery playground, where only the most stalwart of the Chargers ventured at playtime to kick a ball around and have a half-hearted, ritual punch-up.

It was cold in Robert Bates's workshop, and he had put on an extra jersey underneath his overalls. He had left the bungalow's warm kitchen after breakfast, waving at Joey in his high chair as he passed the window on the way. Mandy had been spooning cereal into Joe, but she had not looked up to smile at Robert, and his face was grim as he unlocked the big sliding doors and turned on the lights.

We can't go on like this, he thought, as he set to work on Pat Osman's little Fiat. All the warmth had gone from their relationship, and although he knew that Mandy had not come to terms with Joe's handicap, not really, he wished she would at least talk to him, share the hurt and the disappointment. It was as though someone had died: the Joe they'd brought home in triumph, the son they'd begun to plan a future for. We have to accept that it's not going to be like that, Robert thought bitterly, and we need to grieve together.

Mandy poured all her time and love into the one-year-old child, who couldn't walk, or even sit up by himself, and made only limited sounds that were nowhere near the beginnings of speech.

'But look at his eyes, Bridget,' Mandy said often. 'You can see from his eyes that he's bright. It's all there, I know it is. It's only a case of working hard with him. We shall get there, I know we shall.'

Bridget agreed with her, not having the heart to disagree, and continued to bring little Poppy to play with Joe. Poppy Standing was like quicksilver, everywhere at once, and Joe followed her with his eyes, laughing and waving his arms in delight. She was unusually patient with him, placing toys on the special tray in front of his chair, and repeatedly picking them up when he knocked them flying with his uncontrolled movements.

'Bad Joey!' she would say, rebuilding a tower of bricks for Joey to demolish once more with a crow of success.

And now it was nearly Christmas, and Robert felt no sense of pleasurable anticipation. He went into his small, partitioned office to telephone for spares from Tresham, and saw on his desk the photograph of Mandy and Joey, taken a couple of days after the homecoming from the hospital. She looked so happy, thought Robert. I'd do anything to bring back that smile.

But Mandy continued to prepare meals, make beds, go out to her hairdressing appointments, get up to Joe when he screamed in the night, and return to the warm bed, turning away from Robert's arms and lying rigid with her face to the wall.

The depot in Tresham took a long time answering the telephone, and Robert looked idly out of the window, where tiny, isolated flakes of snow were hanging in the air, almost without the weight necessary to take them to the ground. He wished he had someone to talk to. It was one of the disadvantages of working for yourself, on your own. Perhaps she blames me, he thought, not for the first time. But what could I have done, more than I did already? Maybe I should have been firmer about her giving up work sooner, spent more time at home so she didn't go on working rather than being bored and lonely. If, maybe, perhaps, thought Robert, tired of all the useless speculation about what might have been.

He gave the depot the details, and the friendly store-keeper wished him a happy Christmas. 'Have a drink on me mate,' he said. 'I'll see you again after the New Year.'

The only happy Christmas I'm likely to get, thought Robert, is down at the Arms, and I shall need more than one drink to get in the mood.

Bridget Reilly bathed Poppy and gave her supper, leaving Susan to put her into bed. She had a quick shower herself, and then set off on foot for the village, heading for the Osmans' house. Pat Osman was having a make-up party, and Bridget thought she might pick up a few last-minute presents.

It was bitterly cold, and the sky had cleared. A sliver of moon and sprinkle of stars gave enough light for her to see her way down the long, shadowy avenue, and she was not in the least bit nervous. At home in Ireland, in the village where she was born, she walked about in the dark by herself all the time.

She passed Bates's Farm, and saw a light shining from the front room window. Must have been a shock for the old couple, she thought, although they've been very good with

Mandy lately. Poor old Mandy, she was far from adjusting to it yet. Not sure about Robert. It's quite difficult to know what he's thinking. He doesn't wear his heart on his sleeve, young Robert – unlike his cousin Dan . . .

Bridget walked on, quicker than before to keep her blood circulating. As she passed the vicarage, she heard thin voices singing, 'In the bleak midwinter, frosty wind made moan . . .' She shivered, and wrapped her scarf closer round her ears.

The Christmas wreath on Pat Osman's door was bright and colourful in the porch light. Scarlet berries, bows of ribbon, small, gold-sprayed fir cones, all sparkling and welcoming the ladies to Pat's party. Bridget took off her coat and scarf and joined the others in the warm sitting-room where Pat had laid out her wares.

'Mandy coming?' Bridget said.

Pat shook her head. 'I did ask her,' she said, 'but she made some fairly feeble excuse. She's very depressed these days, poor kid, and not surprising.'

And then they were into the intricacies of colourways and skin textures, and everything else was forgotten.

Robert worked late in the garage, putting off the time when he would return to the bungalow for his tea. The invoices were piling up, waiting for Mandy to type them out and send them off, and Robert shuffled them round, aware that some should have been sent off weeks ago. Before the bad news about Joe, Mandy had taken a pride in keeping the accounts and books in good order, but now Robert hardly dared to mention the subject.

Tea was on the table, and Joey in his high chair, chewing a piece of apple. He grinned at Robert as he came in, and Robert ruffled his hair and kissed the top of his head.

'Don't make him choke, Robert,' said Mandy.

'Should he have a piece as big as that?' said Robert.

Joe answered the question by choking violently and

beginning to go blue in the face. Mandy rushed to pat him on the back, and when this failed, she picked him up and held him upside down, giving him a good thump. The piece of apple flew out on to the floor, and she righted Joey, cuddling him and calming him down. 'See?' she said sharply to Robert.

'My fault, I suppose, like everything else,' he said.

Mandy didn't answer, and Robert sat down at the table. He took a few mouthfuls of food, and then pushed his plate away. 'It's no good,' he said. 'I'm not hungry. Maybe I'll eat it later.'

'Off down the pub again?' said Mandy, as Robert reached for his coat.

'Shan't be long,' he said, and went quietly out of the back door.

There were very few people in the pub, and Robert stood at the bar, talking to Don Cutt.

'How's the family, Robert?' Don said.

'OK thanks,' said Robert. 'I expect you'll be busy later on. Isn't it the Christmas draw tonight?'

Don Cutt confirmed this, and reflected that Robert had changed the subject pretty smartly. What was the lad doing down here at this time of the evening? He busied himself with setting out glasses and refilling gaps on the shelves.

The door opened and Robert's cousin Dan walked in. He had a new leather jacket, and his hair had been carefully brushed into shape. He looked at Robert, grimy and still in his overalls. 'Rob? What are you doing here? Mandy gone out?'

Robert shook his head, and didn't smile. 'Nope,' he said, 'just thought I'd come down for a quick half.'

'What are you doing later on?' said Dan. 'Is Mandy goin' to this party thing of Pat Osman's?'

'I don't know,' said Robert. 'She didn't mention it.'

Dan paid for his cigarettes, and offered one to Robert.

'Don't smoke, thanks,' said Robert. 'You should know that.'

Dan laughed. 'Mind on other things,' he said. 'Did you know that Bridget has chosen to go to this party on her last night before goin' home to Ireland for Christmas? What a waste!'

Robert ordered another beer from Don Cutt. 'Make it a pint,' he said.

Dan frowned. 'Why don't you come with us? Some of the lads are going over to Bagley later on. I could pick you up.'

Robert shook his head and took a long drink. 'I'm all right, Dan,' he said. 'Don't worry about me.'

An hour passed, and Robert still sat on the bar stool. 'Shouldn't you be off home for your tea?' said Don Cutt, not wanting to set up yet another pint for Robert.

Before Robert could answer, Foxy Jenkins came over to the bar. 'What you goin' to have, Robert?' he said. 'Don't like to see an empty glass.'

Robert accepted the offer, and raised his glass to Foxy. 'Cheers,' he said. 'felici . . . felicita . . . well, you know, Fox . . . happy Christmas.'

Foxy looked at Don Cutt in surprise. The publican said nothing, just shook his head warningly.

'How about a game of darts, Robert?' Foxy said, taking the hint.

But Robert refused, saying he'd been doing a lot of close work and his eye was not in. He slumped with his elbows on the bar, and Fox drifted away, looking worried.

Colin Osman and Peter Dodwell came in together. They had become friends, united in their efforts to preserve what they saw as village tradition and heritage, to the amusement of the dominoes school in the Arms.

'Hi, Bob,' said Colin Osman. He ordered drinks, and included another pint for Robert.

'How's Joe?' said Peter Dodwell. His own small son was

his constant delight, and he felt sorry for Robert. But he couldn't find the words to express his sympathy, and just nodded when Robert muttered a vague reply.

Colin Osman stepped in, bright and breezy. 'We're planning a regatta, Bob,' he said. 'It'll be just for the children, some time in late summer, when things go a bit flat after fêtes and garden parties are finished.'

'Good idea,' said Robert, without interest.

'Not too many regattas these days, so Dodders and I thought we'd have a revival. Can we count on your help, Bob?'

Robert had not the faintest idea what he was talking about, but he took a deep swig and said, 'Course you can. Anything I can do to help. You know me, good old reliable Robert Bates.'

Colin raised his eyebrows but made no comment. 'Come on, then, Dodders,' he said, 'let's go and do some strategy planning.' He and Peter Dodwell drifted away, leaving Robert at the bar.

The pub filled up, and Robert retired to a corner with his glass. He saw his father come in, and moved so that his back was towards the bar. Fred Mills and the domino school at the next table asked him to join them, but he declined, accepting their offer of another beer instead.

The draw was carried out noisily, with much chaffing and mock complaints of result-rigging, and Robert laughed along with the rest, not sure now what he was laughing at, and not really caring. He watched his father leave the bar, and then got to his feet.

Time, gentlemen, PLEASE!' yelled Don Cutt. His voice reverberated round the pub and made itself heard even over the hubbub of the celebrating crowd.

'Give us a quick one, before I go,' said Robert, propping himself up against the bar.

Don Cutt shook his head. 'Too late, Robert,' he said, 'and anyway, I think you've had enough for one night.

More than enough,' he added, as he watched Robert swaying away towards the gents.

Michael Roberts, a hard-drinking man himself, nodded self-righteously. 'If 'e was a son o' mine,' he said, ''e'd not be down 'ere knockin' it back and wastin' 'is money. And 'is hand isn't goin' to be very steady when 'e's working on people's cars tomorrow mornin', is it?'

'Just as steady as yours, driving tractors and handling machinery,' said Don Cutt sharply.

He watched Robert emerge and look myopically around the pub. Most people had gone home, and Bronwen Cutt was gathering up empty glasses and plates. Tom Price stood by the fire, finishing his beer and talking to Bill Turner. He turned and saw Robert making unsteadily for the door.

'All right, then, Robert?' he called.

'Fine, fine!' said Robert, waving his hand in an approximate farewell.

Bill Turner frowned. 'He doesn't look all right, Tom, do you think we should take him home?'

'No, he's not driving, only got to find his way through to the bungalow. He can't come to any harm, and the cold air might sober him up a bit.' Tom sighed. 'Things are not good, there, you know, Bill,' he said.

'But what can we do?' said Bill. 'He doesn't want to talk about Joey or Mandy, so we can only bide our time and hope to God they don't go under.' His voice echoed Tom's, frustrated and helpless, out of his depth.

Bridget had stayed much longer at Pat Osman's than she had intended, seduced by the warmth and light and friendly gossip. They'd talked about Mandy and Joe, of course, and most of the women said they'd offered to babysit and that, but were a bit scared because Joey was different, and they weren't sure how to handle him. So they hadn't asked him to play with their children, except when Mandy stayed

251

with him, in case they did the wrong thing. They all agreed it was very difficult.

The moon and stars were now covered over with a thick layer of cloud, and Bridget was glad she had brought her torch. She walked quickly, the heels of her high boots clacking on to the road. Round the pub corner, she checked off, along the Green . . . over the bridge . . . and then she stopped dead.

There was a dark shadow by the gate to Bridge Cottage, now empty and silent. She stood quite still, and then shone her torch at the figure, the powerful beam picking out a white face, familiar and at the same time distinctly odd.

'Robert!' she said. 'What are you doing there? Shouldn't you be at home by now? Are you ill, or something?' His face had a definite greenish tinge, and Bridget walked up to him, relieved that it was Robert and not some mad rapist lurking in the shadows.

He stared at her and smiled foolishly. 'Ah ha, fair maid!' he said. 'What lucky chance has brought you my way this dark and stormy night?'

Bridget laughed, and put out her hand to steady the swaying Robert. He grabbed it, and before she knew where she was, Bridget was enveloped in a tight embrace and Robert was planting beery kisses all over her face.

'Robert!' she yelled, and struggled to break free, her glasses falling to the ground. But in his drunken ardour Robert was strong, and he held her even tighter, fumbling with the buttons of her coat. She twisted her head to one side, and screamed as loudly as she could.

'Christ, what was that?' said Bill Turner to Tom, as they came out of the pub door. Bill set off at a run towards Bates's End, and Tom followed more slowly, puffing a bit.

Bridget continued to struggle and shout, and now she was beginning to cry, appealing to Robert to let her go, and, for God's sake, not to be so silly. Just as Bill lumbered over the bridge and realised who the struggling couple were, Robert suddenly let go of her and turned away. He held on to the gate and, leaning over, was violently sick, groaning and swearing that he was about to die.

'You all right, gel?' Bill said, picking up Bridget's glasses and handing them to her.

Bridget nodded. Her hand was trembling, making the torch beam shimmer and shake. 'Yes thanks,' she said. 'The stupid bugger's drunk. We'd better get him home somehow. What's he doing down here, anyway?'

'Probably thinks he still lives here,' said Tom Price, who had caught up with the action and now pulled Robert upright, supporting him under both arms.

'Wish I did,' said Robert indistinctly. 'We were happy here. I want to go home, take me home. Where's my Mandy? Take me home to Mandy, please . . .'

Tom Price took charge, and sent Bill off with Bridget to see her home safely while he manhandled Robert as far as the pub car park, where he bundled him like a dead sheep into the back of the Land Rover, and set off for the bungalow, praying that Mandy would be well and truly asleep.

Joey's tentative wail had increased gradually to a full-blooded yell, and Mandy surfaced from sleep with a sigh.

'You go, Robert,' she said. 'Your turn.'

She realised after a minute of continuous yelling that Robert had not gone to Joe, and turned over in bed to berate him. He was not there, and she thought, good, he's on his way. But Joe went on screaming, and she got out of bed quickly, wide awake now and her irritation rising.

'Robert! Surely you can pick him up or . . .' Joe's bedroom was empty, except for the red-faced baby, and Mandy lifted him up, making soothing noises and quietening him down in seconds.

Well, where is he? she wondered. She went along to the kitchen to warm up some milk, still carrying Joe, and met the sorry sight of Tom Price supporting a collapsing, whey-faced Robert through the back door.

'Oh, my God,' Mandy said, and her eyes were bright and hard. 'Well, here's Daddy come home to us at last, Joey boy. What a comfort.'

She allowed Tom Price to get him undressed and into bed, and then she assured Tom that she would be fine, shutting and locking the door behind him as he left, embarrassed and apologetic, as if it was his fault.

Loud snores were already rumbling through the bedroom door, and she banged it shut, gave Joey his milk, and then crept into the cold sheets of the spare bed. She could still hear the snores, and put her hands over her ears. She had never felt so alone.

CHAPTER FORTY-TWO

For the first time ever, Ivy Beasley, Doris Ashbourne and Ellen Biggs had agreed to spend Christmas Day together.

'It'll have to be at Victoria Villa,' said Ivy. 'You can't expect us to come down to your draughty little hole, Ellen.'

'You're welcome to come up to MacMillan,' said Doris, 'But I'm not such a good cook as you, Ivy.' The truth was that neither she nor Ellen wanted to have the responsibility of the full Christmas meal, and were banking on Ivy's bossiness and pride in her culinary skills to win the day.

'Well, there you are, then,' said Ivy. 'Best come about twelve, and we'll have a glass of sherry.'

Ellen took a long time to dress on Christmas morning. The mention of a glass of sherry spelt a proper occasion to her, and she did not want to let Ivy down.

'Mind you,' she had said to Doris, 'Ivy would be 'appiest if I dressed meself in black and sludge from 'ead to foot. "More appropriate, Ellen Biggs" – I can 'ear 'er saying' it.'

Having nothing really sober to wear, Ellen selected a turquoise tweed skirt which had once had a jacket to match, and was well provided with pleats for comfort. To cheer it up a bit, she wore a whitish silky blouse with a lace collar, and over it a rich, purple mohair jersey. This last garment she had had to wrench from the grasp of Renata Roberts at the jumble sale, and only by hanging on like grim death had she finally won and bought it for twenty well-spent pence.

Christmas morning was cold and raw. All the snow and frost had gone, leaving a biting wind and muddy roads. Ellen locked her back door and, carrying her slippers in a plastic bag, set off slowly down her path and out into the avenue. She never stirred without her stick these days, frightened of losing her balance and falling. One of Ellen's recurring nightmares was of falling in the house and lying on the floor, cold and bruised, no one knowing she was there.

She shuffled along, feeling slippery patches over the bridge and slowing down to pick her way around them. I suppose I should ask about them alarm things you put round yer neck, she thought. Ivy's always nagging me.

Once over the bridge, she stopped, leaning on her stick, to get her breath. 'Christmas Day,' she said aloud, 'and the village looks as dead as a doornail.' The Christmas morning service had been at Waltonby this year, one of the three-parish group, and in Ringford only the midnight bells had marked the day as special. No wonder I feel so tired, thought Ellen. Them bells woke me up. They never think of folks who might be asleep, that Reverend Brooks and 'is lady wife.

By the time Ellen reached the Standing Arms, there were strong sounds of Christmas cheer coming from an open window. Might 'ave known they'd be busy in there, she muttered. And that set her thinking about the story she'd heard about Robert being drunk and disorderly, and jumping out on Bridget Reilly in the dark, and . . . Even Ellen, who loved spicy gossip more than anything, could not bring herself to think of Robert, whom she'd known since he was a baby, behaving badly. That Bridget must have encouraged him, she thought. Typical Irish.

She looked back over the Green towards the river. The water glinted grey and cold between the bare willows, and beyond the park Ellen could see the tall chimneys of the

Hall. No comforting spirals of smoke came from them, and she remembered Susan Standing saying they'd be away for Christmas, gone to stay over at Waltonby with Mr Richard's brother, where there'd be plenty of help looking after Poppy. Don't know what she'll do if Bridget decides not to come back, Ellen thought. I dare say it'll be another nanny as quick as possible, poor little mite.

Avoiding a large, muddy puddle outside the bus shelter, Ellen crossed the road to Victoria Villa. Plenty of smoke coming from the chimney here, she was glad to see. Before she could lift her hand to the knocker, the door opened, and not Ivy, but Doris Ashbourne appeared, smiling in welcome.

'Happy Christmas, Ellen,' she said. 'Come on in.'

In an atmosphere quite unlike Victoria Villa's usual polished chill, the three friends settled down to enjoy themselves. Ivy had surpassed herself, and finally, after chocolates and nuts and glacé fruits, she had ordered Doris and Ellen into the front parlour, where they were amazed to see a real fire leaping in the grate. Ivy disappeared to make the coffee.

'She did us proud, Doris,' said Ellen, patting her stomach and leaning back in the most comfortable chair.

Doris nodded, and sat in a more upright position, good for the digestion, close to the window.

'You'll not feel the warmth there, Doris,' said Ellen.

'Makes me cough,' said Doris, 'if I get too close to the heat. I'm quite all right here, thank you, Ellen.'

Ivy carried in a tray of coffee things, and set it down on a side table. 'Black or white, Ellen?' she said.

'Pardon?' said Ellen, who knew perfectly well what she meant.

'Do you want it with or without milk?' said Doris patiently.

'She knows,' said Ivy, looking fixedly at Ellen. 'Well?'

'I'll take it white, thank you, Ivy,' said Ellen, with

exaggerated politeness, 'and just a few grains of sugar, if you please.'

The warmth of the fire and the comfortable armchair began to have a soporific effect on Ellen, and Ivy gently took the cup from her hands as her head drooped and her eyes closed. She whiffled quietly, and Ivy and Doris sat without speaking for a few minutes, listening to Ellen and the deep ticking of Ivy's mother's wedding clock, and the hissing of logs on the fire.

'It's very peaceful here, Ivy, just what Christmas Day should be,' said Doris. 'I'm sure we're very grateful to you.'

'We have to count our blessings, Doris,' said Ivy. 'There's many folk not enjoying Christmas at all, I don't doubt. We should thank God for his mercies.'

Doris looked a little embarrassed. She was a regular worshipper, but would never dream of speaking in a religious way outside the church. She cleared her throat. 'I hope Robert and Mandy and little Joe are enjoying their Christmas,' she said. 'They weren't at Midnight Mass last night, I noticed. I could see Olive and Ted looking round for them, but they didn't come.'

Ivy shook her head. 'It's a bad business,' she said. 'Mind you, I blame that Bridget girl, she's flaunted it ever since she came to Ringford.'

'Flaunted what, Ivy?' said Doris innocently.

'Don't be cussed, Doris, you know perfectly well what I mean.'

'Peggy Palmer said poor Robert was in a terrible state next morning, when he came into the shop.'

'Trust Peggy Palmer to gossip,' said Ivy. 'It can only make things worse, and anyway, she has no call to discuss anyone's morals, what with her own in such a wilful mess.'

'But she's been a good friend to Mandy and Robert,' persisted Doris, anxious to be fair. 'Mandy talks to her when she doesn't talk to her own mother. And Peggy's always been fond of Robert, even since he found Frank that dreadful time.'

Ivy stood up and went over to the window. She began to speak in a low voice, her back to the room.

'As you know, Doris,' she said, 'Robert means as much to me as if he were my own child. I don't believe he could do a wrong thing to anybody, not if he was in his right mind. He was drunk, we know that, and he's not one for drinking too much. Something's very wrong there, and it'll be up to them to sort it out. But if you ask me . . .'

Ellen snorted and choked, and woke herself up. 'We do ask you, Ivy,' she said, 'don't we, Doris?'

Doris frowned at her, and turned back to Ivy. 'Go on,' she said. 'What were you going to say, Ivy?'

Ivy had not looked round, and she continued as if there had been no interruption. 'If you ask me, our Mandy has gone too far. She's all for Joey, night and day, and there's nothing left for Robert. I've watched, and so has Olive, and now something's happened like we knew it would.'

Ellen shifted in her chair, straightening her hair and sticking out her legs to catch the warmth of the fire. 'What's to be done then, Ivy?' she said. 'You're the brains in this room.'

'Nothing,' said Ivy, 'unfortunately. Nothing at all.'

'Yes, there is,' said Doris, surprising herself. The other two looked at her expectantly.

'We can pray,' she said, and fumbled for her handkerchief to cover her confusion.

It was nearly dark when Ivy's front door opened and Doris and Ellen walked carefully down the path to the wrought-iron gate.

'Goodbye, then, Ivy,' said Doris, 'and thanks again.'

'Yep,' said Ellen, 'ta very much, Ivy, that was the best Christmas I ever had, and that's the truth.'

Ivy shut the door behind them and went back into the warm room. She sat down on the comfortable chair and put her feet up on the fender. Well, that went off all right, she thought.

I should think so too, said her mother's voice in her head. You watched me put on a Christmas spread often enough.

Ivy felt her shoulders tighten. I don't want to talk now, mother, she said.

Please yourself, Ivy Dorothy, said the voice.

Perhaps because it was Christmas Day, there were no more jibes, and Ivy sat in silence. She thought of Doris and Ellen, and wondered what she would do without them. It was the best Christmas I have had, too, she thought, and closed her eyes.

CHAPTER FORTY-THREE

'My dear Mandy,' the letter began, 'I hope you had a lovely Christmas, as we did here in Ireland. My family made such a fuss of me, you'd think I'd been away for years. The weather could have been better, but you can't have everything!

'Now, Mandy, I have something to say to you that I probably couldn't say to your face, but as I am almost certainly not coming back to Round Ringford and more than likely won't see you again, I've plucked up my courage to say it in writing.

'You may have heard, or at least heard rumours, of what happened on the night Robert got so drunk. If you haven't, then I'm sorry, but you have to know, so that I can make you see straight, and stop anything worse happening.'

Mandy stood at the kitchen window, Joey banging a saucepan lid on the floor behind her, and Robert in his clean overalls disappearing up the garden path towards the workshop. This was the only letter the postlady had brought, and seeing Bridget's handwriting and an Irish postmark, Mandy had put it aside to read after breakfast. Now she stared at it, transfixed, the words jumbling up, running into one another. She rubbed her eyes and continued to read.

'That night, when I was walking back from Pat

Osman's, I saw Robert lurking around Bridge Cottage. As soon as I saw his face, I knew he was drunk, and thought he might need some help. When I got near to him, he grabbed me and kissed me, and tried to do more. But I struggled and yelled, and Bill Turner and Tom Price came running, and that was it. Robert was sick as a dog, and Tom took him home.'

Mandy sat down heavily on a kitchen chair. She had known none of this. No one had even hinted that there was more than just a sick, drunken Robert to cope with. Why? Why hadn't they told her? Oh God, Bridget of all people. My best friend . . . and probably not coming back. She read on, seeing that there were still a couple of pages of Bridget's neat script.

'All this was nothing, Mandy, nothing at all. Except for why Robert had been drinking all night and got himself in that state. And why he needed some loving so badly. Please forgive me, Mandy, for saying all this. But I've thought for a long time that you were not handling some of it very well. Joey, yes, nobody could be a better mother to him. I'd never have had your patience. But you've forgotten Robert.'

Of course I haven't, how could I? thought Mandy, looking over towards the workshop and feeling an unaccountable pang at the sight of Robert on his back, his knees up and his head under Peggy Palmer's car. She turned to the last page of the letter.

'He needs you, Mandy. God, I'm beginning to sound like some old bag of an agony aunt! But it's true. He's Joey's father, and he feels terrible about it too. I've seen him wanting to help, and you pushing him away. Well, if you're not careful, Mandy Bates, you'll push him right away, for good. That's my last word, and I don't expect you to reply. I shall miss you a lot, and Poppy and little Joey. Not Madam Standing so much! And then there's Dan. He talked of coming over to Ireland for a holiday, so maybe he will.

And then again, maybe not. My family want me to stay here, and I think it can never be quite the same again for me in Ringford.

'Anyway, Mandy, lots of love. I hope you'll understand. Yours, Bridget.'

Mandy sat staring at nothing for several minutes, until Joey, sensing something wrong, began to cry. She got to her feet and lifted him into her arms, holding him up to the window so that he could see out.

'Look, Joey,' she said, tears streaming down her face, 'look, there's Daddy, mending the car. Look, he's waving, can you wave back?'

She took his little hand and waved it, hardly seeing Robert through her tears.

Peggy walked up the narrow footpath at the side of her garden and through the small wooden gate that led to the bungalow and Robert's workshop. She had wondered whether this short cut would be used too much, once Robert had got his business going, but it hadn't worked out that way. Most people arrived at RB Engineering by car up the lane between the shop and the playing fields. Mandy came to see her often with little Joe, and Peggy was always glad to welcome them, looking forward to the day when Joey would be able to toddle down the grassy path by himself.

Hope Robert's fixed it, she thought, crossing the yard. Her car was outside, but she couldn't tell whether it was finished. There was no key in it, and she walked into the big workshop. It was tidy, productive-looking, and empty. There was no Robert, not in the inspection pit, nor in his office on the telephone.

Must have gone into the house for a coffee, or something, Peggy thought. Not like him to leave everything unlocked, though.

'Robert!' she called. 'Anybody about? Robert?'

There was no reply, and Peggy stood undecided in the middle of the yard. She needed her car to go to the wholesaler's, and would have to get back soon anyway, to relieve Mary York in the Post Office cubicle.

I could go to the bungalow, see if he's there, she thought, but held back, reluctant to trespass on Mandy's privacy with a matter of business. She thought she could see Robert through the kitchen window, but she still hesitated. I could come back later, dash out for a few minutes at lunchtime, she thought, and turned away to walk back down the path, not worried, but puzzled at the oddness of it all. There were a dozen possible explanations, but she still felt vaguely uneasy.

Buttoning her pink checked overall, Peggy came out of her kitchen and back into the shop, saying as she came, 'That was a fool's errand, Mary, not a soul up there. Perhaps I can dash up again before . . .' she stopped, seeing a woman at the Post Office cubicle window. Peggy stepped behind the big counter, instinctively taking refuge, and the woman turned.

'Good morning, Mrs Palmer,' she said quietly. 'I'm Joyce Turner, in case you didn't know.'

Mary York's face was a study, and as she reached for her jacket from its hook in the cubicle, she began speaking rapidly. 'All shipshape, Peggy,' she said. 'Everyone's been in for their pensions, and I've totalled up. We need some more first-class stamps, and Jean Jenkins' new allowance book has come.'

She came out of the cubicle, nodded desperately at Joyce, and crossed quickly to the door. 'Bye, Peggy,' she said. 'See you next week. Morning, Mrs Turner . . .' She grabbed her bike from where it leaned against the stone wall and fled as if the devil were in pursuit.

Peggy looked at Joyce, and could think of absolutely nothing to say. And then Joyce began to laugh.

'Oh dear,' she said. 'Oh dear, oh dear, poor Mary. I think she was expecting a punch-up or something.' She stopped laughing, and looked hard at Peggy, who had not even smiled.

'I need some writing paper,' she said, 'and it seemed a good idea to get it from you. I can't pretend you're my favourite shopkeeper, but we have to meet sometime, so it might as well be now.'

Peggy was dumb. She could not remember feeling so completely at a loss, and forced herself to take a writing pad and envelopes from the rack and put them down on the counter. 'Ninety pence, please,' she said in a strangled voice.

Joyce produced her purse, and counted out the exact amount. 'Can I have a bag, please?' she said.

Peggy moved stiffly, putting Joyce's purchases in a paper bag and pushing them over the counter towards her.

'Thanks,' said Joyce. 'Good morning.'

As she left, Peggy heard her mutter something. It was loud enough to hear, and was without doubt meant to be heard.

'Well, I don't know what he sees in the woman,' Joyce said. 'Still, there's no accounting for taste.'

CHAPTER FORTY-FOUR

Robert, with his back to the kitchen window, had not seen Peggy standing uncertainly in the workshop yard. Earlier, however, he had caught sight of Mandy and Joey waving to him, and seeing Mandy's face, had left Peggy's car and come running into the bungalow.

Now Mandy had gone through to put Joe down for his morning rest, and Robert sat at the kitchen table with the sheets of Bridget's letter spread out in front of him.

'What is the point?' he repeated. It had been a nonsense, nothing at all, best kept quiet. Whatever possessed the silly girl to write all this stuff to Mandy and upset her so deeply? Robert had never seen Mandy so racked, not even when they'd had the dreadful news about Joe. As the wrenching gulps and sobs had taken hold of her, Robert had put out his hand, and held hers until she had quietened down.

I've never felt so bloody helpless, he thought now, listening to her faltering voice singing Joe's special going to sleep song. What's the good of telling her there was nothing in it, that I was drunk and stupid? She knows that.

And then it came to him, quite suddenly, as if someone had drawn back a dark curtain. She was weeping for Joe, crying out all the terrible sadness that she had kept hidden all this time. It's not much to do with me and Bridget, he thought, though he was honest enough to admit to himself that rumours circulating in Ringford would not be likely to help either of them. It's because of Joey, and not wanting to look forward, and what it's done to us, to Mandy and me. That's why she's in such a state.

He stood up as she came into the kitchen, her finger to her lips, and shut the door carefully behind her.

'He's gone off, I think,' she said, without looking at him, 'but you never know. He looks as if he's asleep, and then as soon as I stop singing, he opens one eye and . . .'

She couldn't go on, her voice cracking, halting. Robert looked steadily at her, all his love and pity for her there in his face for her to see. 'Mandy,' he said, 'Mandy, love,' and she came round the table and into his arms.

They stood like that for a long time, and then Robert gently pushed her away from him, smoothing back her hair and touching her wet cheeks with his fingers.

'We'll be all right, Mandy,' he said. 'We're a family now.'

CHAPTER FORTY-FIVE

February came and went, the most dismal month of the year, with its driving rain and bitter winds, shutting down the village and confining social life to whist drives, evening classes, carpet bowls in the village hall, and the last rounds of the darts tournament in the pub. And then, just when winter seemed to be going on for ever, the wind changed, the sun came out, and with it the drifts of daffodils by the river, planted in memory of Richard Standing's mother, who loved them more than any other flower.

Jean Jenkins looked across the breakfast table to where Foxy was mopping up yolk of egg with a piece of bread. He'd been out early, seeing to the lambs. It had been a dreadful season, with nearly half the lambs dying out in the fields from persistent cold, stinging rain, and now that the weather had turned, it was hard work recouping losses and making sure of the remaining stock.

He came back in for breakfast after the children had left the house. Even young Eddie had been collected by a neighbour for his morning at the village play group.

'Never known anything like it,' Foxy said, holding out his mug for more tea, 'and we're not so badly off as some of them hill farmers in Wales.'

'Olive Bates says Ted's at his wits' end, tryin' to cope with only young Dan, and Robert much too busy now to give him a hand.'

'Ted Bates don't want to pay,' said Fox, without sympathy. 'He got so used to cheap labour with Robert, he don't realise how things have changed.'

'Well,' said Jean, clearing plates and stacking them on the draining board, 'It's been an unlucky time all round for them Bateses. Funny how it goes like that. It's not long since they 'ad that gorgeous wedding, and Robert plannin' his business and everything goin' right. And then wham! Makes it hard to believe in any sort of God, don't you think, Fox?'

Foxy looked away, out of the window and into their immaculate back garden. The cherry tree was in full bloom, and a blackbird sat swaying on the top branch. He could hear the liquid song change to an alarmed squawk as the Roberts' cat, mangy and neglected-looking like the rest of the family, sprang into a rapid ascent up the flowery branches after the bird.

'Too late,' said Fox with relief, as the bird flew off.

'I don't agree,' said Jean sniffily. 'It might just be that they need some help and understanding from the village, instead of looking the other way, which is what most of us have been doing.'

'I didn't mean . . .' said Fox.

'And anyway,' continued Jean, getting into her stride, her firm, large legs planted solidly in front of the sink as she washed the dishes with a great deal of foam and spray, 'It's not that folk don't care. As far as Joey goes, none of us know anything about 'andicapped children, and Mandy don't give anyone a chance to learn. He's not goin' to fall to pieces if somebody else looks after him for a bit, is he?'

Fox had switched off, and was scanning the racing pages. 'It's the National on Saturday,' he said. 'I quite fancy Zeta's Lass. Might be worth an each-way bet.'

Jean banged the scoured frying pan down on the draining board, and turned to face Foxy. 'Bugger the National,' she said, and Foxy stared at her. She very seldom swore.

'It's got to be done,' she said. 'It can't be put off any longer.'

'We got a couple of days,' said Fox. 'National's not till Saturday.'

'Fox!' Jean said warningly. He shrugged. 'Go on then, woman,' he said.

'It's time I had a word with Mandy Bates,' she said. 'After all, what do I know most about? That's it,' she said, without waiting for Foxy to answer. 'Children, that's what. I shall go round this morning.'

'God 'elp us all,' said Fox, and dodged out of the way.

From the wide shop window, Peggy Palmer could see Bill cutting the grass in the children's play area on the far side of the Green. The Parish Council had re-seeded it a year ago, and with proper attention it had become a smooth, green space for the younger ones of the village. Trouble-makers in their teens still jumped over the low fence and sat on the swings, smoking and kicking out at each other as they pushed the iron chains to their limits. But there were plenty of people coming and going across the Green now that the weather was warming up. The hefty lads and leggy girls had so far not sat there long enough to do any real damage.

It had been a busy morning in the shop, pensions and allowances handed out, and the shelves of Easter Eggs were nearly empty. A trip to the warehouse for me this evening, Peggy thought, straightening the much diminished display of packeted seeds. She had noticed an increasing urgency in the way village gardeners were turning out their green-houses. They cleaned and washed down with special solution, set out seed trays and buckets of compost, went into huddles over pints in the pub, discussing the best varieties of this and that, like punters waiting for the off.

Peggy noted down items needing replacement: long grain rice, cornflakes, crisps – always crisps – and those new, delicious biscuits that Ivy Beasley had said she'd need

270

to dip into her savings to buy. Old bat.

'Morning, Peggy, light of my life,' said Bill, after a quick look round the shop to make sure they were alone.

Peggy blew him a kiss from the safe side of the counter. 'You look chirpy this morning. Cutting grass must be more fun than I thought.'

'Ah,' said Bill, 'but there's more reason than that.' He stopped, and grinned infuriatingly at her.

'Out with it then, Billy boy,' said Peggy, not very sweetly.

'It'll all be through by July or August,' he said. 'Joyce is making it as easy as possible, not contesting anything and agreeing on tricky things like her being impossible to live with and that. The solicitors say there should be no problems.' He looked at her frowning face, and said, 'Well, aren't you pleased, gel?'

'It's sad, though, Bill, isn't it, just a bit sad?'

Bill's smile faded. He looked down at his hands and spread out long brown fingers. The narrow gold band which he had accepted from Joyce on their wedding day had dug itself in to his hard skin. It glinted up at him, reflecting the shop lights.

'Yep,' he said, 'of course it is. But it would be much sadder to go on with it when it's dead. Dead and buried, Peggy, and even Joyce knows it now, thank God.'

Well, why am I not delighted, whooping with joy, then? thought Peggy. Further conversation was frustrated by the shop bell jangling, and Ellen Biggs struggled in. Bill walked quickly to help her, and then fetched the chair from the Post Office cubicle for her to sit down and catch her breath.

'What's up with you two?' she said. Neither said a word, and Ellen took the hint. 'Right then, Ellen Biggs, mind your own business. Could I trouble you for a dish-cloth, my dear?' she said. 'One of them stockinette ones, please.'

★

It was Jean Jenkins' morning for cleaning at the Hall, and she planned to call on Mandy on her way back. She strode up the chestnut avenue, breathing deeply, cheered by the bright new leaves and pink flower candles opening in the sun. Avoiding the chained-up sheep dog which barked at her in a frenzy of excitement, she walked across the cobbled stable-yard and pushed open the heavy, black kitchen door.

She found Susan Standing in the kitchen, supervising Poppy, who was having a brave stab at washing up tiny cups and plates from a dolls' tea set in the big stone sink. Puddles of water stood on the floor round the chair on which Poppy was standing, and the front of her cotton teeshirt and frilly skirt were soaked.

'Ah, Jean,' said Susan, 'just the person. We need some towels, don't we, Poppy darling, and I dare not leave her for a second in case she drowns!'

Jean smiled, and thought privately that a bowl of soapy water out on the grass might be a better idea. She said nothing, however, and set off upstairs to fetch towels from the cupboard.

'Still no luck with a new nanny, Mrs Standing?' she said over her shoulder as she left the kitchen. It was common knowledge in the village that one after another hopeful applicant had been for interview at the Hall, and Mrs Standing had rejected every one.

'It's my belief,' Jean had said to Fox, 'that she's got a taste for motherhood at last, and just don't want another woman taking over her precious Poppy.'

Jean was not far wrong. Susan Standing felt quite differently about this last, late baby. She had cheerfully handed over the others, now so big and so independent, but little Poppy was special. She played with her for hours, sat her on a tiny Shetland pony and walked her up and down the grass in the orchard, while the child laughed at the jolting ride, and dug her fingers into the creature's thick, wiry mane. Richard Standing did not know what to feel about it all. He, too, was besotted with the child, but he could see difficulties ahead. There were functions to be attended, where he needed Susan by his side, and sometimes that meant nights in London, away from the village for perhaps two or three days. Some kind of live-in girl would be vital, he thought, but Susan refused to discuss it.

'Would you like me to change her, Mrs Standing?' said Jean, returning with an armful of towels.

'No thank you, Jean, we shall go and find a nice clean dress, and then whizz in to see Grannie in Bagley, shan't we, my precious,' Susan said, and gave her damp daughter an affectionate squeeze.

'Before you go, Madam,' said Jean, reverting to a formality she hadn't used for some time, 'may I have a word? It's just something I wanted to put to you, an idea, and that.'

'As soon as we get this little slippery fish dry, I shall be pleased to listen, provided it doesn't take too long.' Susan Standing left the chair standing in pools of water, and carried a protesting Poppy out through the swinging green baize door and off down the echoing passage beyond.

Jean Jenkins began to mop up.

CHAPTER FORTY-SIX

Fred Mills, rheumaticky and deaf, walked slowly with the aid of his rubber-tipped stick, down his garden path and along to the end of Macmillan Gardens. The sunshine had tempted him out, and he planned to call at the shop to collect an ounce of shag for his evil pipe. Ahead of him, he could see Jean Jenkins coming down the avenue from the Hall. She's a good gel, that Jean, he thought. Works hard and don't grumble.

'Yoo hoo! Fred!' It was Doris Ashbourne, buttoning up her beige mac which doubled as a lightweight coat in early summer. She walked smartly down the Gardens to catch up with Fred, and he waited, leaning on his stick.

'Mornin' Doris,' he said. 'You goin' to the shop?'

Doris nodded, and slowed down to keep in step with the lame old man. 'Lovely morning,' she said. 'Makes you feel like dropping everything and going for a long walk in the woods.'

'Long time since I went walking in the woods,' said Fred gloomily. Then his memories began to take over, and he smiled. 'It were a grand place this time o' the year, though, Doris. You ask our Ivy . . .'

Doris stared at him. 'What do you mean, Fred?'

They had reached the front gate of Victoria Villa, and Fred stopped. He stared up at the lace curtains, a knowing leer crossing his old pixie face. 'She weren't always such a miserable old maid, yer know, Doris,' he said.

'You aren't sayin' . . .' Doris could not bring herself to complete her sentence. The idea of Ivy and Fred Mills walking in the woods, and . . . but no, it wasn't possible. Not our Ivy.

They had reached the shop steps, and Doris took Fred's arm.

'Got yer interested there for a minit, didn't I?' he said. 'No, she never did walk out with nobody, though it weren't for the want of some tryin'. She were too young for me, o' course, but she were quite a good-lookin' gel in her youth. Not pretty, mind, but nicely set up, and always clean and neat. Still, 'er mother put paid to all that, wicked woman.'

They struggled up the steps, and were hailed by Jean Jenkins coming at a run across the Green. The Jenkins terrier saw her and rushed joyfully out of the Gardens, straight across the road, narrowly missing instant death as Robert Bates sped by in Colin Osman's Rover.

'Doris! Can I 'ave a word?' Jean's bulk finally caused her to slow up, and she sat down on the bench in the bus shelter. Doris saw Fred safely into the shop and then returned to sit by Jean.

'What's up, then?' she said.

Jean hooked her fingers into the terrier's collar and made him sit down. 'Stay,' she said, and the dog looked at her, his eyes all faithful obedience, but alert, in case he could slip away unnoticed.

'I've got this idea,' she said. 'I discussed it with Mrs Standing, and she's willing to help. I read about it in my magazine, and I reckon it'd be just what's needed for Joey Bates. And for Mandy, come to that,' she added darkly.

Doris settled on the hard bench. It was going to be a long job. It always was, when Jean started on one of her stories.

' . . . and so, we'd 'ave to get advice and that,' said Jean, several minutes later. 'But with one or two other kids in nearby villages needing special help, we could make a start. The idea is to get two or three mothers with normal tots, and they come and the mothers help, and you have a little playgroup that's not too big or frightening. All the kids play together, and the mothers chat, and they reckon it's good for everybody.'

'I wouldn't call Joey abnormal,' said Doris defensively. 'He's just a bit backward, that's all.' But even as she said it, she knew that wasn't all, and that Jean was right. A big, rumbustious playgroup like the one in the village already, wouldn't do for Joey, but in a small group there'd be other kids for Joey to play with and learn from, and those kids would soon see that Joey was a person, not something different and scary.

'It would be in his own village, of course,' said Doris. 'I reckon you're on to something there, Jean.' Jean Jenkins smiled and replied with her usual honesty.

'Can't claim the credit, Doris,' she said. 'It's been done in lots of places and works well, they say. All depends, really, on getting mothers with normal kids to take part.'

'Where do I come in?' said Doris, not beating about the bush.

'Well, with you having had the shop and being used to figures,' said Jean, 'we thought you might take on the accounts. There'll be a bit of money to handle, and we'll need to do some fund raisin'. Mrs Standing says she'll see Mr Richard about renovating the big barn round the back of the Hall, and even agreed to let Poppy come along.'

'Precious Poppy?' said Doris.

Jean nodded, 'Yep,' she said. 'I reckon I got her in a good mood.'

Jean's next stop was the bungalow, where Mandy was dusting the sitting-room, Joey sitting in his special chair with a tray laden with toys fixed to the front. He was strapped in, but even so had slipped, his head hanging, his grin one-sided.

'He looks tired, Mandy,' said Jean. 'Shall I take him out of his chair? It must be exhaustin' for him, holdin' himself up being' such an effort.'

Mandy moved quickly to Joey's chair and began to unbuckle the straps. 'No, thanks, I can manage,' she said.

Jean Jenkins narrowed her eyes and, confirmed in her purpose, began to tell Mandy about her idea.

'No need for you to go traipsin' into Tresham every day with the little chap,' she said. 'If we could get this goin' in the village, you and Robert could forget that daft plan to move to town, and you could stay where you belong.'

Belong? thought Mandy. She hadn't thought of that.

'Joey's a Bates,' said Jean Jenkins, reading Mandy's thoughts. 'It'll be up to Ringford folk to do their best for 'im. And they will, Mandy, if you give 'em a chance. I've spoken to Doris already, and she's quite happy to give a hand. And you couldn't object to Joey goin' to playschool with Poppy Standing, could you?'

'Where are the other handicapped kids coming from?' said Mandy.

'Don't know yet,' said Jean. 'It has to be sorted out by the authorities, that does, but I do know there's a little chap lives in Waltonby who doesn't walk nor talk yet, and he's nearly four. Then my sister in Bagley knows a tiny one they reckon is nearly blind, poor scrap, living the other side o' Fletching. Anyway, that's all to come. Just now, I need to know whether you and Robert would give it a go, if I can set it up?'

Mandy was quiet for a minute, then nodded, and said that she would discuss it with Robert and let Jean know. 'Here,' she said suddenly, surprising Jean by holding Joey out towards her, 'will you hold him for a minute while I put on some milk to warm?'

Well aware of what this meant, Jean Jenkins took Joey

277

carefully, and folded him, like a limp parcel, in her big arms. 'Come on, Joseph Bates,' she said. 'Come to your Auntie Jean, and let's have a lovely cuddle.'

CHAPTER FORTY-SEVEN

Just about the time the children broke up for their summer holidays, some setting off with their parents for foreign fortnights, and the Roberts boys to stay with their Auntie Susan in Telford New Town for as long as she could stand it, the weather changed from sunny days and showery nights to constant downpour, with little relief.

Ringford struggled under the heavy rain, and gardeners became discouraged at the lack of sun, moaning that they'd have nothing decent for the Horticultural Show if it went on much longer. 'Still,' said Fred Mills, 'we're all in the same boat, Ivy.' He chuckled at his apt choice of phrase, but Ivy did not smile. She said that if anyone asked her, she would say the weather would sort the men from the boys, and those who had garden produce good enough to win prizes would be those who had the skill.

The Green was permanently sodden, and Ellen Biggs was fed up with trudging up and down the lane to the shop with wet feet, tired of juggling with an umbrella and a shopping bag, and the magazines she had to return to Ivy.

'What do y'do with them, Ivy, anyway, after you've read 'em and I've read 'em?' she said.

'Take them into the hospital, of course,' said Ivy. 'Some of us do think occasionally of those less fortunate than ourselves.'

Jean Jenkins ignored the weather, and pressed on with meetings at the Social Services Department, recruiting willing hands in the village, and keeping up Susan Standing's enthusiasm for the project. Bill Turner produced a distant relation at Waltonby, a reliable builder who was prepared to do the work on the barn for more or less cost, as his contribution to the project. It was this builder's niece, a lovely elfin child of two, who had vestigial sight, and he was quietly glad of the chance to help.

Richard Standing was another matter. Returning from London one rainy evening, when work on the track at Watford Junction had slowed the trains to a crawl, he got himself a gin and tonic from the refreshment buffet and slumped down in his seat, watching the misty, dismal countryside move slowly by. He gulped his drink and turned the pages of his *Standard*, trying to find something he wanted to read.

His attention, however, kept wandering, and his mood deteriorated. No doubt Susan would be wondering what had happened to him, what he was up to. God, how bloody infuriating it was! He glared at the pretty girl sitting opposite, and she rapidly lowered her eyes to her paperback.

What had Susan said about supper? Oh yes, they would have to have it as early as possible. She had a meeting with the Playgroup committee. Well, at this rate she'd be lucky to get there before it finished. Richard's spirits raised a fraction. He was not at all keen on Susan's latest enthusiasm and he blamed wretched Jean Jenkins for the whole thing.

'You must be mad even to have considered it, Susan,' he had said. He contemplated the idea of the comings and goings of strange cars and minibuses, and noises of all sorts emating from the old barn across the yard, just when he wanted a bit of peace and quiet. And once they were in, there'd be no getting them out. Before they knew it, they'd be wanting more space, and a playing field, and then there'd be great coaches, and sports days and parents' evenings and God knows what!

He grunted in disgust, and the pretty girl looked up at him in alarm. He shook his head and smiled at her. 'Awful nuisance,' he said, 'just when I'd promised to be home early.'

The girl did not reply, or smile, but hunched herself over her book in an unmistakable snub. Richard's mood worsened. Bloody Jenkins woman, she was at the bottom of it all. Why couldn't Susan have said no straight away, and carried on with her plan to take little Poppy to the Montessori nursery in Fletching? He didn't fancy her mixing with all those . . . well . . . with all those . . .

The train jolted suddenly and stopped, its engine reduced to a gentle idling. They were nowhere, no houses, no factories, no platform, nothing but the flat, rain-soaked fields of Bedfordshire. Richard got violently to his feet and bought himself another gin and tonic, returning to his seat with a deep frown of annoyance and frustration.

Now he had time to think anyway. He took a large mouthful of gin, and followed it with a handful of disgusting, over-salted peanuts. He was very hungry. Yes, well, now he had time to think it out, and he was coming rapidly to a very firm conclusion. It had to be stopped. Enough was enough, and Susan would have to see his point of view. It had to be stopped before it had gone too far.

The train began to inch forward, and as the gin worked its way into Richard's bloodstream he began to feel marginally better. Yes, that was it, now he knew what to do. With luck, he would be home now before Susan went off to the bloody meeting, and he could put her straight before she got in any deeper.

He smiled again at the pretty girl, and this time was not at all bothered that she looked straight past him as if he was not there.

★

'You are not going to believe this,' said Jean Jenkins, coming into the kitchen and slamming her folder of papers down on the table.

Foxy could see that she was near to tears, and got up from his chair. 'What's gone wrong, my duck?' he said, going over to put on the kettle.

Jean slumped down on one of the kitchen chairs, and put her head in her hands. 'Mrs Susan Standing has only gone and backed out, backed out of the whole thing, lock, stock and barrel!'

'What!' said Foxy, genuinely amazed. Susan Standing had seemed so keen on the project, and he'd heard her working on Mr Richard round by the barn one afternoon when he'd been stacking logs. Surely she couldn't mean it?

'She had the grace to look very unhappy about it,' said Jean, 'but she was quite definite. Said Mr Richard had been worried about the "possible implications" of having what would amount to a school in 'is back yard. And although it would be nice for Poppy, she'd soon be big enough to move on to the next school, and then there'd be no real connection between them and the playgroup. No reason, she said, for it to be at the Hall rather than anywhere else!'

'Did she have any suggestions of where else?' said Foxy.

'Village Hall,' said Jean, 'though even she must know it's pretty booked up, what with the other playgroup, and upholstery, and keep-fit, and over-fifties bowling, and that new Dabblers club got going by Mrs Ross. God knows what they do there, but it meets every Friday morning. So the Village Hall would be useless.'

'Well, bugger me, never mind,' said Fox, completely at a loss. He felt angry with the Standings and sorry for Jean, knowing how much work she had put in. And his anger was even greater because he knew there was nothing he could do, being an employee of the Standing estate and having to keep on the right side of them.

He put a mug of tea in front of Jean, and leaned over her

282

to kiss the top of her head. 'Never mind, my duck,' he said. 'We'll look at it again in the mornin' and see what we can do. We're not givin' up now, Standings or no bloody Standings.'

CHAPTER FORTY-EIGHT

Peggy Palmer opened her eyes and, as always, looked across at the curtained window overlooking the village street. Filtered golden light streamed through the thin material, warming up the white walls of her bedroom. Sunlight at last! She was so used to seeing grey skies and rain beating on the panes that she leapt out of bed in delight and drew back the curtains.

It was a sight to warm the heart of even the most hardened villager. The Green sparkled with early morning dew, every drop reflecting the bright, clear sun. High, belling clouds floated above Bagley Woods, and a song thrush, perched near the top of the big sycamore in the school playground, sang loudly, repeating each note as though to emphasise the change in the weather.

Peggy pulled on old trousers and a cotton shirt, and went downstairs. Gilbert put out her paw and touched Peggy, a gentle, feline hint that usually at about this time she had something to eat.

'Here you are, Gilbertiney,' said Peggy. 'Some nice fish I saved for you.'

The cat sniffed it and turned away. 'Oh, Gilbert,' Peggy said, 'It's a lovely piece of cod! You can't prefer that dreadful tinned stuff?' but Gilbert would not return to the fish, and Peggy, seduced into indulgence by the brilliant morning, spooned out some tinned beefy chunks for the obstinate little cat, who immediately began to eat.

The yard was warm already, and Peggy took her cup of tea and sat on the bench by the back door, soaking up the sun. Her geraniums, nearly rotted away by the constant rain, had perked up already, and the yellow rudbekia flowers in the long border down by the apple trees shone like small satellite suns.

I wonder if Bill is up, Peggy thought. Recently, in an odd sort of interregnum, she had kept her meetings with Bill to a minimum. With the divorce in sight, Peggy had settled back into a contented certainty that all would be well in the foreseeable future, when secrecy and clandestine meetings would no longer be necessary. She was, however, well aware that Bill did not have the same patient view.

By now, the whole village knew that Joyce Turner had left Bill, was living with her sister over at Bagley, and intended to get a divorce as soon as possible. The general feeling was that this was the best possible solution to a problem that had dragged on for years. As for Bill's affair with Peggy, this had been monitored ever since Frank Palmer died, and in its incubation before that by Ivy Beasley, and now the village waited for things to take their natural course.

As Peggy sat in her yard thinking about Bill, he was in his shed thinking about her. He had at last replaced the dead angora rabbits, poisoned in the bad old days by Joyce in a violent fit of jealousy, and three new does were settling into their hutches.

'Wonder if Peggy's up,' he thought, as he filled the water troughs and measured out handfuls of feed. He came out into his garden and looked over towards Walnut Farm, where the rooks were quarrelling and taking wheeling flights in the clear, morning air. He took a deep breath and smiled. He had made plans, and with any luck he could put them into operation soon. He propped open the shed door with a piece of pitted ironstone.

Once the children's regatta was out of the way, it would be the Horticultural Show, and then in no time Bonfire Night and into Christmas. The village year had a natural momentum, punctuated by traditional events and the farming year. Bill could scarcely believe that he would soon be a free man, with Joyce starting a new life in a way he could never have thought possible.

Better get on, he thought, back in the house and clearing away his big mug and breakfast plate. Mr Richard had given him the morning off to get the river path roped off for the regatta. Colin Osman and Peter Dodwell had recruited others, and their idea had been well received by young people in the village. Peggy had done a roaring trade in toy boats for the last couple of weeks.

'What's the use of having a river if nobody makes use of it?' Caroline Dodwell had said to Mandy Bates. Mandy had replied that she vaguely remembered Ted Bates telling her that years ago they used to have races with little wooden boats on the August Bank Holiday.

'It was only for the village children, Ted said, but there was a lot of competition to win, and some of the bigger boys got quite nasty. He said Tom Price always used to take the most prizes, with a heavy old boat that looked like Noah's Ark. I reckon it'd be fun to get it going again.'

There had been much concern about the weather, and tentative proposals to change the date, but Colin Osman and the Reverend Nigel Brooks had protested that the forecast was good, that the Lord would look kindly upon them, and now Bill glanced at the sky and reckoned it was set fair.

He loaded up his old van with stakes and rope, and drove slowly down Macmillan Gardens. Old Fred was out in his garden, his head wreathed in tobacco smoke. He leaned on his garden fork and waved at Bill, who shouted 'Grand morning, Fred!' Fred did more leaning than forking these days, but his garden still looked trim and neat, and now the weather had changed Fred would be out there most of the day.

'Will it last?' yelled Bill, wondering if the old boy could hear.

He parked his van by the bridge, and began to unload. Ten minutes later, an excited Colin Osman and Peter Dodwell joined him, and together they put up the rope barrier and strung the school bunting along the line of willows. The sun continued to shine, and the men sat down on the river bank with cans of beer.

'Looks all right, I reckon,' said Bill.

'Very festive,' said Colin Osman.

'Very,' said Peter Dodwell.

They contemplated their handiwork in silence, and drank the cooling beer. Then Bill rose to his feet, and set off towards the bridge. 'Better mark the starting line,' he said, 'and the finishing post best be up by Ringle Den.'

'Ringle Den?' said Colin Osman who, though only recently a Ringford man, prided himself on knowing all the local names.

'It's just a thicket of bushes on the bank,' said Bill. 'A lot of courtin's been done there. The river's made a shallow pool, so it'll be easy for Robert Bates to hook in the boats. William Roberts is helping him, which could go either way. You're on duty at the start, aren't you, Colin?'

Colin nodded. He had planned it all out on his computer. Starting times, handicaps, entry fees, prizes for each race, all had been carefully worked out, and now he pulled out printed sheets of information for the spectators.

'You've certainly gone to town there,' said Peter Dodwell admiringly.

Bill remembered the old days, when Grandad Price got them all lined up by the bridge, and then everybody ran and yelled and screamed as the boats bobbed along the river, to be pulled out by their owners at the end. It had worked all right then, without computers, thought Bill, but he said nothing.

Jean Jenkins stood the twins in front of her and gave them the once over. 'Gemma,' she said, 'show me your teeth.'

Gemma flashed her a quick, guilty grimace. 'Go on up,' said Jean, 'and do them properly this time.'

Amy escaped retribution, and smiled smugly. 'I did mine,' she said, 'first thing, but then Warren pushed me out of the bathroom, and there wasn't time for Gemma to do hers.'

'Hm,' said Jean. 'There's bin plenty of time since.' Always stick up for each other, them twins, she thought, as she packed her basket with sandwiches and biscuits and cans of drink. She was looking forward to the regatta. Everything had been so difficult lately, what with Mrs Standing scuppering the special playgroup plans, and then not finding anywhere else suitable. Foxy had told her to leave it for a while, something would be sure to come up. But she saw the summer almost gone, and her hopes for starting in the autumn vanishing fast.

'Come on, Foxy,' she called, and with Gemma's teeth now sparkling white, and little Eddie resplendent in clean shorts and teeshirt, his blond hair flopping silkily over his eyes, the Jenkins family set off for the river. Warren was down there already, helping William and Robert Bates, and as Jean marched down Macmillan Gardens at the head of her tribe, holding tight to Eddie's warm little hand, she could see a number of people already gathered under the willows.

Mr Richard and Susan Standing were on the bridge, with Poppy excitedly pointing at the boats and wriggling to get free of her father's restraining hand. It had been arranged by Colin Osman that Richard Standing would officially open the regatta by firing a starting pistol for the first race.

Richard looked at the water, running fast with all the

summer's rain, and remembered the time, long ago, when he had rashly proposed marriage to the Barrett girl from Walnut Farm, and been firmly pushed into the icy water for his pains.

'Richard?' said Susan. It was time to start, and Colin Osman handed him the pistol. He fired it into the air, Poppy screamed with delight, the boats were released and started swiftly, taken by the current past the cheering onlookers, and the children's regatta began.

Mandy had walked down from the bungalow, Joe well propped-up with cushions in his pushchair, and although his small head almost always drooped to one side, he smiled constantly, pleased with the air of excitement and the unusually large number of people about the village. Mandy had protected his eyes from the sun with a bright blue baseball cap, and he waved his arms in greeting and delight when he saw Poppy Standing rushing around the green chasing the Jenkins terrier, once more on the loose.

'Joey do it,' Poppy said, holding out her hand, inviting Joe to join in the chase.

'He will one day, Poppy,' said Mandy, swallowing hard, 'won't you, my pet?' She leaned over and planted a kiss on the top of the bright blue cap, and walked on to join Peggy on the river bank, gripping the pushchair handle a little tighter.

The regatta was a huge success. Robert Bates's quiet authority quelled any dispute about the winners, and a local rule was quickly made to allow any grounded boat to be pushed off and started again. William and Warren were thoroughly biased retrievers of sunken boats, standing up to their thighs in the cold water, and having a marvellous time. When Andrew Roberts' homemade yacht won its race, William splashed Warren in triumph and got a clip round the ear from his father as a result.

All the races were finally run, and it was time for speeches. The new Challenge Cup, given by Don Cutt, stood twinkling in the sun on a card table, and Mrs Standing was presented with a bouquet of flowers, not for doing anything very much, but because she always received a bouquet at village events.

'Now, ladies and gentlemen, and, most importantly, children,' began Richard Standing. He forgot no one in his thanks, and was just turning to present the Challenge Cup to the overall winner when there was a shriek and a splash, and Poppy Standing, in her voluminous flowery frills, disappeared from sight under the weedy, flowing water, now cloudy with stirred-up mud.

There was a moment of complete silence, and then pandemonium. Richard Standing plunged in and was immediately bogged down by his heavy shoes, and Susan Standing began to run like the wind along the bank. She had been talking to her mother, and not noticed Poppy straying off down the river path, picking daisies and talking to herself.

But quickest of all was Robert Bates. He waded in, lifted up the limp, choking child, and carried her quickly to the bank. There he pushed aside anxious villagers and gently pressed and squeezed until the swallowed water had all come up, and Poppy stopped choking. She lay in her mother's arms, still and quiet, but breathing, with her eyes closed, as Richard drove his big car across the Green at speed. They disappeared off towards Bagley and the Cottage Hospital.

'What a rotten end to a lovely afternoon,' said Peggy, walking gloomily back across the Green with Bill. Everybody had given a hand in clearing up, and a subdued Colin Osman had thanked them all for their help. He had shaken his head in a puzzled way. 'You'd have thought,' he said, 'there were enough people about to see the child on the bank.'

'It just shows,' said a tart Ivy Beasley, as she walked back to Ellen's Lodge for a cup of tea. 'It just goes to show that you can't trust children near water. They'd all forgotten why river races were stopped in the first place.'

'I 'adn't, Ivy,' said Ellen, unlocking her front door. 'It was over at Fletching, weren't it, on their stretch of the Ringle. Awful tragedy, they said, a lively child, and only three years old. Still, I think that Poppy's goin' to be all right, thanks to our Robert.'

Ivy nodded. 'Thanks to Robert indeed,' she said, 'and I hope the Honourable and Mrs Richard Standing will be duly grateful.'

CHAPTER FORTY-NINE

Peggy had slept badly, waking in terror as in her dream she dragged a limp, dripping child to the bank of the river and, turning it over, saw Frank's face. And then when she drifted back into a fitful sleep, began the dream all over again, and without being able to stop it, turned the waterlogged body once more and saw Joyce Turner, eyes open and staring, but unquestionably drowned.

At about four o'clock, she got out of bed in desperation. She went over to the window, drew back the curtains, and looked out at the village. It was no longer dark, and a chilly half-light enabled her to see the empty street. The idly flapping rope on the school flagpole was the only thing that moved, and a thin mist hung over the river, spilling out across the Green.

Nothing there to cheer me up, she thought, and went downstairs to make a cup of tea. Perhaps if I read a book, I'll be able to go back to bed in a while and sleep without dreaming.

Peggy sat down at the kitchen table and lifted Gilbert on to her lap, opening her book but finding it difficult to concentrate. Frank, Bill, Joyce . . . Still the same old guilt, she thought and, too depressed to read, she shut her book and put her head down on her folded hands. She closed her eyes and dozed until the starlings under the eaves began to chirp, one joining another, slowly swelling to the daily chorus, and the grey light of dawn brightened with the first sight of the sun.

Gilbert woke her, jumping off her lap and departing noisily through the cat flap. Peggy felt stiff from her awkward position and stood up, stretching painfully. 'It's about time,' she said aloud, 'that I made up my mind. That's half the trouble. Some positive decisions are called for. Nobody's going to do it for me. Poor old Bill is the most patient of men, but even he must be getting fed up.'

Feeling more cheerful already, she opened the back door, allowing a few tentative rays of sunlight to stream in.

In spite of its chilly beginning, Sunday was a perfect day. As the sun came up, early morning mist vanished, and the sky cleared to a cloudless china blue.

'Too bright too soon,' said Fred Mills, standing on his doorstep and looking round the gardens. Jean Jenkins' bedroom curtains were still drawn, and there were no signs of life. Beats me, thought Fred, how they manage a lie-in with all them kids. Still, Foxy's a good father, and they do what they're told most of the time. He looked across to the Robertses'. The big Alsatian dog was barking, deep, echoing barks, straining against his chain in the back yard. Fred heard Michael Roberts cursing at it, telling it to shut up, and then a loud thump and a whimper which Fred wished he hadn't heard.

The church bell began to ring for the early morning Communion service, and as Fred watched and puffed his pipe, Doris Ashbourne's front door opened, and she emerged, smartly dressed, ready for worship. She called out a greeting to him as she went past. Nice woman, thought Fred. Pity I ain't a few years younger.

Movement from Bill Turner's house caught Fred's attention, and he waved as he saw Bill coming out of his gate. Bill was heading in Fred's direction, and as he came close, smiled and saluted the old man cheerfully. 'Morning Fred,' he said. 'What d'you reckon, then? Thought I'd try for a bit of fishing today. I can't remember when I last got out my rods.'

Fred shook his head. 'Too bright, boy,' he said. 'Still, it 'on't last. You could well be lucky this afternoon. Where you goin', then?'

'I might try Flasher's Pool. Haven't been up there for a long time.'

'Nobody has, to my knowledge,' said Fred. 'We 'ad some good fishin' there years ago. Did I ever tell you about the time I caught that grit ole pike?'

Bill nodded hastily. He knew the story so well he could have repeated it back to Fred, word for word. Now he said, 'I do remember it well, Fred. But before I forget, could you lend me your old fishing basket? Can't find mine anywhere. I reckon Joyce chucked it out some while ago.'

Fred nodded sympathetically. He had witnessed many occasions when Joyce Turner, consumed with irrational rage and resentment against Bill, had taken armfuls of his clothes and belongings, especially anything he particularly valued, and dumped them in the dustbin just before the binmen came, giving Bill no opportunity to retrieve them.

Bill followed Fred into his musty-smelling, shabby house. A fine layer of dust covered everything. When Fred's sister had been alive, they'd had a home help to keep the place clean, but when Fred was left alone he could not bear the woman scuttling round his home, getting under his feet, and shifting him from room to room while she cleaned.

'I can do it meself,' he said to her finally. 'Thanks for what you done, missus, but I shan't be wantin' you no more.'

The authorities had sent a young woman to find out if Fred really meant it, and when he reached for a convenient lie and said Jean Jenkins had promised she'd give him a dust round once a week, the young woman nodded sympathet-ically and went back to Tresham to make an optimistic report.

Fred climbed his narrow stairs with difficulty, and called to Bill to come and help. He had opened the door of the landing cupbord, and a tangled assortment of accumulated junk fell out.

'Damn me,' said Bill. 'I didn't mean to cause you all this trouble, Fred. Better let me give you a hand to tidy up.'

The brilliant morning progressed. Doris came back from church with Ivy Beasley, and the two women made coffee and sat on wooden kitchen chairs on Doris's porch. They watched Michael Roberts, spruced up and smiling, set off for the pub. Colin Osman and Peter Dodwell walked past the Gardens on their way to a meeting at the Village Hall, carrying neat files of papers setting out plans for a safer and more spectacular fireworks party.

'They don't learn,' said Ivy Beasley.

'They will,' said Doris, 'when they've been here a bit longer.'

'Our Robert's always done the fireworks. Never been any complaints.'

'No harm in letting them have their meetings,' said Doris with a smile. 'Keeps them out of mischief, and Robert will get on with it just the same, when the time comes.'

Mr and Mrs Ross, neatly turned out in their Sunday best, stepped off the footpath which had brought them from the river and across the Green to the village street. They joined the road at the bottom of the Gardens, carrying their little dog in case he should be contaminated by something nasty near the bus shelter. As they disappeared from sight, Ivy Beasley said, 'Creatures of routine, them Rosses, you could set your watch by them.'

'Which reminds me, Ivy,' said Doris, getting to her feet, 'I must put the potatoes on. Will you stay and have a bite with me?' She knew she was on safe ground. Ivy's roast would be sizzling nicely in a slow oven, awaiting her return.

Fred Mills, covered with dust and grime, finally found the old fishing basket and with a whoop of triumph dragged it out and handed it to Bill. 'There y'are, boy,' he said. 'I knew it was in there somewhere.'

Bill helped Fred put back all the boxes and packets, old photograph albums and worn-out boots that might come in useful, agreeing that it was best not to throw anything away. 'Come on, Fred,' he said. 'It's too late to go fishing this morning. I'll buy you a pint, and then get going after dinner.'

He brushed down the old man, waited for him to find his cap and lock up as if they would be gone for days, and they walked at a snail's pace down to the pub. 'Good God, boy,' said Fred, stepping into the public bar with relief, 'we've earned a pint this mornin', I reckon!'

Peggy had stayed after church to talk to Sophie Brooks, the vicar's wife, about the proposed W.I. outing to the Potteries, and one thing had led to another, so that by the time Peggy passed by the pub, Bill Turner was emerging, cheerful and smiling after his couple of pints with Fred.

'Morning, my gel,' said Bill, taking her arm. In such a public place it was usual for Peggy to avoid any physical contact between them, but this morning she made no attempt to shake him off.

She smiled up at his ruddy face, and said, 'I hope you'll be getting something to eat now. All that beer sloshing about inside you is no good at all.'

'Nice of you to consider the inside of my stomach,' said Bill grandly, 'but it's used to my wicked ways, after all these years. I'm going home for my usual Sunday dinner of bread and cheese, and then I'm goin' fishin' at Flasher's Pool.'

'Fishing?' said Peggy. 'First time I've heard of you

fishing.'

'Lots of things you don't know about me,' said Bill. 'Do you want to come? I could teach you how to hold the rod . . . and that.'

They had reached the end of Macmillan Gardens, and Peggy disengaged her arm. 'If you get much further than a deckchair in your back garden, I shall be very much surprised!' she said, and walked on home, smiling to herself.

After a salad lunch, Peggy put on gardening clothes and went out to clear out some border plants, already dying back with the end of the summer. She had been cutting out and tidying for half an hour or so when she looked up and saw Bill's van going past the end of the passage. So he has gone fishing, she thought. Bet he doesn't catch anything.

She started on the Michaelmas daisies, but her heart wasn't in it. Gilbert was fast asleep on the grass, soaking up the warm sun, and Peggy put down her shears and stretched her back. Done enough for one day, she persuaded herself. No point in overdoing it.

She returned to the kitchen and washed her hands. These trousers are grubby, she thought, and went upstairs to put on a clean skirt. Not allowing herself to think much about anything, she sprayed her best scent behind her ears and on her wrists.

Gilbert had woken up and was miaowing at the foot of the stairs, and Peggy went to the fridge to get some milk. Right, she thought, putting down a brimming saucer. Better lock up, I suppose, though I shan't be out long.

She put her doorkey in the pocket of her skirt, and went down the passage, emerging into the sunlit street. There was nobody in sight, except for the Jenkins terrier nosing along the gutter for ice-cream papers and fragments of crisps.

Peggy set off smartly, as if she had some perfectly reasonable objective in view, like taking a magazine to

Doreen Price, or delivering an emergency loaf to Ellen Biggs. She was, however, carrying nothing and, aware of her empty hands swinging at her sides, she began to feel conspicuous. She put her hands in her skirt pockets and quickened her pace, anxious to get out of the village as soon as possible.

Flasher's Pool, Bill had said. Peggy knew that it was about two miles away, across a couple of fields the Fletching side of the village, where the river wound through the valley, making pools of quiet water where the bends were extreme.

The cut stubble in the cornfields shimmered like silk, and as Peggy walked carefully, trying not to scratch her bare legs on the sharp stalks, rabbits scattered and pigeons flew up from feeding on spilt grain. It was very warm, heat reflected up from the field, and Peggy stayed close to the hedge, grateful for the shade of spreading willows by the stream. It would run eventually into the Ringle, so she knew she was on the right track. A moorhen squawked, making her jump and she paused, watching the clear water running over tree roots and smooth stones. She saw an inviting smooth patch of short grass by the stream, and the remains of an old wooden gate, now permanently anchored shut by a fallen branch. Could this be where Bill had said he used to bring Joyce for picnics when they were first married? A familiar train of thought began, but Peggy erased it firmly, and continued on her way.

She scrambled through a broken wire fence, up the slope of the disused railway embankment, and walked on the footpath, glad that the vicious nettles were beginning to die back. The spinney of beech and hazel trees along the line petered out for a few yards where an old blue brick railway bridge crossed the widening stream. Peggy walked carefully down by the side of the bridge, setting off along the side of another stubble field. From the top of the embankment she had seen an old white van parked at the end of an overgrown green lane, and knew that Bill had arrived at Flasher's Pool from the other side of the valley. She imagined him, serious and self-contained, bent over his fishing rod, tying on the wriggling worm to attract the innocent and unsuspecting fish. Well, thought Peggy, I am far from innocent and unsuspecting, and she hesitated, but only for a moment. She pushed through a cluster of thick, concealing knotweed, and arrived at the far side of the pool.

Bill did not see her at first. He was stretched out on a bed of flattened long grass with his hands behind his head, staring at the sky. He had propped up his rod at an angle, and the line floated idly on the calm water.

Peggy walked round the edge of the pool quietly, hoping to surprise him. But her foot snapped a dry, dead branch, and Bill sat up, shading his eyes from the sun. He saw her, and got to his feet, saying nothing, not even smiling. She stopped, unsure now of her welcome.

Then Bill put out his arms, and she walked on, until at last Bill was kissing her in a way that made up for all the weeks of abstinence.

'Sit down here, Peggy,' he said, and they sat on the warm grass by the edge of the river pool, holding hands.

'Look at that old bee,' said Bill, and Peggy followed his gaze to a swaying purple foxglove growing in the willows' shade. She watched as a huge soft bumble bee settled on the lip of one of the trumpet flowers. It preened itself, and then in an ecstasy of buzzing pushed its way up into a nectar-filled heaven.

'Oh crumbs,' she said, as Bill put his arms around her again and gently moved her back on to the grassy bed.

'Dear Bill,' she said, and then, 'Bill, it's been rather a long time . . .'

'Don't you worry, gel,' said Bill, breathing faster, 'it's like riding a bike . . . there . . . you never really forget, do you . . . take it easy, my little love . . . Oh God, Peg, I do love you.'

The bumble bee, drunk with pleasure, stumbled out of the flower and zoomed happily off over the pool, where Bill's float submerged in sudden agitation. A large perch had taken the bait, but Bill's attention was elsewhere.

CHAPTER FIFTY

The spell of warm weather ended in a spectacular thunder-storm which kept Joey awake all night, and in the welcome cool of the next morning, Robert Bates opened up his workshop. He had to fix a new exhaust pipe to Peter Dodwell's car, and he called on Mandy half way through the morning to give him a hand.

'Careful now, Mandy. Don't let go until I tell you,' said Robert.

Just as well Joey isn't trotting all over the place, thought Mandy grimly. There are some compensations. But she knew this was rubbish, even as she thought it, and smiled across at the little chap sitting in his special chair where he could watch his dad at work. He loved everything to do with cars and the workshop, and Robert had set up a small garage with cars and petrol pumps and a car wash on the special tray attached to his chair. He could manage quite a passable 'brrmm brrmm' now, and with his more dextrous right hand guided his cars in and out on endless missions.

'Shan't be able to do this much longer, Rob,' said Mandy.

He smiled at her, and finished the job quickly. He was just advancing a greasy finger towards one of Joey's cars when the telephone rang.

'Good morning, sir,' he said, mouthing 'Standing' to

Mandy.

The conversation was brief, and Mandy looked enquiringly as he put the telephone down. 'Not another shunt in the Merc, I hope!' she said.

Robert shook his head. 'No,' he said slowly, 'he wants me to go up to the Hall when I've finished here this evening. Says he has something to say, and he'd like to say it personally.'

'Well, I expect it's to thank you for fishing Poppy out of the river,' said Mandy, lifting Joey out of his chair and walking off towards the bungalow. 'Thank goodness the little mite is running about again. Gave us all the fright of our lives, didn't she, Joey?' She disappeared through the kitchen door, and Robert got back to work.

Richard Standing opened the door to Robert and motioned him inside. Robert had washed and changed, and stood self-consciously in the cool black and white tiled hall. He hadn't been in here since the Sunday School treat tea when he was seven. It hadn't changed at all. Splendid portraits of Standing ancestors looked down on him with expressions varying from stern to bucolically cheerful. Tall vases of flowers stood on richly polished tables, and the door into the pink drawing room was open.

'Hello Robert!' called Susan. 'Come on in, we're in here.'

Robert walked across the hall, the heels of his best shoes clacking on the tiles, and found Mrs Standing and daughter Poppy, and the irritable Yorkie terrier, at the moment curled up asleep on his velvet cushion.

'What will you have, Robert?' said Richard Standing.

'A beer would be nice, if you have one,' said Robert, thinking it as well to be honest. He couldn't abide sherry or gin, or whisky either, come to that.

'Now then, Poppy,' said Richard, when they were settled, 'are you going to give this to Robert? Be careful with it, darling.'

He handed Poppy a white envelope, and she bounced into Robert's lap, almost crushing the envelope before he could get hold of it. Robert gently lifted her up and held her close, then looked down at the envelope and saw his name.

'It's a thank you from Poppy and all of us,' said Richard. 'I don't know what we would have done, if . . .' He couldn't finish, and looked away and over the park while he composed his face.

'There was no need, sir,' said Robert, 'no need at all, it was nothing. I just happened to be in the right place.'

'Robert dear,' said Susan, with unusual warmth, 'why don't you open it?'

Robert fumbled with the envelope and eventually had it open. He withdrew a sheet of paper and a cheque. The cheque was for a large amount of money, and the letter was even better.

'Somebody at the door, Fox,' said Jean Jenkins. 'You go, will you, I'm just doin' these potatoes for tomorrow. I shan't have no time in the morning.'

Fox got up and found Robert Bates standing on his doorstep, grinning from ear to ear. 'Come in, Rob,' he said. 'You don't need to knock.'

'Hello, Robert,' said Jean, as they walked into the kitchen. 'How's the family? Nothing wrong, I hope?'

Robert pulled the envelope out of his pocket. 'Thanks, Jean, everybody's fine. I hope I'm not interrupting anything, but I had to come straight here from the Hall to give you this.'

Jean took it and opened the flap suspiciously, peering inside.

'Go on, pull it out,' said Robert, winking at Foxy.

Jean looked at the cheque, widened her eyes, and started to read aloud.

'Dear Robert, Susan and I wish you to know how deeply grateful we are to you for rescuing Poppy from the river.

Of course, we always knew that all children are precious, but this has given us considerable pause for thought, particularly myself.'

'Huh,' said Foxy.

Jean frowned at him, and carried on reading. 'I have seen very clearly how fortunate we are to have our little girl, whole and happy, bringing joy to our lives. We have thought a great deal about you, Robert, and Mandy and Joey, and in a small attempt to express our gratitude, we would like you to accept the enclosed cheque as our contribution to the special playgroup. It will, we hope, help towards the conversion of Hall Barn, which we now wish to donate for this worthwhile purpose for as long as it is needed.'

Jean's face was streaked with tears, and Foxy put his strong arms around her. Robert cleared his throat, and said, 'Calls for a celebration, this does. How about meeting later at the pub, if we can get babysitters?'

'You're on,' said Foxy, and much to Jean's tearful amusement, he put out his hand and shook Robert's warmly. 'Well done,' he said. 'Bloody well done, boy.'

CHAPTER FIFTY-ONE

On the second Saturday in November, after firework night and before Ringford Stores went into top gear for the Christmas trade, Peggy Palmer sat in her bedroom, gazing at the photograph of her late husband, Frank.

'What do you think, then, Frank?' she said. 'It's not too late to change my mind.'

She looked at herself in her dressing-table mirror. 'Fair, fat and fifty-four wouldn't be a bad description,' she said, seeing plump shoulders and well-rounded bosom. Her new petticoat was pure white, encrusted at the top with lace, and trimmed with a tiny rosebud between her breasts. 'Very virginal, Peggy Palmer,' she said, 'and most inappropriate.'

In front of her, laid out neatly on the flowered china tray that had been her mother's, was an array of new make-up. A tinted moisturising foundation, pink blusher for her cheeks, blue eye-shadow and dark brown mascara for her lashes, all carefully chosen in Tresham for this day. Peggy picked up the tube of foundation and squeezed a small blob into the palm of her hand. She looked at it in disgust, and pulled a tissue from the box on her dressing-table. She scrubbed the pastel pink blob from her hand and threw the tissue into the waste bin under her dressing table. Then she lifted up the china tray and swiftly tipped the collection of untouched make-up to join the offending blob.

Reaching for her Boots all-purpose cream in its plain white jar, she opened the lid and proceeded to stroke it into her cheeks, chin and forehead, just as she did every other, unspecial, morning. A few quick dabs with an ageing powder puff and a practised sweep round her lips with an almost exhausted pale lipstick, and she looked again into the mirror.

'That's better,' she said, and began vigorously brushing out the carefully styled hairdo which Mandy had taken far longer than usual to achieve. Her spirits rose. On a coathanger, suspended from the outside of her wardrobe hung a new suit, pale grey, soft wool, with a gently flared skirt and long, loose jacket. Peggy stepped into the skirt, pulled in her stomach, and closed the zip. The skirt hung in flattering folds round her legs, which were still shapely and firm. She slipped her feet into plain black shoes with a small heel, not too high, but conferring a little elegance. The jacket felt light and warm, and Peggy turned to look at her full-length reflection in the wardrobe door.

'Not bad,' she said. 'At least I look like me.'

On the bed lay the hat. Or The Hat. It was a deep rose pink, and had a small veil which the shop assistant had said Peggy could either pull down over her eyes – 'A touch of mystery, dear!' – or fold back over the small brim. She picked it up, and put it squarely on her head. She could have sworn she heard Frank laugh.

'Absolutely right, Frank,' she said, and took off the hat, putting it down on the bed, intending to forget it at the last minute.

'Perfume,' she said, and gave herself a few squirts of the same scent which had done such splendid service that day by Flasher's Pool. She looked round her bedroom, and knew that there was one last task, the most difficult one of all. Her watch told her it was time to go downstairs to wait for Tom Price, but she lingered, took a glance out of the window and saw that a small crowd had gathered. William

306

and Warren, Gemma and Amy with Jean Jenkins, all dressed up and clutching cameras; old Fred, warmly wrapped in scarf and gloves, Mr and Mrs Ross, carrying their little dog.

Peggy felt tears in the offing, and sniffed. A handkerchief, she thought, and took a small, folded square of fine cotton from her drawer. She opened her handbag and checked the contents. Not much needed for such a momentous event, she thought. And then, because there was nothing more she had to do, and because Tom Price had drawn up in his newly-cleaned car and was hooting outside, Peggy picked up the photograph of Frank, kissed his smiling face, and put it firmly in the top drawer of her dressing table. She ran down the stairs as if fleeing from wickedness, and almost collided with Ellen Biggs, who had come into the kitchen through the back door.

''Allo, my dear,' Ellen said. 'Don't you look nice. I shall see you later, when you get back from Bagley, but I just brought this for a bit o' good luck. You deserve a bit, God knows.'

She held out a small box, and Peggy opened it carefully. Inside, half covered with brownish cottonwool, lay a silver brooch, well-polished to a twinkling gleam. Peggy lifted it out and saw that it was a tiny four-leaved clover.

'Ellen,' she said, and choked.

''Ere,' said Ellen, 'let me pin it on for you. You're all of a dither, and no wonder. There, that's it.'

Peggy looked down at the little brooch, and then put her arms round the stout Ellen, kissing her warmly on her wrinkled cheek. 'I shall treasure it, Ellen,' she said. 'always.'

Louder hooting galvanised Ellen into action. She brushed a stray hair from Peggy's shoulder, and then propelled her firmly through the dark shop, naturally closed on such a day, and out into the winter sunshine, where a small cheer greeted her.

Tom opened the rear passenger door for Peggy, but she shook her head, and took the seat next to his. She wound down her window, and laughed at William and Warren, doing a mock march round the bus shelter to the familiar Mendelssohn melody. 'See you later!' she called, and waved like the Queen Mum. 'Well,' she said to Tom, who teased her gently, 'it is my day, isn't it?'

Panic, and an urgent desire to tell Tom to turn round and go straight back to Ringford, assailed Peggy half way to Bagley. She tried to empty her mind, but saw again and again the top drawer of her dressing table closing over Frank's face. She felt a flicker of pain up the left side of her neck. Oh no, not a migraine, not today, please God, not today.

Tom turned to look briefly at her, checking that she was all right. He saw that she was not, and put out a large brown hand to take hers, small and shaking. 'Everything's fine, Peggy,' he said. 'He's a very good man, you know, a very good man indeed.'

This sustained Peggy until the car drew up outside the register office in Bagley, when she began to shake again. She allowed Tom to hand her out of the car, and took his arm. Panic and the desire to run set in again, but she followed Tom's guiding arm up the steps and into the solemn interior.

And then it was suddenly perfectly all right, safe and proper. Bill's broad back and tall, straight figure dominated the small group of friends waiting for her. He looked at her pale face, and smiled in his warm, reassuring way, just as he had on the first day they met, hundreds of years ago when she and Frank moved into the Post Office Stores.

'Here you are, then, my lovely gel,' he said. He sniffed. 'Mmm . . . nice scent,' he said, and squeezed her hand.

After the blessing which followed, in St Mary's Church,

Round Ringford, the Reverend Nigel Brooks stood happily in the chilly wind, his white surplice billowing in front of Mrs Peggy Turner as she stood holding her husband Bill's arm, smiling wholeheartedly at the photographer. The photographer was, of course, Colin Osman, and he was determined to do a professional job.

'That'll do, boy, I should think,' said Bill, feeling a shiver through his wife's arm. He looked down at her and, watching her face light up in a way he had not seen before, impulsively took her in his arms and gave her a loving, husbandly kiss. Colin Osman knew a good opportunity when he saw one, and snapped away, thinking to himself that here was a dead cert for the Kodak competition next year.

The church had been full. Peggy had issued a general invitation to the village and they had all come. The hymns were familiar old favourites, and the ancient building reverberated to a volume of sound not heard for many years. Now the aisles buzzed with excited conversation as the congregation waited to join Peggy and Bill in the Village Hall for what Peggy had called their wedding breakfast, and Bill had described in the Arms as, a bloody good knees-up.

'Off we go, then, Mrs Turner,' said Bill, and Peggy had a momentary vision of Joyce, young and pretty, all in white on Bill's arm. She banished it, but in that moment knew that it would always return, however seldom.

The Village Hall was a miracle of silver bells and multicoloured balloons. 'No hope of flowers at this time of the year,' Doreen had said to her wedding sub-committee, Pat Osman, Mandy Bates and Sophie Brooks. They had spent hours cutting out cardbord bells and covering them with silver foil, tying on white ribbon streamers to float in the warm air of the hall. Bunches of balloons had been willingly inflated – and some exploded – by William and Warren, armed with balloon pumps and boundless energy.

Ellen and Doris had provided enough embroidered table-cloths to serve a battalion, and Ivy Beasley, prodded and goaded by Ellen Biggs, had grudgingly produced tiny bouquets of dried flowers for each table.

'It's all legal and above board now, Ivy,' Ellen had said. 'Joyce is safely settled in Bagley, and bin seen walkin' out with that widower of 'ers, so what is there to jib at?'

Ivy had done what was asked of her, but in private conversation with her mother she had confessed to a lingering dislike of her blossoming neighbour.

The wedding sub-committee had surpassed itself on the catering. 'Good hot victuals is what we shall need in November,' Doreen had said and, once everyone had found seats, steaming plates of juicy roast beef, crisp, golden potatoes and every possible trimming, were set in front of hungry guests. Peggy and Bill, side by side at the top table, talked to their neighbours, and sometimes whispered quietly to each other things that were for their ears only.

When the plates were all empty and the Village Hall windows steamed up, shutting out the darkening November day, Tom Price got to his feet.

'Now, what did I say, Tom,' said Bill.

'No speeches, Bill, that's what you said, but o' course I shan't take notice of that!' A round of applause, and cries of 'speech! speech!' greeted this.

Tom's speech was not long, but it was sincere and heartfelt. The hall was very quiet, and as Tom came to his conclusion, Peggy touched the four-leaved clover, small and silvery on her grey jacket.

'If you ask me,' said Tom, 'and there I quote someone who shall be nameless . . .'

There was a delighted laugh from the hall, and eyes turned to the impassive face of Ivy Beasley.

'If you ask me,' repeated Tom, 'I would say Peggy and Bill Turner stand a good chance of a truly happy marriage.

They're not young and foolish, nor are they old and incapable . . . '

Ivy Beasley frowned, and Michael Roberts pierced the air with a shrill wolf whistle.

'So I give you a toast – Peggy and Bill, God bless them.'

The guests stood and drained their glasses, and loudly echoed the toast. And in the silence that followed, a small childish voice was heard.

'Peg'n Bill,' said Joey Bates, to his mother's intense delight.

Bill replied with moving dignity, and declared a ban on further speechifying, and in due course Tom left to collect his car and bring it round to the door. He had arranged to take Peggy and Bill and their luggage to the London train in Tresham, and thereafter their plans were secret.

Waved off by what seemed like the entire village, Peggy and Bill leaned back and laughed at the antics of William and Warren, capering about in front of the car and brandishing toy pistols in a mock hold-up. 'Yer money or yer life!' they yelled, as Tom accelerated and the car moved off down the village street.

'Hey, Tom, we want to go to Tresham!' said Peggy, as they turned off down Bates's End and cruised over the bridge.

Neither of the men replied, and then Bill said, 'You got it, then, Tom?'

Tom nodded, and brought the car to a halt outside the cemetery gate.

'Come on, Peggy my love,' said Bill, opening the door and holding out his hand. Tom got out too, and handed Peggy a small bunch of white chrysanthemums, cool and sharp-scented. She looked at Bill, and he smiled.

'We've got one more thing to do, gel,' he said and, while Tom returned to the car, he took Peggy's arm and they walked together into the cold, colourless winter cemetery. Then Peggy knew where they were going, and was not sure she could cope.

Frank's grave was neat and tidy, the headstone still new-looking and the inscription sadly fresh and crisp. 'FRANK ARTHUR PALMER, beloved husband of MARGARET.' Peggy and Bill stood hand in hand, silent in the half-darkness.

Peggy gathered all her strength, stepped forward and placed the flowers in the waiting vase. She kissed the tips of her fingers and gently touched the cold marble. Then she stepped back and tucked her hand into Bill's.

'Time to go,' he said. 'Cheerio, boy. I'll look after her, never fear.'

They walked through the iron gate, and found Tom had the car door open ready for them.

'All done, then, Tom,' said Bill. 'Sit tight, Mrs T.' He turned to Peggy, and smiled. 'He drives this car like a bloody old tractor,' he said.

POSTSCRIPT

Another New Year, thought Bridget Reilly, picking up the post from her doormat in Enniskerry. She had applied for another nanny job, but in Ireland this time, and sorted anxiously through the pile of cards and letters. There was nothing for her except a newspaper, carefully folded and enclosed in a brown paper wrapper.

'What's this?' she said, handing the rest of the post to her mother.

It was the *Tresham Advertiser*, and there was a note from Dan Bates inside. 'Thought you might like to see this – best love, Dan.'

Bridget looked puzzled, but turned the pages and came to the announcements. One entry had been circled in red, and she gave a whoop. 'How about this, Mum!' she said, and handed the paper over, jabbing at it with an excited finger.

The announcement came as a complete surprise to both of them, and Mrs Reilly smiled delightedly at her daughter. She read out the small paragraph:

'How wonderful, dear,' she said. 'What lovely news!'

And so it was, as Ellen Biggs stoutly asserted to Ivy and Doris, sipping their tea in Victoria Villa. Well worth celebrating with another slice of Ivy's excellent lemon sponge.